MW01129256

FLY GIRL

FLY GIRL

———◆———

Bill Hellman and Sali Gear

© 2017 Bill Hellman and Sali Gear
All rights reserved.

ISBN-13: 9781548622886
ISBN-10: 1548622885
Library Control of Congress Number: 2017918333
CreateSpace Independent Publishing Platform
North Charleston, South Carolina

This work of fiction is dedicated to the memory of Commander Bud Gear, US Navy fighter pilot, decorated hero of the Second World War, Navy test pilot, husband, and father, and to his courageous wife, Sally, and the incredible legacy they created.

CHAPTER 1

BIN THUY AIRBASE, SOUTH VIETNAM, 1965

———◆———

JUNE WAS JUST THE SECOND month of the rainy season in Vietnam, and it was already shaping up to be a record-breaker. Rain would fall around the clock, days were gloomy, nights were dark, and water was standing everywhere. Bin Thuy had been built by the US Air Force, Red Horse Civil Engineering Battalion, in the southern part of the country on drained rice paddies. At the time, it was far more important to get the airbase operational than to worry about future rainfall and/or other issues that might be important at an airport.

A single Air Force C-130A cargo plane sat alone away from the hangars and other activity on a large paved square known as the Hot Pad. It was a location where aircraft could load or offload cargo or personnel while still having their engines turning if the need arose, and if cargo operations required an increased level of security, the Hot Pad could accommodate that. Tonight was a case for the latter, as forty heavily armed US Marines formed a perimeter around the aircraft while the aircrew stood out of the rain on the aircraft's lowered ramp. The only light came from the red aircraft cabin lights, and they cast an eerie glow around the back of the plane.

Soon a few vehicles approached, and more security personnel exited the covered trucks. Men from the security force were looking around from under their rubberized camouflaged ponchos and occasionally talking, oblivious to the time or weather.

Major Gayle Morris, the Aircraft Commander, was growing impatient. He knew a storm was raging to the north of his route, and he wanted to get off the ground as soon as possible.

Morris turned to his Crew Chief, Master Sergeant Don Tucker, and simply glared at him. Tucker knew the look well. They had been flying in and out of Vietnam together for over a year. Before Morris could ask, Tucker walked off the ramp into the downpour.

"Who is talking to the convoy?" Tucker asked. "Ten minutes or less" came the reply. Tucker turned around without answering and went back to the shelter of the aircraft.

"Ten minutes!" he yelled. "Get it ready."

Without talking, the crew dispersed and set about getting the aircraft ready to depart. Morris frowned as he followed his copilot and flight engineer to the cockpit.

Major Morris and the Master Sergeant were the only members of the six-man crew who knew exactly what the cargo would be. The others might speculate, but nobody asked or discussed it aloud.

They had all been part of aircrews carrying classified cargo, and they knew the drill. No talking to anyone who might come aboard unless it was specifically about something they needed or needed to know. No questions or comments about the load. Not even among themselves.

Sometimes the cargo would be personnel. Usually CIA or some other covert group. Sometimes it would be material. It really didn't matter to anyone in the crew. It all paid the same, and besides, they were only going as far as Anderson Airforce Base in Guam, where they would be replaced by another crew who would take the aircraft to its next destination. Wherever that might be.

A short time later, a small convoy approached. In all there were three vehicles. No cargo-handling equipment and no cargo pallets.

More Marines exited the vehicles and soon two men walked up the ramp carrying a locked gray box the size of a large suitcase. They stopped on the ramp to shake off the rain then walked toward Tucker. The box had no markings, just two locks; two steel, serialized ordnance seals; and four wire bands.

The box was placed on the deck between the wheel wells, and the Loadmaster secured it using four nylon cargo straps. Twenty Marines came aboard and found seats for the trip. They were all carrying their primary weapon, the standard issue Colt M16, a M1911 sidearm and a small rucksack. They would be staying with the cargo to its ultimate destination. In all, it would be a three-day trip to a government weapons storage facility in Carlsbad, New Mexico.

The Troop Commander was a young black Marine Captain named Otis Reed.

MSGT Tucker saved the Captain the trouble of seeking him out. "Is everybody onboard?" Tucker asked. The Captain nodded as he reached out to shake Tucker's hand. Then he handed the Master Sergeant an envelope that held a troop manifest and a classified message regarding the cargo that would only be opened by the Aircraft Commander in the event of an emergency.

Tucker raised his left arm and made a circling motion. It was his signal for the ramp to be closed. The men standing security in the rain saw the plane's red interior lights slowly disappear beneath the towering tail of the C-130.

The security perimeter was pulled back, and several men returned to the trucks. One by one the blacked-out cargo plane's four turbo-prop engines roared to life, and the rain and standing water was blown in every direction. No identification lights on the aircraft were illuminated, and appropriate to this classified mission, the aircraft would leave with no external lights until they reached their cruising altitude.

In the cockpit Major Morris spoke to the Bin Thuy tower while his copilot started the short taxi to the takeoff end of the runway.

Security personnel on the ground followed close by as the aircraft taxied into position.

MSGT Tucker passed through the cargo bay with the Loadmaster. They were both shining powerful flashlights on various areas of the interior of the aircraft. Once they were sure everything was in order, the Loadmaster took a seat near the ramp, and Tucker climbed the two steps to the cockpit and plugged his headset into the aircraft's intercom system.

"All set in the back," he said. There was no answer, and Tucker didn't expect one. With the brakes holding the C-130 back, all four engines were throttled up to near maximum rpm. Then without warning the aircraft lunged forward as it started to roll. Rain streaked across the windscreen, and the dim lights marking the edge of the runway were a blur as the aircraft accelerated. Forty seconds after Morris had released the brakes, the wheels of the aircraft left the ground, and the Air Force C-130, and crew known only by their call sign, "Valiant 06," flew into the stormy night, never to be seen or heard from again.

CHAPTER 2

GULF OF OMAN
PRESENT DAY

———◆———

As THREE NAVY F-18 FIGHTER jets formed up over the Gulf of Oman, Lieutenant Rawley West eased her aircraft into position on the right side of the formation, just as she had done dozens of times during this deployment.

She looked at the other planes and couldn't help thinking this would be the last time she would see this beautiful sight. She caught herself thinking of her next life, then stopped and focused on the task at hand. Formation flying at 350 knots was no place to daydream, and she knew that.

Over her radio she could hear the flight leader talking to the aircraft carrier *Abraham Lincoln* using a brevity code, a one- or two-word message that let the carrier know several things about the flight or mission without transmitting any details over the radio. Passing the word "Dolores" might mean they had departed a certain landmark. Passing "Caroline" might indicate another milestone in the mission was complete. Brevity codes changed regularly and were usually common words such as models of automobiles, names, or some other list of words. Based on the short, coded voice messages, the carrier would also learn everything important about the flight's return: condition of the aircraft, including remaining fuel, or if any ordnance failed to deploy. These were just two things that were significant for planning purposes.

The flight of three had just completed a bombing sortie over Afghanistan, and it was exactly the kind of mission that made Rawley long for a new way of life. Dropping bombs on an often-unseen enemy wasn't her favorite activity. Rawley was a fighter pilot, not a bomber pilot, and unfortunately the glory days of dogfighting were long gone. Close air support was at least more challenging, but unless it was a spontaneous emergent requirement, those missions normally went to the Marine Corps or Air Force A-10s. Now she had made a choice to leave this world behind. She had accepted a nonmilitary flying position that would have her slowing down and flying closer to the action.

Most pilots would kill to be where she was right now, but they didn't know what she knew, and few had the experiences she had been afforded growing up. Her father, Bud West, had also been a Navy fighter pilot, who saw action in the Vietnam War and later served as a Navy test pilot. When the war ended, he returned to his home state of Montana, where he used his flying skills to establish a very successful mountain flying business.

While working in that business, Bud flew all over the Rocky Mountains and the Pacific Northwest and from western Canada to Alaska, providing any service that required an aircraft or pilot with his skills. The job normally entailed flying sportsmen into and out of tight areas in the wilderness, and occasionally he would train other pilots.

Before he joined the Navy, Bud had married his childhood sweetheart, Sally Peigen. Sally was a direct descendant of the great Blackfoot war chief Crowfoot, and her grandfather was the last Blackfoot war chief, Kinistook. Sally had always embraced her Blackfoot heritage, and Rawley's given middle name, Peta, was Blackfoot for "Golden Eagle," a name that would prove to be more than appropriate. While Bud was flying, Sally managed the cattle ranch they had built on the Front Range of the Rocky Mountains.

When Rawley was old enough to sit a saddle, Sally would take her on horseback into the mountains, often for days at a time. Through these experiences Rawley would become an accomplished rider while also learning the ways of the Blackfeet. Rawley learned to ride, hunt, fish, and shoot, but mostly she learned to be a survivor, and those instincts had served her well. Surviving is exactly what carrier pilots did. Every flight was a new challenge, and pilots were often forced to find new and creative ways to save themselves and their aircraft. Now Rawley was making her final flight as a Navy pilot. It had been seven years and some months since she finished flight school. She had made several deployments, and other pilots held her in high regard. A "good stick," they would say. Seven years and a few thousand flight hours all coming to an end with this next landing, or what naval aviators called a "trap."

As they approached the *Abraham Lincoln*, Rawley mentally went through her checklist while listening to the flight leader communicate with the carrier. Passing down the right, or starboard, side of the *Abraham Lincoln*, Rawley took one last long look at the deck of the boat that had been her home for so many months. She could not help but wonder if she was making a mistake.

The flight leader called the break as he entered a sweeping left-hand turn that would take them into a set pattern until each aircraft was in line to land. Rawley watched as the number-two aircraft rolled left, then she mentally counted her interval before banking around into what was referred to as the downwind leg. As she banked left, she watched the tail hook and landing gear deploy on the F-18 in front of her. She heard the pilot transmitting his remaining fuel in pounds. On the giant ship, they would calculate that into total aircraft weight, then set the appropriate tension on the arresting wires. Too little tension and they risked losing the jet overboard; too much tension could damage the aircraft. Like everything onboard precision was part of every aspect of carrier operations.

She slowed her plane and fell into position behind the second aircraft. She could hear the landing signal officer, or LSO, over the radio, talking to the flight leader. She lowered her landing gear and tail hook then instinctively looked at her airspeed and added power to compensate for the added drag. During a normal carrier landing, the 25,000-pound fighter would go from 150 nautical miles per hour to a dead stop in nearly 300 feet.

She saw the first aircraft jerk to a halt as the tail hook grabbed the arresting wire. Seconds later the deck was clear, and the second plane touched down.

Rawley was next. Another quick check, wheels down and locked, hook, flaps, airspeed. She went through every item mentally in a split second. She scanned her instruments and the carrier deck ahead.

She took one last glance at her fuel. She saw the light of the Fresnel lens and anticipated the first call from the LSO. She squirmed back into her seat and pulled her harness tight.

As she closed on the carrier, more information flashed through her mind than most people process in an hour. Rawley was now about three quarters of a mile from the stern of the giant floating airfield when her radio came alive with a familiar voice.

"Pocahontas. Call the ball."

"Roger, Ball," she calmly replied. Rawley's callsign was a nod to her Indian heritage.

Names were never used over the radio. Just call signs. Some were fitting, and some were confusing. Some call signs were befitting a warrior, such as Viper or Thunder, some were borderline unflattering. Like most nicknames, you never picked it, it picked you.

While making the appropriate calls, Rawley continued the rapid scan of her instruments and the indicators at the stern of ship.

At all times she maintained her focus on landing and resisted the urge to be distracted by the constant activity on the deck of the carrier as she made her approach. Aircraft were being catapulted from the bow of the ship one after another. To the port, or left, side of the carrier and low to the water, a large helicopter slowly moved along with the ship. Steam from the ship's plane-handling equipment blew across the deck. Dozens of personnel in colored shirts were moving everywhere interacting with aircraft in one way or another. A massive elevator was moving aircraft to or from the ship's hangar deck below. Discipline ruled the day, and mistakes were never tolerated. If a pilot allowed him- or herself to become distracted for even a split second, that could spell disaster.

As she flew over the fantail of the great ship, it gently rolled from side to side, but that was transparent to carrier pilots. She managed the power to control her sink rate. Her eyes were on the Fresnel lens, and she listened intently for advisory calls from the LSO. Her rate of descent, line, and glide slope were just a few things the LSO watched as aircraft approached the deck. The process was an orchestrated event where every aspect was controlled.

At any moment the command to "bolter" would signal her to initiate a "go-around." In a split second, she would need to respond by adding power while climbing away from the ship on a specific heading. But that wasn't happening today. Not on what would likely be her last carrier landing.

As Rawley's F-18 fighter jet pounded onto the deck, the robust landing gear flexed to absorb the crushing impact, and she instantly increased to full power. If she missed a wire or anything failed, she would need full power to avoid crashing off the end of the angled deck. Rawley's tail hook grabbed her target, the third of four cables spaced fifty feet apart on the steel deck. The "three wire," as it was commonly referred to, brought her aircraft to a bone-jarring stop in just two seconds. She eased the power back to idle and folded her wings. On command from a plane handler, she raised hook, and other deck personnel disengaged her from the arresting wire. Once free from the cable, she was directed out of the landing area, where her aircraft was quickly chained to the deck. This entire sequence happened in less than one minute.

Rawley powered the twin turbines down, then raised her canopy. She was facing toward the bow of the ship, and she could see a few members of the flight deck crew walking toward her. Leading the way was a young woman wearing a brown shirt. The woman was smiling broadly, and as she came near, she raised her right hand in a salute. The woman was a petty officer who had been Rawley's assigned "plane captain" since before this deployment left port. Rawley stood up and returned the salute, then she took one last lingering look at her surroundings as she drew a long breath and slowly let it out.

Camaraderie in naval aviation is extremely high, and everyone on deck knew this was her last flight. Anyone not actively engaged in landing or launching aircraft gathered around. Rawley looked down at the rainbow of shirts and familiar faces. At sea this was her family, and she was leaving home all over again.

Before Rawley stepped down from her plane, she uncharacteristically removed her helmet and shook her long, black hair free. As she climbed from the plane, pilots, crewman, and deck personnel surrounded her. She was an important part of this squadron, and she would be missed.

After a short speech by her squadron commander, everyone gathered around Rawley for one final photograph in front of her aircraft. As the crowd dispersed, Rawley was left standing with her commanding officer. "You know you'll miss this about a minute after that COD leaves the deck."

"I already do," she said. "There's nothing like it in the world." Rawley looked over the expansive carrier deck. Then lamented. "I admit I'm torn. I love this life, but how soon before I'm sitting at a desk and not flying at all." She said it as a statement rather than a question.

The commander just nodded, knowing that was true. "A fighter pilot can't fly forever. It's a young man's game, Rawley; you take what you can, when you can, and where you can." With that he turned and walked away, leaving her to her thoughts.

He didn't say it, but her commander was envious. She was a young warrior going closer to the fight.

As Rawley took one last look around, the smell of jet fuel was in the air, the wind was in her face, and the activity carried on. Planes were still being launched and recovered simultaneously. Jet engines roared, and men and women in colored vests were everywhere performing their tasks. It was like a frantic stage play set to the sound of thunder. It was truly a unique world, she thought. And soon it would be just another memory to log away.

CHAPTER 3

———◆———

RAWLEY HEADED TO THE SQUADRON ready room for debriefing, and once again she was greeted with catcalls and cheering. Every pilot shook her hand or slapped her back, wishing her well and promising to meet sometime in the future to drink and tell stories. From there she would clean up and get mentally prepared for the long journey back to Virginia. Sadly, it would all begin with one last catapult, or "cat shot," riding in the back of a propeller driven, C2 COD mail and logistics plane. She would be sitting backward with no window, no view of the signals. No responsibility. The ultimate indignity for a Navy fighter pilot.

Rawley quickly made the rounds, finishing administrative details and saying good-bye to a few friends, including her mentor and former commanding officer, Captain Arlen Cooper. In Navy jargon Cooper would be referred to as "seasoned." That was just a polite way of saying he was an Old Guy. He was on his last deployment, and after thirty-five years in the Navy, he knew a Flag was not in his future. A Flag signified the rank of admiral, a coveted milestone he would not achieve. Flying was always competitive, but now pilots were amassing huge numbers of combat missions in support of high-profile combat operations. Promotions required achievements that would set you apart from the crowd, and as the war on terror dragged on, high-ranking personal awards were commonplace. The slightest blemish on a military record meant you would be lucky to see thirty years and the rank of O6, or "captain," as the Navy called it.

Cooper had a blemish. An errant bomb dropped by a pilot under his command had caused collateral damage. By the time the inquiry was finished, he may as well have dropped the bomb himself. The enemy lines and rules of engagement changed daily it seemed, and since the rules were a political tool drafted by civilians they were rarely as simple as black or white. The US military was under the boot of an administration that had little interest in this or any other war, and the current president inherited a winning situation and had managed it into near chaos. Mistakes on the battlefield were common, and poor leadership at any level meant innocent people would pay with their lives. Men and women in leadership roles like Cooper paid in other ways.

Rawley knocked on Cooper's door, then walked in.

"Whoa, what if I was naked?" Cooper said, feigning indignity.

Rawley laughed as she looked around the relatively large stateroom. "I would have just confirmed the rumors I've been hearing for years."

"It's a great rumor, and I started it!" he said.

Arlen paused and looked at her for a moment, hoping it would not be the last time.

"Tell me one more time why you are doing this?" Cooper asked.

"Well," she started, "I thought I knew, but now I can't really sum it all up."

"Tell me again how you met this recruiter." Cooper motioned for her to sit.

Rawley smiled as she remembered the mysterious stranger who started her on this path out of the Navy. "It happened in Hawaii," she said, "while I was getting fuel. I was at flight operations at Hickam Air Force Base, and this guy approached me and asked where I was headed. He asked what I had been flying and where. Questions like that. Nothing crazy." She continued. "Then he showed me his credentials and said he was recruiting pilots to fly for the government in less conventional roles in support of the war."

Cooper leaned back in his chair and relaxed as Rawley continued to describe her chance meeting.

"I wasn't really interested at first, but the more he talked, the more it appealed to me. And anyway," she said, "I'll be flying a desk like you when this deployment is over, you know that." She paused as if to let her friend and mentor dispel that idea. He did not.

And then her eyes lit up. "It's mountain flying," she said. "Right down in the terrain. No more loitering on station, hoping to be called. And I'll be learning a trade. Learning a trade!"

"What do you call this?" Cooper asked.

Rawley stopped him before he could complete his thought. "Look, my father has been flying in the mountains for years, and he has made a very good life out of it. It's what I want to do. I'll just be doing it on a whole different level."

"How is your father?" Cooper asked.

"He's great!" Rawley offered.

"Unfortunately, I can't share with him exactly what I'll be doing next, but I'm sure someday we can discuss it. And besides, If I can just fly for a few more years, I can leave the government and go to Alaska or maybe work with my father. Bush pilots will always be in demand." Rawley stopped talking and took a deep breath and then slowly let it out. She had summed it all up after all, she thought. "What are you going to do when this gig is up?" she asked as she relaxed into her chair.

"I am going to fly an air ambulance for a friend. A converted G5 that will get at-risk combat wounded where they need to be faster."

Rawley tilted her head back. "Really."

"Hey, just because I'm not flying now doesn't mean I've given it up," he said.

Rawley nodded her head at the thought.

"What made you want to fly, Rawley?" Arlen asked. "Are you doing it for of your father?"

Rawley was shaking her head and smiling. "How much time do you have, and what do you have to drink?"

Arlen turned to a small cabinet next to his desk. "This is strictly for medicinal purposes, of course." He pulled a small bottle from the bottom drawer. "The hypothermia brandy! Never leave port without it." Arlen poured a small amount into two coffee cups and handed one to Rawley.

"To all things that fly," he said, raising his cup to hers. "Your story."

Rawley took a sip then again slid back into the uncomfortable vinyl office chair. "When I was very young, my mother started taking me to a place in the mountains on horseback. It's a natural clearing surrounded by rocks and tall pines with a creek running next to a nice grassy area perfect for landing aircraft.

"She told me it was called Apistotooki, and it was both sacred and magic to the Blackfeet. A healing place, she said.

"On one trip when I was nine, I think, we were there alone, as usual, sitting near the fire, and she had been telling me tribal stories she learned as a child. Then she stopped and told me to follow the plume of smoke into the sky and make a wish. I told her all I could think of was that I wished my dad could be there. About ten minutes later, I heard a sound coming from one end of the valley, and just like that, my father appeared in his old silver Cessna 185."

"The sun made it glow as he came nearer, then he cut the engine and glided in like a bird right between the trees and rocks. I must have seen him come and go from the ranch in that plane a hundred times, but I was mesmerized. He bounced a few times, then rolled to a stop right in front of us. My life was never the same after that. I flew with him every chance I got, until one day I was just flying everywhere I could just to be flying."

Rawley stopped talking and took a sip of brandy while still remembering that day in the mountains.

Now the room was quiet except for the ship's perpetual hum from constantly running machinery. Cooper sat forward and put his hands on his knees, then looked Rawley directly in the eyes.

"Nothing," he said, and then paused. "Nothing happens by chance. And I'm not talking in some deep, spiritual sense. Be careful what you wish for." Then once again he paused while still looking directly at her.

"This is not some mountain-flying adventure delivering fisherman to a trout stream. It's dangerous. The aircraft are slow, unarmed, and unsophisticated. The people you are sharing the cockpit with are not you. For the most part, they are general-aviation pilots, dreamers looking for some bullshit adventure." Cooper watched her face as he spoke, and he could tell his warning was falling on deaf ears.

"I'll stop." Cooper relaxed back into his chair. "Just remember," he said, "if anything should ever go wrong…"

Rawley knew exactly what was coming out Cooper's mouth next, and as he spoke she followed along mentally like she had heard it a thousand times.

"Flying is an art form," Cooper said, finishing his thought. "A dance between man and machine. Stay light on the controls, and if you do go down, fly it until it stops moving."

Rawley had in fact heard it word for word more times than she could count. Her father had been saying it for years. It was probably the first words out of the mouth of the first pilot who crashed and lived to tell the story.

Cooper stood up, hugged Rawley, and physically turned her toward the door to avoid an awkward good-bye. "Be vigilant and be tough," he said as she walked out of his stateroom.

Rawley raised her right hand into the air as she walked out, but she never looked back. She had two hours to grab her bags and report to the ready room. She had a long trip ahead, but the next chapter of her life was beginning now, and she was finally excited. No more second thoughts, no more apprehension.

CHAPTER 4

OCEANA NAVAL AIR STATION, NORFOLK, VIRGINIA

———◆———

RAWLEY'S TRANSITION FROM NAVY PILOT to civilian was a fast and unceremonious process. Navy personnel who finished a career or retired would be honored with a military ceremony to mark the end of their service. There would be awards and gifts, speeches and anecdotes. Family and friends would gather to share in the milestone event, and then there would be another celebration that included drinking and more stories. In contrast, Rawley was ending her career the way most service members ended a deployment, and that in itself was always an awkward transition after eight to nine months of having every minute of every day planned, scheduled, briefed, and debriefed. Married personnel would normally return to a functioning household, a welcome home party, and loved ones. For others, it meant simply leaving work and returning to an empty apartment or a familiar bar.

For persons leaving the service before retirement, such as Rawley was doing, there would be documents to sign, equipment to return, and then…without fanfare or circumstance, it was simply over. A few short good-byes and gone. As Rawley walked to her car, she stopped, turned, and took one last long look at the nondescript concrete-and-metal hangar that had been her workplace for nearly half her military career. As she stood there. she remembered the words of a retiring commander she once knew: "Leaving the Navy is like pulling your finger out of a bucket of water. In an instant, it's like you were never there." Rawley tightened her jaw then finished the long walk to her car.

Rawley's route home took her east down Atlantic Avenue along the boardwalk and through the prime tourist area of Virginia Beach. As she drove she passed two monuments, one dedicated to Naval Aviation and another dedicated to Naval Special Warfare. Soon the hotels along the beach gave way to homes. Most were refurbished beach cottages, some more than sixty years old and a few much older than that. The homes were tightly packed together, and parking was at a premium. As she turned down the narrow street to her oceanfront duplex, she could see little had changed. Surfers were walking to the beach or returning to their cars, and others were walking, jogging, or riding bikes. In her driveway sat a familiar car, and Rawley could not help but smile.

Aubrey Hodges was a Navy Blackhawk helicopter pilot, although the Navy version of the airframe was called the Seahawk. Rawley and Aubrey had been on opposite deployment schedules for at least three years, and they kept each other's affairs in order when the other was away.

As Rawley walked through the door, she could see Aubrey coming from the kitchen with two glasses in one hand a pitcher in the other. "Welcome home and bon voyage?" Aubrey said as she leaned forward to kiss Rawley on the cheek. "Change and meet me on the beach." Aubrey handed Rawley one of the glasses she was holding then filled it with rum punch.

It was a short walk to the beach across an elevated boardwalk that crossed the dunes to an area known to locals as The North End. This area was usually devoid of tourists unless they were renting one of the local homes. Locals and surfers were ever present, but the crowds never seemed to make it this far from the vacation hot spot at the southern end of Virginia Beach.

"I got your cryptic message," Aubrey said. "What's going on, and why are you home early?"

Rawley looked out across the ocean as she spoke. "I met a guy who offered me a job." Then she looked down the beach to the south. "The timing was right." Rawley shrugged as she sipped her drink. Now they were both looking out to sea at the ships entering and leaving the Chesapeake Bay.

"A tall, dark, and mysterious guy?" Aubrey asked.

"No, more like my dad's age. But mysterious, yes! I was refueling in Hawaii, and we started talking."

"So, what's the job, or should I ask?" Aubrey leaned back on one elbow and looked at Rawley.

"Contract flying in Afghanistan at first," said Rawley. "Do you think I'm crazy?

"Let's see. You're leaving the cockpit of an F-18 with all the backing of the United States Navy and guns and missiles to fly, what?"

"I don't know exactly," Rawley said. "I know what I've seen over there. No jets. I am crazy, aren't I?" Rawley also leaned back. She looked at her empty glass, then held it out to be refilled. "I did stay in the reserves. It was a last-minute decision. I wasn't going to, but you know the deal."

Aubrey shook the ice in her glass, then tossed the cubes into the sand before refilling her own glass. "No sense watering down the rum. How long before you leave?"

"I have to be at Langley Monday," Rawley said.

"Two days to drink, one day to recover!" Aubrey said as she stood up and brushed the sand from her legs. "I know a young ensign who would love to be our designated driver!"

"Pilot?" Rawley asked as they walked back toward the house.

"FO," Aubrey said, shaking her head. "Another pilot would just be drinking."

Officers who filled positions other than the pilot on naval aircraft were designated as flight officers and often referred to as FOs. The term, often pronounced "foe," wasn't derogatory; it was simply another military label.

CHAPTER 5

CENTRAL INTELLIGENCE AGENCY, LANGLEY, VIRGINIA

———————

AFTER WHAT SEEMED LIKE AN abnormally long verification process that included photographs, fingerprints, briefs, and document signing, Rawley was finally sent through the main gate at CIA headquarters with an escort who took her to an unmarked door at the rear of the largest building in the compound.

"Welcome to Langley, Miss West!" The receptionist seemed a bit more enthusiastic than she expected. She didn't actually know what to expect, she just didn't expect an enthusiastic secretary at this early hour.

"Call me Rawley," she said as she reached to shake hands.

"Oh, yes, I know!" the young girl said, without offering her name. "I know all about you. I've read your entire file. All the women around here are very excited to have you onboard. We don't have too many women flying in the field."

"How many women are there?" Rawley asked.

"Actually, you are the first. Let me show you to the briefing room," she said as she turned and walked away.

As Rawley followed her guide through the halls, she couldn't help but think how austere things looked for an organization with such a long history. And no women pilots! she wondered. Is that possible?

The young girl stopped at another unmarked door. Her enthusiastic demeanor seemed to fade. As she turned toward Rawley, she began explaining the procedure. "As a contractor in indoctrination, you don't have access to very much around here. This area is where you will always come if you need anything. The bathroom is right there." She pointed.

"In here you will be briefed on your training phase. After the brief I'll take you to admin and get your paperwork in order. That is of course if you decide to stay with us," she said rather bluntly.

OK, Rawley thought. Maybe people changed their minds around here. As a former Naval Officer, she wasn't used to having choices.

Rawley shrugged, then turned and pulled the door open and stepped inside.

The room was small and not well lit. There was a long wooden table with a white board at one end and nothing on the walls.

Already seated were five men. Recruited pilots like her, she assumed. They all stood up to say hello. Nobody offered a name, so she followed their lead. Rawley stood five foot eight, and she noticed all these men were shorter and much heavier than her.

They looked like an odd group for pilots, she thought. They were quiet and fairly reserved and none in what she would consider great physical condition. She was used to much more arrogant, boisterous, and physically fit pilots. They looked at her, she looked at them. After more than seven years in the Navy, she knew exactly what they were thinking. Hair, face, tits. Unless they were gay, in which case they were likely appalled by her wrinkled appearance and tangled hair.

Soon the door opened, and two more men came inside, followed by another man with a handful of file folders. As the new arrivals sat down, the other man walked to the end of the table. He looked around at the room as if studying everyone and then called for the brief to begin.

There was nobody else in the room, but on his command, the white board lit up, and a map appeared. It was one she knew too well.

"Afghanistan. This is where you will be flying," he said, without looking at the map. "If you decide to stay, you will be deployed here for nine months to a year for your first assignment. No negotiating that.

"In that time," he said, "you may fly four to five days a week, maybe more, depending on the operational tempo of the forces in-country."

He paused briefly, and after looking around the room, he continued. "We maintain twelve pilots in this theater of operation. That includes a mixture of government employees and contractors. We lose on average two to four pilots a year."

After a short pause for effect, he went on. "Those losses are a result of aircraft failures, enemy ground fire, and primarily pilot error. Mistakes!" he said emphatically. "Mistakes made by pilots with more hours than anyone in this room.

"The terrain is unforgiving, and the locals will not be happy to see you if you survive a forced landing. You will be required to fly day and night in all kinds of weather." Again, he stopped talking and looked around the room.

"You will be flying a variety of unpressurized aircraft. You will be flying low and slow, using terrain for cover when you can, but mostly in the open.

"You are not," he stressed, "combat pilots. You will never be the first choice for air support in known hot areas; however, some of our aircraft do have gun pods for that purpose." Each time he paused, he looked at the faces of those seated at the table. Rawley listened but did not look at the man giving the brief. Instead she also studied the faces of the other men in the room, a habit she had acquired from giving and listening to countless operation briefs with new, young pilots. She was immune to the theatrics and drama. Voice inflections for emphasis just annoyed her, and right now she was greatly annoyed. Flying was inherently dangerous. Flying in a warzone therefore must be more dangerous. Enough said. She thought.

As she looked around and the brief continued, she could already see the first quitter. And if he didn't quit, she might suggest he find other work for his own safety and the safety of anyone who might fly with him. She knew the look. The fidgeting and white knuckles on curled fingers told her all she needed to know.

"You will be flying surveillance missions," the briefer said. "And you will be ferrying ground branch personnel as required. This is mountain flying at its finest!"

A hand went up, but the briefer raised his hand in protest. "Save your questions." He looked around. "The only thing I want to know is if you are ready to go to the next level. Take the next step."

"Any quitters?" he asked. "It's yes or no, right now. That simple."

The men looked at each other, and then they all seemed to fix their gaze on Rawley. Rawley ignored everyone now and just looked at the map. She wasn't really listening; she was reminiscing. Remembering routes she had flown and landmarks used by the FAC, forward air controllers. And she recalled days she spent loitering overhead.

Finally, the silence was broken, and one man slipped his chair back. As he stood up, he began to speak. The briefer stopped him midsentence. "No explanation required; nothing to talk about," he said. "Please step outside, where you will be met and escorted to debriefing."

Rawley watched as the man left the room. Her instincts were correct. She was happy. She knew that man had made the right decision.

"OK. No one else?" the briefer asked. "That guy probably just saved his own life. And maybe some of yours."

He began again. "Here's the process." His tone was much less ominous now, as if he was satisfied at having made a man leave the room. "You have some admin work to take care of. Next of kin, wills, creds, stuff like that. You have a few days to report to our flight school. Obviously you are all skilled pilots—that's why you are here—but nothing you have done has prepared you for what's in store.

"Your first stop is in Montana," he said as he again looked around the room.

Rawley thought it was odd they would go to Montana and not Alaska, but she kept that to herself.

"You'll fly in the Rocky Mountains, the Great Plains, then up to Alaska, and on to some weapons training in Arizona. If you do crash and happen to survive," he said, "shooting skills might come in handy."

"If at any time during the training you decide it's not for you, just tell your instructors, and they will tell you what to do next. One last thing," he said, again raising his voice for added emphasis.

"This school is highly classified, and that includes the location, the staff, and the curriculum. That means nobody needs to know where you are going or what you are doing. Understood?"

Heads were nodding the affirmative.

"This is the CIA," he said, "but you are not 'spies.' You don't need to have code names or backstopped cover stories. You just need to learn to offer less information when you are talking to anyone, including friends and family. In the folder in front of you," he said as he pointed, "you will find a clearly worded confidentiality agreement between you and this organization. It's more comprehensive than the first one you signed.

"Read it, understand it, and sign it," he said with an air of finality. "You will be monitored, and you will be prosecuted if you violate that agreement." With that the briefer left the room, and the secretary walked back in.

She looked at Rawley and smiled. "If you will all follow me," she said, "we will get you on your way. School starts in five days."

CHAPTER 6

SHELBY, MONTANA

———◆———

As Rawley approached the small town of Shelby, Montana, she could not help but feel nostalgic. She grew up 150 miles to the south, where most small towns looked alike. A gas station, a store, three bars, and a stoplight. Shelby had a population of nearly 3,500, so around here it was like the big city.

Rawley wasn't going to the Shelby airport but instead had been directed to a private field outside of town called Buffalo Lake. The Buffalo Lake airstrip was typical for Montana, nothing more than a grass strip and a few old wooden buildings. No matter how austere, it was considered an airport in this state. Lined up near the runway was an assortment of old aircraft. At a modern airport, the decades-old and weathered planes might have looked out of place, but here they were as common as a pickup truck. Aircraft were used for everything in Montana. They delivered fishermen to remote lakes and streams, in the winter they delivered hay to stranded cattle, they searched for lost vacationers, and they delivered mail and served as ambulances. By the time Rawley was eighteen, she had seen it all from both left and right seats of a variety of aircraft. Some had two engines, some had one, some were large, and some were small. Some of the aircraft were specially modified or prepared for mountain flying, and some had no business being there at all. Along with her father, she had seen or done everything a pilot could do with an aircraft under ideal conditions and in weather that was far from ideal. Like the US Postal Service, her father was never deterred by rain, sleet, snow, or dark of night.

She had seen people rescued and cattle saved and flown into and out of a hundred places nobody in their right mind would even consider taking an airplane. And there had been accidents. Blown tires, wings clipping trees, and engine failures. Through it all she witnessed her father's cool and often eerily calm handling of whatever came. He was the consummate professional pilot and a phenomenal flight instructor. By the time Rawley began flying from the left seat as the pilot in command, she had received the finest education any pilot could hope for. She had experienced rugged, mountainous terrain, the Great Plains with its brutal, constant-changing winds, and long cross-country flights to some of the busiest airports in America. Before Rawley graduated from college, she was qualified, or "type rated," in numerous aircraft, including floatplanes and multiengine aircraft.

Those experiences served her well as a Navy fighter pilot, especially when it was time to "go to the boat," as they referred to the aircraft carrier. While others may have been shocked at how small it seemed, to Rawley carrier landings were far from challenging. A flat, open deck always facing into the wind, arresting wires to stop your aircraft, a clear path ahead if you had to go around, visual cues, and a calm, familiar voice to guide you in. Added up it was far less difficult than landing a heavily loaded cargo plane on a steep, sloped airstrip at a high altitude or on a rocky creek bed in the winter.

The Navy was behind her now. She had made nearly six hundred carrier landings, seen combat while piloting the most sophisticated fighter jet America owned, and flown missions that included close air support and precision night bombing. Her future flying would be far from that world. She was coming back to the kind of flying she was destined to be part of, a mountain pilot with the added element of being in a war zone. She knew everything she had done as a pilot had led her to this moment in time. Her father was always proud of her, but she knew this would make him happier than anything she had done yet. This was his world, his kind of flying. If only she could share it with him. She still had not told her parents she was leaving the Navy. In her last message, she just said she would be extremely busy and they shouldn't worry if she didn't communicate with them for a few weeks.

The recruiter never mentioned training in Montana. Flying here meant there was always a possibility of a chance meeting with her father or someone she knew. It was Big Sky Country, but the aviation community in Montana was small by any measure, and worse, this was his backyard. Oh well, she thought, deception was part of her life now. He would surely understand.

She would discuss the potential issues with the staff, she thought. But no sense dwelling on that now. Rawley pulled up to the main building, and a cloud of dust passed over her car. As the dust cleared, she thought of her in-briefing instructions. She looked around, breathed in deep, and let it out slowly. Always her way of calming any nerves she might have. She knew this was the start of a whole new life, a familiar one, but different just the same.

As she stepped out of her rental, she looked around, subconsciously counting cars. Eleven she counted; maybe she was late, she thought. She pulled her long, black hair back into a ponytail, grabbed her flight bag, and walked toward the building marked Office.

As Rawley came through the door she was met by another happy receptionist, and again no name offered. Just a friendly greeting.

Rawley handed her the package of paperwork she had been given, and the woman pointed out the coffee and directed her down the hall to the briefing room. As she walked in, heads turned toward her. She recognized everyone from the meeting at Langley and at least one new face. She took the initiative and went to each pilot, offering a handshake and her name. All the men said hello, and she couldn't help but notice they had clammy hands. Indicators, she thought.

Rawley took a chair in the back of the room and pulled another chair close for her feet. In contrast to the others, she was relaxed and obviously at ease as she leaned back against the wall. This was an environment she could live with. Old planes and mountains!

As she looked out the window at the Rockies, the door opened, and five men filed in.

Rawley dropped her feet to the floor and looked to the front of the classroom. As she looked at the men standing before her, she was dumbstruck. The first man to begin speaking was someone she had known since she was a child. In fact, she knew all these men. They seemed to avoid eye contact with her as they shuffled around. She was confused, but at the same time, it all made perfect sense. If this school was the best, these men epitomized that.

The only man speaking was someone she had known as her uncle Bart. A man she had flown hundreds of hours with, even before she graduated high school. She had known all these men growing up. They were family. What was going on here, she wondered.

"Welcome aboard, everyone," Bart said. Then he looked directly at Rawley as he began talking. She tried to capture the gaze of the other men, but still they avoided eye contact.

"No need to discuss anyone's background; we have read your résumés," Bart said. "You have already been told, but I'll say it again. This school is classified. What happens here stays here. We have been providing this service to the government since 1975. These men behind me have been flying here since the early sixties. We are anonymous and hide in the wide open. We want to keep it that way."

No shit thought Rawley.

"The boss will be here in a few minutes, and he'll explain the way we work and more of what you can expect. You may have noticed one of you is missing. He quit already," said Bart.

"This work is not for everyone. This is not fun flying. It's not recreational flying. You are leaving here to fly in one of the most challenging and unforgiving environments on earth, and it also happens to be a war zone at the moment. That makes it twice as dangerous.

"Wars create exceptional circumstances," he said. "Exceptional circumstances call for extraordinary measures. As the operator of a mobility platform, you may be the only chance of survival for Americans or our coalition partners in imminent danger."

"That means you must fly your aircraft into seemingly impossible locations and then get off the ground and out of harm's way. You might be overloaded; you may have an aircraft with degraded capabilities. Read that as one engine out or engines with less than full power available. We create those situations here."

As Bart spoke, Rawley was still trying to make sense of it all.

She had been sent to what was described as the best bush-flying school in the world. The men standing before her were like family. They all had worked for her father in his flying business, yet nobody acknowledged her. It seemed like a surreal situation. If this had been going on for all these years, how could she not have known that? Was she that unaware of her surroundings? That naïve?

Before she could complete her next thought, the door opened. Rawley held her breath, then swallowed hard. In her heart she now knew who was coming through the door, and she was not wrong. It was Bud West. Her father. Although they talked on the phone often, she had not seen him for almost two years. And now here he stood. Rawley leaned back and once more drew a deep breath. She had watched him enter rooms her entire life, but it was as if she was seeing him for the first time. She wanted to stand up and embrace him. She was confused. Should she stand, stay seated, say anything? She leaned back in her seat, and she could feel her jaw tighten.

Her father appeared as relaxed and confident as ever. He was everything the new pilots sitting before her were not. Bud nodded to everyone, including her, and began to speak.

"This day will start with a familiarization flight in the mountains. You will find Montana terrain is very similar to Afghanistan; that's why you are here. You may or may not return to this location each night. You'll fly for two weeks locally in the mountains and plains. The final two weeks will take place in Alaska. There will be cargo and passengers.

There will be emergency scenarios. Everyone will progress at their own pace. We want you well trained and safe." Bud paused.

"Everyone will be exposed to different aircraft and situations. Graduation is not assured," he said.

Rawley had barely heard him speak. Her mind raced as she replayed countless details from her childhood. How many times had she participated in these training scenarios? How many pilots had been trained while her father pretended to deliver fishermen and campers into the mountains or to teach someone to fly?

Bud finished talking and turned toward the door. Then he paused, and Rawley leaned forward. Was he going to acknowledge her?

"I want to leave you all with this bit of advice," he said.

Rawley opened her mouth, and the words just came out. Bud stopped talking.

"Flying is an art form," she said in a low but audible voice. "A dance between man and machine. Stay light on the controls, and if you do go down, fly it until it stops moving."

The other students looked at Rawley as if she had committed some kind of sin. Bart and the other instructors looked at Bud. There was a pregnant pause, and then Bud smiled broadly. "Well, that's a lot better than what I was going to say." "We need to write that down."

Then he looked at the other students. "You would all do well to remember those words, it's good advice." And with that, he left the room.

Bart took over as the other instructors also filed out after Bud.

A roll-up map was pulled down, and Bart began to point out the landing sites. They could hardly be called runways. Most were nothing more than dry riverbeds this time of year. There was at least one icy glacier and a few county roads.

Rawley unconsciously mouthed the names of the locations as Bart went through each one. She had landed at every one of these places at least once while growing up. She would be reliving her childhood, she thought. This entire situation was like a scene from a strange movie.

Why all the subterfuge? she wondered. Why couldn't her father just tell her the truth? By default she was practically part of this business. How many men would she meet in this new life who had flown with her and her father in this secret endeavor?

Enough thinking, she thought. Time to fly!

Bart finished with the map and issued his first mission orders.

"On the ramp," he said, "you will find seven aircraft. In the cockpit you will find everything you need to know about that airframe. Pick a plane, go through it, and preflight it. Make sure it's ready to fly.

"Learn the numbers," Bart added. "We live or die here by Vso and Vmc. Knowing those will keep you alive."

Every aircraft ever flown has a set of numbers, or in aviation terms, *V* speeds. There were fourteen in all, though not all applied to every aircraft. Those numbers had designations such as Va, maneuvering speed, or Vne, the speed the aircraft should never exceed. By flying within those parameters or numbers, a plane should be safe to operate. When an aircraft exceeded those numbers, they had a tendency to crash. Vso and Vmc referred to stall speed in landing configuration and minimum control speed, respectively. Landing in the mountains often required extremely slow approaches. It was a fine line between extremely slow and a stall. Once a plane stalled, or quit flying, there was little chance of recovering. Especially close to the ground in the thin mountain air.

As everyone stood up to leave, Bart looked at Rawley. "There's a Twin Otter out there, young lady. Why don't you get that ready, and I'll be along shortly."

"One last thing," Bart called out as he left the room. "We don't create problems for you to find. That's a good way to end up dead. There will be enough issues without us making trouble. The planes are in great shape, but do a thorough preflight."

—◆—

CHAPTER 7

As Rawley left the room, she looked around, hoping to catch a glimpse of her father but he was nowhere to be found. She wasn't surprised, just hopeful. She thought about looking for him but changed her mind. Better to just go along, she guessed. Besides, she would be flying with Bart soon enough and he would tell her what was going on. Hopefully.

No matter how hard she tried, she could not stop the flashbacks that kept finding their way back into her thoughts. Like the time her favorite plane was destroyed in a landing accident on the Missouri River.

It was a beautiful Husky on amphibious floats. Her father had let her and a girlfriend fly it to a class party at Flathead Lake the summer before her senior year. What an entrance they had made. After a requisite low pass, they circled around and made a text book landing, then taxied to the water's edge in front of the party.

Rawley was very angry when she discovered the man who crashed the Husky had left the wheels down while landing on water. What a rookie mistake, she thought. And why was he flying the plane in the first place? Now she knew it had to be part of her father's business.

And there were other incidents and accidents, and her father never seemed to react the way she might have expected. Now it all made sense—and it had gone on right under her nose.

Rawley walked with the group toward the planes then stopped and let the others walk ahead. She looked at each aircraft. None were familiar. They used to be like old friends, she thought. Every plane held memories. These were all strangers to her. Friends she had not yet met. With their huge balloon-like tundra tires, the planes looked more like caricatures or airplanes from a children's cartoon. They had cargo pods, and some had net doors, while others had no doors. There were no fancy wheel fairings, no elaborate paint schemes, and no plush interiors. If there was anything on the inside or outside of the plane that could be removed without affecting safety or airworthiness, it was gone. Even a single pound removed meant a pound of cargo could be added or another passenger or maybe fuel.

All the planes showed transfer marks or scars from contact with rocks, tree branches, or bushes. To most people, and even some pilots, these planes might have looked like they were done, ready to be scrapped. To Rawley they were magic carpets to a world full of excitement and wonder. Every landing, every takeoff in the mountains would be like a singular event unlike the last landing or the next. There were always new challenges and new dangers and in the world of flying, there were few parallels.

Rawley steadied her gaze on the de Havilland Twin Otter. Compared to the other aircraft, it was a monster. On normal wheels the tail stood twenty feet in the air. On tundra tires the aircraft towered over the small Cessna it was sitting next to.

Rawley walked beneath the wings of the Otter and looked over the entire exterior of the aircraft paying particular attention to the control surfaces and especially the wing tips. Most of the wing tips were composite or plastic, so they would break away without damaging the wing structure in the event of a tree strike. Compared to the others, this plane looked quite new.

She could tell from the exterior handles around the cargo door that the aircraft had been used for skydiving at some point in its life or maybe still. Another clue was the roll-up cargo door. That was popular for skydiving but not a normal modification for cargo operations.

The Otter was sitting on three thick wheel struts. One in the nose and two jutting from the airframe's bulbous midbody. It was the only aircraft there with a nosewheel. All the others were referred to as taildraggers. That meant two wheels forward and one small wheel under the tail. She scrutinized each landing strut, looking for any sign of damage or fluid leaks. There were none to be found. The tires were obviously new. They even smelled like new rubber, and the painted-on markings could still be read. She knew it made sense to start this kind of training with new rubber. There was no roadside service in the mountains. If your aircraft needed to be repaired to come home, you were doing the repair, and that included changing tires.

After dragging a large stepladder to the plane, Rawley finished the preflight then scaled the side the plane to gain access to the cockpit. The cockpit had a smell of its own, and she knew it well. Her mind was filled with abstract thoughts as she looked over the switches, knobs, and controls. Rawley stopped and looked out toward the other planes to see if her father was walking around or if any of the instructors had come outside. She didn't see him, so she went back to what she was doing.

On the copilot's seat were all the logs and other information she needed. She then turned around and looked back at the hollow shell of a fuselage.

Strapped to the deck were a large ladder, a spare nosewheel and main tire, a toolbox, an axe, and a hydraulic jack. Behind the copilot's seat was a large first-aid kit and next to that a bag full of blankets. Let's hope all these things are not needed, she thought.

"Numbers, numbers," she said aloud. She fanned the aircraft manual to the information she needed. She knew the twin Otter fairly well, but it had been some time since they had enjoyed each other's company. She went back and forth between the manual and the panel, remembering as she went. She looked up at the engine controls, switches, and circuit breakers. Then she reached up and put her hand on the throttles.

Nothing too hard here, she thought. And, it was just a fun flight anyway.

CHAPTER 8

As Rawley systematically went through the preflight checklist, she looked up and saw Bart a few feet from the nose of the aircraft. He was standing with his hands on his hips and smiling from ear to ear. He never changed, Rawley thought. His thick black hair seemed to never grow, and she had never once seen him without a large bushy mustache. Rawley smiled as she looked down at Bart. For a moment they just looked at each other, then Bart came to the right side of the aircraft and climbed aboard.

"What in the hell is going on?" she asked.

Bart leaned across the cockpit, and she met him halfway. He grabbed her with both arms and squeezed her tight.

"Welcome home, jet pilot!" he said. "Is this thing ready to fly?"

"It's ready if you are," she responded. Rawley scanned left to right around the cockpit, and Bart did the same.

Other planes were starting, and one was already taxiing to the runway. After putting on her headset, Rawley continued through the checklist, then she pulled her door shut.

"Clear!" Rawley yelled through a small window. It was meant as a warning to anyone nearby that she intended to start the engines.

She began the starting sequence for the left engine. A puff of gray smoke came from the exhaust as the propeller slowly turned, then the Pratt and Whitney turbine roared to life. Instantly the noise from the smaller planes vanished. Rawley looked to her right. Bart reached out for his own door and yelled, "Clear!" again. In a few seconds, the right engine was spinning.

Rawley scanned the instruments, and Bart instinctively did the same.

Using common CRM, or cockpit resource management skills, they backed each other up without speaking. Although Rawley had not flown the de Havilland for some time, it was all coming back. When Rawley pulled the toggle switch to energize the avionics, her headset immediately quieted the outside noise and panel lights illuminated. At the same time, her compass needle and artificial horizon came to life.

Rawley looked at the fuel level and engine-status indicators. Everything looked normal.

They buckled up while still watching the instruments. Rawley adjusted her seat, and so did Bart. They were both getting comfortable and ready to fly. Rawley would be the pilot in command, but Bart could assume control in an instant if required. It didn't matter how experienced the other pilot was or how many hours each of them had in the aircraft. It was just good practice. Especially considering the kind of flying they were there to perform.

At most small airports in Montana, planes often came and went in radio silence, but with all the planes departing at the same time, the radio was alive with pilots announcing their departure intentions. For now, all the planes were on a common radio frequency known as UNICOM, the same frequency often shared by other small airports nearby. To avoid confusion pilots would start their announcement with the airport identifier followed by their aircraft type and then what they intended to do after departure. Soon all the aircraft would be flying off in different directions, and once away from the field, they would no longer be talking to each other.

One plane was left to takeoff, then Rawley and Bart would head to the takeoff end of the runway.

"Where are we going?" Rawley asked.

Bart turned toward her to speak, even though his voice could only be heard through the headset. "Let's head toward Choteau. We can burn some fuel and pick up some weight. About five thousand pounds to be exact." He looked to the right. "Clear to taxi," he said.

Rawley looked left and ahead then advanced the throttles. The big plane surged forward then lumbered along toward the airstrip. The balloon tires caused the aircraft to wobble right to left as it rolled along.

Rawley continued to scan left, right, and ahead. Bart had a checklist in his hand, and he was double-checking everything and positioning the flaps for takeoff. The empty plane didn't need much help from the flaps to get off the ground, but it was on the list. Bart set the transponder to 1200. The code would be broadcast and indicate that the airplane was operating under visual flight rules, or not on an assigned route. Transponder codes were of no consequence to other pilots unless they had the proper equipment to receive the signal. If they were equipped, they could see where an aircraft was in relation to their own position to aid in collision avoidance.

When operating in controlled airspace, a transponder was required for safety. Each aircraft in that airspace would be assigned a four-digit number or discreet code that allowed air traffic controllers to identify them from the other aircraft.

Rawley stopped the Otter perpendicular to the runway so she could see both ends of the field. The aircraft rocked forward then settled back when she touched the brakes. Bart and Rawley looked in every direction but lingered longest looking to the right and up for landing aircraft. It wouldn't be the first time a plane returned unannounced immediately after takeoff, and they didn't want to take any chances. Rawley applied the emergency brake and performed a "run-up" of both engines. It was a procedure where the engines' RPMs were increased to near full power while holding the aircraft in place. She and Bart would check all the gauges and look at the engines for abnormal exhaust color or other abnormalities. It only lasted a few seconds. Hopefully any anomalies would be detected on the ground rather than during the initial climb.

Satisfied they were ready, Bart keyed the microphone and announced their departure. "Buffalo Lake traffic, De Havilland departing two three." The numbers "two three" indicated the direction they would be departing. In this case, 230 degrees, or southwest. Announcing Buffalo Lake would distinguish the field from others on the same frequency. Once again Rawley looked first left in the direction she would be leaving then to the right and up. Satisfied no aircraft were landing, she rolled the big twin-engine plane onto the grass strip.

"Let's try a short field take off and high-performance climb," Bart said.

Rawley shot him a glance then pushed the throttles to full power while holding the brakes. An odd way to start a FAM flight, she thought.

The nose of the aircraft went down, and the engines screamed. She released the brakes, and the aircraft lurched ahead.

"Not quite a cat shot," Rawley said.

"Airspeed alive," said Bart.

Rawley looked ahead, and Bart called out the speed. Still using good CRM procedures, Bart announced sixty knots, and the plane was already trying to fly. That was just one characteristic that made the de Havilland DHC-6 a perfect plane for short field operations. With a stall speed of fifty-eight knots, it meant this aircraft would look like it was hovering if landed properly in slow flight. It also meant the plane would be leaving the ground at a relatively slow speed if allowed. Rawley pulled the yoke back, and they began to climb. She pulled back harder, and nose went even higher.

Bart continued to read off airspeed and altitude. This version of the DHC-6 could climb at 1,600 feet per minute, and in the length of three football fields they had already climbed to an altitude of 350 hundred feet. A takeoff like that would get them out of any mountain landing site they might use. Bart was satisfied that Rawley could still handle something with propellers.

"Level off at 1,500," he said.

Rawley pushed the nose over as Bart brought up the flaps, then she pulled the power back. Bart looked over the panel and dialed the radio to 121.5. That was the emergency and hailing frequency that most general aviation aircraft monitored when they were not on an assigned radio channel.

Rawley leveled off and turned toward Choteau. In the air over Montana, Rawley didn't need a map or GPS to navigate. She knew every road, every knoll, and every body of water. For a split second, she tried to remember the last time she had flown in Big Sky Country. It had been too long, she thought.

CHAPTER 9

———◆———

RAWLEY MADE ANOTHER SCAN OF the instruments, then the airspace ahead, to her left, then turned to Bart.

"OK," she said. "What gives?"

Bart looked at Rawley. He was still smiling. "It's not too complicated," he said. "Your father wants you to take over the family business one day, and he didn't want to ask you to leave the Navy."

"That's it?" Rawley said. "That's all this is about?" she asked.

"Well," Bart said, "it's almost that simple. Obviously you're a badass carrier pilot, but you need some street cred to play in this world, so he cooked up this plan to get you here of your own free will. That's it." He shrugged.

"Free will!" She said. "I was recruited! A guy approached me and brought me into this web of lies."

"You mean that nice man in Hawaii." Bart laughed. "He kind of works for your dad."

"Works for my dad? You mean like he was sent there to find me?" she asked.

"Pretty much," said Bart.

"Holy shit!" Rawley said, shaking her head. "Cooper was right."

Bart looked out the right side of the plane. "If you mean Arlen, he was in on it. He's how your dad kept track of you. They go way back to the Navy days."

"No way!" said Rawley. "He tried to talk me out of it."

"No, no," said Bart. "He was just checking your convictions. If your heart wasn't in it, your dad would have pulled the plug and made the job offer vanish before you went too far."

"You guys are a school. The job is the CIA. And I was hired by Gryphon Aviation," she said.

"Technically," Bart agreed. "But remember, we are a contractor to the CIA. We are employees of Gryphon Aviation; that's who holds the government contract. And Gryphon Aviation—is your father."

Rawley was quiet now. She was processing the information. She instantly remembered a painting in her father's home office. A flying dragon over a Navy aircraft carrier. A gryphon. Her father's squadron symbol in Vietnam.

She looked out the window ahead and then down. Her mind was spinning, but she maintained her situational awareness. Multitasking was her best trait, and this information was demanding a lot of brain cells right now. "Are we really going to Choteau, or am I going some-place else?" she asked sarcastically.

Bart laughed again. "Yeah, we're landing there. We can get some coffee while they load the plane."

"How about we just park this thing and start drinking?" she said.

"That's a damn fine plan also," said Bart.

"What's the load?" Rawley asked. "Or should I ask that?" Rawley maintained her sarcastic tone.

"It's concrete and lead. We artificially weight the planes to add an air of excitement. You'll love it!" he said, with a fiendish accent.

"Wouldn't it be safer to do that later in training?" Rawley asked. "I mean, I don't know where you found those guys, but they don't look like they are ready to land on asphalt, and max weight won't help."

Bart turned to Rawley as he spoke. "Those guys are a product of government recruiting, dear, and ultimately not our employees. Whereas," he said, "you are more along the lines of what we bring in." He paused. "And anyway, they won't touch this plane for two weeks if they are still around. The weights for you, killer. This is your check ride, baby!"

Rawley looked at Bart and mouthed some profanity.

"What?" Bart asked as he tapped his headset. "Nothing coming through."

Rawley looked ahead, and she could see Choteau on the horizon. "Give me ten degrees." She was referring to the flaps.

She eased the power back then rolled the aircraft trim wheel forward to compensate for the flaps. Bart visually checked the flaps then dialed up the Choteau weather information. They both listened to the AWOS, or weather broadcast. It was updated hourly, and based on the wind, they would choose a runway that would have them landing as close to into the wind as possible. The wind here was the same as Buffalo Lake, 15 gusting to 20 miles per hour at 230. Choteau and had 2 asphalt runways—5 and 23 and 14 and 32. The wind direction dictated the shorter runway of the two.

"Straight in on two-three," she said.

"Why don't we swing around, take one four, and try a little crosswind?" said Bart.

"This really is a check ride," Rawley said. She didn't protest; she just banked right and set up for a crosswind landing. There was not a plane in sight near Choteau. She could see that, miles out. Fighter pilots had incredible vision, and her eyes were still young.

Bart continued to scan while dialing up the Choteau UNICOM. No chatter on the frequency confirmed Rawley's observation. No aircraft were landing or taking off. Bart made the appropriate radio announcement, and Rawley turned into the left base. She looked down at the short runway then scanned every direction. Landing on runway 14 would give Rawley almost a direct crosswind. It would require some piloting, but this aircraft could easily handle it. Bart's hands hovered near the yoke while he continued to look for traffic. His head was on a swivel while Rawley concentrated on the aircraft. Bart had always been great to fly with, she thought. She always felt safer just having him in the plane.

They were seconds from touchdown and Rawley was using the controls to crab into the wind then just as they were touching down she aligned the plane with the runway and began a rollout just off the centerline as she reversed pitch on the propellers. "OK. What's with the secrecy and the ridiculous effort to keep everyone nameless?" she asked. "Tell me that's not for my benefit."

The reversed pitch and brakes stopped the aircraft in less than three hundred feet. It was a better than average land and hold short maneuver, even though Bart had not asked for it.

Bart smiled and said, "Nicely done." Then he answered her question. "Security around here has been for your benefit since you were seven years old."

"What do you mean by that?" she asked as she taxied toward the ramp while announcing over the radio that she had cleared the runway.

"When we first started this business, we were pushing through a lot of government pilots like the guys in this class, and most worked for counterdrug operations in Central and South America," he said.

"We weren't too savvy about security back then, and we tended to befriend everyone." Bart still looked in every direction as he spoke.

Rawley came to a stop on the ramp and began shutting down the aircraft while Bart talked.

"We had put through about twenty pilots that year, mostly ex-military. We thought they were doing surveillance or spotting for counterdrug forces," he said, looking out the window for his friend.

"It turns out they were mostly undercover guys who would be seeking employment with the cartels. They needed to have our kind of flying skills to make their cover believable. We provided those skills." His voice trailed off as he saw two men he recognized walking toward the plane.

He opened his door and waved.

"Let's walk," he said to Rawley. Bart climbed down and approached the men.

"Confirm the weight, and put the *A* package in," he said. "And make sure it's tight; we are going into the mountains."

The men looked at Rawley as she approached, and she felt like she should say hello or something, but they just nodded to Bart and turned around before she could get close enough to say anything. There was no need for any more discussion. They had done this more times than they could count, and they knew the policy. No talking to anyone who might be flying with Bud's pilots. Bart started walking toward the airport office, and he picked up the story right where he had left off. Rawley matched his pace and listened.

"These guys were living undercover on a government salary, and most saw an opportunity to make a hell of a lot more money," Bart said.

"It wasn't long before it became obvious that the pilots we trained had skills far beyond anyone who was already flying for the bad guys. Somebody talked, and one thing led to another, and a couple of Colombians showed up. They were looking for your father, but first they cased the town, the house, the hangar, and your school. We missed all that because we were flying all day, every day."

Rawley was all ears. She was trying to remember that time.

"That afternoon," Bart went on, "we landed, and there at the hangar were these two slimy bastards in their leather pants and silver-tipped boots.

"They came over, and they were all smiles. They asked to talk to your father in private. He walked a short distance away with them following. When they stopped I could tell by the body language there was some bullshit going on.

"The conversation ended, and Bud looked shaken. I'd never seen him look that way before," Bart said.

"The Colombians left, and I asked Bud what the hell was going on. It turns out, they made some demands, and to ensure they got what they wanted, they threatened your life. They told Bud enough to make him believe they could get to you any place any time. Honestly, we felt stupid and vulnerable."

Bart stopped talking as they went into the building on the edge of the field. There were a few people inside, and Bart seamlessly picked up a different conversation like he had been talking about it all along.

"I want you get that left strut checked," Bart said as he walked toward the coffee.

Rawley just said, "OK," going along with the ruse.

The two people in the building looked at Bart and Rawley. They both said hello then went about their business. Bart poured a cup of coffee, and Rawley declined.

They walked back outside, and Bart picked up right where he left off.

"Bud was pissed," he said. "Mostly pissed at himself. He said he was going to fly those two up into Canada near Medicine Hat and pick up a load of dope then fly them down to Northern California.

"We were kicking ourselves in the ass and trying to find a way out. Calling the police was a bad idea, Bud thought. These assholes were ruthless, and if they were arrested, there would just be more coming."

"He had agreed to take off at two o'clock, and he assured them he would cooperate to ensure your safety."

"Bud told them they needed to take the DC-3 and he would have to get it ready. As we walked to the plane, Bud told me to take your mother to Rocking Horse plateau and be ready for whatever came. He said to tell her it was like an Elk hunt and plan accordingly.

"The Colombians returned, and soon your father was flying away," Bart said. "I figured I had about three hours to get your mother and drop her at Rocking Horse. I couldn't leave a plane there, so she would be alone." Bart paused.

Rawley felt like she was hearing the plot of some Hitchcock thriller. "Then what happened?" she asked. "Wait! Do you mean the DC-3 that's burned up at Rocking Horse?"

Bart nodded. "Yeah, that was ours. Honestly, it was a wreck before the fire, so it wasn't a real loss." He smiled.

"Anyway," he said, "I told your mother what was happening. She grabbed her long gun and then you, and off we went. You just thought it was the biggest adventure. I flew her into Rocking Horse and dropped her off."

"Oh my God!" Rawley exclaimed. She was beginning to remember.

"Your mother felt you were safest with us, so we would know exactly where you were," said Bart.

"I flew out over Kildare Range so I could keep an eye on Rocking Horse. About an hour before sundown, your father appeared.

"He was flying about eight thousand feet. He told the Colombians they would have to go down the east side of the mountains because the plane had no oxygen. When Bud was about two miles from Rocking Horse, he screwed with the mixture, and the engines started missing, then they both shut down. He said it got a little chaotic on the plane. Those two Colombians didn't know whether to shit or go blind. They were yelling at your father to do something. He was pretending to try and restart while gliding that bird right toward Rocking Horse."

Bart's voice went up and down. It was as if he was reliving the moment as he told the story. "Only your father could glide that big son of a bitch into Rocking Horse and live to tell about it.

"He went in wheels up and sat it down flat. It was a real nice crash landing," he said. "I flew toward him after seeing the plane go down."

"There was smoke and dust and a trail of engine parts all across the plateau, but the plane was mostly intact. It seemed like an eternity before your father emerged. Behind him were the two Colombians, one of them obviously pointing a weapon at your father."

Rawley interrupted him. "We left my mother there alone!"

"Well, it was a desperate situation, sweetheart, and it called for the first team," he said. "No rookie was going to resolve that mess, and your mother was the best damn shot in this part of the state. Where do you think you got your skills?"

"What happened next?" asked Rawley.

"Well, I told you to look outside and help me find goats, and then I dove for the ground, thinking I might distract the guy with the gun long enough for your mother to get a shot off."

"Oh no!" Rawley said. "You're going to tell me my mother shot someone?"

"Oh, hell no," said Bart. "Not one. She killed both those SOBs. A head shot on the first guy and center mass on the second."

Rawley couldn't talk. She drew a long, deep breath. "We...are talking about my mother, right, Bart?"

"Hell, Rawley, you know those Blackfeet," he said. "They're killers; they fought everyone from here to Minnesota, including their friends.

"I circled around to pick up your parents, and by the time we landed, they had a damn fine barbecue going. Those two Colombians burned in a plane full of dope. It was a real tragedy. Your mother made me fly us all to Apistotooki right then," Bart said.

"She said she wanted to cleanse her spirit or something. Between you and me, I think she was just bragging to old Crowfoot."

CHAPTER 10

———◆———

RAWLEY WAS STILL TRYING TO grasp the reality of what she had just heard.

Bart finished the story as they walked back to the Otter. "We made some calls and thought things through. It was too good a business to abandon, so we just made some changes.

"It all may seem a bit melodramatic, but we control everything. And I mean everything, including that brief you got at Langley."

"Oh no," Rawley said. "That cheesedick works for you?"

"Well, he works for the government, but he answers to us," he replied. "He owes your father a hell of a debt. Bud loaned him that new Husky we had when you were—

"Don't tell me that guy crashed the Husky?" she asked.

"Oh yeah, he crashed it all right," said Bart. "He wanted to take some rancher's bimbo daughter on a little flying picnic on the Missouri, and he left the damn wheels down. When they touched the river, the Husky flipped right over on its nose then it tumbled up on the bank. Nobody died, but it was the saddest damn day ever. The plane was totaled, and that girl's parents sued the shit out of your father."

"Damn!" Rawley said. "If I had only known that, I would have broken his nose."

"I like the way you talk, kid!" Bart said as he slapped her back. "This business calls for doing just that on occasion. You are going to fit right in!

"Let's get this load in the air," Bart said. "Your parents are waiting at Apistotooki. Lunch should be just about ready when we get there."

Rawley climbed into the Otter then went aft to check the load. She wanted to confirm its location and make sure it was secure. If that much weight even shifted, it could crash the plane. She confirmed the location by doing a quick weight and balance. The calculations were within limits for the aircraft, so Rawley felt confident she could fly it in and out of any mountain landing area, including Apistotooki. Rawley threw her leg over the center console and climbed back into the right seat.

"Aren't check rides normally performed at the end of training?" she asked Bart as she settled into her seat.

"This is the end," he said. "You have other places to be."

Rawley started the plane, checked the ramp around her, and started rolling toward the runway. She could tell from the airport flag and some other indicators she would be taking off on 23. Bart listened to the weather anyway. The plane had a much different feel with the weight onboard. Instead of wobbling side to side, the aircraft seemed to bounce.

"I'm going around twice," Rawley said. "I want to see what a normal landing feels like with this weight." Rawley was talking while looking at instruments and setting the plane up for takeoff and scanning the field for other aircraft.

Normally she might have ignored the published checklist and gone through the procedure from memory, but the situation was different now. The de Havilland DHC-6 400 series was rated for a maximum take-off weight of just over 12,000 pounds. Based on their fuel burn coming from Buffalo Lake and the added cargo, she put their weight right at 11,200 pounds.

Bart was watching her systematically going through the checklist. "I see that Navy training kicking in," he said.

"Well," she said, "Louis Pasteur said it best. Chance favors the prepared mind."

"Was he a pilot?" asked Bart.

Rawley just smiled.

After another run-up, Rawley was ready to fly. She made the appropriate radio calls and then positioned the Otter onto runway 23. Just as she was about to push the throttles forward, she asked Bart to watch the cargo and make sure it stayed in place when they accelerated. She didn't mind being overly cautious. The men who loaded the weight were unknown to her, and who knew what forces the tie-downs had been exposed to over the years. It was a well-used plane, and of course, Bart was right, there was her Navy training. It was hard to push that aside. The Otter bounced down the runway, and at the appropriate airspeed, Rawley eased back on the yoke. The aircraft rotated, and in no time Rawley pushed the nose over and leveled off at 1,500 feet.

"Nothing happening back there," Bart said as he turned around.

Rawley announced her departure from Choteau and intention to stay in the pattern. "Choteau traffic, de Havilland turning left crosswind two-three."

After flying the left downwind, Rawley announced over the radio she was turning left base to final. Bart gave her full flaps. She was scanning instruments and her surroundings and mentally preparing to stop the aircraft in as short a distance as possible.

Bart keyed the mic and announced over the radio, "Choteau traffic, de Havilland final, land and hold short, two-three Choteau."

Rawley had one hand on the yoke and one hand up on the throttles. She eased off on the power and manipulated the yoke to control her rate of descent. She knew it was important to avoid going into what was known as ground effect before the wheels made contact with the asphalt. If that happened the aircraft would float down the runway, using up valuable landing space. Here at the airport, that would be of little consequence. In the mountains it would mean going to full power, making a steep ascent, and going around.

Going around was a common maneuver and often the safest choice, but it did tend unnerve passengers who might not understand the nuances of safe aircraft operation. The Otter was heavy, and Rawley could feel it. As she came over the runway numbers, her eyes were fixed on the exact spot the wheels would touch down. Navy pilots are trained to land in a box, and Rawley was doing that before the Navy. She could land on a dollar bill if there was a bet involved. As always Bart's right hand hovered near the yoke, and his left hand was up near the throttles behind Rawley's.

It wasn't critical here, but in the mountains with two pilots onboard, it would be silly to not take every precaution. It would also be silly to not practice given the opportunity. Bart read off the airspeed as they slowed for the approach. The balloon tires of the main gear touched down, and Rawley pulled the power back enough to cause the aircraft to squat. Rawley knew the main landing gear was firmly planted on the ground, and she reversed the propeller pitch and accelerated to full power. At the same time, Bart pulled the lever to raise the flaps. This would rapidly change the airflow over the wings and help the aircraft resist ground affect.

The nosewheel went down hard, and the propeller noise changed to a familiar chopping sound. The landing struts were getting a serious workout as the aircraft came to a complete stop. Rawley changed the propeller pitch to idle, and they sat for a moment. Rawley looked out the left side of the Otter, and Bart looked out the right side. They had used up less than 260 yards of runway coming to a complete stop. Bart nodded approvingly.

"OK," he said. "Let's see what we can do getting out of here."

Rawley announced over the radio that she was performing a back taxi on runway 23 while she turned the aircraft around. She rolled to the end of the runway and turned right onto the taxiway, then she spun the plane around until they were facing the runway. They could have easily taken off from where they were, but she didn't want to feel rushed. She went through the checklist again and double-checked every gauge and switch setting.

Bart lowered the flaps then visually checked each wing. She would execute this takeoff just as she had leaving Buffalo Lake. The intent was to get off the ground and climb as quickly as possible without stalling the aircraft.

The takeoff was flawless, and Bart was happy. Rawley was also happy. Military pilots were graded on every maneuver while working up to deploy, and this was just another test of her skills. An extension of her military life, she thought.

She took a course to the southwest, climbing at a rate of just 500 feet per minute. Choteau was almost 4000 feet above sea level, and she would be landing at 7000 feet above sea level. Apistotooki was a thirty-minute flight from Choteau in the Twin Otter. Compared to the flight from Buffalo Lake to Choteau, the plane was quiet. Rawley was thinking ahead to the landing at Apisto and going through everything from the approach to the go-around procedure, should that come to pass. She was used to thinking far ahead of the plane, and being prepared meant being safe. She was scanning the instruments and thinking about where she would divert in an emergency. At a fuel burn of fifty-five gallons per hour per side, Rawley was mentally calculating the impact of the short flight on her weight. She decided they would be approximately 385 pounds lighter when the wheels touched the ground.

CHAPTER 11

———◆———

BART WAS WATCHING THE SCENERY go by while occasionally scanning the instruments and watching Rawley. He could see she was occupied with the aircraft and thinking ahead. It was a habit she had formed long before she joined the Navy. Finally, Bart spoke up.

"I know it's been a while since you went into Apisto," he said. "We'll overfly at eighty-five hundred and come in off a left downwind, and if we have to go around, we'll climb straight out to eight thousand feet, turn to two eighty, and head west of Baldy. Sound good?"

"Good," Rawley said. Baldy referred to Mount Baldy. It wasn't the highest peak in Montana by far, but at 7,500 feet above sea level, it was clearly visible from a long way off. The peak of Baldy was just one mile from the middle of the landing area and 500 feet higher than where they would touch down. That was close by any standard but still far enough to allow for a straight climb out, and they only needed to gain 501 feet to clear the top. They would be climbing at a rate that should give them a 700- to 800-foot buffer.

The clearing at Apisto was 200 to 500 feet wide. There was a little more than 1500 feet of useable landing area and another 300 feet before the first obstacle. A shallow stream ran down the middle of the narrow valley. It wasn't a box canyon, but it wasn't wide open at the ends either. Several Indian tribes had inhabited the canyon and the surrounding area at different times throughout history, primarily because it was defensible and extremely difficult to get to.

Even now it was part of the largest unroaded wilderness area in the state of Montana, known as the Front Range. The closest civilization had been the mining boomtown of Silver Rock, six miles to the southeast. Silver Rock was just a ghost town now and had not been inhabited since 1931. Rawley's mother learned about the canyon when she was just a child. Tribal elders would tell stories of how the Blackfoot Confederacy would move across the plains following the great bison herds and make camps in different places along the Front Range of the Rockies.

In the summer months, they would go into mountains and camp in the shadow of Mount Baldy. The canyon known as Apistotooki was holy to the Blackfeet. They believed the stream had healing powers. Sick members of the tribe or wounded warriors were brought here to heal or begin the journey. If they left this earth, their lifeless bodies would be positioned beneath the rays of the rising sun as they came through the towering pines. The Blackfeet believed the spirit of the deceased would follow the rays of sunlight to their reward, thus the beginning of the journey. When Sally was a young girl, that was just one version of many stories the elders would tell.

Sally didn't care if the legend was true or not. After seeing the canyon at sunrise for the first time, she embraced the belief and knew when the time came her mortal remains would rest here while her spirit rode a ray of light to heaven. Bud never questioned her beliefs, and now that Rawley was old enough to understand, it was a given she would fulfill her mother's wish if Bud could not.

Growing up, Rawley had come to Apistotooki many times with her mother on horseback. It was a two-day ride from their home, but the distance never mattered. If their timing was right, they would enter the canyon at sunup and see the beams of light coming through the trees. Together they would make camp, and Sally would tell stories by campfire, just as she had heard them as a young child. Sally was proud to pass her Blackfoot heritage on to her daughter, and Rawley listened intently no matter how many times she'd heard the same story. It was here that

Rawley learned to fish and hunt and appreciate her American Indian heritage.

Rawley leveled off at eighty-five hundred feet and turned toward the approximate location of Apistotooki based on her relative position to Mount Baldy. Bart was in instructor mode and couldn't help but remind Rawley of the little things she needed to think about as they got closer to landing. She was an accomplished pilot with experience far beyond those who normally came here for training, but Bart was conditioned to teach and Rawley was respectful enough to listen and go along.

As they closed in on the valley, they could clearly see a solid plume of white smoke rising above the tree line and rocky walls that defined Apistotooki Canyon. That meant two things. No wind, and her mother was burning extra wood to guide her in.

"Keep your mind on the task here, and I'll read off airspeed and altitude during the approach," Bart said.

Rawley didn't answer. She just nodded without taking her eyes off the smoke. She turned to a heading that would bring the smoke plume down the left side of the aircraft and give her a clear view of the landing area. She couldn't help but flashback to the carrier. A precision approach and precision touchdown on a small patch with no margin for error. In her mind's eye, she could see exactly where the wheels needed to meet the ground at Apisto.

Off to her left would be a pyramid-shaped rock the size of small car sitting alone and just past that another large rock shaped like a dinner table. She would touch down exactly between those landmarks, she thought. Not a foot before and not after. If the wheels weren't firmly on the ground when she passed the tabletop, she would go to full power and execute a go-around.

She was purposely not talking now and giving all her attention to landing the plane. Five more minutes, she thought, then she would call for full flaps and adjust her airspeed to ninety-five knots. She was making another quick scan when Bart broke the silence.

"What ever happened to your college love interest?" Bart asked.

Rawley turned and looked at Bart. "Seriously?" she asked. "You want to discuss that now? Right now?"

"Well, I was just curious. I mean, if you don't want to talk about it, then don't."

"Is distraction part of the check ride?" Rawley asked.

"He dumped you, huh?" said Bart as he looked out the right side of the aircraft.

"No. He didn't dump me!" Rawley said, clearly perturbed. "Are you familiar with the Aboriginal custom of not saying the name of those who have passed?" She paused. "Give me full flaps."

Bart pulled the flap actuator, and the flaps came down to forty degrees. Bart again turned to the right and watched the flaps slowly extend. Then he turned to check the other side. Full flaps caused the plane to rise, and Rawley instinctively pushed the yoke forward while turning the trim wheel for nose down.

"Oh, hell! Is he dead?" Bart asked.

"He is to me," Rawley said as she passed directly over the canyon.

She looked down and could see her father's favorite airplane. It was a shiny 1956 Cessna 185. The plane was unpainted except for the tail, and that was international orange. Depending on the season, the aircraft might be on amphibious floats, skis, or tundra tires, like it was now. Rawley noticed that her father had parked it as far to one end of the canyon as he could get it. She had overshot on one landing here in her entire life, which resulted in a small dent in a wingtip, and it was obvious she would never live it down. She could see her parents waving, two horses, a pack mule, and more dogs than she could count.

"Mom rode up, I guess," Rawley said.

"Looks like," said Bart.

"How many dogs?" Rawley turned into the left downwind leg.

"Oh, Sally doesn't say, and we don't ask," Bart said as he twisted his butt into the seat and tightened his harness.

Rawley saw that out of her peripheral vision and asked, "Anticipating a hard landing?"

"I don't want to go through the windscreen if you have another landing like you did at Deer Lodge." Bart smiled.

Rawley shook her head. "I guess Dad is reminding me about his favorite faux pas of mine. You see where he parked."

Rawley gently banked left and adjusted the power to eighty knots. She was sinking now and kept her right hand on the throttles. Bart called out the airspeed and altitude. Rawley worked the rudder pedals and yoke. As she continued the turn, she visually picked up the exact spot where the wheels would touchdown.

She could see the pyramid and tabletop. Dogs were chasing each other through the stream.

Bart was now saying the speed and the altitude every fifty feet. They were nearly lined up when Bart asked, "When's the last time you saw him?"

Rawley smiled but didn't answer. "You'd better tighten that harness" was all she said.

Bud and Sally never took their eyes off the big plane now that it was lined up to land. Bud was behind Sally, his arms locked around her. The noise from the two Pratt and Whitney turbines echoed through the canyon.

"That will wake the dead," said Bud. Then he began to talk her in as if Rawley could hear him.

"More power," he said. "You're a little low..."

In the cockpit Rawley was already putting pressure on the throttles when Bart said, "Sixty-five knots." The published stall speed for the Twin Otter was fifty-eight knots with full flaps. At this altitude and weight, it would be a little higher.

The plane was sinking fast, and she put the slightest backpressure on the yoke and the nose came up slightly. Sally was saying a silent prayer, Bud was still talking to himself, and Bart was calling out the air speed. This close to the ground, altitude no longer mattered. The only thing Rawley cared about now was getting the main wheels on the ground first and not stalling the plane.

A nosewheel strike here would be catastrophic. It was near two in the afternoon, the sun was behind them now, and the canyon was full of shadows. As they sank toward the ground, the trees seemed closer than ever. Rawley's attention was on one thing now, and that was the exact spot she had picked out. She knew she had a good line and a perfect sink rate, and she felt a great sense of calm.

CHAPTER 12

———————◆———————

THEY WERE LESS THAN A second from touchdown and Rawley knew she had the landing nailed. She eased the power back, and the plane settled the last few feet. She pulled the yoke, and again the nose rose slightly as the big main wheels touched the ground. The plane bounced then came down hard. Rawley was reversing the thrust of the props while trying to hold the nosewheel off the ground until they slowed. Bart also had his hands on the yoke now. He knew they weren't going around, so he retracted the flaps. Rawley knew she had a few hundred feet to spare, so she stopped in a much less aggressive manner than she had at Choteau. The plane rocked side to side and continued to bounce as it rolled out and the powerful reverse thrust forced the nose down.

With all three wheels firmly on the ground, the big Twin Otter rocked to a stop at Apistotooki. Bud raised both arms in the air, Sally clapped, and dogs barked and ran back and forth around the plane.

Bart said nothing, and Rawley began shutting down as she silenced one engine and then the other.

She had not been here in over five years. It was good to be back, she thought. She breathed in deep and slowly let it out as she relaxed into her seat.

Rawley pushed her door open. The smell of burned jet fuel still hung in the air. The only noise Rawley could hear now was the slow-moving stream. She looked up at the towering rocks to her left and then panned right down the canyon to Mount Baldy. She could see her mother standing by the fire attending to a pot that hung over a camp-fire. Her father and Bart were walking toward each other. No matter how long she had been away, she still recognized every rock and every tree. She turned to climb down from the Otter, and several dogs ran up to greet her.

As Rawley came around the nose of the aircraft, she could see her father and Bart talking and her mother was walking towards her with arms reaching out. Rawley hastened her pace. Although she talked to her parents by phone as often as possible, she had not seen either of them in over a year, and that was in Virginia. They said their trip was for pleasure, but now Rawley couldn't help but think it was for some government business and since her perception of the family business was a facade, who knew what was real and what was not? And did it really matter? She herself was prepared to embark on a lifestyle that would require deceiving her family and friends about work and travel. That fact alone would make it difficult to judge her parents' motives. She always knew they were special but perhaps they were even more special than she imagined. They were certainly cunning or conniving, although that seemed a bit harsh.

"Welcome home!" Sally said as she put her arms around Rawley and squeezed her tight. Bud came near and he was also smiling, beaming actually. The mood was light and happy, and with so many questions answered, Rawley actually felt a sense of relief. Bud wrapped his arms around the two women he loved most in life. Dogs were at their feet, but nobody seemed to notice or even care. "You must be starved, dear," her mother said.

"Of course I'm hungry Mom." Rawley said. Saying anything else would be crazy. Sally just assumed everyone was always hungry. Rawley saw Bart walking toward the fire, and she couldn't help but think about their last words in the plane.

Now Bart was looking into the pot on the fire.

"Rattlesnake stew?" he asked. "Roadkill? Tree bark? What's for lunch?"

Forever the comedian Bart kept every situation light. He saw the humor in everything no matter how dire the situation. He had survived countless airplane crashes. First in the Army and Vietnam, where he flew a Cessna L19 Birddog, a small fixed-wing observation plane, then later in Alaska, where he established a one-man flying business of his own. Bud would say that Bart had ice water in his veins when it came to facing danger, and Bart would attribute his heroic and happy demeanor to being divorced more times than he was married.

Sally put her hand on Bart's back as she walked up to him. "You are a card. That's dinner, and your lunch is in the cooler." It had already been a long day, and Bart knew Sally meant beer.

Rawley looked around the valley and saw a familiar friend staked out near the trees, and when she made eye contact with her horse, the chestnut mare began throwing her head in the air and scraping the ground. Rawley called out her name as she walked closer, and Wildfire became more active and snickered loudly as her head bobbed up and down. Rawley heard her mother call her name, and she turned around. Sally tossed Rawley an apple. Rawley twisted the apple in half, knowing it would be a problem for her mothers' horse if she didn't have a treat for both of them. On a day full of memories, seeing Wildfire was nothing but a catalyst for more reminiscing.

Rawley was given the mare in the summer before she started high school as partial payment for working as a cattle wrangler at the Clement ranch. Wildfire was just five years old and stood a little over fifteen and a half hands. She was full of fire and energy, and Rawley had to win her trust. If Rawley wasn't flying, she was on her horse. Together they traveled a few hundred miles that summer exploring the Garnet Range, and they made more than a few trips with Sally to Apisto. When Sally wasn't riding in the mountains, she taught equestrian eventing and western-riding skills to many of the local adults and children. Rawley took part whenever she could, and she learned every aspect of riding, including jumping, cross country, and western-riding skills. After giving the two horses the apple, Sally's mule, Jade, began braying loudly in protest. Jade was an extremely strong and stout jack, or male, who had sired many off-spring around the state. His roots could be traced to the famous jenny Royal Gift and sire Knight of Malta.

Unlike most mules Jade had a relatively pleasant disposition. Sally had a way with animals, and Jade was no different. She could calm him with a word, and he would move heaven and earth if she asked.

As the four sat around the fire and ate lunch, Bud finally addressed the strange events of the day.

"I know Bart filled you in on everything," Bud said. "I hope you don't feel betrayed, but I think you will agree you've done everything you could do in the Navy." Bud knew from experience the cycle of life of a Navy pilot. First you fly then you facilitate others' flying. It was a source of deep frustration for most pilots.

Rawley was quiet, but she shrugged as if to say she was fine with the situation. "So far I'm where I want to be," she said. "It was a great first day on the job."

"What next?" Rawley asked. "I'm going to Afghanistan, aren't I?"

"You are," he said. "Here's the way it works." Bud paused and took a long breath, then slowly exhaled. A family habit Rawley recognized.

"We are the fixed-wing aviation training and support for CIA low-intensity covert operations and DEA. At any given time, we have around twenty pilots in our employ all over the world supporting various things and another ten or so flying part time." Bud stopped and took a long drink from his beer.

"Are we really losing four pilots a year?" Rawley asked.

"Government theatrics," Bud said, shaking his head and looking at Bart.

"I heard one guy left the room," Bart added.

"You weren't scared?" Sally asked.

"Well," Rawley said, "I knew I couldn't get back in the squadron, so..."

Bud picked up where he left off. "You have some training to do, but once that's finished you'll be put into the rotation. We provide aircraft and skilled pilots. Our customers provide tasking." Bud shrugged. "That's it. It's lucrative, it's edgy, and you get to fly."

Bud looked at Rawley. He was overwhelmed with pride and pleased at the way she was handling the situation.

"In Afghanistan or wherever you go, you're our eyes on the ground," said Bart.

"Fly some ops, get your feet wet, and tell us what you think. You are replacing Gilbert Adams. He's retiring," said Bud.

"Gilbert Adams?" Rawley said incredulously. "Our Gil Adams, from Butte?"

Bud and Bart smiled and nodded.

"I can't believe he's still flying," she said. "What is he, eighty?"

"Seventy-two," said Sally. "Seventy-eight," said Bart.

"Seventy-two," Sally countered. "And that's not old!" she added.

"He got his beard tangled in the controls or stepped on it or something, got distracted, and knocked the nosewheel off a two oh six, landing north of Kandahar." Bart said as he looked back and forth at Sally and Bud.

There were short periods of silence, then Rawley would ask a question about the business and Bud would answer. As Bud talked Rawley looked around the camp, counting in her head.

"Don't count the dogs," Sally said, without looking up from the book she was reading. "It's rude."

Rawley looked at her father, and they both smiled and shrugged.

Bart was back at the cooler and asked if anyone wanted a beer then tossed one to Rawley without waiting for her response. They spent the rest of the afternoon talking about Rawley's adventures in the Navy and reliving memories. The day dissolved into twilight, and after a hot meal that included venison and home grown vegetables, it was time to think about going to bed.

The canyon was getting dark, and the air was dry and brisk away from the fire. Sally added wood to the fire then asked Bart where he was sleeping.

"You know I don't camp," he said. "I think I'll just drink too much and climb into that Otter."

Dogs laid around the fire. Some were asleep, some were alert, but when Sally moved every head came up, and tails went in motion.

Sally gave Rawley a long hug. "I'm glad you are home, dear. I brought your sleeping bag and a thermal pad. It's there." She pointed toward the pile near the cooler. Then she pulled her coat back and handed her daughter a Ruger .357 revolver. "Your father and I will be in the plane if you need anything." She turned to leave, and Bud and Bart jumped to their feet.

Sally hugged Bud. "I'll be right along," he said.

And then she turned to Bart. "Don't fall in the fire again." She said as she placed her hand on his chest. Bart touched her hand and smiled. She then went by the horses and headed toward the Cessna. Every dog followed Sally as she walked.

CHAPTER 13

———•———

THE FIRE WAS FADING, AND everyone had made their way to bed. Rawley lay on her back and looked up at the clear, black sky filled with endless stars. She was reminded of walking on the deck of a blacked-out ship at sea. The stars seemed to go forever. There were shooting stars and satellites moving across the sky. As a child she would try to find as many constellations as she could before fading off to sleep. Her mother had taught her the names of every star formation, including their Blackfoot names. When Sally wasn't telling Rawley a story, they would lay quietly and listen to the flowing stream and other sounds of the forest. The wind through the pines was like music to her ears.

When Rawley was very young, she would sometimes fear the night and move as close to her mother as she could get. Sally was intuitive and knew she must calm her daughter's fears before Rawley could fully appreciate the beauty of this special place. Sally would tell her the spirits of the great Blackfoot warriors would watch over them until the sun once again shined through the towering pines. Sally made it sound believable, and Rawley learned to sleep without a worry or care.

On one occasion a wolf pack entered the canyon. Sally's dogs and the horses alerted her to the danger. Rawley was awakened by the abnormally bright glow of the fire, and when she reached for her mother, she was not there. Two dogs sat nearby, and when Rawley stood up, they came close and stayed at her feet. Rawley called to her mother, and Sally answered back immediately. Rawley saw that she had her back to the fire, looking toward the tree line. Rawley was unaware of the danger, and Sally's voice did not betray her concern. The wolves moved on, and Rawley was soon sound asleep next to her mother.

As Rawley aged Sally would discuss the true dangers of the wilderness, and Rawley learned that her mother was always on guard keeping her safe. When it was time, Rawley assumed the shared responsibility of standing a watch. She learned to enjoy the time spent alone with her thoughts, and later in the Navy, while standing watch at sea, she would think back to those times with fond remembrance.

Rawley was drifting off to sleep when once more the nagging question returned. Why did Rip disappear? If something had happened to him, she would know. He was just gone and staying away for reasons only he must understand.

For a moment she thought about the way they had met at college and the fun they had shared. Eventually she pushed the thoughts away, as she had conditioned herself to do and soon sleep found its way to her clouded mind.

CHAPTER 14

———◆———

THE NIGHT IN APISTOTOOKI PASSED quickly, and Rawley opened her eyes to find herself among the beautiful rays of light coming through the pines. She could smell bacon and coffee, and there was a familiar sound coming from her father's plane. She could not help but smile as heard the unmistakable voice of the late country singer Marty Robbins, accompanied by her father. Country music and Montana were like a hand in a glove, and her father loved the music of the famous ballad singer. Bud was doing a preflight, and Bart was doing the same to the Otter.

Her mother said good morning and handed her a cup of coffee.

Rawley looked around and saw dogs eating together from a large metal pan. The horses were eating grain, and Jade was baring his teeth as if he was grinning.

Sally seemed to always have an endless amount of energy. The camp, like her home, was orderly, and she fostered a sense of calm and relaxation when it was needed and a sense of urgency if that was required. She was leader and taskmaster when she had to be and a source of sound advice for anyone who might require direction. Rawley watched her with admiring eyes and could not help but think how fortunate she was to have been blessed with such a family.

Bart was obviously in a jovial mood as he walked toward the fire. "Let's eat!" he shouted. Sally handed him a plate and told him to help himself, which he did. "How did you sleep?" Bart asked Rawley.

"Great!" she said. "What's on the agenda for you?" she asked Bart.

Bart shook pepper on his eggs, and Sally made a plate for her daughter as Bud walked up. He went straight to his daughter and bent to hug her.

"Good morning!" he said. "Hope your butt is up to a few hours in the saddle."

Rawley just smiled and nodded. "That's my agenda, I guess."

Now they were all eating breakfast, and Bud finished telling Rawley what lay ahead.

"When you get back to the ranch, come by the hangar and you can get familiar with our operation."

"You should leave for Alaska Friday or Saturday," he said. "You'll be flying there for a few days then going to Arizona for some defensive-weapons training. You'll probably enjoy that more than flying. The school is run by some ex-Special Forces guys. I hear they know how to have fun."

"Maybe you'll find something to take your mind off that other guy," Bart said.

Rawley didn't answer. She just looked at him and shook her head.

"I'm going to introduce you to a very nice young man when we get back to the ranch," Sally said as she moved around picking up.

"No nice young men!" said Rawley. Sally was normally not a matchmaker, but lately she had made no secret that Rawley was getting older and most young women her age were married with children.

Rawley had successfully avoided such entanglements by staying busy with work. Not having the Navy as an excuse might prove to be a challenge, but Rawley would find a way to turn off anyone her mother might send her way. She always had.

After a quick breakfast, Bart jumped up and said his good-byes. Rawley was helping her mother put most of the camping equipment in her father's plane when the de Havilland roared out of the canyon.

Rawley couldn't help but look up when she heard him go to full power. Bart was off the ground in no time and soon climbing away into the clear blue sky.

Bud walked up to the Cessna and took a quick look in the back to make sure everything was secure. "We have a surprise for you when you get home," he said. "I know it's hard to go cold turkey off flying a jet."

Rawley smiled. She loved surprises, and her father seemed to always come up with something good.

Bud gave Sally a long hug and a kiss. "Be careful coming down," he said. A minute later he was rolling toward the southern end of Apistotooki.

Compared to the Otter, the 185 sounded quiet as it barely took any power to taxi to the end of the clearing.

Just as Rawley had done more than twenty years before, she held her mother's hand as Bud flew off in his shiny antique Cessna. The old plane effortlessly climbed away, and within minutes Apistotooki was quiet save for the running water flowing south through the canyon.

Sally and Rawley packed the remains of the camp, and Jade was loaded for the ride back to the ranch. As Rawley saddled Wildfire, the mare was clearly ready to go. She was tossing her head and scratching at the ground. Sally made a final walk around the camp, and Rawley looked around the canyon. She wanted this memory like so many others to be etched in her mind.

CHAPTER 15

THE RIDE DOWN TO THE ranch was often a two-day event. Sally had many friends along the way, and depending on the weather, they might over-night the horses in a friend's corral or a stall. Sally always used the trip to catch up on the latest goings on, and when Rawley was young she would get to spend time with friends she normally did not see outside of school.

The trail passed very near the popular ghost town of Silver Rock, and visitors would always take pictures of the two as they passed by. To most people Sally looked like a character from an old western movie, with her long black hair in braids and tanned leather clothing. She would have Jade in tow with his packs, and behind them a young girl on a spirited mare. Running in every direction, there were always dogs. Sometimes a few, sometimes more. The dogs were Sally's constant com-panions. Occasionally Sally would stop and talk to visitors while letting the horses rest, and other times they would just pass by on the outskirts of town.

Sally knew Rawley was anxious to get home, so she intentionally shortened the ride into a one day event.

The final hours of the trip home passed quickly, and soon the two came to a small clearing above the ranch. Rawley rode up next to her mother and stopped as she had done so many times before. They had both seen this sight more than a thousand times, and it never got old.

Before them lay Warbird, the name Rawley's father had given the family ranch.

Warbird sat on fifty thousand acres at the base of the Rocky Mountains. Twenty thousand acres were leased out to produced hay and wheat. The rest of the land was used for cattle. The herd varied in size and make-up, but on any given day, there might be three to five thousand head of beef cattle on the ranch. Warbird ran Hereford and Angus livestock. Both breeds had thick hair coats and were well suited to the harsh Montana winters. Warbird ran a small herd by Montana standards, but the real business was flying, and the ranch was well suited for both.

Away from the main house and facing north and south was a lit 3,500-foot asphalt runway, and off the east side of the runway sat a climate-controlled, 30,000-square-foot hangar. It was there that Bud kept his office and several aircraft, old and new.

On the west side of the runway and closer to the ranch entrance, there were three silos, a fifteen-stall barn, and a variety of storage buildings for hay, grain, and equipment. Behind the ranch office, there were two snowplows used to keep the roads and runway clear in the winter and several horse trailers of various sizes. Set back away from the house and barn, there was a three-thousand-square-foot bunkhouse for ranch hands and a common dining area for Warbird employees. There were several stables, a round pen, and a large corral that led to a loading area for shipping cattle. Across from the ranch office was a large covered riding arena where Sally rode or held training year-round.

From the main ranch entrance, there were two roads. One led to the working area of the ranch, and the other went around all the buildings and ended at the house. The main house was a faded yellow one-story structure with an attached four-car garage. Parked nearby were several 4x4 trucks and a few ATVs of various sizes. This was the only home Rawley had known growing up. It was a great life, and Rawley never took that for granted.

Sally reached out for Rawley's hand, and Jade brayed impatiently. "Your father will be waiting." Sally rode forward, taking the lead. Sally led Rawley and Jade down the well-worn path that would take them to the barn. Once there, Jade's load would be removed then the horses cared for. Although Rawley had been away, everything was as familiar as if she had been riding yesterday.

"I have a lesson soon. When you are done with your father, we'll have lunch."

"OK," Rawley said. "I'll see you at the house." Rawley turned Wildfire out in the pasture behind the barn, then she walked toward the hangar. As she approached she could see the doors were partially open.

So many memories, she thought as she stepped inside. The aircraft her father had collected over the years were lined up in two rows. There were eleven in all. Active aircraft, or those still in use, to the left, and on the right, it was like a museum. The aircraft there were old, and a few were rare. There were two biplanes, a 1930 Waco and a 1952 Boeing Stearman. As a child she loved the open cockpit and wind in her hair, and later as a pilot, Rawley would fly both any chance she got. There were two Piper Cubs that had been on scientific Arctic expeditions, one on big tires and one on skis. The rarest of the collectable fleet was a Red 1933 Lockheed Vega, one of only six in the world and the only one with a famous past. It was not the plane she used to cross the Atlantic, but Amelia Earhart's name was scratched into the cockpit. Rawley's favorite plane came to Warbird on a trailer long after its flying days were over. As a child she would sit in the cockpit and dream of great flying adventures. It was the Canadair F-86 Sabrejet Jacqueline Cochran had used to break the sound barrier in 1953. Jackie Cochran broke many barriers as a pilot, and Rawley dreamed of doing the same. Some of the other aircraft were newer and still in use. There was a 1960 Cessna 185 on floats and a newer 185 on skis. There was also a Cessna 206 on amphibious floats and an Aviat Husky on big tires.

"Reminiscing?" Bud asked as he walked through the open door.

"A little," Rawley said.

"Come outside." Bud turned and walked back toward the sun. "Your coming-home present is arriving in about five minutes."

Rawley caught up to Bud and they walked on to the ramp. Rawley looked to the north, and she could see two bright landing lights of a small jet descending toward the runway. Bud and Rawley watched as the aircraft touched down and decelerated before turning back toward the hangar.

"It's a Cessna Mustang," Bud said. "Respectable cruise speed and about eleven-hundred-mile range at max weight. We'll get you checked out in it before you leave for Alaska."

"I love it!" she said, putting her arm around her father. "But I would have been happy with another Husky."

"I know, but this will get you around quicker, and you have places to go and little time to waste," Bud said as he walked toward the aircraft.

CHAPTER 16

———————————

RAWLEY HAD BEEN IN BUD'S office many times over the years, but now it felt different. Everywhere she looked clues pointed to something much larger than the small flying operation portrayed by her father.

"Coffee?" Bud asked as he walked in the room.

"No, thanks," Rawley said, shaking her head.

Behind Bud's desk was the large painting of a gryphon flying over an aircraft carrier. Bud slipped the painting to one side to reveal a map of the world. The map had several colored pins, mostly in the Middle East, South America, and Africa.

"Each one of these pins represents an aircraft," Bud said as he sat down behind his large oak desk. "The planes and number of people vary depending on the tasking."

Bud pointed to the filing cabinet to the left of his desk. "In there we keep all the details. The second drawer has everything you will need to be concerned with for now. You will find information on the pilots who'll be working for you in Afghanistan and a list of assets."

He handed Rawley a folder from his desk. "Look at that list." He leaned back in his chair and put his feet up. He was pleased at the person his daughter had become. She was a great pilot with combat experience, and a she was a leader. He could not ask for more than that. Rawley quietly looked over the list.

"That represents our long-range logistics assets," Bud said. "Mostly jets we lease or just fly for the government. Three Bombardier Globals in various configurations, two Citation Tens, and a G5 converted into an air ambulance. We also have contracts for other aircraft if we need them."

When Rawley heard "air ambulance," she looked up and smiled.

"What?" Bud asked.

Rawley just shook her head. "Nothing," she said, thinking of her conversation with Arlen.

"If anything bigger is required, there are other contractors, and of course the Air Force, who provide those aircraft. We have an East Coast hangar in Edenton, where we can paint, repair, and reconfigure aircraft," said Bud. "It's a nice, quiet place away from prying eyes."

"I've been there," Rawley said. "Edenton, I mean. What's in Alaska?" Rawley laid the folder back on Bud's desk.

Bud put his feet down and reached for another folder then handed it to Rawley.

She opened the folder as he began to explain. "We keep five aircraft up there," he said. "Two in Kodiak. A CASA 212 and Pilatus PC12. Both used by the government for everything from moving people and cargo to parachute operations. You need a little time in both. Those and a Caravan are our primary aircraft where you are headed.

"We also have a 206 on amphibs and a PC12 in Anchorage and another 206 in Nunavut that gets changed between wheels, floats, and skis depending on the season and the need. We have four pilots and two mechanics full time and contracts for anything else we need." Bud again put his feet up. "We provide various training curriculum depending on who we are teaching or what's requested. Pilots usually finish here and go there for two or three weeks." Bud paused for a moment. "We have several landing areas that are challenging but relevant, and we also deliver supplies to some out-of-the-way places. It helps the locals and gets our pilots some good experience flying logistics routes. We do it as humanitarian aid or something like that. It's training and a tax write-off. Your mother's idea," Bud said, with a smile.

"Who runs things up there?" Rawley asked.

"Another ex-Navy pilot," Bud said. "Susan Williams. She flew C-130s at a couple of VRC Squadrons and Pax River." Pax River was short for the Navy's air station at Patuxent River, Maryland. It was home to the US Navy Test Flight Center and Special Operations Wing, tasked with airborne submarine communications and tracking.

"Susan comes from an Alaskan flying family, knows the state well," said Bud. "Her mother was the first woman to fly for Alaska Airlines." Bud paused and watched his daughter's reaction.

"I don't know the name, but I'm sure we'll be fast friends," Rawley said. "What happens in Arizona?"

"Mostly shooting and survival," said Bud. "We have a contract with some former SEALs and Marines near Yuma. They put all our pilots through a short course. It gets everyone proficient with the weapons we keep in the aircraft and sets the tone for the environment you're headed to."

"Sounds fun," Rawley said.

"We also run a desert-flight syllabus there when it's needed," Bud added. "We generally just go down from here for a few weeks with a couple of planes."

Rawley leaned back in her chair and looked around the room. A few weeks ago, she thought she would get some training and report to Afghanistan as a CIA contract pilot. Now she was getting a business brief from her father.

"Well," she said, "when do I get started, and what's next?"

Bud again put his feet on the floor and leaned forward. "Your mother isn't going to be very happy if you race out of here. How about four or five days at home? It will give you time to go through the files and put some time in the Mustang. I'll give you the number of the pilot who's checking you out in it. Your mother would like to see her sister in Salt Lake. How about running her down there on Friday?" Bud asked as he headed for the door.

Rawley shrugged. "Sounds like a plan. You said Gil crashed a 206. What are those used for?"

Bud stopped in the office doorway and turned around. "We have four of them full of electronics for picking up cellular and other signals." Then he paused again and looked at her. "Welcome home," he said.

"Is there anybody I should avoid or situations I should be aware of?" Rawley asked as she moved toward the filing cabinet.

"It's all in there," Bud said. "We've had a few guys get crossed up with the law. Some threats. Goes with the territory." He was smiling as he left. "I think your mother wants to have lunch in about an hour."

Rawley pulled the Afghanistan files and spent thirty minutes looking at the personnel. The only name she knew was Gil Adams. He was a lifelong friend of the family and a famous early Montana aviator. He had mapped the first commercial routes through the Rockies as a teenager and delivered mail, medicine, and visitors to remote ranches in an open cockpit Stearman. He was also the one who taught her to fly her father's biplanes. He had always seemed old to her, but she never thought of him as too old to fly. Like Bart he was the consummate aviator and adventurer.

Rawley made her way to the house by way of the covered arena where her mother was teaching riding, then by the ranch office to say hello to old friends.

As she entered the house, she could see her bags had made it from Buffalo Lake.

"We turned that car in at Shelby," her father said. "You can find keys to anything you want to drive there by the door. The big yellow Ford is your mother's dog limo; you may want to leave that one alone."

Rawley just smiled as she looked around the house. She could see not much had changed. After her father left, Rawley walked to the fireplace and looked at a photo on the mantle. It was the only picture, and she saw it had been moved to a place where it was partially obscured since the last time she had looked at it. The photo had been taken when she was six years old at an air show in Great Falls, Montana. It was her and her older brother standing near a Navy F-14 from the squadron VF

84. Rawley looked at the photo for a few minutes, and as always her eyes filled with tears.

"Your father won't say it, but we think about him every day." Rawley's mother had come into the room without her noticing.

"So do I," Rawley said as she touched her eyes.

"Put your things away; we'll have lunch," Sally said as she touched her daughter's shoulder.

Rawley took her bags to her room, and as she opened the door, she could see could everything there was also just as she had left it. It looked like a shrine to women in aviation. There were photos everywhere of famous women pilots from around the state, the country, and the world.

Everywhere she looked there were memories and books, including a well-worn paperback titled "Night Witches," the account of Russia's most famous World War Two women aviators and their exploits against the Germans. Her favorite poster from an airshow she had attended as a child in Billings, Montana was there also. It was there she had met the Navy's first female F-14 pilot, Kara Hultgren.

It was a meeting Rawley would never forget. Soon after she would be heartbroken to learn Kara was killed in a carrier-landing accident. In another photo Rawley was in the cockpit with Helen Adams, Gilbert Adams's older sister. When Rawley was twenty, and at her mother's request, she flew Helen, one of Montana's original female pilots, to a WASP reunion in Washington, DC. The WASPs, Women's Airforce Service Pilots, were an all-woman pilot organization founded by Jackie Cochran to ferry military aircraft during World War Two. Their purpose was to free men from the administrative duties of delivering aircraft so they could fight. In all there were 1074 women involved, and Rawley met many of them at the reunion. It was another unforgettable event in her short life, but the real value was sharing the cockpit with a living legend. More than 25,000 women applied to join the WASPs, and less than 1,200 were accepted. Rawley would never forget the stories or what it felt like to walk among some of the most courageous women in America.

There were other photos as well, including several of Wildfire through the years and many from her time at Georgetown University. Photos from college meant photos of Rip. Seeing his face brought back feelings and questions, and, as always it caused her to pause. On a shelf near her bed Rawley saw a stack of letters she had written home over the years.

As she fanned the letters she could see her mother had kept them in order and that made her smile. One letter caught her eye and she pulled it from the stack and began to read it to herself. It was her thoughts after her first training flight in a jet in Kingsville Texas.

Dear Mom,

Today was a FAM hop to begin the transition to jets. It was an adjustment having a new instructor, new instrument panel, and learning a new scan. It was me in the front with two jet engines whining behind me...so much power at my fingertips, I can't help but feel as if I am on a strong horse. Crazy maybe, but like prior to jump class, all I have to do is open my fingers so it may take the reins.

Transitions are aggressively subtle, a contradiction. The instructor was supposed to demonstrate the taxi, takeoff, etc., but he had me do the entire thing. Just prior to starting my takeoff roll, I began to appreciate the power, and when I advanced the PCLs, power control levers, to full power, I found I could not hold the plane back. We quickly accelerated to 100 knots, and in no time we were at 900 feet. I did my instrument scan then a quick scan outside. The instructor was giving me instructions, and all around I could see other aircraft performing maneuvers. An A4 Skyhawk was to my right, and about a mile ahead, another A4 was performing a straight dive. That was all I needed to see to remind me how important it is to stay aware. Closure rates are rapid, and visibility is essentially limited. After a few maneuvers, we returned to base to practice landings. I had to think ahead and remind myself to not pull the nosewheel up as we neared touchdown. My instructor told me to accept the impact. After only a few times, it was normal, and painful, but I did accept it, and I will continue to do so. When I finally did a full stop landing, I felt physically and a bit mentally drained, but my instructor's comments were encouraging. Tell Dad his training is paying off. I know there are challenges ahead, but I will do whatever it takes to get through this. I know I am supposed to be here. I found a horse to ride at a local stable. Her name is Chesapeake. She needs her feet trimmed, but she is a pleasure to ride.

All my love,
Rawley

After a few days at home that included a check ride in the Mustang, a daytrip to Salt Lake City with her mother, and several business discussions with her father, Rawley was ready to take the next step in her new life. She was excited by what lay ahead and felt a great sense of pride in her family.

CHAPTER 17

———————◆———————

RAWLEY MADE A CALL TO Susan Williams before leaving for Alaska. She would meet Rawley in Anchorage, where they would leave the Mustang. It seemed funny departing from the home ranch on what could prove to be a greater adventure than going off to the Navy. She was now a key part of a family business that was anything but conventional. Bud and Sally met Rawley at the hangar, where she was getting everything ready.

"What's your flight plan?" Bud asked.

"Climb out to the south then over to Port Angeles, Washington for fuel, then Juneau and on to Anchorage. Susan is meeting me there with the CASA," said Rawley as she pushed her bag into the plane.

Rawley first hugged her mother, then Bud, before climbing into the Mustang. Bart walked out of the hangar and joined her parents as she closed her door.

Bart, Bud, and Sally walked away from the plane and watched together as Rawley taxied to the north end of the runway.

"What do you think?" Bud asked Bart.

"Well," he said, "I think she has some demons to slay. One, anyway."

Bud nodded in agreement. As the Mustang raced by and roared into the air, the three waved. Rawley rocked her wings to say good-bye.

Once in the air, Rawley checked in with ATC and picked up the first waypoint in her flight plan. Alone with her thoughts, she couldn't help but think about flying in the Navy and how uncomplicated this was in contrast.

Port Angeles, Washington, was on the Straights of Juan De Fuca in the northwest corner of the state. She would get fuel and lunch before going to Alaska. Rawley had been to this part of Washington State just a few times, and it always seemed to be raining, foggy, or both. Today she was anticipating beautiful weather and a great view of Mount Rainier and all the other snowcapped peaks.

Eight hours after departing Warbird, Rawley was on short final for Anchorage International. The sun was going down and the outside air temperature was fifty-five degrees.

Once parked, Rawley grabbed her bag and walked toward the flight operation's office for civil aviation. On the ramp, there were nearly a hundred aircraft of every type and size. Several large corporate jets and a variety of bush planes too numerous to count. Most were old Beavers or Otters and many Cessnas. Several were on amphibious floats. There was also a long line of helicopters and activity everywhere as cargo was being loaded or unloaded. Anchorage was a launching point for destinations throughout Alaska, and it was busy around the clock.

Rawley stopped for a moment and took it all in. When she turned back toward the main building, or FBO, she could see a woman walking toward her. She could tell from the file photo it was Susan Williams.

As she came near, Susan stretched her hand out and smiled. "Welcome to Alaska!" she said.

"Thanks," Rawley said. "I've been looking forward to it."

"Other bags? Susan asked.

"I have everything I need for now, and I'm buying if you know a place," Rawley replied.

"I know a place; it's a short walk," said Susan as she turned around. "First time in Alaska?"

"It is," Rawley said.

"The Lagopus is just around the corner."

"Lagopus?" Rawley asked.

"State bird. Flyers' hangout," said Susan. "Usually a gathering of who's who around here." Before she opened the door, Susan stopped.

"This is a fun place, but don't make eye contact with anyone you wouldn't mind killing later. Some of these guys can be hard to shake," Susan said.

"I know the type too well," said Rawley.

"I know all these guys," Susan said. "Too many are walking a tight-rope with the law or have other significant issues. You'll know right off, and if you want to break contact with anyone and they won't leave, just bring up the weather. I'll know what to do."

"Great plan," said Rawley as they walked in.

CHAPTER 18

THE LAGOPUS PREDATED STATEHOOD. THE Ellis brothers, a couple of Alaskan aviation pioneers, opened it in 1935. From the beginning, they provided for all the pilots' needs, including food, a place to sleep, a place to meet, and of course a place to drink. Over the years it was the scene of a few hundred wedding parties, too many memorial parties for lost pilots, and thousands of other celebrations. There was fun and some occasional drama. When the pilots weren't flying, they were drinking, and drinking led to arguing that sometimes came to blows. The current owner was Verlie Davis, and she ran the place with an iron fist. She had spent thirty years operating the Lagopus while dispatching seaplanes from her office upstairs, and she knew how to handle pilots, lumbermen, and self-important adventurers. Whether they were young or old, rich or poor, she treated them all the same. Crossing Verlie always came with a penalty and being banned from the bar was a fate worse than death. When Verlie talked men listened.

Each time the door opened, everyone in the front room instinctively looked to see who was coming in. Such was the case when Rawley and Susan walked in. The Lagopus was divided into three separate areas. The entry was through the main bar. To the right was a larger room that was often used for private parties or music and dancing on the weekends, and to the left there was a narrow hall that led to showers and bunkrooms that were normally rented by the hour or day.

The walls were covered in Alaskan aviation memorabilia, and one section behind the bar was dedicated to pilots who had met their fate. If they were killed flying, the date, type of aircraft they were in, and location were written somewhere on the photo. Verlie had initiated that practice after hearing one too many arguments about who died where, when, and how.

Rawley looked around the dimly lit room and couldn't help but smile at the collection of characters. As Susan moved toward the bar, there were catcalls and questions. "Who's your friend, Susan?" they yelled out.

Several men and a few women were standing at the bar, and maybe forty others were seated at tables around the room. Verlie saw Susan and came around the end of the bar to embrace her.

Susan hugged Verlie then introduced her to Rawley. "Verlie Davis, Rawley West," she said.

Verlie smiled and hugged her tight. "Bud's daughter?"

Rawley smiled back and nodded her head. "I am."

At least one drunk poked his head into the mix to say hello, but Verlie chased him off.

"Welcome to the Lagopus, dear! Drink, get some food, and look around," said Verlie. "Your first night here is on the house. Check the walls in there." She pointed to her left. "You'll find some photos of your dad when he was a young man."

"What about Bart Chambers?" Rawley asked.

"Oh, heavens yes, he's in there. He should be behind the bar by now," she said with a laugh. She was still talking as she went back to serving customers. "I banned him for a month once for running a bordello in my bunk house, another month for an illegal poker game, and another month just for good measure."

"You were just mad because he shorted you on the profits," a man said as he turned to face Rawley. He held out his hand. "Rance King. I flew with your old man in the Navy. How's the cattle business?" he asked.

"Profitable," said Rawley as she moved away. "Excuse me, I'll be right back."

Susan called out, "What are you drinking?"

"Cuba Libre, please. Extra lime," Rawley said as she made her way to the back room. Many eyes watched her as she left the bar area, not for any specific reason, but mainly just because that's the way it was here. A lot of men and a few women. Alaska's curse.

Susan walked in as Rawley slowly walked past the thousands of photos on the wall and handed her a drink. Most of the photos were black and white, wrinkled, and poorly framed or not framed at all. It was like looking at the history of the de Havilland Beaver, the bush pilot's workhorse since the '40s.

Rawley sipped her drink as she scanned the walls, and Susan left her to walk the room alone. Soon she stopped and sent a text message to her father. She typed, "Rance King?" and hit send. The answer came back in seconds and made her smile.

"RK OK. Don't believe anything Verlie says about me. V engaged to Bart. But shot him. Have fun, be safe. My best to Susan and V. Dad."

Rawley walked back into the bar and directly to Rance. She held out her hand. "A pleasure to meet you," she said.

Rance smiled. "Checked in with your pop didn't you?"

"Technology is a wonderful thing," said Rawley as she set her empty glass on the bar.

"So, tell me some war stories about you and my dad," Rawley said as she motioned for a refill. The night passed quickly, and Rawley found Rance a great deterrent from unwanted attention. Soon it was just Susan, Rawley, and Rance, and Verlie behind the bar on a stool.

As the conversation died down, Rawley looked around the bar, then at Verlie.

"Dad said you shot Bart," she said.

"Right in the ass," Rance said, before Verlie could speak.

"Well," Verlie said as she looked at Rance with a frown, "I asked him to marry me, and he said yes." She paused. "Then, I guess he had second thoughts. I found him fooling around with my cousin in the back. So that was that."

Verlie shrugged. "And no!" she added. "I didn't shoot him. I shot the lamp, and he was hit in the ass by some broken glass. And, if it wasn't sticking up in the air and uncovered, he wouldn't have been hit at all."

Everyone laughed. Rawley raised her glass to Verlie and smiled.

"How is he?" Verlie asked.

"He's great," Rawley said.

"I'm guessing he hasn't changed," Verlie said, with a far off look in her eye. "Another round." She poured drinks for everyone. "He was just back from the war. He was handsome and wild and fun and heroic. I knew he'd never settle down. But what the hell? Every woman needs at least one man like that in her life. What about you, Rawley?" She slid the drinks across the bar.

"There was a guy," Rawley said as she took a drink. "I didn't shoot him, but I did leave him with nice scar to remember me by."

"Annie Oakley said it best," said Susan. "You can't be afraid to love a man and you can't be afraid to shoot him either. Or something like that."

"A toast to love!" said Rance as he raised his glass. "And to the Ellis brothers! Those visionary barnstormers who gave us this fine establishment!"

"Salud!" they said as the four glasses clinked together.

"If Bart didn't marry you, who did he marry?" Rawley asked.

"That old liar has never been married," said Verlie. "He just says that."

Rawley smiled and shook her head.

"So, what are your plans?" Verlie asked Rawley.

"I forgot to ask," Rawley said as she turned to Susan.

"A cargo drop at Prudhoe, then a government job out of Kodiak. A floatplane recert and some other stuff. Just flying around Alaska," said Susan.

Verlie handed Rance a camera and motioned for the women to join her behind the bar. "A tradition!" she said. "It will hang in a place of honor!"

CHAPTER 19

———◆———

MORNING CAME QUICKLY, AND BOTH women were feeling a little hungover. A common theme in Alaska. At breakfast Susan explained the entire business, including training and the covered aviation operations they ran in Alaska.

"As far as anyone here is concerned, we are just another flying company doing anything we can to make ends meet," Susan said. "Aircraft come and go around here, and pilots change hats as often as most people change their mind, and nobody is surprised by anything they see at an Alaskan airport, so we just hide in the wide open and blend in." She reached for her coffee.

Rawley was eating and listening. Susan went on. "We have an office and a dispatcher in Pelican. It's a nice, out-of-the-way seaplane base near Juneau. We usually don't have a plane stationed there. It's really just a place to hold records for the endless state and federal inspections."

The front door opened, and Susan stopped talking as she looked to see who had just walked into the bar.

Rawley could tell from her face she wasn't happy. "Weather problem?" Rawley asked.

"Perceptive," said Susan. "Just a landmine I stepped on a long time ago. I should have been a lesbian."

Rawley couldn't help but smile. "Where to next and when?" Rawley asked.

Susan adjusted her chair to put her back to the room, then continued. "We'll take the CASA up to Prudhoe and drop some supplies. It's loaded now. We can spend the night, then head on down to Kodiak. We have a military airdrop in two days. A SEAL team water jump."

"How often do you do that?" Rawley asked.

"Usually one a month," Susan said. "They also have a training area north of Nome on the Nuluk River. We normally land the CASA on a road up there if we can, and if not we make a few trips with an amphib twin Otter we contract."

As Susan talked Rawley was looking at photographs on the wall near their table. One photo caught her eye, and she could not help but stare at it. Susan could see she was distracted and turned to see what she was looking at. Rawley stood up and walked toward the photo.

It was a group of men wearing heavy white-and-black camouflage parkas. The photo was dark and grainy, and they were gathered in front of the Lagopus. Most of the men had long hair and thick beards. Rawley stared intently at one face in particular. Like the others the man had a thick beard and he was wearing sunglasses and a ball cap. Then she pointed at the photo.

"Who are these men, Susan? Do you know?"

"I was here when that photo was taken," Susan said. SEALs mostly. That was about six or seven years ago. Why?"

"SEALs. Are you sure?" Rawley asked.

"Definitely. I picked them up in Barrow and brought them here to meet an Air Force C-17 then they headed back to Virginia I think. Do you know any of them?" Susan asked.

"No," Rawley said, shaking her head. "Just a coincidence. A doppelganger, I guess." Rawley took a photo of the photograph with her phone, and as she turned around, she could see Susan's unwanted friend making his way to the table.

"Well," Rawley said, "it's clouding up. Shall we, uh—"

"Leave!" said Susan as she slid her chair back. She gathered her things, then held her hand up as if to say stop. The man was smiling and opened his arms, offering a hug, but Susan stepped sideways and put a table between them.

No words were spoken as the two women left the bar. Susan pulled her cellphone from her pocket and called Verlie. "Hold my tab, will you, Verlie? We had to make a hasty exit." Susan listened then laughed before bidding Verlie good-bye and hanging up.

At the airport Rawley walked around the Casa 212 as part of the preflight inspection.

The 212 was a nonpressurized cargo plane initially built for military use, but several were in private service around the world moving cargo and passengers. As they walked around the twin turbine aircraft, Susan discussed the specs and characteristics.

"OK," said Rawley, "let's fly!"

CHAPTER 20

FORWARD OPERATING BASE, KEJAHN, AFGHANISTAN

---·◆·---

THE SCENE IN THE BASE operations center was frantic as always. Every day brought news of a new threat from some new faction or an intelligence report to be acted upon. Kejahn hosted a large joint quick-reaction force, or QRF, made up of Air Force, Navy, and Army Special Forces and a contracted security force that protected the base from insurgents. Within its perimeter there was a single seven-thousand-foot runway, three large hangars, and a main building, or OP Center. The OP Center took three years to build. It had four floors to accommodate workspace and a comfortable living environment for the nearly six hundred personnel assigned there. The main building was large enough to house a small shopping mall, and with the majority of its hardened structure underground, it was nearly invulnerable to a conventional attack.

Twenty-four hours a day, seven days a week, over three hundred men and women manned satellite communication terminals, computer terminals, and UAV control stations in three shifts. The main operations floor was a maze of workstations, cables, and monitors. The walls were covered with flat-screen televisions and clocks labeled with the region or city they represented. The largest clock on each wall was different in appearance from the rest and easily distinguished. That clock was local time.

Over five thousand messages a day were read and acted upon by the twenty-two military commands and government organizations represented within the OP Center, commonly referred to as kilo juliet, or kay jay. There were three flag officers, nineteen command equivalent officers, senior government officials, and thirty-two liaison officers assigned full time to the center. They all answered to a single four-star Admiral or General who reported directly to the Secretary of Defense. Also housed at kay jay, but separate from everyone else, was the command center for the Central Intelligence Agency operations.

Throughout the day there were briefings and planning conferences, and task orders were generated. There were also post mission debriefs and active missions being monitored in real time.

Due to countless incidents of stress-related issues with personnel at kay jay and other bases with similar op tempos, there were two full-time psychologists and human-behavior experts monitoring the morale of those assigned to the base. Security was tight, and in many areas where compartmented information was handled, movement was restricted and controlled. Many personnel were segregated from the general populace for personal security reasons.

It was at kay jay that the most valued human-intelligence operators in the theater worked and lived. Their identities were protected by code names and disguises, and they were often unknown even to each other as they would come and go under the cover of darkness or through one of the many restricted passageways that provided cloaked ingress and egress. History had proven time and again that no technology could or ever would replace or make human intelligence obsolete. The men and women who filled these roles placed duty above personal safety, often working alone among the enemy to gain bits of information, like pieces of a puzzle that might later save lives. At kay jay they were known simply as Task Force Zebra, or TF Z.

The current head of Task Force Zebra was Dave Mayer. He was a member of the senior executive service and a former CIA field operative and ex-Navy pilot. Under his command he had twenty operatives who serviced over two hundred covered insurgents who traded information for money and other things they might require. It was a full-time job that required constant attention.

TF Z maintained three personnel on communication watch at all times who monitored secure radio frequencies, satellite emergency beacons, telephones, open radio bands, and several text message systems used by the military and government field operators. Coded messages and voice messages in the clear could come in at any time if operators were compromised or suspected compromise. Communication by any means was often the difference between life and death. The primary mission of the joint quick-reaction force at kay jay was to respond to these urgent requests for extraction.

Dave Mayer was at his desk reading messages when his secure phone rang. Mayer knew the voice at the other end well. It was his counterpart at CIA headquarters, Brick Wellen.

"Dave, it's Brick. How are things?"

"Great, what do have for me?"

"Probably nothing, but we are picking up bits and pieces about an American nuke that's been found and available, and some folks in your theater are involved in the conversations. You do know we've lost sixteen nukes since the fifties, mostly in the Atlantic. Which one do you think they found?" Mayer asked.

"Based on what we are piecing together, it's small, and it's associated with a Vietnam-era plane crash somewhere in Asia. The only thing we can come up with here is a diver-delivered weapon lost during the war. The aircraft was on the first leg of the trip when it disappeared, but its route should have been well away from any land mass or islands. The loss was all but buried after a drawn-out search."

"A small bomb?" Mayer asked in a skeptical tone.

"A SADAM actually," Brick said referring a small nuclear weapon made for special forces during the Cold War.

"Those things were filthy. If it broke open, we should be able find it from the sky." Mayer said.

"I agree it should be glowing, but we have been looking and had no luck yet. I'm just giving you a head's up is all. You'll be getting a list of guys talking in your area. How about stepping up monitoring around there, and if you hear anything interesting, let me know."

"All right, send details. We'll catch up later."

"I'm sending you a message now," Brick said. "Out here." With that, the line went dead.

Mayer opened the message and looked at the three names and details of their intercepted phone calls. Two names he knew well. Muhammad Sersi, a British-born Afghan, and Bloom Fournier, a German National who had come on the scene recently in Afghanistan. Both were well educated and listed as "capture not kill." It was the only reason a drone had not visited them. They were known to possess vital information, and this news just made their capture even more vital.

Mayer typed out a surveillance order that would make collection against these specific targets a priority and hit send. A minute later he would receive a receipt confirmation message from the signals intelligence liaison officer, who would then generate a task order for all collection platforms in the region.

CHAPTER 21

———•———

THE THREE-HOUR FLIGHT TO PRUDHOE Bay was uneventful and offered a beautiful view of the state as they cut across central Alaska. Susan and Rawley talked about the Navy and life and flying.

Susan also talked about the influence of her mother's flying exploits, and Rawley talked about her father. "How did you get into this?" Rawley asked.

Susan looked at Rawley. "My mother and Bart were best friends for years," she said. "Bart encouraged me to fly and then join the military, which, like you, I did after college." Susan stopped, then turned to Rawley. "Mom is also Verlie's cousin."

"Not the infamous cousin?" Rawley asked.

"Oh yeah," said Susan. "The one and only. Alaska is always good for a scandal or two."

There was a long silence as Rawley took everything in. "Have you been to Afghanistan with the company?"

Susan shook her head. "No, I must admit I'm very comfortable right here." She said as she dialed the weather for Deadhorse airport.

Prudhoe Bay was on the horizon. A gated, restricted area protected all the oil activity, and the town that served the industry was called Deadhorse. The entire area was surrounded by tundra, and in the summer months, the terrain was too soft to support equipment, so any new construction took place during the winter while the tundra was frozen. Building supplies were usually stockpiled in warehouses near the airport at Deadhorse during the summer. During that time there were constant resupply flights and trucks coming and going from Juneau and Fairbanks.

Tourists often made the two-day trip from Fairbanks by bus to see the tundra, the Arctic Ocean, and the Northern Lights. All the lodging, entertainment, and commerce centered in the area around the airport. Like most places in Alaska, the most prosperous and influential citizens were those who provided food, lodging, and especially alcohol.

As they taxied to the cargo area, Rawley looked out the side window at the different planes sitting around the ramp. Off to one side were three obviously wrecked aircraft. Two were nearly identical Lockheed Electras like the one flown by Amelia Earhart on her final flight.

"Wow!" she exclaimed. "Unlucky place for the Electra."

Susan looked to the right. "Both overloaded and compounded by pilot error. That C-46," Susan said, indicating the wreckage of a large cargo plane, "was over thirty years old when its nose gear collapsed on touchdown. We slid halfway down the runaway on the belly. It was fairly benign, happily."

"We?" Rawley asked as she looked at Susan.

"Bart and my mother were flying, and I was in a jump seat. That was the end of Grizzly Aviation's cargo business," Susan said. "After that Mom started flying for Alaska Airlines, and Bart…" Susan paused again as she often did. "He went down to Montana to fly with your father."

Rawley looked back at the plane as they passed by.

Once they were parked, the aircraft was offloaded, refueled according to Susan's instructions, and repositioned back to the flight line. The FBO, or flight base operations building maintained a list of people looking for a cheap flight or a free ride out of Prudhoe. Mostly oil-field workers trying to get back to Fairbanks for a week of rest and relaxation, which of course was just code for drinking and women. They always paid in cash and generally carried nothing but a small backpack. Too many pilots would bring them along for the cash even if it meant overloading their aircraft.

Susan always looked at the list but rarely took any passengers or cargo that wasn't manifested by the contracting officer she reported to. Mostly she was just looking for a familiar name.

The next day the sun was up at five, and the women were preflighting the plane by seven. They had another good weather day for the flight to Kodiak.

Susan checked her phone for any messages from Pelican, and soon they were in the air, flying south with Rawley in the left seat.

"We are going to take a less direct route," Susan said as they climbed out of Deadhorse with Rawley at the controls. "Pick up one ninety-five, and level at forty-five hundred."

"I can do that," Rawley said as she adjusted the power and scanned instruments.

"We will be flying down a route unofficially known as Alaska's 'Trail of Tears,'" Susan said as she scanned the horizon for other aircraft, even though none showed on the traffic-alert instruments. "Too many guys flying around without transponders, so do keep a look out."

"Ominous name," said Rawley.

"It was the primary winter route for years. It's littered with crash sites," Susan said as she looked at some notes she had made on her knee-pad. "Mostly Beavers and mostly fatal." Susan was referring to the de Havilland DH2. "The early planes had the battery installed right under the fuel tank, which was installed right under the pilots' seats. Nobody survived those crashes." She shook her head.

"What's the biggest killer up here?" Rawley asked.

"Overloading and fast-changing weather," said Susan. "So many of these guys will fly in fog, pushing the limits, then one day...they get closed out in a canyon, and there's no room to turn around and no climbing out. When that happens, you can cancel Christmas." Susan shook her head and stared at the panel, like old memories rushed in, and she couldn't clear them away.

Then without looking up, she continued. "I've lost three boyfriends and a fiancé like that."

"I'm sorry to hear that," Rawley said sincerely.

"Well, one thing Alaska has is an endless supply of men, so you celebrate their life, you mourn the loss, then you move on. All that tends to happen rather quickly up here. And all those lost souls end up as photos on a wall at the Lagopus or some other bar. An Alaskan tradition for pilots and fishermen."

"What about you?" Susan asked. "Boyfriend?"

Rawley looked out the side window and shook her head. "Too busy." she said.

"Well there was a guy." "The photograph?" Susan asked.

"No, just a similarity." Rawley was shaking her head. "Honestly I met him in college and I haven't seen him in more than seven years."

"We were inseparable then one day he just disappeared. Vanished."

Rawley shrugged and Susan frowned.

CHAPTER 22

———◆———

THE FLIGHT TO KODIAK WAS just an hour longer than they had flown the day before. Susan loved to talk, and Rawley didn't mind listening.

"Tell me about the jumping," Rawley said.

"We'll have a brief with the jumpmaster around ten a.m. tomorrow," said Susan. "They normally have about twelve to fifteen jumpers. It will be a single-pass freefall into the water about a half mile from the airfield. It's not complicated. You fly left seat, I'll do everything else. They jump from anywhere between thirty-five hundred and twelve five. We'll have a crewman onboard for the jump. One of our guys will fly in and meet us."

Rawley nodded. "Sounds easy enough."

Susan checked in with Kodiak and confirmed she had the weather. After she completed the landing checklist, she started to explain more about the event.

"We can park at the coast guard ramp or GA," Susan said, referring to the general aviation area. "The SEALS prefer GA so they can avoid going through another gate. It also makes it easier for us," she said. Rawley nodded as she looked at the Kodiak approach instructions.

Like many coastal airports in Alaska, Kodiak was situated right on the water and had an adjoining seaplane base. As they were on short final, Susan could see their Cessna 206 with its distinctive orange tail tied up at the seaplane docks.

"Brett's here," she said as the CASA touched the ground. "You'll like him. Also ex-Navy and just back from Africa."

"What did he fly?" Rawley asked.

"Rotary guy," said Susan. "Hawks mostly." She meant the Navy's H60 variant, the Seahawk.

As they taxied onto the ramp, Rawley was getting directions to a parking spot. Brett Jones was standing there with his hands in his pockets. In contrast to most pilots in Alaska, Brett was fit, well groomed, and drank in moderation if at all.

As soon as the engines started shutting down, Brett had the cabin door open and was climbing aboard. "Welcome to Kodiak!" he yelled out.

Brett made a quick walk-through of the small cargo bay and then pulled a belt and harness out of a box. He would be wearing the harness during the jump to ensure he didn't accidently leave the aircraft.

"Test the lights," he said.

Susan showed Rawley the switch for the jump lights. "Red before the ramp goes down, then green to jump," she said as she cycled the switch. By now Brett was sitting in the cockpit door, looking back into the cargo bay.

"Red," he said as the light illuminated. "Green, and off. The plane's ready, ladies! I have three rooms across the street."

Susan was finishing the shut-down checklist. Rawley reached her right hand back to Brett. "Rawley," she said.

"Brett. Nice to meet you," he said. "How are Bart and your dad?"

"Great," Rawley said as she climbed out of the seat.

Brett filled them in as they walked. "We are briefing on the plane at nine. Wheels up by ten, fifteen jumpers, one pass, and everyone is getting out." Brett shrugged. "That's it."

He added, "We've been invited to meet a few of the guys later at the Snowshoe."

"The Snowshoe?" asked Susan. "Since when?"

"Since the Goldrush burned down," Brett said. "Cigars and sawdust floors aren't a good mix, I guess."

It was an hour later when Rawley walked out of the hotel. Looking across the airport, she could see Womens Bay and far off to her left, snowcapped mountains. Every vehicle that passed by was a truck of some sort, and every vehicle had a layer of dirt. Most of the vehicles were pulling into the Snowshoe bar across the street. Rawley watched for few moments then walked that way.

As soon as she walked into the Snowshoe, Rawley could tell who the SEALs were. They weren't rowdy or boisterous; they just looked different than anyone else. Even in this environment, where all men tended to be rugged, they stood out. She didn't see Susan or Brett, so she walked up to the bar and ordered a drink, then approached the SEALs. Like most bars she entered, men watched her every move. It was the same with the SEALs, except they also watched everyone else.

"Are you guys jumping tomorrow?" she asked the group.

"We are," the man closest to her said as he reached for her hand. "Who are you?"

"New pilot," Rawley said.

"Where's Susan?" someone asked.

"She'll be here, I'm sure," Rawley said as she looked at each man. Like most special forces operators, they all had beards and longer hair than anyone in the military. Most of them had blond hair, and even in this environment, they were tanned as if they had just come from a vacation on the beach. They stuck together at the bar and rarely talked to anyone they didn't already know. Unless you were a woman, and there were always women. Even in Alaska, where the ratio tended to be five men to every woman, the SEALs always seemed to have women hanging around. The only men in the bar they interacted with were the bartenders, bouncers, and bar owners.

Rawley had a lot of experience with team guys, as they were often called, from her time in the Navy. She knew exactly what they would say.

She knew the topic of sex would come up within minutes, and she knew at least one would invade her space. And soon.

Rawley sipped her drink as she looked around the bar. Typical of any bar frequented by the military, the walls were covered with decals from Army, Navy, and Air Force squadrons and other military units, including the generic SEAL and UDT stickers. Like a brand these decals were put up wherever the military drank.

One SEAL was reaching out to her with another drink. Rawley knew he would soon be standing too close to her, and in no time, she was right.

Like an interrogator he was asking one question after another. Where are you from? How did you become a pilot? Have you been here before? How long are you here for? Married?

Rawley kept her answers short. If she had learned anything from her time in the Navy and being in a world dominated by men, it was how to carry on a conversation while saying nothing, offering nothing, and never appearing to be overly impressed by anyone.

Her aloof attitude quickly drove most men away except SEALs and Marines, who were always more persistent. They had a never-say-die approach to everything, and if there was more than one, they would back off and allow someone else to try. Most women would be flattered by the attention, but Rawley looked at it like a game. She knew who they were, what motivated them, and what the next move would be. After talking for nearly an hour, they still knew nothing about her except her name.

Rawley was on her third drink when Susan showed up. Upon seeing her the SEALs all cheered and raised their glasses in a salute.

Susan smiled and was clearly familiar with all of them. The guy closest to the bar handed her a drink, and they all toasted. Rawley raised her glass and joined in. The atmosphere instantly turned more festive.

"We've been talking to your friend, but she's pretty guarded," one of the men said.

Susan just smiled and looked at Rawley. "Any weather issues?"

Rawley laughed. "Not yet, but you know there's a storm here someplace."

"Let's hope!" Susan said as she raised her glass.

Susan kept the conversation going, and Rawley moved into the circle to discourage any drunks who may have built up the courage to approach her. Another learned trait from the Navy.

Women came and went, and their only interaction with Susan and Rawley were dirty looks and an occasional snide remark. The night was winding down, and a few of the SEALs had already paired up and left. By now Rawley was strictly passive, listening to the endless stories and watching. Always watching. The door. The crowd. Those closest to her. The only partiers more vigilant than her were the men in her perimeter. She felt safe here, and she was. As she set her last empty glass on the bar, the only man who had not engaged her all night came close. Rawley saw his reflection in the mirror behind the bar.

"Quite a demotion, isn't it?" he said, as he also looked at her reflection.

Rawley looked at him but didn't answer.

"I mean, Hornets to a CASA?" he said.

Rawley turned slowly and looked up at that man standing in front of her. He was taller than the other men and slightly more groomed.

"Have we met?" she asked.

"On the *Eisenhower* about two years ago," he said. "You were providing CAS to my squadron when we went into Chora, Afghanistan."

CAS referred to close air support. Attack aircraft would loiter overhead on call in case the men on the ground needed help to suppress enemy fire. It was a mission Rawley had performed countless times. And one she had loved.

Rawley smiled and held out her hand. "Good memory," she said. "Sorry I don't recognize you."

"It's cool. I'm John," he said as he reached for her hand. "You weren't beating your...uh...chest or offering much, so I thought I'd just stay out of the conversation," he said.

"Thanks," said Rawley. "Good SERE school training." SERE was survival-and-escape training that all pilots and most other military members went through to prepare them to deal with interrogation should they ever be captured. "I don't need to throw all that out. I save it for when I'm around pilots or someone who might actually be impressed." She smiled.

The others were oblivious to their conversation. By now the bar was raging with noisy drunks and louder music.

Rawley looked at Susan and motioned in a way that any Navy pilot would recognize as the signal she was leaving, or as she would call it, punching out.

Susan stopped talking midsentence. "See you in the morning. Be careful leaving here," she said.

Rawley nodded. She turned to John, who was standing by but not talking. "My hotel is across the street. Would you mind walking me out of here just to uncomplicate my exit?" she said as she looked at the crowd of rowdy drunks between her and the door. John smiled and put his arm around her, then parted the crowd as he led her from the bar.

CHAPTER 23

———————•———————

THE SUN WAS JUST COMING up in Kodiak. As Rawley and Susan approached the plane, two black four-wheel-drive trucks full of olive-drab parachute bags pulled up to the CASA, followed by a white government bus. Rawley looked at her watch.

"They're always early," Susan said as she headed toward the open ramp at the back of the plane. "They may be hungover and hurting, but they are always early!"

The SEALs came off the bus and started unloading gear from the trucks. Brett was walking off the ramp as Susan approached.

"The plane's ready," he said. He handed Susan a clipboard that was used to preflight. Due to the fact that nearly every pilot in Bud's employ had a background in military aviation, things ran very much like they did in a squadron. Records were complete, and every line of a published preflight was checked. Happily, that translated to a very good safety record.

Rawley was walking around the aircraft out of habit when she stopped at the ramp. Susan handed her the clipboard.

"Up early?" she said to Brett. He just shrugged.

"We missed you last night," Rawley said as she looked over the pre-flight checklist.

Brett laughed. "Two female aviators and bar full of SEALs. I knew someone was going to need a clear head this morning. And the SEALs have a nasty habit of punching pilots when they drink."

Rawley smiled. Susan turned back from watching the SEALs offload. "I'll fly right seat and be Aircraft Commander of record. Brett, you'll be running things in the back. We'll get the rest from the jumpmaster. Questions?"

"No," Rawley and Brett said in unison. It occurred to Rawley that Susan was suddenly very straightforward and businesslike. She liked that. The first jumper to come aboard walked up to Susan. Rawley recognized him from the night before.

"I'll be the jumpmaster for this event," he said. "I have fourteen plus me. We had a brief this morning." He unfolded a chart.

Rawley and Brett moved closer, and everyone exchanged greetings.

"Here's the DZ." The jumpmaster was pointing to an area in Womens Bay just a mile offshore from the airport. "There will be two big RHIBS and four smaller inflatables on the drop zone lined up into the wind, if everything is a go. That will also be the loss of com signal for clear to jump. If for any reason we are not clear to drop, the boats will move away from each other. We can loiter until things get straightened out. The jump altitude will be four thousand feet, and everyone is going off the ramp in one pass. Cool?" he asked as he looked at each of the pilots.

Rawley, Susan, and Brett nodded to indicate they were good with the plan. The jumpmaster handed Susan a piece of paper that listed the drop-zone coordinates, frequencies, and call signs and a second piece of paper that had a list of jumpers.

"I have the NOTAM in my bag," Susan said, referring to the "notice to airman" message that notified anyone flying around Kodiak of the jump location, altitude, and time. "The wind is approximately out of the east, so we will set up about three miles west of runway seven until we are ready to go. It's about five minutes from there to the DZ."

The jumpmaster nodded his approval then turned away to join the rest of the men coming aboard.

They were all dressed in black immersion suits and wore a light-gray parachute. Every man also wore a flotation vest over another vest with ammunition magazines and other equipment. Under each man's left arm was a short automatic rifle, and on one leg they wore holstered handguns.

Those who were at the Snowshoe acknowledged the women or walked up and said hello. Rawley took out her cell phone and looked at the photo of the photo she had taken at the Lagopus. She thought for a moment about showing it to one or more of the SEALs, then she hesitated and put it away. It was just a nagging thought she preferred to get out of her head. Two men were taking a headcount as Rawley and Susan went to the cockpit.

"Everything we need is in the nav computer," Susan said. "I'll handle the radio, if that's ok. This whole event will happen kind a fast."

"Sounds good," Rawley said.

Susan double-checked everything according to the checklist while Rawley buckled her harness. Flying with passengers and dropping jumpers was new to Rawley, but clearly this was old hat to Susan. In the back Brett was taking another headcount and talking to the jumpmaster.

Although the faces changed, the sequence of events was always the same and Brett was very familiar with the procedures. Safety was paramount, and the more prepared they were, the safer they would be. Water drops from this altitude meant the jumpers would line up in the center of the aircraft from front to back and run out in a single file. The jumpers would open their parachutes after a five-second count then follow the man in front of them as they made a long descending *S* turn down to the water drop zone, where they would land facing into the wind.

Brett would be off to one side of ramp, wearing a safety harness secured to the plane. He would count parachutes as they opened and report that number to the cockpit. In turn that number would be relayed to the drop-zone safety officer, or DZO as he was called. On the DZ, others would also be counting. This redundant behavior would ensure every man was accounted for.

The aircraft had barely left the ground when Brett got up and signaled the jumpers to get ready. "Ten minutes!" he shouted, while also holding up ten fingers. All the SEALs were on the floor and seated near the front of the cargo bay. One by one they rose then instinctively paired up and began checking their partner's equipment. As soon as the jump-master had been checked, he motioned to Brett with his hands for the ramp to be opened. At the same time, he was shouting to the jumpers to warn them. Brett keyed his microphone to communicate with Susan. He was talking and nodding, then he repeated the jumpmaster's warning while pushing the switch that opened the ramp.

As the back of the CASA opened cold air and bright sunlight flooded the otherwise dimly lit aircraft. Brett squinted as he put on his sun-glasses, and the jumpers finished their checks and donned helmets if they had not already done so.

The ramp was still going down when the jumpmaster and his assis-tant lay down on their bellies on opposite sides of the ramp and looked out over the edge to find the drop zone. The icy air stung their faces through their balaclavas, and they soon abandoned the effort.

In the front Susan was looking at yet another checklist of prejump instructions, and Rawley was circling the aircraft in the prescribed hold-ing area at four thousand feet while setting up the aircraft in accordance with Susan's instructions.

The DZO checked in on a secure frequency. "Sabre, this is Iceberg… Clear to drop."

"Roger, Iceberg, five mikes," Susan said as she also looked over the instruments. She then switched to internal com and keyed her mic. "Ready in five?" she asked Brett.

Brett held up five fingers toward the jumpmaster then his thumb to ask if they were ready. The jumpmaster looked at the line of jump-ers and held up his open hand to indicate five minutes. Each jumper raised his thumb to indicate the affirmative. After seeing every jumper acknowledge he was ready, the jumpmaster turned to Brett and gave him the thumbs up. Then he walked to Brett and looked at the altimeter Brett wore on his wrist.

"Good to go back here; give me a red light," Brett said.

"OK," Susan said to Rawley as she pointed in the direction of barely visible RHIB boats on the drop zone.

"Looks like about zero eight five to line up from here. Turn in four, three, two...turn to oh eight five."

Rawley repeated the heading as she turned the CASA to eighty-five degrees on the compass.

"Maintain ninety knots; you have it from here," Susan said. Then she made a final call to the Kodiak control tower. "Kodiak Tower, Sabre. Can we get a clear to drop?"

"Sabre, Kodiak Tower. You are clear to drop. Winds zero seven zero at one five, scattered at two thousand, broken at eight thousand, altimeter two niner point seven zero."

"Two niner point seven zero. Sabre," Susan said in response.

Rawley and Susan both moved the barometric pressure dial on their altimeters slightly. "Four thousand feet, three minutes to drop zone," Rawley said over the internal com.

Brett held up three fingers, and all the jumpers did the same. All eyes were now on the jumpmaster as he was lying on the ramp looking ahead at the boats. Without looking up he motioned to the right and held up five fingers.

"Five left, five left," Brett said over the com.

Rawley adjusted her course five degrees to the left. The jumpmaster looked back toward the line of SEALs and held up two fingers in a pinching motion to indicate "stand by," then he pointed to the light that was still showing red.

"Give me green," Brett said over the com. Instantly the jump light changed.

"Women!" Brett yelled out to no one in particular. Then he keyed up again. "Stand by," he said.

In the front Rawley checked her speed and concentrated on the heading and altitude.

Susan called the tower. "One minute to drop." The tower acknowledged then retransmitted the message for aircraft in the vicinity. Susan watched the boats on the DZ in case they moved to abort the jump then made a quick scan for traffic. "All clear," she said.

The assistant jumpmaster motioned the jumpers toward the back of the aircraft. Then the jumpmaster stood up. Rawley felt the aircraft settle slightly in the back and instinctively put her hand on the throttles. Susan looked at the throttles and nodded her approval. As the first boats in the drop zone came into view from the ramp of the CASA, the jumpmaster turned to Brett and saluted. Then he turned back and executed a headfirst dive off the ramp. In seconds every jumper ran and dove out in a line and then opened his main parachute after a five-second count. The last man out was the assistant jumpmaster, and he slapped Brett as he went by. The aircraft shuddered momentarily as approximately four thousand pounds left the cargo bay. "Jumpers away," said Brett, over the com.

Susan called the tower to report jumpers away, and immediately she could hear over the Kodiak UNICOM frequency an announcement to anyone flying near Kodiak that there were jumpers at four thousand feet one mile east of the tower.

Brett was counting chutes as the aircraft went into a slow right-hand turn to circle the drop zone. Brett counted, then counted one more time. "Fifteen parachutes," Brett said.

Before Rawley completed a second circle around the DZ, Susan could see the jumpers landing in the water next to the rubber boats. "We just orbit until they release us," Susan said as the radio came alive.

"Sabre, Iceberg. All jumpers accounted for; you are free to go. Thanks for the lift."

"Roger, Iceberg, we're clear."

By then Brett had closed up the back and come forward. "Since this is training, ladies, I know a wonderful lunch spot in King Salmon. With an even more wonderful raven-haired beauty serving. We can get a little low level through the Lake Clark Pass with the float guys. It will be real dangerous—you'll love it!"

"Give me a heading," Rawley said.

"Turn southwest and climb to forty-five hundred, Captain."

Brett directed Rawley, and Susan checked in with the tower. "Kodiak Tower, Sabre departing VFR to the southwest at four thousand five hundred."

"Sabre, Kodiak Tower, altimeter two niner point seven two, squawk one two zero zero, good day!"

"Two niner seven two, one two zero zero, Sabre." Susan signed off with Kodiak and handed Rawley a chart and checked instruments.

After returning to Kodiak, Rawley spent the next three days flying various low-level routes around western Alaska with Susan and made several water landings with Brett. She was experiencing weather and terrain in ways she had never imagined.

On the fourth day, Rawley was at a hotel near the Nome airport when she awoke to a message from home. A company aircraft had been lost in Afghanistan. There were no details, just instructions to leave Alaska as soon as possible and head to Arizona to complete abbreviated weapons training. She acknowledged the message then began to pack.

A minute later her phone rang. It was Susan. "I heard the news. The Mustang will be on the flight line by noon," she said.

"Thanks, Susan." Rawley said. "I'll be right down. What's the flight time to Anchorage?" Rawley asked.

"You are going by charter. It's faster that way. I'll run you over to the airport." Susan hung up before Rawley could ask if she had any details.

At the Nome airport, Brett and Susan bid Rawley a safe flight. Then she boarded a charter jet, and she was off.

CHAPTER 24

FORWARD OPERATING BASE, KEJAHN, AFGHANISTAN

———◆———

DAVE MAYER WAS READING MESSAGES when there was a knock at his door.

"Come in," he said.

Jack Lerner from signals intel walked in with a note in his hand. "I have something that will interest you." He took a seat. "We picked up a conversation between Sersi and another local who is well known to us. The guy Sersi was talking to was giving us info for over a year, and then disappeared. Apparently he's back, and they were talking around something that could be a large bomb available outside the country. The text of the conversation is in your inbox now."

Mayer looked at his screen, found his mail, and opened a new message from SIGINT. He read through the text twice then hit forward and passed it to Brick Wellen at Langley. "Put a clamp on this," he said as he looked up from his screen. "TS SCI Special Access." He referred to a classification of top-secret compartmented information, one of the highest levels of classification. "Keep it between us. You don't know who worked the guy when he was active, do you?" Lerner looked down at the notes he had brought in.

"The Kraken."

Kraken was a code name for a specific CIA case officer, usually shortened to CO, Rip McGuin. Mayer picked up his phone and dialed a number. "Have the Kraken come up right away. Right, he's in the building. Find him personally." Mayer hung up the phone. "OK, I'll talk to

Rip. Start getting everything ready for him to go out. Com plan, beacon, secure cell. Get a good location on the worm."

Worm was an internal term given to insurgents who traded in information. Lerner turned to leave as Mayer's phone rang. "Brick?" Mayer asked, assuming he would call the second he read the message. "You read that? The guy Sersi was talking to is a worm we've used in the past. The CO that worked him is still here." Mayer listened as Brick discussed the possibilities of getting more intel from an informed source. "OK," Mayer said. "Send me an OPORDER. I'll brief our guy and get him in the field ASAP." Mayer listened again as Wellen finished the conversation. "Got it." Mayer said then he hung up.

Ten minutes later McGuin was knocking on Mayer's door as he pushed it open. Mayer jumped up and reached for his hand. Everyone who interacted with them held case officers in the highest regard. They took substantial risks, and everyone knew it.

"I have something for you," Mayer said as he sat back down.

McGuin moved to a chair. He was thirty years old, a SEAL-trained, civilian CIA field operative, very fit with a large unkempt beard and long, twisted dark hair. His face was tanned, and his clothes were baggy, well worn, and strictly Afghan. Under any circumstances he could easily pass for a local. He spoke or had a working knowledge of several local dialects, and he had nearly four years of experience in the region.

"What do you have?" Rip asked as he leaned back in the chair.

"We intercepted a conversation between Sersi and a worm named Achmed. His phone number came up as a match with a guy you worked before." Mayer handed McGuin a printed copy of the message he received. "Intel and SIGINT will be ready to brief you in an hour or so. Listen to the tape, make sure he's your guy, then come and tell me what you plan to do and what you'll need. Langley is sending an OPORDER; we'll get you out immediately. This is important."

McGuin was taking it all in and nodding while trying to remember the exact identity and details of previous meetings with Achmed. "What's the end game?" McGuin asked. "Grabbing Sersi?"

"No," Mayer said. "He's more valuable to us when he's on that damn phone. We have reason to believe there is a Vietnam-era bomb, a SADAM, on the market or coming on. Possibly one lost flying out of Vietnam and never recovered. We want to know all the details." Mayer stopped talking.

"Is that a nuke? Did we lose a lot of those things back then?" Rip asked, half-jokingly.

"It was on a C-130 bound for the US, and the plane disappeared without a trace," Mayer said. "If the weapon's been found, we need to know where it is or where it's headed."

McGuin stood up to leave. "OK," he said. "Give me a couple hours to sort it all out, and I'll be back."

CHAPTER 25

———————◆———————

IT WAS MIDAFTERNOON AS RAWLEY entered the final approach at Yuma, Arizona. From Yuma she would head to a small town east of Buckshot on the Gila River. It was there a group of ex-special forces operators from the Army, Navy, and Marine Corps ran a comprehensive weapons and tactics school for qualified government employees and private contractors. The school was known simply as "the Site." Bud had been sending pilots to the Site for over ten years.

Rawley knew Yuma well. She had been there many times as a Navy pilot for bombing and close air support training. On top of that, all the services sent their special forces personnel to the Yuma Marine Corps air station for freefall and tactical jump training.

For military and government personnel, there was always a party to be found in Yuma. Her mission was different on this trip, but the thought of connecting with an old friend or two did cross her mind. Of course that would mean questions to answer, or avoid.

As soon as she parked at the general aviation ramp, she could see a woman walking toward her who looked out of place at the civilian airport. She was wearing a tan flight suit, and her long blond hair was tied into a tight ponytail. She was very fit, and there was a sense of urgency in her gait.

Rawley was gathering her things when the woman approached. "Rawley West?" she asked as she extended her hand.

"I am," Rawley said.

"Joan Vega. I'm here to fly you to the Site. We'll be going in that," Joan said as she gestured toward a flat black Hughes 500 helicopter. The helo was far from typical. It had N numbers to indicate a civilian registered aircraft, but it was outfitted with a FLIR, forward-looking infrared pod, all the doors were removed, and there were platforms on each side normally used by snipers. Protruding from the right side was a hard mount over the crew door for attaching a fast rope or rappel lines. Joan barely took a breath before going on. "You've only got three days, so we will be flying right into a downed aircraft scenario. One of the guys will brief you on the way." Joan reached for Rawley's bag. "May I?"

"I have it," Rawley said as she processed the information.

"Do you need to use the head before we go?" Joan asked.

"That would be great," Rawley said. "Navy?"

"Excuse me?" Joan said.

"You said 'head'; it was just odd."

"Oh," Joan responded. "Marine Corps. I flew a Cobra for a while, then I heard about this job, so here I am."

As they walked into the FBO, Rawley could see a man she assumed was the "guy" Joan spoke of. He was also dressed in a tan flight suit and talking to a woman at the desk. She was laughing, and he was clearly working hard to impress her. Rawley walked by without saying anything.

When she came back into the lobby, Joan and the other guy were talking. He saw Rawley and held out his hand. "Roy Boone," he said. "Welcome to Yuma."

"Rawley," she said. "Nice to be back, I think."

Roy laughed then grabbed Rawley's bag. "That's it?" Roy said in reference to her small bag.

"Traveling light," Rawley said as she reached to take it back.

"It's about a thirty-minute flight. I'll brief you on the way. Your plane will go in our hangar," Roy said, walking away.

Rawley was in the left front seat, and Roy was in the back. Joan isolated them on the intercom. While they flew toward the training area, Roy talked about the event that would take place when they arrived.

"The situation is this," he started. "We will land on a live range. You are the only shooter. Your mission is to get from the helo to a position of cover approximately fifty yards from the plane. You will exit and go straight out, engaging the enemy as you see them. We are using pop-up and moving targets. Those will be controlled on the range, so they will roll out or pop as you move to cover. Just do what you think you would do, and keep your weapon pointed downrange. Try and hit each target with no more than two rounds." Roy was talking fast, and his voice was emphatic. "You will have two thirty-round magazines. Plenty for this drill." Roy paused only long enough to take a breath. "I will be right behind you as you move."

Rawley was listening and nodding as Roy talked.

"You will have two weapons in your plane, but you are just using this today." He handed her a short-barreled Colt M16A4 automatic rifle then two magazines. The bolt was back on the rifle, but Rawley checked the weapon anyway. "You know how to use that?" Roy asked.

"I do," Rawley said as she looked it over.

"We'll get you on some more modern weapons like you'll have in Afghanistan, but that thing is simple," Roy said, referring to the A4.

"As soon as we land, step out of the helo, lock and load with the muzzle pointing downrange. I'll say "go" and you're off. If at any time I call "Cease Fire" just put your weapon on safe and point the muzzle down and forward. Use your instincts as you move." He said. "Think survival. Think about killing the threat as it appears because they want to kill you. If you can get to cover your chances of staying alive go way up." Roy paused again. "Questions?"

"None right now." Rawley said as she briefly turned back to look at Roy.

"We don't expect you to run through this just do the best you can." Roy said as looked forward out of the helo.

"Ten minutes." Joan said over the intercom. Then she turned a switch on the panel that again isolated her and began talking to someone on the radio. Rawley couldn't hear the conversation but she assumed it was the range as it was coming into view. She could see at least six buildings along the winding Gila River. She could see several cars and trucks and people standing on line and shooting at various ranges near the buildings. "Don't get distracted." Roy said. Shoot for center mass and don't pass targets that aren't down unless I tell you to." Rawley was still nodding as Roy spoke. Roy was silent for a moment then started again as Joan began to flare the helicopter and sink into to the range. "Standby!" Roy said in a more intense voice as a cloud of dust rose up from the rotors strong downdraft.

Joan flared hard then the helicopter met the ground. Rawley took a long breath then let it out. She pulled her head set off and dropped it next to her seat. Her heart was racing as she stepped out of the helo.

Rawley pushed a magazine into the weapon, let the slide go forward and turned the selector switch to semiautomatic. Joan was lifting off as Rawley's feet touched the ground. Rawley took a knee and covered her face with her left hand. Dust and grass swirled into the air and the sound of the helicopter was deafening as it departed. Roy was directly behind Rawley observing her every move and the second she appeared ready he yelled, "Go." The range instantly came alive with the sound of automatic gunfire from every direction. Rawley was on her feet and she immediately leaned into the weapon and engaged two targets that were twenty feet ahead of her. First the left then the right. The targets went down. Four shots two kills. She could see what she believed was her objective ahead. A berm with a few trees. To her it looked like the only plausible cover on the range. She was moving toward it when two moving targets appeared. One from right to left and another coming directly toward her. She fired again and both targets went down. Four more shots. She was counting in her head. As she moved she was scanning from right to left when three more targets popped up. Two side by side and straight ahead and one off to the right. Rawley took a knee and engaged the two on the left then the one on the right. She was sure half her rounds gone. In an instant she was up and moving forward.

Just a short way to go she thought. Behind her there were six men observing and controlling the targets and pyrotechnics. Two followed close with video cameras capturing the entire event for debriefing. Nobody talked but they had seen this scenario many times and they were impressed. Rawley was less than sixty feet from what she assumed was cover when three more targets appeared moving fast from left to right then stopped. The sound of automatic gunfire intensified. Rawley opened fire working from right to left as she again dropped to one knee. The last target raced back to the left as Rawley fired. Her rounds kicked up dust but they did not find the mark. She fired once more as the target went behind a painted wooden barrier with a large red X. "Don't shoot the X!" Roy yelled out.

Rawley knew she had a few rounds left but she pulled her second magazine from a pocket and quickly put it into her weapon. She stayed down and watched the area where the target had disappeared. Suddenly from her right, four targets stood up side by side, and Rawley used her right thumb to switch to full auto. She opened fire with two short bursts in a sweeping motion but only one target fell. Rawley pushed the selector back to semiauto then carefully engaged the remaining targets. Once the last one fell she moved quickly to cover. Just as she stopped at the berm she heard a shrill whistle and all gunfire stopped. "Cease Fire Cease Fire! The range is cold." Roy yelled. "Clear your weapon and make it safe!" He said

Rawley lowered her weapon and moved the selector to safe. She dropped her magazine and pulled the charging handle and locked the bolt back then bent down to pick up an ejected live round. "Damn!" Roy exclaimed. "Who taught you to handle an A4?"

Rawley didn't answer as she looked back surveying the distance she had covered. It was only then she realized how many men were following her. Rawley was sweating and her ears were ringing. She looked at her hands. They were dirty from the expended gunpowder and dirt. They were also trembling. When she did a double take at her hands one of the men spoke up.

"Adrenaline." He said. Rawley looked in his direction but didn't speak. Then he said it again. "It's just adrenaline. That's why your hands are doing that. It will pass. Good job." He said as held out his hand. "Dennis Biggs."

"Rawley." She said as she shook his hand.

"We know. Obviously." He said as he looked her up and down. "Sorry about your clothes but we kind of figure it's better to buy new clothes then to warn you about this drill. Glad I didn't show up in heels." She said as she handed the weapon and magazine to Roy. The remaining men were introducing themselves as an authentic yellow Jeepnie straight out of the Philippines pulled up. The men climbed into the back and called out to Rawley. "Let's go Commander!" Said one of the men.

"Lieutenant, or Ex Lieutenant." Rawley said. "Whatever. You're buying." Three men said practically in unison then laughed. Rawley sat on the hard bench seat and looked around. The Jeepnie was standard transportation in the Philippines. It was built on a stretched jeep frame and had a covered seating area in the back with facing benches for passengers. It was perfect for moving people around on the desert ranges. Perfect for this crowd thought Rawley.

"We had it shipped over." The man closest to her said as they pulled away from the range. "We'll debrief later with the video we have." Roy called out from the front of the Jeepnie. "We have a room for you. Get cleaned up and we can—" "Drink I hope!" Rawley said cutting him off.

A resounding "Yes!" came back from all the guys.

CHAPTER 26

———————◆———————

THE JEEPNEY CAME TO A stop in front of the main building, and everyone climbed out.

"Your bag is in your room," Roy said as he came up behind Rawley. "Follow me; I'll show you where you're staying."

Roy walked through the main building and out the back door to a small cottage. Parked in front was a small SUV. "This is your place. It has everything you'll need," Roy said as he unlocked the door.

Inside Rawley looked around. "Now I'm impressed," Rawley said.

"Privileges of ownership," Roy responded, with a smile.

"Ownership?" Rawley asked.

"Bud is the majority owner of this place," responded Roy. "This is his private cabin. I guess you didn't know."

"There are a lot of things I still don't know," Rawley said as she opened the closest door to a bedroom. Roy walked down the hall, opening doors and pointing out amenities. "In here you'll find a washer and dryer. And that room is an office," he said, pointing to a door down the hall. "You'll find a secure phone and fax in there and secure Wi-Fi throughout. You have some messages in the main office now from Bud. They came in about ten minutes ago. Not urgent, however. Get cleaned up and come to main building. There is a community dining hall and a bar. If you need wheels, the key to that SUV is on the counter, along with all the information you'll need here." With that, Roy turned to leave the cottage. "Nice shooting, by the way," he called over his shoulder.

Rawley dropped her stuff and threw some water on her face to clear the fine desert dust that had bronzed her artificially before heading to the bar Roy had advertised.

As she came through the back door of the main building, she could hear what sounded like a party. She let the noise lead her to a room off one hall and entered what looked like every ready room or team room in the military. The walls were covered with photos and memorabilia from all parts of the world. There were group photos from the ranges and some images that captured the explosions going off. All the men in the pictures wore tan pants and load-bearing vests or body armor. All had facial hair, owing to their line of work, and most wore a baseball cap from someplace they had been or from a weapons vendor. In a few of the pictures there were women, also dressed in tactical clothing and holding weapons. Ten men and two women were in the room drinking and talking over each other.

"What'll you have?" someone called out to her from behind the bar.

"Rum and Coke if you would!" Rawley yelled back.

"Coming right up" was the response.

"Make it a double," she added.

"We always do," replied the bartender.

As Rawley came closer to the bar, two men moved and made room. She looked at the two flat-screen televisions directly behind the bar as video began on both. Then she saw the same helicopter she arrived in flaring as it approached the range. A second later she saw herself stepping out of the helo. A cheer went up, then the noise died down. All attention was on the video.

"We can debrief in private if you prefer, or just get it over with." The voice was Roy. He was now standing behind her.

Rawley raised her glass as if to concede permission. The room became totally quiet except for the sound coming from the television. Rawley watched as she systematically engaged targets that appeared. Each time a target fell, there was a cheer at the bar. As Rawley and Roy walked past the first two downed targets, Roy called for a pause. Both videos stopped on the scene. The video on the left was taken from a vantage point directly behind Roy and Rawley. The second video was from the right and just behind the firing line.

"Look at the base of the targets," Roy said. "Weapons. If they were shooting at you, they have weapons and ammo."

Rawley nodded.

"It's a pure judgement call." Roy continued. "If you can carry it, grab it. You don't have a lot of fire power in your plane. If you are alone, it's one thing. If you're not alone, have one person collect guns and ammo. Help may not arrive quickly. Roll it." Roy said as the videos continued. "From here there isn't a whole lot to say except to reinforce good habits. There aren't any shooting schools in the info we have on you, so naturally...we are all dying to know where you learned to handle an A4."

Rawley just smiled. "If you knew my mother, you would understand" was all she offered on the subject as she turned back to the bar and held up her empty glass. The videos ended, and the screens went black then the screens came back to life. On one screen there was a compilation of skydiving movies and on the other, rock climbing. The man behind the bar turned up the stereo, and the speakers came alive with '70's rock 'n' roll. In an instant the conversation in the room returned to a dull roar.

"The other ranges will be shutting down soon, and this place will get real busy and loud for a few hours," Roy said. Everyone who walks through that door knows the drill. "Nobody asks questions, and you don't share anything you don't want to share."

"Fair enough," Rawley said, raising her glass. Rawley found a table in the corner of the room where she could be alone with her thoughts. She had several.

Roy left the room then returned with a manila envelope. "It came in from your dad earlier. I'll give you some time, then I'll fill you in on the schedule," Roy said, before returning to the conversation at the bar.

Rawley opened the envelope and found it was a few details of the downed aircraft. Nothing compelling about the accident. It appeared to be a forced descent into terrain possibly due to mechanical issues reported by the pilot before they lost com. One fatality, the body had been recovered. A familiar story, especially among bush pilots. Rawley recognized the name from the list she had read at Warbird, but she did not know him personally.

Just as Roy had predicted, the door opened and the room filled with other shooters who had spent the day on the ranges. They all glanced at Rawley as they made their way to the bar. They ranged in age from twenty-five to fifty. They were dressed in khaki pants, black shirts, and assault boots. Some were fit, and others looked soft. Rawley looked at the message again. At the bottom was a handwritten note from her father that made her smile.

Roy called out to her from the bar and held his glass up to ask if she was ready. Rawley nodded the affirmative. As Roy sat down, he gestured toward the envelope. "Bad news travels fast. We heard about the accident. Jim was a great guy. You know him?"

"Never met," Rawley said, shaking her head.

"He was ex-Air Force. He came through here several times."

"Family? Kids?" Rawley asked.

Roy laughed and shook his head. "Divorced multiple times, probably a few kids. His last girlfriend moved out with all his shit before he deployed. Most everybody working over there is somewhat dysfunctional...I mean, well, not everyone of course," Roy said as he tried to walk back his comment.

"It's cool," Rawley said, stopping him. "I'll fit right in." She reached across the table in a toast.

Roy just smiled and shrugged.

"What's next?"

"A few of the guys who sat through your video are your instructors. You are getting serious attention. They are all experts, all ex-military, with lots of time downrange. Tomorrow you will get handgun all day. Long gun the next, then we'll do some move-and-shoot drills with both weapons, and you'll be done. It's short and sweet, but you have skills, so it should suffice." Roy stopped and emptied his beer. Rawley finished her drink as well. "Dinner will be ready soon. It's served buffet style next door. You can eat in here or over there or back at your place. Whatever makes you happy."

Another night went by quickly, and soon the sun was coming through the windows. It was not even seven o'clock when the gunfire could be heard coming from one or more of the ranges.

Rawley made her way to the main building in search of coffee, and she found the place was packed with shooters doing the same. Everyone said hello or good morning as they passed. It was a very friendly atmosphere, considering the testosterone in the room. Rawley went through the food line and found a table.

"Can I join you?"

Rawley looked up and saw a face she recognized from the night before. Rawley pushed the empty chair back with her foot. "Have a seat."

The man held out his hand and introduced himself. "Mike Crabbe. Most everyone here just calls me Buster." "Buster?" Rawley asked. "A frogman thing, not important."

"Ok, you know we met last night around midnight," Rawley said as she peppered her eggs.

"Oh yeah. Hope I didn't piss you off with my opinion of women in this business," Crabbe said.

"Been hearing it my whole life," Rawley said. "Besides, I'm just a pilot getting some survival skills."

"That's why I'm here," said Crabbe as he dug into his breakfast. "I'll be your handgun instructor. There's no rush, but when you're ready, I'll pick you up and we'll head to the range. I prefer to bypass the usual instruction methods and go straight to shooting. I'm sure you've seen enough video lectures to last you."

"I have indeed." Rawley smiled.

"I've spent a lot of time with your colleagues, and they don't wear anything standard, so just dress to be comfortable, I guess. You got one old guy who looks like he's going to the rodeo, if that works for you. See you in a bit."

Rawley just smiled as Crabbe pushed his seat back. "My godfather," she quipped.

"What?" Crabbe asked. "Rodeo guy. He's my godfather."

"No shit?" Crabbe said, shaking his head as he turned to leave.

"No shit," Rawley said under her breath.

An hour later Rawley was on the range. Unlike the range she had arrived on, this one was all sand, clear and flat, with four rows of steel targets set at different distances from the firing line. There was a table and a bench at one end and a high grassy berm at the other. There were a few men already prepping targets and opening ammunition cans. Crabbe walked up and handed Rawley a nine-millimeter handgun with the slide locked back. "That's a Glock 19, nine mil, fifteen-round mag, low recoil." Then he held up a black nylon vest. "Some guys like to wear this while they fly. It will hold your handgun and a few magazines, and it's more comfortable than a holster. You're right handed, so your weapon will be on your left side above your waist while seated. It keeps it off your hip and out from under your arm. If it's not comfortable, it won't be on your body, and if it's not on your body and you crash, you'll never find it. Your rifle will be in a bag between the seats, held there by a carabiner. If it's not secured to your seat, it will become a projectile when you hit the ground."

Rawley nodded in understanding, taking it all in.

"Everything we do here is about your actions after a forced landing. This knowledge and your actions will save your life and those with you. Hopefully." Crabbe paused, and Rawley smiled.

"We are going to assume you can move away from the plane and shoot," Crabbe said. Then he took a long look around the range and down the firing line. "Range is *hot!*" Crabbe yelled out. Everyone involved raised a thumb to indicate understanding of the active status.

"Put your vest on, and I'll show you some things about your weapon."

After some instruction Rawley was ready to start shooting. Her first task was to hit five steel head plates, as they were called, from twenty feet. Crabbe took his position behind her, and on his command she drew her weapon and began firing from left to right.

CHAPTER 27

ON HER FINAL DAY OF range training, Rawley woke early and couldn't help but think how exhausting weapons training was both physically and mentally. She thought about what lay ahead, how different life was from her time in Navy, and how quickly it was behind her. The light was just coming through the windows when her phone rang.

"How's it going down there?"

"Great, Dad. I'll finish up today then be ready to go."

"OK. Take the Mustang to Virginia and get your house and affairs in order, and I'll meet you next Friday for a final brief before you fly out."

"See you Friday, Dad. Give my love to Mom."

"OK then, out here," her father said. Then the phone went dead before she could say anything else. She looked at the time again and decided to skip breakfast and go for a run to clear her head.

There was a chill in the air as the sun continued to rise, and it felt good to be running again.

As she walked toward the range, she could hear gunfire coming from everywhere on the property. She had only been shooting for two long days, but she could distinguish the different weapons in use. As she stopped at her assigned range, she took one long breath and slowly exhaled as she looked at the men setting up targets. The range was automated, with numerous scenarios available. There was an aircraft cockpit and an old Suburban on the firing line. They were obviously used to simulate various situations. Sitting off to one side were other vehicles, including an ex-military Humvee and a limousine.

This morning Roy and a few others she did not recognize joined Mike Crabbe on the range.

"Good run?" Roy asked.

"Yeah, it was a nice change of pace."

"Great," Roy said as he walked out onto the range to inspect target placement.

"Everyone gather around," Crabbe called to the others who had come along. "Rawley, these guys are passengers. They are civilians, like you. One is armed, the other two are not. You are going to execute a forced landing, and just like the drill when you arrived, you will fight your way to the yellow flag you see downrange. When you get there, it's over. You will start from the left side of the cockpit, and the others will exit the aircraft from the other side and come around the front of the plane to join you. Every one of your aircraft in-country have a bag like this." Crabbe held up a green bag about the size of a small suitcase. "This bag has magazines, a radio, and smoke. Never leave your downed aircraft without it."

Rawley was nodding as Crabbe spoke. "When I say go, you will engage the threats as you see them. Once you are together, you start moving. Don't pass any target that does not go down unless I tell you to. Any questions for me?"

Rawley shook her head then looked at the three men who would join her. She could see two men with weapons.

"OK, everyone, take some time and talk about what you plan to do. Clear that handgun, and leave it on the bench," Crabbe said to one of the men before walking to join Roy on the range.

They all introduced themselves, then Rawley took charge. "I'll cover as you come around," she said. "I'll be on one knee; come behind me and do the same." She looked at the one guy that would be armed. "How many rounds do you have?" she asked.

"Two mags, thirty rounds," he said.

"What's your background?"

He looked at the others. "Good question," he said. "I am an OGA moving from one base to another."

"Ex-military?" Rawley asked.

"I am," he said.

"Should I be giving you my long gun and backing you up?"

"When you get over there, don't fly anyone without knowing their background, and yes, you should let the most experienced shooter lead the way if there's time for that kind of discussion. That said, for this purpose, no," he said. "I'll follow you."

"OK," Rawley said. "Take my left side so you're clear of my brass. I'll cover ahead and right; you take the left flank. You guys," Rawley said as she looked at one of the other men, "watch behind us as we move. I'll give one of you the bag. If I go down, everybody do the same thing. As we pass targets that are down, look for weapons. Pick up any weapons and magazines you see, but don't fall back, and if you are not familiar with the weapon you pick up, keep it pointed down and your finger off the trigger. Everyone cool?"

All heads nodded.

After three range scenarios, five hours had passed. Rawley was back in the main building for a final debriefing with Roy and Crabbe.

"Handguns aren't your strong suit," Crabbe said. "When you get back to the US, come down for a few days, and we'll make you as good with that as you are with an assault rifle. Good luck over there."

"I'll bring my mother," Rawley said. "She can show everyone the finer points of the long shot."

"Look forward to it," Roy said.

"Joan will be landing soon. She will fly you back to Yuma when you're ready. Be vigilant over there."

"You know it." Rawley said as she left the room.

CHAPTER 28

FORWARD OPERATING BASE, KEJAHN

———————◆———————

THE TF Z BRIEFING ROOM was a secure room within a limited access space with seating for just ten people. There was a flat-screen television on the end wall and a camera connected to a secure line direct to Langley. From here a thousand human intelligence operations had been launched. Seated at the table were Dave Mayer, Rip McGuin, and Jack Lerner. Brick Wellen was listening in and watching a video feed from a secure room at CIA headquarters. When the screen lit up, the image was that of Achmed Zumo, with his many aliases listed below his face.

"We confirmed Zumo's identity by voice match," Lerner said.

Then Rip McGuin summarized his interaction with Zumo in the past. A map came up showing the general locations where the cellular signals were located. Rip turned toward the camera so he could talk directly to Brick. "I've met Zumo in this region before. It's always been safe to move around if you're aware. I plan to jump into a deserted area ten miles from the destination and get picked up by a small indig group we have working the area. They will drop me in the village of Chagar Raz. It's a mountainous village large enough to blend in and come and go. A lot of trading goes on there, so transients are common." Rip stopped there and looked at Mayer. The detailed information was strictly for Wellen's benefit.

"How do you expect to make contact with the guy?" Wellen asked.

"SIGINT will be tracking his cell, and they will give me a vector," Rip said, looking at Lerner.

"Once he sees me, he'll either make contact or sound the alarm. That's about as complicated as it gets." Rip paused again.

"What do we have on this guy?" Wellen asked, referring to Zumo.

Rip again looked directly at the camera. "His family is safe in America. He was scheduled to come in also but disappeared."

"As you all know, it's not uncommon. We believe he has another wife and family, or had. It's always something with these guys, but he isn't going to compromise himself at this point. He'd die a real horrible death," Rip said as he turned to Mayer.

Mayer looked at the camera. "We have your list of questions, and you'll have your answers before Rip is recovered. Anything to add?" Mayer asked.

"None here," Wellen said. "Good hunting." The light on the camera went out, indicating it had gone dead.

Mayer turned to Rip. "I have your egress plan and other details. How soon can you leave?"

Rip looked at the clock on the wall. "I'll be jumping two hours before sunup, so I'll be out of here by midnight tonight."

"Think about bringing him in or terminating him if it comes to that," Mayer said. "Let's not risk anything."

Rip nodded but didn't say any more.

Mayer slid his chair back then stood up and reached for Rip's hand. "Good luck, son" was all he said before leaving the room.

Rip looked at Lerner. "I have some prep to do with your guys, then I'm going to the gym. If you need me later, that's where I'll be." Everyone involved in this business had their own way of coping with stress, and Rip preferred to workout. Besides keeping him fit, it occupied his mind.

The evening passed quickly, and it was time for a final brief and gear check. Rip McGuin would leave the main building through an entrance guarded by American contractors, and from there he would go into a tunnel that led away from the cluster of buildings in the camp to a secure aircraft hangar near the airstrip and away from prying eyes. No matter how loyal the locals who worked on base were, any information could be turned into money or favors, and movement of troops or individuals was a commodity.

In the hangar Rip waited for the all clear, then he moved from a darkened room to a single turbine Pilatus PC12. Like most aircraft used in Afghanistan, the aircraft had been modified with a roll-up cargo door to support parachute operations. It was also useful for aerial resupply. The windows were blacked out, and the aircraft had no outer markings. It was painted flat gray with a broken black line down the side. Although its appearance looked old and weathered it was actually quite new.

Two of Bud's pilots would be flying this mission. Both had extensive military flying experience and knew Rip well from previous operations. As always, Rip preferred to brief on the plane prior to departure, and tonight was no different. Rip went to the cockpit and pulled a map from his coat. "Joe, Caleb," he said.

The pilots stopped their predeparture checks and turned around. "Hey, Rip. Long time, brother!" Joe said as he extended his hand. "Whatcha got for us?"

"I'd like to HAHO into this location right here about ten miles from Chagar Raz," Rip said, pointing to an area he would use as a drop zone. HAHO was short for high altitude, high opening, meaning he would open his parachute soon after exiting the aircraft then using the wind glide over a great distance to his destination under canopy. It was a good way to get into an area clandestinely since the roads were always watched and an aircraft would get attention any time of day or night.

Joe and Caleb listened intently as Rip spoke. "I'd like to exit around fifteen thousand feet about here." Rip again referred to the map. "Here are all the details." Rip handed Joe several papers that included the desired exit point, predicted winds aloft, radio frequencies, and deconfliction information to avoid any blue-on-blue issues should they encounter a coalition aircraft. In addition, there was a short list of prowords and their meanings.

The prowords for this event would indicate "wheels up" or "jumper away" or when a specific point was passed during insertion. During an operation such as this, the QRF, or quick-reaction force, the SIGINT OP Center, and an appropriate member of the human intelligence office, or HUMINT, would monitor the insertion phase every step of the way.

Joe handed Caleb the com plan, and he looked over the route. "Give us a few minutes we'll tell you when we need to roll," Joe said, without looking up. As Joe entered information into his flight computer, Rip looked over his parachute and other equipment. He was traveling light for this op, which he hoped would last no more than a week. Rip carried an AK47 that was purposely corroded and worn looking on the outside, and a wool bag common to the region with a few essential items.

He also had a false dental mouthpiece to hide his upper teeth. Nothing would look more out of place in this part of the world than straight white teeth. He also carried ten thousand dollars, five thousand Afghan rupees, and an ATM card. If there was ever trouble, currency could mean the difference between life and death.

Joe turned in his seat and looked at Rip. "We could do it easily in an hour as the crow flies. I think we'll wander north then swing back and pick up a crosswind track toward the exit point. That will keep us the farthest from Chagar."

Rip looked at his watch then back at Joe. "Off in twenty?" he asked.

"Twenty it is; get comfortable," Joe said.

Rip took a seat on the floor and propped his rig under his head then stared at the roof of the plane. His thoughts wandered back to a girl and a summer day sailing on the Chesapeake Bay, and then he drifted off to sleep.

"Thirty minutes! Thirty minutes!" Rip pulled back as he awoke to Caleb shaking him. "Man, you were out," Caleb said as he turned toward the cockpit. "He's up." Joe gave the thumbs-up but didn't look back.

Rip sat upright and rubbed his eyes. He looked at his watch and shook his head.

Caleb handed him a portable oxygen tank. "Take a hit off that. It'll clear your head. We're climbing to drop altitude; better get suited up." Caleb attached his harness to a cargo point.

Joe was following his flight plan and climbing to fifteen thousand feet. Once he was at the drop altitude, Joe would slow to one hundred knots and check in with the OP Center.

Caleb came forward to let Joe know they were ready in the back. Joe was just leveling off and slowing down when he keyed his mic. "Victor Able, Victor Able, Tango Seven."

"Tango Seven, you are loud and clear; send your traffic."

"This is Tango Seven, Orchid. I say again, Orchid."

"Roger, Tango Seven, I read Orchid.

Tango Seven, Victor Able, Rose, I repeat Rose."

"Understand Rose, Tango Seven clear."

"Orchid" was the proword that let everyone monitoring the operation know that the aircraft was ten minutes from the drop point, and the reply "Rose" confirmed they were clear to proceed.

Joe switched to intercom. "Clear to drop; go on my command."

Caleb cupped his hands over his headphones and listened. "Stand by!" he yelled to Rip.

Rip moved to the back of the aircraft and pulled the rolling door up. The cold air rushed in, and Caleb moved toward Rip and put his hand on Rip's shoulder. The landscape below was pure blackness. There were just a few dim lights coming from the small camps spread around the mountains.

Joe watched the exit point close in on the aircraft's navigation system, and he made small corrections to ensure he was precisely in the correct position for the drop. "Stand by to drop, drop," he said over the intercom.

Caleb slapped Rip on the shoulder, and in an instant Rip dove headfirst into the night. Caleb immediately looked out and down, trying to get a glimpse of Rip's parachute, but there was nothing to see. He pulled the cargo door down and returned to the cockpit.

Joe was in a turn heading away from Chagar Raz and other areas of civilization in this area. "I already passed jumper away," Joe said. Caleb nodded as he turned on a beacon receiver that would pick up Rip's signal once he activated it.

Under canopy Rip checked his heading then pulled his night-vision goggles from their pouch. He would be gliding for the next twenty-five minutes. Next he activated his homing beacon for five minutes. That only served to let the OP Center and the drop aircraft know he was alive and on his way.

CHAPTER 29

———◆———

THE FLIGHT FROM YUMA, ARIZONA, to Norfolk, Virginia, was one Rawley had made numerous times while she was in the Navy. This trip was slower and more relaxed but still the same. Same scenery when you could see the ground, same familiar fuel stop in Oklahoma, where there was stale popcorn, lukewarm coffee, and hot cookies at the FBO, a combination that never sat well with Rawley's stomach but was hard to resist. The weather was mostly CAVU across most of the country, an aviation term meaning no clouds and unlimited visibility. It was a great day for a flight across America at twenty-three thousand feet. As she began her descent into Norfolk, the sun was already low in the sky behind her. She was trying to remember the last time she had flown in there. It was before she deployed but seemed like forever.

When she checked in with Norfolk Approach, the voice was a familiar one. She liked that. It was like a building block in the process of coming home. The stay would be a short one, but it would be nice to not jump up to fly or shoot for the next five days. That much she knew. Of all the places she had been stationed or visited while on active duty, Rawley preferred this location because it was smaller and far less crowded than her other option, which was San Diego. Norfolk and Virginia Beach were part of a metro region known as Hampton Roads, and the area was part of what was considered the birthplace of America since it also encompassed the Jamestown Settlement.

Hampton Roads was rich in American history and played a vital role in the American Revolution and Civil War. Hampton Roads was also home to the US Navy Atlantic Fleet, and Virginia Beach hosted a master jet base, Oceana Naval Air Station. That meant aircraft carriers and Navy fighter jets. All Navy pilots passed through here eventually, either as a duty station or for training. Rawley had spent a total of five years here. She had a small house on a crowded street at the beach, and the Atlantic Ocean was her front yard. It was a sharp contrast to Montana. There were no mountains visible in any direction. No rivers nearby, no cattle ranches, and winters were typically short and mild by any standard. As she taxied to the FBO at Norfolk International, she could see the red sky to the west and a storm coming from the north.

She knew Aubrey was flying, and she could have called any number of friends for a ride home from the airport, but she was in no mood to talk. She just wanted to be in her own bed and hear the waves breaking on the shore. In the taxi Rawley made a mental list of everything she needed to do before leaving Friday. She had done this several times during her Navy career, and for her it was a simple process due in part to the fact that she hadn't amassed a lot of anything, including clothes or personal possessions.

Like most single Navy pilots Rawley's age, her home was relatively austere. In fact, it was more a crash pad than a typical home. It was just a place to sleep when you were in town and store your things while you were away. When she wasn't deployed or on a det, as it was called, she would spend the majority of her free time riding a horse she leased at Calypso Run Farm. It was a local Equestrian facility owned by a retired female Navy pilot. The owner was among the first women to fly fighter jets in the Navy, and like Rawley's mother, she also rescued dogs. She had been a mentor and friend to Rawley, Aubrey, and many of the young women who frequented the farm. She briefly thought of going for a ride, but that would just spark questions she was not prepared to answer. Everyone expected her to be deployed right now, and she would just leave it at that.

It had only been weeks since she left the carrier, but the Navy already seemed a long time ago. It was funny how such a significant part of her life could go by so fast and then be over. It was like turning the page of a book. She looked at the few photos she had on her walls. Most were from her time in the Navy and a few from Warbird, and there were a few plaques the Navy was so fond of handing out. The week passed quickly, and the sun was once again setting on what she expected to be her last night at home for some time. She opened the windows facing the ocean and made herself a rum and Coke. The waves were breaking, and there was a storm cell offshore. As she sat in the fading light and felt the wind in her face, she could smell the ocean. She closed her eyes, put her head back, and breathed in deep. She had come to love that smell, and she wanted to remember it.

She had just sat back and cleared her mind when her phone rang. She looked and saw it was her father. After an hour-long conversation, she made another drink and sat alone in the dark. Then, as usual, her mind drifted to a place she didn't want to go. She picked up her phone and found the photo she had taken of the men standing in front of the Lagopus. She was bothered by how familiar one face looked, and again she found herself wondering where Rip had gone to and why he stopped communicating with her.

The next morning Rawley was on the beach as the sun came up, like she had done so many times before. Most of the locals and surfers shared the same ritualistic habits of greeting the sun. In the distance she could see two warships and one freighter heading to sea. She was just one mile from Cape Henry Lighthouse, and that marked the southern point of the entrance to Chesapeake Bay. Ships bound to or from Norfolk and Baltimore had to pass there, so something was always going by.

The week passed quickly, and by the time her father landed in Norfolk, she had already loaded her bags in the Mustang. Based on their last conversation, she knew they would be flying to the company facility in Edenton, North Carolina, then on to Dulles, where she would board a flight for Abu Dhabi in the United Arab Emirates. From there she would be picked up by a charter plane and be taken to Kabul, Afghanistan. The entire trip would take forty-eight hours or more, including a one-day layover in Abu Dhabi.

When Bud arrived at the FBO in Norfolk, he found Rawley looking at weather. "How's it look?" he asked as he walked up behind her.

"Hey, Dad!" she said as she embraced him. "It looks good. You need anything before we go?"

Bud shook his head then turned to go back to the lobby. In no time they were climbing out over the Chesapeake Bay, expecting a turn south then a twenty-minute flight to Edenton. Designated as the Northeastern Regional Airport, the glory days of the Edenton Airport were long gone. It was built during the Second World War as a Marine Corps air station, and for the next twenty years it was home to fighters, bombers, and trainers. Now it was primarily a general aviation airport that served aviation enthusiasts, a shipping operation, and a few crop dusters. The town itself was well off the beaten path, with a small historic district that attracted a few thousand visitors each year. Edenton's most famous past resident was the notorious pirate Edward Teach, also known as Blackbeard. One of Blackbeard's many wives lived in Edenton, and whenever he was in town, he was merely regarded as a businessman who frequently traveled away from home.

Bud built a hangar at the airport that was large enough to hold three of the largest corporate jets made. It was there that they might do maintenance or change registration numbers or livery markings without drawing attention. The airport was three miles south of the town and somewhat isolated, but Bud's aircraft always came and went well after dark to maintain a level of anonymity.

As Rawley lined up for runway one nine, she was looking south at the Chowan River, and beyond that there were tobacco fields as far as the eye could see. She could see the hangar ahead and off the right side of the runway. She had seen it many times, but she had never given it any thought. Thanks to the "business friendly" policies in North Carolina, many small airports in the region had large buildings or industrial complexes nearby or on the field, so the large hangar at a small rural airport was hardly uncommon.

As Rawley taxied Bud dialed a number on his cell phone, then after a short conversation, he put his headset back on. "Pull straight in," he said. As they approached three men came into the hangar to direct the Mustang. Rawley slowed the plane then when directed she rolled to a stop next to a very large plain-white corporate jet. As she shut down, Rawley was looking up at the aircraft. She had seen many private aircraft, but nothing as large as this. "It's a Bombardier Global 8000," Bud said. "It will do just under point nine Mach for seventy-nine hundred miles with a reserve."

Named after Austrian physicist Ernst Mach, the term defined the speed an aircraft might attain given the local environmental conditions, specifically temperature. Mach 1 was 700 miles per hour and .9 Mach approximately 685 miles per hour. That kind of speed required swept wings and power. The Global 8000 had that and more.

Bud was also looking at the aircraft. "Change of plans, by the way. You'll be flying over with it tonight," he said.

"Sounds good to me," Rawley said. "Nice plane." She went through the aircraft shutdown checklist for the Mustang.

Bud took Rawley around and introduced her to the crew who manned the facility then introduced her to the two men she would be flying with to the UAE. Like her they were both ex-Navy jet pilots. Rawley liked that.

Ry Parkland introduced himself as the aircraft commander. "We'll go wheels up at ten p.m. tonight. That'll put us in there around fifteen hundred local," he said.

"OK," Rawley said, then she looked at her watch and turned to Bud.

"We have much more to discuss about business and procedures. Let's go in the office," Bud said as he started walking away. Compared to Bud's ranch office, this place was little more than a desk and a few chairs.

"Are you ready for this?" Bud asked as he opened his briefcase and began laying out folders.

"As ready as I can be," Rawley said as she took a seat at the table.

"We'll go through some of this together, and the rest you can read at your leisure. We can start with tasking." Bud shuffled through the folders and pulled the one he was looking for. Nearly two hours passed before Bud suggested dinner. Rawley was more than ready for a break. It was a lot of information to digest, but she knew it was important.

"I know a great restaurant in Edenton." Bud put his arm around Rawley as they walked. "I'm proud of you," he said. "I've always been proud of you."

Rawley didn't respond, but she squeezed him tight. Bud didn't say much during the drive to Edenton, and Rawley was watching the houses go by. She could understand why Bud chose this area. Like so many small towns in America, it was like time progressed but the area did not. Nobody would suspect a business tied to the CIA or any government clandestine operation might be going on here. And even if they did suspect, who would they tell? Who would care? Life here was always simple, and anything that went on out of the ordinary was just fodder for gossip.

By nine o'clock, Bud and Rawley were back at the hangar, and the preflight of the Global was nearly finished. Bud seemed a bit agitated, and Rawley was feeling a little uneasy. She had seen this side of him many times. Like the day she left for college, then when she left for flight school, then her first cruise, and pretty much any time she was leaving for something new. He hated to see her go. She knew that. But at this point in her life, going away was exactly what she did. Rawley hated being tied down, and this new adventure was already appealing to her. She rarely discussed it, but she thrived on the dangerous aspects of flying in a war zone, and she well knew there would be danger where she was going.

By 9:45 Bud was keeping himself busy in the office and listening to old country music. Rawley called her mother, but the conversation was short. Her mother had always seemed to be more understanding and supportive of Rawley when it came venturing out into the world, and if she worried she hid it well. Bud had brought her into this, but he clearly had issues that only he could resolve. Finally, the time came. The big hangar doors began to open, and the tow tractor was attached to the nosewheel of the Global. Rawley was at the stairs leading up to the aircraft when Bud approached.

"Be safe, be tough, and be vigilant," he said.

Rawley looked at her father, and many things rushed through her mind. After a short hug, she turned to leave then stopped and turned back to face Bud.

There was a long pause while they looked at each other. "Why didn't you just ask me to join you?" she asked.

Bud's jaw tightened, and he shrugged. "Your mother said it had to be your idea or nothing. We just wanted to open a door and see if you walked through."

Rawley said nothing. She just nodded then continued up the stairs. At the top of the stairs, she paused one more time and looked back at her father. "Thanks for the job, Dad." One last wave and then she pushed the button to retract the ladder.

Ry and his copilot, Jeff, were in the cockpit. Rawley closed the door and pushed the lever down to lock it. She could see an indicator light that told her it was locked in place. Jeff yelled from the cockpit to also confirm it was locked.

Rawley went forward to watch the startup process. Jeff read items aloud, and Ry looked at every switch and knob as they were called off.

"Make yourself comfortable," Ry said. "There is food in the galley, movies if you want, and a bed in the way back. You'll be up here with me in four hours."

Rawley watched the two men go through the checks for a few more minutes. "Wake me if I'm not up," she said, then she found her way to the bed. She could hear the big turbines start, but that was the last thing she heard. She was fast asleep before the wheels left the ground.

———•———

CHAPTER 30

AFTER JUST A FOUR-HOUR NAP, the Global was already halfway to their destination and the sun was up. Rawley scanned the panel as she stood behind the left seat. She could see they were at fifty-five thousand feet with a speed over the ground of nearly eight hundred knots.

"Tailwind!" she said as she continued to look at the big glass panels full of information.

"Big time," Ry said.

Jeff slid his seat back and climbed out. "You know where I'll be."

Rawley sat down and got comfortable then opened the operating handbook for the aircraft. She was looking over the characteristics of the plane and operating parameters. "Impressive," she said.

"It is," Ry said. "We just traded up from a Global 6000. This one is actually leased by the government; we just operate it."

"So, tell me your background, Ry," Rawley said as she leaned back into the seat. For the next three hours, Ry and Rawley talked about the Navy and flying and the specifics of flying as a contractor in Afghanistan and other parts of the world. Rawley learned more about what lay ahead from Ry than she had from anyone else, including her father. This new job was clearly never boring, and there was a large assortment of aircraft to fly. That had appealed to Rawley since she was young.

As they closed on Abu Dhabi, the radio traffic became constant. They were given vectors to clear restricted airspace and then vectors for recognition, and then there was other traffic to avoid. The skies were extremely crowded in this part of the world, and they were covering a lot of sky rapidly.

By now Jeff was back in the cockpit. He took his place in a jump seat behind the copilot's chair and put on a headset.

"Jeff, we are getting a priority message. Can you handle that?" Ry said as he turned to look back.

Jeff rotated his seat to face a communications station that had been a custom install on this aircraft. After a few minutes, he handed Ry the printed message. Ry read it then handed it to Rawley.

"Rawley, it looks like we are cleared to Kabul. Jeff, look at the nav and fuel, and make sure we are good. Take us down the gulf, and turn up at Gwader, then over Turbat, then direct."

"OK, stand by," Jeff said as he started pushing buttons on the navigation computer.

A few minutes later, Jeff handed Ry the revised route and fuel data. "Easy day." he said. "I'll request the weather on the route and coordinating instructions for Pakistani airspace."

"And I'm going to take a nap." Ry said, pushing his seat back.

As they turned north over the port of Gwader, Rawley had a rush of flashbacks. It was now just twelve weeks since she last flew in this airspace between the boat and her assigned CAP, or combat air patrol, loiter station. She would cross the beach south of the Port City of Gwader then fly up the Iranian border to a tanker waiting just inside Afghan airspace. From there the flight of three or four would check in with controllers and go to one of the many CAP loiter locations, depending on coalition activity. Time and again they would burn fuel in a holding pattern that spanned several miles before going back to the tanker then on to the boat without engaging the enemy. At this point in the war, most bombing and airstrike activity was handled by drones whose primary operators sat thousands of miles away.

Rawley was looking silently out and down from the right side of the aircraft when Jeff touched her arm. It snapped Rawley back from her daydreaming.

"Where did you go?" Jeff asked.

"Back to the reason I'm sitting here, I guess," she said as she scanned the instruments.

An amber light flashed on the panel in front of Jeff. "Message coming in," he said. "Can you grab that?" Rawley pushed back and rotated her chair to the left and reached for a message as it printed out. As she read it, she began to smile. "Good news?" Jeff asked.

Rawley handed Jeff the message, and he read it aloud as Ry came back into the cockpit. "Gil Adams sends. Inform Rawley standing by Kabul with two armed Tractors for immediate departure."

Then Jeff handed the message to Ry. Ry was back on com and reclined in the jump seat. "Gil Adams," Ry said. "There's a character for you."

"My godfather," Rawley said as she went back to looking out the aircraft.

"No shit," Jeff and Ry said, in unison.

"No shit," Rawley said, then she just smiled. Rawley turned back to look at Jeff. "It says 'Tractor.' Like a crop duster Air Tractor?"

"You haven't seen one gunned up?" Ry asked.

"No," Rawley said shaking her head.

"They are modified to carry gun pods, rockets, bombs, you name it," Ry said. "Deadly mothers."

"Kind of a modern-day Skyraider," Jeff added, referring to the Douglas AD1 Skyraider made famous in the Vietnam War as a mainstay for close air support. "We just took delivery of them to provide immediate support for the food and water convoys. Kind of a first response with more payload than an Apache and cheaper to maintain than a Warthog."

Rawley nodded and imagined the prospects of flying an armed aircraft again. "I saw we had some gunships, but that wasn't what I envisioned."

CHAPTER 31

———◆———

Rawley had not seen Gil Adams for several years. She knew from Bart that he had been in Afghanistan for at least four years off and on as chief pilot on site for her father's business. Bud had warned her that he might not be happy about leaving, and the decision would be hers alone. Although Gil had recently had an accident, her father and Bart didn't seem overly concerned about his age or ability, and she dreaded the thought of ending any part of his flying career. She would just have to wait and see for herself.

It was four in the afternoon in Kabul, and the trip from North Carolina was coming to an end. The speed and comfort of the Global had made the nine-hour flight pass quickly. Rawley had never once landed in Afghanistan, although she had overflown the country from border to border many times. She knew the Kabul airport layout from countless aerial photographs and briefings. There was a single eleven-thousand-five-hundred-foot runway with civilian operations on one side and military operations on the other, making security a challenge if not impossible. Hills and mountains surrounded the airport and city of Kabul. The airport was a magnet for rebel and antigovernment activity. No matter how tight security was, there always seemed to be some incident or incursion going on, and a large mortar or rocket could be lobbed to the airport from any number of elevated locations near the northern edge of the field.

As they lined up for their final approach, Rawley could already see the Air Tractors. They were clearly militarized but still seemed very much out of place among what looked to be about a hundred helicopters of various size and origin. Afghanistan was a melting pot of fixed-wing and rotary aircraft that ranged from the most modern to flying antiques. Contractors and the Afghan military were flying surplus helicopters and aircraft from around the world. Crashes were as common as an auto accident in Los Angeles. In every direction there were abandoned airframes. Some were wrecked; some were just parked and cannibalized for spare parts. It was like a museum for ex-Soviet aircraft.

As the wheels of the Global touched the ground, Jeff was already on the phone, discussing fuel and passengers. He made it clear they would be leaving within the hour and had no desire to loiter at the airport.

"We are picking up some passengers, fuel, and bolt," Ry said. "It's been fun."

Rawley reached for his hand. "Thanks for the ride."

"I'm sure we'll cross paths again. Be safe," he said as they rolled to a stop.

Rawley opened the door, and a cool rush of stale smoky air blew into the aircraft. It was like a mix of burning rubbish, dust, and something rotten. Two Afghan airport officers approached the aircraft as a fuel truck pulled up, followed by a small white pickup. Rawley watched as a Gil Adams stepped from the truck. Just the sight of Gil caused a rush of memories.

He looked exactly as she remembered and exactly as she expected. He was wearing worn, faded jeans, tan cowboy boots, and the same leather flight jacket he had worn for more than fifty years. On his hip he had a leather holster carrying an Ruger Blackhawk 44 magnum, and on his head a sweat-stained gray Stetson. If the world thought of Americans as cowboys, Gil Adams was a walking, talking confirmation of that belief. With his rugged looks and weathered attire, he was the consummate image of the American cowboy and a barnstorming pilot of days gone by.

Rawley couldn't suppress her smile or her excitement as she rushed down the stairs and into his outstretched arms.

Gil hugged her tight then lifted her off her feet and swung her around. "Welcome to Cowbool, darlin'!" Gil said. His voice gravelly as ever. Gil had always had his own way of pronouncing words and describing everything. He was a character, and Rawley loved it.

She took a step back and looked Gil over from head to toe. "You didn't step on that beard," she said as she reached out to grab hold of the long, gray mane hanging down to his waist.

"Trimmed the damn thing, and no I didn't step on it. You've been poisoned by that cadet bush pilot, Bart. I got it tangled up in the yoke landing in a thirty-knot crosswind. You'll see," he said. "You're in for some wild-ass flying, sweetheart! Nothing like that sissy Navy jet stuff."

"That's what I'm here for," she said.

"Good! Good! We're covering a little convoy in the morning. Get your gear, and we'll get you settled and checked out in our new toys. Toss your bags in the back." Gil motioned over his shoulder. "I'm too old to be carrying any damn bags. Even for you!" Gil said as he wheeled around and headed toward the pickup truck.

Rawley turned, and Jeff was there with her bags. She thanked him, and they exchanged good-byes for a second time.

Rawley tossed her bags in the back as instructed then climbed into the truck. Gil handed her a well-used stainless-steel Colt Commander 45 Automatic. "I think you'll find this to your liking. It's loaded, with one in the tube," he said.

Rawley pointed the pistol at the floor and press checked the weapon to confirm it was loaded. Gil nodded his approval.

"Thanks, Gil," she said. Then she held it up and looked it over. "It looks like the same forty-five my mother has."

"It's your mother's," Gil said. "She sent it over, along with some other stuff I have back at the office. We unpacked a few things according to her instructions, and now the place looks like a tribe of Indians moved in."

Rawley just smiled. As they drove toward the coalition compound, Rawley's head was on a swivel taking everything in.

"These relics are mostly for show," Gil said as they drove past row after row of former Soviet Hind Mi-25 and Mi-35 helicopter gunships. "Most aren't airworthy. The US bought 'em, but they came with no logistics support and timed-out engines. Our tax dollars at work." Gil shook his head.

CHAPTER 32

—————◆—————

As THEY APPROACHED A SECURITY gate, two American Marines and two Afghan police came out from behind a mound of sandbags. One of the Americans waved them through as he raised the security bar.

Gil waved back and went through without slowing. "You're in the green zone now. Feeling safe?" Gil asked. "Well, don't get too comfortable or complacent round here, darlin'. Green don't mean shit!" His voice trailed off as they passed several concrete bunkers. "I'll take you to the shop, then we can check out the Tractor." Rawley was quiet as she looked around. Even here at the airport, she could see a country ravaged by years of continuous warfighting.

History indicates Afghanistan was inhabited over fifty-two thousand years ago. As time and humans evolved, the trade routes ran through the country, making it strategically important to whatever power happened to be ruling at that time. Afghanistan was considered the gateway to India and was central to the silk trade and commerce between China and the Mediterranean. Over time as many as twelve empires established capitals within the borders of Afghanistan. Wars had been fought and civilizations decimated only to be rebuilt under a new flag. Afghanistan's most famous conqueror was Alexander the Great. After defeating Persia in 330 BC, Alexander's forces fought the Battle of Gaugamela, making him king of all Asia.

Since that time, Afghanistan had endured hundreds of wars and changes in ruling parties. Assassinations of kings and rulers were commonplace, and boundaries were established then contested, until finally in 1880 the Russians and the British outlined what is now modern Afghanistan. Formalization of the nation's borders did little to stem the constant struggle for control of the country. As families fought for the right to rule Afghanistan, war has often bled across their borders into Pakistan and India, creating other issues.

In modern history, the USSR invaded Afghanistan in 1979 for what would turn out to be a failed ten-year war, waged primarily against the Islamist Mujahedeen. The countries that supported the war on both sides mirrored the allies of the Cold War, the United States and its allies on one side, and Russia and its allies on the other. After considerable Russian losses and pressure from the US and other countries, Russia withdrew their forces. The reasons for the invasion have been a matter of debate for many years, and in the end the only visible result was the flooding of Afghanistan with weapons of modern warfare. Killing was now mechanized and efficient.

Today an American-led coalition was here fighting. The current war would be justified as part of the Global War on Terror inspired by the 9/11 attacks on the American World Trade Center and the Pentagon but with no finish line to cross and no despot to vanquish. The success of the GWOT would long be debated. The goal, if there was one, was to root out evil wherever it could be found. The only certainty here was that Afghanistan was a wounded, war-torn nation with an unpopular leader, a weary populace, and an insurgent force that was stronger than ever.

As Gil drove down the protected green zone flight line, Rawley broke from her trance. "Tractors?" she asked.

Gil pointed ahead at four aircraft sitting under awnings near a heavily fortified and guarded hangar. "Your pop didn't tell you about these, did he?" Gil was beaming like a proud father as he turned toward the aircraft. "He wanted me to keep you out of them for the time being."

Rawley smiled and shook her head. "He wants me to send you home," Rawley said, without looking at Gil or even pausing. "He said gunships. I assumed he meant surplus Broncos or something, but not crop dusters."

"They ain't no crop dusters, darlin'. Least ways, they ain't no more. They just showed up last week. They got a few twenty-millimeter rounds, some rockets, and a lot of seven point six two in two wing pods."

Rawley was nodding and thinking. "What's their role over here?" she asked as they came to a stop in front of the first aircraft on the line.

"Purely convoy support and suppression until the real help arrives," Gil said as he opened his door. Gil put a leg out of the truck then stopped and turned back toward Rawley. He looked at her, and she looked at him in a moment of awkward silence. "What was that you said about me and home?" Gil asked, without looking away. "Are you sending me home?" His voice was uncharacteristically different. He was not brash or loud. He was concerned. He was seventy-two years old, and it was as if he were asking a parent if he was being punished.

Rawley didn't hesitate, and she never broke eye contact. "Dad told me to use my best judgement, Gil. I think sending you home right now wouldn't be too smart."

Gil exhaled and his shoulders relaxed as a smile came across his weathered face. "I can still do this job. I can fly."

"Stop," Rawley said. "Go home when you're ready, or I'll send you home with a flag draped over you, but whatever the case leave here on your own terms." Rawley reached for his hand, and Gil reached for hers. "I know you can fly, Gil. I covered your escape at Laskar Gah last January."

Gil threw his head back. "What?" he said as he remembered his harrowing exit from the Laskar Valley under a hail of rocket-propelled grenade fire. Then his smile turned to a broad grin.

"You were talking to my wingman," Rawley said. She was also remembering. "I didn't know it was you then, but I know now. It all came together when I heard you were here, and then I remembered your voice on the radio. God, that was great flying." Rawley stepped out of the truck. Then she turned back toward Gil. "Someday you'll have to teach me to fly like that."

Gil didn't move for a moment as the events at Laskar Gah replayed in his mind. He had just picked up two OGA operators in a location that should have been secure, but as soon as he started his takeoff roll, the first of many RPGs exploded close enough to shower his side window with dirt and rocks. His aircraft, a single-engine, high-wing, turbine Pilatus tail dragger bounced over the rough terrain as he increased power to maximum. At the same time, Gil keyed his microphone and called for help. A voice answered immediately, identifying himself as a flight of two Navy F/A-18s that happened to be nearly overhead.

As the Navy fighters came down, another RPG exploded, then another as they attempted to bracket the small aircraft. Just as his wheels left the dusty dirt road, Gil pushed his stick forward and went back to the ground. RPGs flew above and ahead right where he would have been had he continued his climb. Then, like a barnstorming performer, he pulled back on the stick and banked hard left into a 180-degree turn. It was as if he had pivoted on the wingtip. His left wing was inches from the ground as the aircraft came around. Then Gil leveled off and accelerated in ground effect before pulling up hard while this time banking sharp to the right as he headed straight for the walls of the canyon. He could feel small-arms fire strike his plane as the first Navy aircraft opened fire on the insurgents.

Seconds before impact with the canyon wall, Gil pushed the control stick to the left and picked up the contour of the canyon as he flew down the sloping embankment, inches from impact and certain death. The stench of vomit filled the plane, and the shock of explosions and jet afterburners drowned out the noise of his own screaming engine. What may have seemed like an eternity for his passengers was over in seconds as Gil climbed up and over the canyon walls to safety. The Navy pilot bid him farewell, and they were gone.

Gil walked toward Rawley as she looked over the massive four-bladed propeller of the Air Tractor. "That plane smelled like a nursery after that," Gil said. "Vomit and shitty pants!" Gil's demeanor was back to normal, and there was a spring in his step.

Rawley just laughed without turning her attention away from the Tractor. "How did you go through that and sound so calm on the radio?" She asked as she circled the plane.

Gil didn't say anything; he patted his left breast and grinned.

"Faith? Heart?" Rawley asked, looking at Gil.

Gil shook his head then reach into his coat and produced a flask. "Mr. Beam," Gil said. With that, Gil turned and started walking away. "Grab you gear and come inside. We'll get back to these machines later."

CHAPTER 33

———— • ————

RAWLEY WALKED INTO THE OFFICE and looked around as she dropped her bags. She could see the things her mother had sent already hanging on the wall. There was a feathered ornament with beads and painted bones, a symbol the Blackfeet believed made you invincible in battle. Gil was sitting at a desk with his feet up. "You'll be working out of an airfield at Kejahn for a few weeks," Gil said as he pointed toward a map on the wall. "That green pin in the middle is the place."

Rawley looked at the map. "I've loitered nearby many times."

"We'll run you up there in a few days after we've had a chance to go over all the things we have going on. The flying there is mostly benign for the skilled and well prepared." Gil continued. "We keep a Caravan and a PC12 there for some airdrop stuff and moving supplies around. The Army SPECOP guys handle all the hairy flying with Hawks and Ospreys. Do that for a couple weeks, then come on back."

Who's flying the Tractors?" Rawley asked.

"Me and another guy coming in from Alaska for now. Your dad's looking for a couple fighter jocks."

"Brett Jones?" Rawley asked.

"The Alaska guy? Yeah, that's his name. You know him?" Gil pulled out his flask.

"Met him in Alaska, did some amphib stuff with him," Rawley said. "I thought he was a rotary guy." She reached out for the flask.

Gil waved her off. "Don't drink this stuff." He motioned toward a cabinet. "It just kills you slow. There's beer in the reefer. Brett's been flying here for a while. He'll be fine." He frowned.

Rawley opened a beer, and before she turned around to ask another question, Gil was fast asleep. Rawley could only smile. She looked around the room. It was dark and dirty. Just about what she expected. The door opened, and a man walked in. He also looked at Gil and smiled then approached Rawley with his hand outstretched.

"Hamid," he said. "I am the head mechanic, head of maintenance, interpreter, and Gil Watch."

Rawley smiled. "I'm Rawley. I read your bio. Most Hamids don't have a last name of Johnson."

"That's because my name is really David Arron Johnson, but around here I find Hamid opens doors and gets me more respect. Happily, my mutt heritage helps me look the part."

Rawley nodded.

"My Ruger does the same thing," Gil said, as if he had never been asleep.

"You are a novelty, my friend," said Hamid. "An American cowboy in the truest sense."

Gil looked at Rawley. "There's some info on the Tractors on that desk." He pointed. "Read up on the plane, we'll go wheels up around nine in the mornin', then join that convoy around ten. We get relieved at eleven by some Army Blackhawks. It's a short hop just to get you in the plane so you can see what they do. Maybe give us an opinion before we start accepting tasking for close air support all over the country."

"Hamid will give you the grand tour," Gil said as he again leaned back. "He'll show you where to eat and bunk for the next two days. We'll do the op tomorrow then get into the admin stuff before we run you up to KeJahn. We got a PC12 and a Cessna Caravan up there servicing the Spooks and some SPECOP guys. Strictly logistics stuff but active. Fly out of there for a few weeks then come on back, and we can turnover."

Gil was repeating his earlier conversation, but Rawley didn't stop him. It was a habit he'd had for as long as she could remember. Just like when she was young, she just listened and nodded, while again looking at the map. She had been over kay jay many times and seen the contract aircraft transiting the valleys. The PC12s were fast and agile like a fighter, and the Caravan slow. But the Cessna could carry a lot of cargo and land anywhere and often did.

"I'll get you settled," Hamid said as he picked up Rawley's bags. "It's close and as secure as you'll find here."

Rawley took one last look at the office and Gil. His head was down, and he was snoring again. He looked peaceful, she thought, and strangely it made her think of home. "Give me the bags," she said as she took them back from Hamid. He didn't resist.

"Follow me," he said.

Hamid went through a door that led to a short, dimly lit hallway. "Communication is in there," he said, nodding at an unmarked door. "You can call home on a secure line anytime. We usually check for messages once an hour. Aircraft operations are monitored at kay jay and a few other places in-country. If someone needs to get an urgent message to us, it comes by courier from the coalition com center here in the green zone."

Rawley tried the door, but it was locked.

"I'll get you set up with access after I show you where you'll sleep. The armory is in there," Hamid said as they passed another door.

"We keep a few weapons in reserve, but mostly everyone has a primary and secondary with them at all times." Primary and secondary referred to a rifle and a handgun. A common military reference.

"We also have a range if you want to shoot, a fitness center, and a makeshift library and lounge."

Rawley didn't speak; she just listened and followed along.

Hamid stopped at another door and keyed the cipher lock. "I'll give you all the info, but this is star nineteen eleven. And here we are!" he said as he gestured around. "We have a common area, a kitchen, and five studios that also have a dinette and private bathroom."

Rawley looked around and nodded her approval.

"This room will be yours for the duration, so make yourself at home," Hamid said as he opened the door.

"Last thing in here," he said as he pointed toward two lights in the ceiling, "if there's a security breach, and there will be, you'll see that red light come on. About five minutes later, or less, twenty guys will be coming through that door. You are standing at the core of a secure bunker right here."

"OK," she said, nodding. "Good to know. I won't lounge around in my underwear." Rawley shrugged.

"Oh, you can," Hamid said, "just expect a lot of false alarms." He smiled. "When the threat is clear, you'll see green for maybe thirty minutes then no lights. It's the same system all over the AO."

Rawley just nodded her understanding.

For the next hour, Rawley followed Hamid around the Kabul green zone as they went from room to room introducing her. One fact that stood out to Rawley was the lack of women in anything but traditional roles such as clerical and medical. It didn't matter to her; it was merely an interesting observation. Like most military women, Rawley was not obsessed with the plight of women's lib fanatics.

She felt you got what you earned, and she never once felt held back. There were plenty of haters who made their feelings known, but she never let them get her down. In fact, they only fueled her desire to succeed.

The green zone also had a large number of civilians working for various news outlets. Some were embedded journalists, men and women who were allowed to go to the forward operating bases then into the field. They were not held in high regard by anyone other than attention seekers and those trying to get close to the females. Having sex with the women who came to report on the war was like playing bingo. Everyone kept score, usually not by names but by affiliation.

It was common to see the letters identifying a news outlet such as CNN or NBC discreetly scrawled near a soldier's bunk. The military women were no different, maybe just more discreet. War was marked by periods of terror and stress and longer periods of boredom, and men and women always seemed to find a way to find relief. Sex on the battle-field was a time-honored tradition that had been going on since the Bronze Age, when the world's first armies, those of Summer and Akkad, drew blood in Mesopotamia over a land dispute around 3000 BC. There were camp followers then, and there would always be.

CHAPTER 34

FORWARD OPERATING BASE, KEJAHN

———•———

IT WAS NINE O'CLOCK AS the helicopter carrying Rawley approached KeJahn. It was a dark but clear relatively moonless night, and the US Army MH60 Blackhawk was traveling blacked out and alone at over 130 knots. Rawley had spent two days with Gil flying the Air Tractors and getting indoctrinated into all the business and management aspects of the job. For the most part, things ran well and everyone just did the tasks they were assigned. It was easy to handle most issues or business at home through video conferencing and secure e-mail.

At the end of the day, the aircraft were just an asset to be used by the customer as they pleased. The air assets supported two customers, but the primary billpayer and priority was the CIA. No matter what the tasking, the aircraft could be redirected on a moment's notice, and it was clear from discussions with Gil that it happened often.

Rawley had a lot on her mind as she sat on the port side of the helicopter directly behind a crewman manning a GAU2B minigun. Although she had seen these helos on the carrier deck many times, it was the first time she had ever ridden in one. The entire crew was vigilant as they scanned out and down through their night-vision goggles, looking for any hint of trouble.

The cockpit was lit by night-vision compliant blue lights, and there were several flat-panel screens displaying images from infrared and thermal sensors. The crew chief had a remote screen in his lap with a joystick, controlling another set of visual sensors. He was slowly scanning down and behind. The biggest threat was a lucky shot with an RPG. It wasn't an everyday occurrence, but it had happened, and RPG rounds could not be foiled by countermeasures.

Like a bullet it was just a dumb projectile that flew in the direction it was fired. It required the shooter to make a SWAG, a scientific wild-ass guess, as to how much to lead the aircraft and how high to shoot to account for the degrading path the projectile would follow. Most times the RPG rounds would pass too low or behind.

"We are about ten minutes out, Rawley," one of the pilots said over the intercom.

"Roger" was all Rawley said in reply. She looked ahead thinking there should be light, but there was none.

She looked forward over the blue glow in the cockpit and still she saw no light or obvious signs of life. "No lights?" she asked over the com.

"There was a mortar attack about forty minutes ago, so they shut everything down" came the response. "The QRF is loitering out here someplace. They will join up in a few," the pilot added.

Rawley nodded but did not respond. She just turned her attention to the rugged, uneven terrain that was passing just five hundred feet below. Another set of eyes, she thought even if she wasn't wearing NODs, a common slang for night optical device or night-vision goggles.

As she turned her gaze back to the horizon, the crew chief tapped her shoulder and pointed to something in the dark. Rawley looked but saw nothing but an endless void and stars. Suddenly an Apache attack helicopter appeared less than eighty feet away at the same altitude. Right behind them and to the side, another helicopter that looked like a Chinook MH47, and slightly back another. She wondered how they could do that and not have their rotors impact each other. People probably wondered how jets flew so close. Sitting here and observing this formation, the helicopters seemed to be a depth-perception nightmare.

They were so close, she could see the faces of the pilots illuminated by the green glow from their night-vision goggles. She felt her aircraft bank slightly right and begin to lose altitude. The other helicopters held a perfect interval as they stayed in formation. Rawley flashed back to her night formation experiences. It was all the same, just different speeds, she thought. The consequences of an error were also the same, and though she had not really thought of it before, it now struck her how much the helicopter vibrated, shook, and shuttered compared to a fighter jet.

She thought her butt and head could go numb on a long mission on a Blackhawk compared the FA-18 that seemed smooth in comparison. In a fighter jet, the pilot is firmly strapped to the aircraft. Acceleration and maneuvers are felt but more as a force of pressure. Helicopters were loud, and the constant noise engulfed you like a blanket. The only crew on helicopters that were strapped in were the pilots. Everyone else was on a tether so he or she could be mobile. Passengers, such as she was now, were usually not attached to the helicopter at all. She also noticed the noise had a constant change of pitch and decibels. In a jet the noise was behind you, more like a low rumble going away. She never once left a fighter jet thinking about the engine noise, just the incredible power of both thrust and weaponry right at your fingertips—a world few would ever know or comprehend.

The helicopter slowed and began to flare for landing. The nose pitched up, and the tail went down. One crewman was hanging out looking down and back from the left side of the helicopter and another was doing the same on the other side. There were no landing lights, no crowds, nobody directing on the ground. Just helicopters landing and even more noise as the rotors chopped the cool air into submission. Dust and small stones swirled around the rotor, creating an eerie circular glow, something she had witnessed from above while supporting operations. Seeing it this close was very different. She thought of that debris passing through a turbine and the havoc it would cause.

Without warning the wheels met the asphalt, and they were rolling forward. Rawley looked back, and she could see the other aircraft maneuver into a line as the Blackhawk she was on took the lead. A minute later the helicopters dispersed, and her ride came to a stop. She could hear the big turbines winding down. Alarms were wailing and lights flashed as pressures dropped and systems shut down.

Like Kabul the air smelled different. There was burning jet fuel and the typical rancid air from a distant fire. As her eyes adjusted, she could now see armed men in every direction. Some were walking, and some were standing guard. A small tractor and two men came from the darkness and took the Blackhawk in tow.

"We'll go this way, ma'am," a crewman said to Rawley as her feet touched the ground.

"What did you say?" she asked, as if her trance was broken.

"This way," he repeated as he started to walk toward a large hangar.

"Don't call me 'ma'am.' You can call me Rawley or anything but 'ma'am,'" she said.

"Yes, ma'am," he said, smiling.

The interior of the hangar was lit with red lights. The illumination was enough to see your way but not bright enough to cast a shadow or aid a far-off sniper. It was there Rawley was met by another man offering his hand.

"Welcome to kay jay," he said, smiling and reaching out. "Nile Liddy."

"Rawley," she said, grasping his hand as she looked to her right at the Pilatus PC12.

"That's our bird," Nile said. "We also have a Caravan here full time, but they diverted to Kabul after the shit hit the fan earlier."

Rawley nodded and as usual generally took everything in without comment.

"Follow me; I'll take you to your quarters. We live in the palace," Nile said, referring to the main building. "It's four stories of hardened security attached by a series of tunnels and covered walkways to this hangar and other parts of the camp. It's safe; you can sleep well," he said. Nile was the first man who had not tried to grab her bags or make any overture that indicated she was anything other than one of the guys. She never missed those little nuances.

After a short walk through a few deserted corridors, they arrived in what looked to Rawley like the hallway of a hotel.

When Nile opened the door to her room and pushed it open, Rawley was instantly reminded of shipboard living, except with all the comforts of home.

"You'll get used to not having a window," Nile said as he looked around.

"I was on a ship, so..." Rawley let her comment trail off as she looked around. She looked up and saw the red and green lights.

"You know what those are for, right?" Nile asked, pointing at the ceiling.

"I do." One thing caught her attention on the dresser, and she walked toward it. It looked like a ledger or a diary.

"It's a kay jay tradition," Nile said as she picked it up. "Everyone who has ever stayed in this room puts their name and a few thoughts in there. You are probably guest number thirty or forty, I'd say."

"OK," Rawley said. "What's next?"

"Here's all the info you'll need to find food, a gym, laundry, and what have you." He handed her a folder. "It's a map to the place.

"Tonight, you can only get to the lounge, the kitchen, and the recreation areas. We are kind of segregated here, you'll find. Two-thirds of this place are inaccessible to us due to clearance issues. There are a lot of spooks working here and layers of classification. You'll be hauling them around, maybe see them at meals and when they are out and about, but our access to their work and living spaces is limited. I'd stay inside the building tonight until you can get your bearings in the daylight."

Rawley was just nodding.

"I will, uh, see you in the morning? Say, nine in the dining room?" Nile asked as he moved toward the door.

"OK, Thanks for meeting me." Rawley said. And with that, Nile was gone.

Rawley looked around the room for a second then picked up the ledger and lay down on the bed. As she turned the pages, she looked at names and comments; nothing really struck her as odd or compelling. Just names, random thoughts, and countdowns until departure. At the top of one page, instead of a name someone had written "The Kraken." No name, no date, no other words. Simply, "The Kraken."

Oh well. In this business and the military, nicknames and call signs were common, or maybe it was just someone being funny, she thought.

CHAPTER 35

———◆———

MORNING CAME QUICKLY, AND THE hallways that were quiet the night before were alive with men and women carrying folders or briefcases going one place or another. Everyone was cordial but seemed preoccupied, and nobody engaged Rawley in conversation beyond saying hello.

As she entered the dining area, she saw Nile sitting with two other men. One she immediately recognized from the personnel records in her father's office, a former Marine F-18 pilot with rotary and Harrier experience. As she approached, all three men stood up. Rawley raised her hand in protest.

"Don't get up, please," she said. She nodded to Nile, then the first man to her left held out his hand.

"Greg Falcon. Scheduler," he said as he stepped back.

"Caleb Smith," the second man said, without reaching for her hand.

"Gentlemen," Rawley said as she took a seat.

"Joe Blume will be in later," Nile said. "He was diverted to Kabul."
Rawley nodded.

"How's that old crop duster doing at Kabul?" Caleb asked, with a hint of sarcasm.

"Gil?" she said. "He's great. He's in heaven now that he has a couple 'crop dusters' to fly around." She reached for coffee.

"Oh well, that old coot's crazy. He'll bend one up before long," Caleb said as he looked around the room. "You ever met him before?" Caleb asked without looking directly at Rawley.

"He's my godfather," Rawley said, showing the same level of interest for the conversation displayed by Caleb.

"No shit!" Nile and Caleb said in harmony.

"No shit," said Rawley.

"How do they look? The planes?" Caleb asked, more to change the subject.

"Nice platform," said Rawley as she also scanned the room. "We took a hop two days ago and spent some ammo. They're a bit slow but capable. When can you get in one and tell us what you think?" She looked at Caleb.

"You're the boss now, so you tell me," Caleb said as he pushed his seat back. "I have a brief in twenty minutes for an extract, so I'll leave you all to talk. I'm picking up a civilian medical team at a village about thirty miles north."

"I'm wheels up at one. Come with, if you are done with the grand tour."

"I'll make a point to be done," Rawley said.

Caleb smiled and nodded to the other men as he left.

"He's a little bitter about the perceived demotion," Nile said as he watched Caleb leave. "He's been the top dog here for a while."

"Well, I'm not staying long, so he can pretend to be in charge again soon enough," Rawley said as she continued to slowly scan the room.

"Looking for someone?" Nile asked.

"No, I've just spent so much time overhead, I never really thought about the scope of this place."

Nile nodded. "The turnover here is huge and these people represent hundreds of small and large companies. They're from all walks of life, every service, every skill set. Some are completely normal, and some are just as socially screwed up as you can imagine. Or, maybe more than you can imagine."

Rawley just smiled. "Greg, what do you schedule?"

"Everything! I am your liaison between the folks who run this place, military airflow, and anyone who might be in an area you would fly to and the team that would come and get you if there's trouble. I do three months on, three off. I just got back, so I'll be your guy."

"Good," said Rawley, nodding.

"I know you just left the Navy, so this place won't be such a mystery," Greg said.

"I go to the OPS briefing every morning at seven then meet you all here at nine. Then another brief after the evening meal. If you need more than what I give you in your oporder and it's classified, we meet in there." Greg pointed toward a small room off the dining hall. "I also direct our planes in Kabul and any company airflow coming and going."

"Busy guy," Rawley said.

"That room," Greg said as he pointed back to the secure area, "has a direct secure phone line to OPS, so we can discuss anything in there we don't want shared with the general populace. More operations have been planned in that room over meals than any other place in this building. Do you know Dave Mayer?" Greg asked.

Rawley shook her head. "Never heard the name. Should I know him?"

"He's the head of Task Force Zebra. Or just TF Z around here. He's our real boss, and he runs all agency activity here. He is also a very old friend of your father's, and he wants to see you at your convenience. I'm surprised your father didn't mention his name," Greg said.

"Well, my situation with my father is odd at best," said Rawley. "Until a few weeks ago, I was a Navy pilot, and I had no idea about anything my father did relating to this work."

Greg tossed his head back and smiled. "No way!" He turned his gaze to Nile. Nile just shrugged but added nothing.

"Since I was very young, I literally thought my father was just a pilot who flew hunters and campers around. Naïve, I know. But the truth was a well-guarded secret."

Rawley turned to Nile. "What's on tap today besides Caleb's flight?"

"That's it," he said.

"I'll show you around a little, but most everything is easy enough to figure out. Communication security here is tight, just so you know," Nile said. "You'll see guys talking on cell phones, and you can video conference from your room. Just know everything is monitored, and blackmail is rampant."

Rawley smiled and nodded. "Fair enough."

"We talk to Bud about every five days to give a SITREP," Nile said, referring to a situation report. "You'll be doing that while you're here, I assume."

"I will," Rawley said as she turned to Nile. "Let's walk, shall we?" She stood up from the table.

"The best time to talk to Mayer is around four, just so you know," Greg said. "That's between briefs for him."

"OK. If I'm back I'll find my way to his office," Rawley said.

Just then the door to the dining facility opened and a loud group of men flooded in. There were fourteen of them, and they all had long hair and wore a mix of clothing that included flight suits, camouflaged uniforms, and civilian clothes.

They were laughing and talking loud as they moved to the food line. Everyone seemed to give way as they passed.

"SEALs?" Rawley asked.

"Good guess," Nile said. "There's about a hundred of them in the compound. They'll find you. You can count on that."

Rawley just smiled and headed for the door.

For the next two hours, Rawley and Nile wandered through the compound and Kejahn headquarters. The enormity of it all was staggering. Although she had seen the briefs and seen the compound from the sky many times, the actual size and scope of the operation was incredible to her. This was a city grown from a camp in the only area within a hundred miles capable of supporting an eight-thousand-foot runway.

The average citizen in America had no idea just how involved the War on Terror was in Afghanistan, and most could not care less.

CHAPTER 36

———◆———

As RAWLEY WALKED INTO THE hangar, she could see the Cessna Caravan had returned. Like the Pilatus PC12, it was gray in color with a broken black stripe down the side and streaked with dirt and dust from landing on unimproved roads and fields. The plane carried several antennas not normally found on civilian aircraft and a roll-up door usually found on planes used for skydiving. Unlike the Pilatus it was a high-wing, fixed-gear aircraft often used for cargo or passengers and popular for short flights in rural and unimproved areas.

Cessna had introduced the aircraft in the early '80s, and since then more than twenty-five hundred planes had been delivered around the world. It so happened the Afghan National Army Air Force was the third largest user of the Caravan behind FedEx and the Brazilian Air Force.

The Caravan was a real workhorse and a popular bush plane if you could afford the price, and that was as much as Rawley knew about it.

She could see Caleb and another man she assumed was Joe Blume standing at the front of the Pilatus. As she approached Caleb turned and walked away, and Joe reached out to shake her hand. "Joe, Joe Blume," he said, smiling.

"Rawley. Nice to meet you."

"I have a package for you from Gil. I understand you two have a history," Joe said as he handed Rawley a small daypack.

"We do," Rawley said. "Thanks, what is it?"

"Just admin stuff we normally pick up once a week." I was there, so I just grabbed it."

Rawley nodded and handed it back to him. "Give this to' Nile, will you?"

Caleb did a walk-around on the Caravan then stopped at the propeller. "The plane looks good, but these props take a real beating landing on dirt. Let's fly," Caleb said as he turned and walked to the left side of airplane. Rawley also took a quick look at the plane before climbing the stairs to her seat.

Caleb looked at Rawley then down at the floor between their seats. "You have a long gun and ammo in a bag right there. There's a Gentex," he said, referring to a standard military ballistic flight helmet. "I usually don't put it on unless I'm landing, but suit yourself."

Rawley opened the bag and looked at the automatic rifle and other gear. She said nothing else as they taxied out to the runway. Caleb handled all communication.

Ascending out of kay jay, Rawley could see several defense posts manned by American contractors and Afghan and coalition troops. The concrete bunkers formed a perimeter around the base, and they were hardened to withstand car bombs and mortar attacks, but none were hidden or concealed in any way. Their obvious presence was considered as much a deterrent as anything. There were still occasional mortar attacks, but the roads leading into the base wound around countless barriers, making effective attacks by vehicle extremely difficult, and attacks by land could be repelled by rocket and artillery fire from within the compound. Troops assigned to protect the base were on guard seven days a week, twenty-four hours a day. It was like a city that never slept.

Once they leveled off, Caleb picked up a checklist and went quickly through the items, looking at every indicator on the panel. "We don't want this thing shutting down without warning," he said, still panning the gauges.

"OK, give me the rundown," Rawley said.

"Here's the deal," Caleb said, handing her a folder. "Our entire op plan is in there. Who, when, where, ingress, egress, and emergency route. The com plan and downed aircraft plan is at the bottom." He pointed at the page Rawley was looking at. "We are squawking IFF."

IFF referred to Identification Friend or Foe and it was used by several military assets including aircraft, maritime or vehicles to help prevent a "Blue on Blue" attack.

"Our IFF works just like the one in the Hornet, except we push this if we have an issue." Caleb pointed to a switch on the panel labeled "DA" and continued. "DA, or down aircraft, means we are in trouble, and that one button summons the cavalry. The installed emergency locator beacon is disabled, and the new beacon is coded and secure."

Rawley said nothing but she was making mental notes as they went along.

"You hit that button, and everyone gets our constant updated position, altitude, and speed. kay jay will know if we're still moving or done for. It lets you fly, or crash, without worrying about communicating."

Rawley nodded.

"The QRF will normally be wheels up ten minutes from notification," he said.

"If you are going down, just look for a soft spot," Caleb said as he scanned down and to the left. "Remember to keep flying, and if you think about it, unlatch your door and tighten your belt before you touch down."

Rawley again nodded and looked at the door handle.

"Just basic ditching stuff," Caleb said.

Then he pointed at two handles at the top of the panel. "These things are the last thing you pull before you depart the plane." He looked at Rawley. "You pull these, and twenty seconds later thermite will burn this plane to the ground. That's twenty seconds to pull and hit the bricks. If you forgot anything, leave it!" he added.

"Thermite?" Rawley asked, reading the label near the handles.

"I don't know what's all in it, but I know a German chemist invented it to weld train tracks together or some such shit. I also know once its initiated it burns hot and can't be extinguished."

"There are three charges in the panel, two over the wings and two more in the back in case any passengers leave something behind we don't want getting into the wrong hands. All our planes are set up the same way. "It's pretty good coverage, so the whole plane will go up, and fast."

"OK, what about routes and SOPs?" she asked.

"The route depends on weather and known activity. We are very vulnerable to random rocket attacks. One lucky shot is about all it takes. I like to fly an arc to my destination and vary the altitude. Quite honestly there's no magic formula," he said. "Nobody tells you how to get there, just where to go, when to be there, and what areas to avoid. If your gut or voices tell you to do something, I'd listen.

"As we close in on our destination, we'll take it down and maybe zigzag in. The bad guys use cell phones to communicate. kay jay and several other places monitor those frequencies. If they hear something that makes them think we are being targeted, they'll call us. It happens."

Caleb pointed to the radio stack. "The top frequency is our company plane-to-plane and general-use com. Next is a coalition frequency. Nobody calls us on that. Next is the kay jay admin freq. We use that coming and going from kay jay only, and it changes regularly.

"This last radio we just monitor. If we are aborted or redirected or need to communicate with the QRF, that's their frequency."

As Caleb talked he turned forty degrees to the right and began a descent. Rawley was still making mental notes while scanning out the right side of the aircraft. She could not get over how different this was from loitering thousands of feet above the ground and relatively away from danger.

Caleb put his helmet on, and Rawley did the same. They were now below two thousand feet, and the rocky ledges were above them on both sides. "Keep your eyes open, and call out anything you see," Caleb said.

"This place has been more or less quiet, but anything can happen. We're landing on that road ahead. We need a recognition signal. Today, two fires about thirty feet apart. They usually dump some oil into the fire to enhance the smoke. We should see that soon."

Caleb pulled the power back and lowered the flaps. The aircraft was being buffeted by the wind rolling off the cliffs. Rawley was watching Caleb as much as she was watching everything else.

"Better see smoke soon," he said. "I'm hugging the right side here so we can egress left."

Soon they could see people standing together, and village structures began to take shape. "Smoke. Come on." Caleb was just talking to himself, and his head was on a swivel. His right hand was on the power, and he leveled the aircraft off at seven hundred feet above the ground. "Out of here in one minute," he said.

"Got smoke!" Rawley said as she pointed ahead. "Two black columns."

She could see Caleb was relieved. "Civilians, doctors, even worse," Caleb said as he slowed the plane more and pushed the nose over. "This should be fast. You keep a watch outside. I'll watch the load." As they passed through two hundred feet above the ground, Caleb pulled the *T* handle to close the inertial separator. "I always do this on dirt. It was intended for heavy rain and ice, but it works good for blowing dust, small animals, and children also."

Rawley just smiled.

"You see anything suspicious, yell out," Caleb said as the wheels touched the ground, then he pulled the power back to idle and then into beta, or reverse thrust. The nose pitched down hard, and the aircraft rolled to a stop. Dust swirled up around the aircraft, momentarily obstructing their view.

As they came to a stop, a small pickup truck backed up to the left rear of the aircraft, and a man in the bed pushed the cargo door up. Six men and two women climbed from the truck to the aircraft and quickly slid forward.

Caleb turned around in his seat, watching the passengers come aboard, and Rawley scanned the crowd for anything that looked like it might be a threat. She subconsciously put her hand on her mother's Colt Commander. She didn't know what she would do from her seat behind a closed door; she just knew she felt better knowing she was armed.

"If something goes bad, there's damn little we can do right now, but just keep watching," Caleb said, watching the passengers load. "Hurry up back there!" he yelled.

Everything Caleb said sounded like an order and made Rawley tighten her jaw.

"Buckle up! Who is Oswald?" Caleb yelled over the noise. One man came forward quickly and handed Caleb his ID. Caleb took one quick look then gave it back without saying anything. There were no seats in the aircraft, just two cargo straps on the floor. It was not their first time in this aircraft, and everyone moved forward and pulled the straps across their thighs. When the last bag was thrown in, the cargo door was pulled down, and one passenger tightened another cargo strap across the bags then took a seat. Caleb turned around then looked to his left and back. One of the locals was off his left wing, waving and giving him a thumbs-up. Caleb looked at the man without returning the gesture.

Caleb pulled the flap lever to 20 percent then advanced the throttle without looking down. With his left foot, he pushed down hard on the left rudder pedal, actuating the corresponding wheel brake.

As Caleb added power, the aircraft came around until he was positioned for takeoff. Villagers lined the dirt road for several hundred feet. The engine screamed as Caleb pushed the throttle forward while holding the brakes. Then with a jerk they surged ahead, and in seconds the Cessna Caravan was passing through the cloud of dirt they raised on landing. As the aircraft raced down the road, villagers turned away from the dust and trash being blown into the air.

Rawley continued to watch outside as they climbed out. Then she looked back into the rear of the plane. The passengers were quiet and crammed together on the floor. Two held rosaries and prayed, and a couple were holding hands. It was a sight she didn't expect, and it was certainly a not a life she could envision for herself.

Rawley removed her helmet and put her headset back on. "Wow!" was all she said.

Caleb was quiet as he looked at her and shrugged. After a few minutes, the aircraft was in level flight high above the jagged rocks below.

"Do we let anyone know we have them?"

"No com needed," he said. "Ops saw us land then climb out. As long as we don't touch that beacon, it's the same as telling everyone we are clean and green! If the headcount is wrong or something worth saying comes up, then sure we can call them up. These guys are a real low priority, but you can call in if it makes you feel better."

For the remainder of the flight, Caleb was quiet. No casual talk, no comments or advice. Rawley knew the attitude too well. She had seen it from the day she entered Naval Aviation. Happily, in this era of modern warfare, more and more women joined the fight and more male pilots treated her as an equal than did not. But the attitude was always there. True equality was a myth. It was just a concept thrown around by the politically correct and senior leadership. She knew it, and she accepted it as the price to play the game.

CHAPTER 37

———•———

AS RAWLEY WALKED INTO THE common area at kay jay, she could see Nile sitting with Greg and Joe. They all stood up as she approached. "Enough of that shit," she said as she pulled a chair to the table.

"Good run?" Nile asked.

"Yeah, it was painless," she said as she scanned the room.

"How was conversation with Caleb?" Joe asked as he reached for his coffee.

"He's an ass," Rawley said. "Great pilot, but he's an ass."

"He treats me the same way," Joe said. Greg and Nile laughed.

"I'll go find Mayer now. Anything on the schedule?" Rawley asked, looking at Greg.

"Yeah, I heard an asset is coming in, but no confirmation, what that means to us is both planes in the air on routes near the expected pick-up point." Greg said as he looked at a note pad he was holding.

Rawley nodded.

"We go out and back essentially. One plane in the morning, one in the afternoon." Nile added.

"If the guy checks in, you'll get instructions over the radio. If it goes into the night or looks like a hot extract, the Army and SEALs will cover it." Greg added.

"OK, Joe, you and Caleb in the PC12, and Nile and I will take the Caravan." Said Rawley as she turned to Nile who was nodding in agreement.

"It's all still in flux, so I don't expect official tasking for hours," Greg said as he stood up.

Rawley slid her chair back. "Greg, how about walking me up to TFZ?"

"Let's go," he said.

As Greg and Rawley headed toward the operations center, she could see activity in every office. "What are all these people doing?" she said, more as a statement than a question.

"Reports and impact statements and on and on and on," Greg said. "We are spending millions daily, and every congressman wants to know where it's going and why."

The outer office to TFZ was simple and unassuming. It wasn't apparent that every operation in this region originated here. Dave Mayer controlled the money, the personnel, and in some cases the fate of Afghanistan from this office.

In the outer office of TFZ, three men and one woman were seated at desks, working on computers. As Rawley and Greg walked in, one young man stood and reached to shake Rawley's hand while nodding toward Greg.

"This is the new head of our air division, Rawley West," Greg said.

"Welcome," the man said. "Bud's daughter, right?"

"I am," Rawley said.

"Great!" he said, smiling. As he picked up the phone, another man raised his hand and said, "Welcome to kay jay," without looking away from his computer screen.

The man who greeted them hung up the phone, and a door at the back of the room opened. Standing in the doorway was Dave Mayer, smiling broadly and motioning them forward. "Come in!"

Rawley stepped forward, and Greg turned to leave. "I'll catch up to you later," he said.

In Mayer's office Rawley looked around and couldn't help but think how much it looked like the combat information center on a ship. Flat-screens lined one wall, all numbered and showing different information or news programs. There was no sound, just captioning.

"Welcome to kay jay," Mayer said. "Can I get you anything? Water, beer, something stronger?"

Rawley was shaking her head before he finished the question. "I'm good, thanks."

"Your father told me you were coming over. I was surprised you left the Navy," he said.

Rawley smiled and shrugged at the comment. "I guess I kind of hit the wall and knew I wouldn't be flying as much as I wanted," she said.

"I flew in the Navy," Mayer said. "With your father."

"Really," Rawley said.

"Yeah, we flew some combat missions, we worked at Pax River together, we did some drinking. Pilot stuff, you know."

Now Rawley was smiling. She never really thought of her father as a young naval aviator doing the things she and countless pilots before her had done. The flying, the partying. It was always life on the edge.

"He saved my life after I went down in Thai Bin. He stayed on-station covering me until Jolly Green showed up. He made about twenty low passes, taking fire every time, then he couldn't get tanked on the way to the boat. He landed on fumes with a plane full of holes. And if that wasn't enough, his hook wouldn't come down, so he got arrested by the net."

Rawley remembered reading the citation, but of course there were no details and her father had never told the whole story.

"I know he was cited, but I have never really known much about it," she said.

"That's his way," Mayer said. "Just a quiet professional. Except on liberty. He left it all in town when we were out!" Mayer was clearly thinking back to better times in his youth.

"I have also never heard any liberty stories," Rawley said, laughing.

"Well, those stories are better left in the past anyway," Mayer said. "So, what are you doing here, Rawley?" Mayer asked. "It's a step down from a career in the Navy, isn't it?

"I'm here because I was just tired of looking down on this place from twenty thousand feet and thought I'd see it up close. I honestly had no idea my father was involved in any way."

Mayer leaned back and listened.

"I felt kind of duped, though it probably shouldn't matter. Just saying," she said as she also got more comfortable.

Mayer locked his hands behind his head and leaned back. Rawley smiled, thinking no woman ever sat like that or started a conversation from that position. She knew it was a prelude to philosophical enlightenment. Something else women rarely engaged in.

"I'm not looking for an explanation, honestly," she said, more as a preemptive gesture.

"OK," he said, "I'll spare you. Anyway, I'm glad you're here," Mayer said as he put his hands down then leaned forward, putting his elbows on his desk.

"Your role here is fairly defined. Your assets serve mine. Our number-one priority is intelligence gathering."

Rawley listened intently for the next twenty minutes as Dave Mayer explained the process of supporting Human Intelligence efforts in Afghanistan and how her aircraft fit into the equation.

When Mayer finally stopped talking, Rawley was leaning back with her arms crossed and her head cocked to the left.

The flight with Caleb felt very administrative and tame compared to the flight operations Mayer described. Her imagination was working, and she felt like she was in the right place at the right time.

Mayer pushed his chair back and stood up. Rawley did the same. She reached out for Mayer's hand, and he stepped forward to give her a hug. "That's from your mother," he said. "My inbox is full of messages from her."

Rawley could only smile and shake her head. "She e-mails you?"

"All the time since you decided to come over. Why?" he asked.

Rawley shook her head, and her mouth was open in disbelief. "No reason. Tell her I'm happy. You know she sent me her forty-five," Rawley said as she turned to the door.

"You gotta love a mother that thinks that way," Mayer said. "We'll have dinner soon, be safe."

Back in the common area, Caleb, Joe, and Nile were again sitting together in a corner of the room. Once Rawley sat down, Nile started explaining what lay ahead.

"When these guys come in, it can be hectic or benign," he said. Joe was nodding in agreement, and Caleb was looking around the room. "There's no timeline; we just need to be ready. The planes are topped off and preflighted.

"Tomorrow we will go wheels up in the morning and stay in the pattern so you can get comfortable with the Caravan while Caleb and Joe cover. Then we'll take the afternoon standby shift. Here's the book on that plane," Nile said as he handed Rawley a binder.

"Sounds good to me." Rawley slid her chair back to leave, and nobody got up.

She sat for a moment, lost in thought. "Do any of the guys get e-mail or text messages from your mother?" she asked.

"I don't talk to my mother. Why?" Caleb asked, in his usual sardonic tone.

"Never mind," Rawley said. "Forget I asked."

"My mother uses Twitter, texts, and about five other social-media platforms, and she's seventy-five," Nile said. "Why? What's up?"

Rawley paused for a moment then looked at Nile. "My mother and I have traded nothing but written letters since the day I left for college. Joe just brought me a bag full of mail from her," she said, looking at Joe.

"I just found out she's a prolific e-mail writer." Rawley shook her head, and the others just looked at each other but didn't comment. With that, Rawley turned and walked away.

"I'll be in the Caravan if anyone needs me," she said.

"Call your dad around seven tonight," Nile added.

Rawley raised her hand to confirm as she left. Caleb watched her walk through the door then looked at the others. "I can't relate to women in this job," he said as he turned back to watching the room. "I never got it in the Corps, and I don't get it here."

CHAPTER 38

———◆———

THE NIGHT PASSED QUICKLY, AND Rawley was up and ready to fly by nine. Her conversation with her father the night before was short and uncharacteristically businesslike. It was the fourth time she had spoken to him since arriving in Afghanistan. He didn't question her decision to keep Gil in place, and he seemed pleased to have her there watching out for what was now a family affair.

As she entered the hangar, Nile was already there looking over the plane. Although she had not flown with him, she knew from conversations he was a skilled pilot with corporate experience but no military background. She also heard he had adapted well to the environment, and he was very loyal to her father.

After a short discussion, they were off the ground, circling the kay jay airfield. Rawley set up for the first of three short-field landings, and Nile backed her up. He was a great resource in the cockpit and much more talkative than Caleb.

The Caravan was a simple aircraft by most standards, and Rawley had no problem learning the nuances of flying it or managing the Pratt and Whitney PT6 turbine engine. It was a common aircraft engine used in many fixed-wing airplanes and helicopters.

It was close to noon when Rawley and Nile returned to the hangar. Caleb and Joe were sitting in reclining chairs along one wall, and in another area of the hangar, the SEALs were staging equipment and weapons.

"New plan," Joe said. "We are down for the day."

It seemed to Rawley like all eyes were on her as she walked past everyone. It was a typical scene here or anywhere groups of military men were gathered. Women were few, and there were always men who would try anything to get in good with them, getting in good meant getting in bed.

Activity in the hangar and TF Z operations was hectic. The word had come in that the Kraken might be coming in and possibly with a prisoner. All communication channels were being monitored, and plans were being made. If he was uncompromised, he would go to any one of the preplanned extraction points he was aware of and activate a beacon that had been planted prior to his arrival.

If he was compromised, any number of scenarios might play out. There were several extraction points around the region he was in, and all contained caches that included a coded beacon, weapons, and medical supplies. The intent was to get to one of these points, call for extraction, and wait if at all possible. The only thing that was certain at this point was that if he did have a prisoner, the QRF and SEALs would bring him in.

The UAV teams kept several unmanned aircraft overhead around the clock, and their reaction time was a quarter of what it would take the QRF once they were notified. Some UAVs were armed with missiles, and some were unarmed. All the UAVs were capable of sending a real-time video feed via satellite back to kay jay, where it could then be retransmitted to anyone who might have a need for the information.

As the day went on, the intel monitors sat patiently waiting for a computer to warn them of an intercepted word or word string that might give them a clue as to when the Kraken or one of the other assets might come in or need assistance. They would also be listening for other information that might mean an imminent attack or terror event anyplace in the world.

The men and women working here were called analysts. They all had different roles that included listening, documenting, and analyzing the bits and pieces of "intel" garnered from conversations or text messages. That raw information went to the next level, where opinions or theories were formulated and passed on to more senior analysts who then briefed those opinions and theories to operational staff who were tasked with disseminating or acting on the information.

It was a task that employed hundreds if not thousands of personnel around the world, and it went on in shifts around the clock every single day of the year. The analysts came from every walk of life and every corner of the world. They were hired for their language ability, their understanding of the geographic area they were assigned to, and their ability to calmly and quickly piece bits of information together. They were scholars and intelligence specialists and former military contractors. At kay jay they worked three months on and three months off.

Every twelve months they would return to Langley or one of the other government intelligence offices where they would have a nine-to-five job and receive training in a normal work environment. They were the backbone of America's intelligence network.

While the gathering went on, Greg sat at his desk in ops, waiting for a task order, and the pilots sat near their aircraft, waiting to be launched. During these alert periods, the waiting was often tedious and sometimes frustrating, but it was the job.

It was after midnight when Greg heard a commotion in the hallway. He jumped to his feet and stopped the first person walking past. "What's going on?" he asked.

"We have an asset coming in around three. The QRF is covering it."

Greg yawned and looked at his watch. He knew nothing would happen at this hour with Rawley or her guys.

In the hangar Rawley was asleep in a recliner near the Caravan when she heard the voices. The SEALs were running to their gear, and the hangar doors were opening.

She knew better than to stop anyone and ask questions. She chose instead to sit and watch. She could hear helicopters and the unmistakable

V22 Osprey turning up as two trucks pulled up to the hangar. The men tossed gear into the trucks and climbed in. As fast as they had arrived, the SEALs were gone, and the hangar was closing.

Rawley looked at her watch. It was fifteen minutes to one. She looked around the hangar aglow in red light, and she could hear the helicopters depart. A second later the noise was gone, and the place was quiet.

Just the sight of the men rushing in then leaving with a sense of urgency got her adrenaline pumping. She knew well the feeling of standing by then being sent out on a moment's notice. In her past life, many a time she would go from sitting in a carrier ready room in silent thought to racing to the flight deck and a waiting aircraft. After climbing into the cockpit and racing through a mental checklist while watching hand signals, she'd be hurled into the sky by the catapult. In mere seconds the aircraft carrier was far behind, and it was her racing to the objective.

Rawley settled back into the seat and exhaled hard. She was a lion once. Now...not so much.

She cleared her head and thought about going to bed. Then she reclined and went back to sleep.

——◆——

CHAPTER 39

Morning came quickly, and Rawley woke up in her room, though she couldn't remember going to bed. She looked at her watch, and it was almost seven. She hoped it would be a normal day and there would be a flight someplace. Anyplace actually. She wondered how the extraction had gone the night before, and she wondered how Gil and Brett were doing with the Tractors after their first flight the previous day. She wondered a lot of things lately, but for the most part, she was content with her decision to follow this path. Occasionally she wondered how her parents could keep so many secrets from her. But those thoughts were fleeting now that she was here and working.

The silence in her room was broken by a knock on the door. "It's open!" she yelled.

Greg walked in carrying an envelope. He held it up as he walked toward her. "I have a good one for you."

Then he stopped and looked at Rawley. "Did you sleep in those clothes?" It was obvious, but he asked anyway.

"Yeah, I did. In a chair in the hangar, in fact," she said. Greg just smiled and handed her the package.

"Pace yourself. Wheels up around ten. Let's talk in the hangar around nine. It's a supply drop in an area too tight for a 130, and we can't get a CASA down here in time." Greg was referring to the Lockheed C-130 cargo plane normally used for such purposes. Rawley just nodded.

"I'll let Nile know," Greg said as he left the room.

Rawley opened the envelope and saw a briefing package, just as she had seen while flying with Caleb.

All the information she would need was written on one page. Call signs, routes, frequencies, timeline, and coordinating instructions. It was a lot of information all neat and organized.

Rawley saw the area for the drop and recognized it from flight briefings she had received on the carrier during past deployments. She knew US forces manned a remote base there while they were clearing a series of caves and tunnels. She also knew the area to be an insurgent hotbed.

The dining area was quieter than normal. Most people worked the night shift while the QRF was out, so many were starting work late, she assumed.

After dining alone Rawley made her way to the hangar. She could hear the activity before she came through the door. A fork truck moved a cargo pallet toward the Caravan, and Greg and Nile were standing near the tail, talking.

They both acknowledged Rawley as she approached. "You look fresh," Nile said sarcastically. Obviously the word had got around that she spent the night in a recliner waiting for something to happen.

Rawley just shrugged. Then she looked up into the Caravan. One pallet was already loaded and rigged with a small parachute. When the fork truck stopped at the plane, two men started rigging a parachute on the second pallet.

"Have you dropped cargo before?" Nile asked.

"Not really," Rawley said. "I left Montana before they got to that."

"Well, that will be a case of beer, then," Nile said, smiling. "I'll have it delivered in your name and bill you."

"Just feel free to let us know if there is anything else you happen to be doing for the first time while you're here."

Rawley couldn't help but notice Nile was more animated than he'd been before. She liked the change. She preferred working with men and women who were more aggressive and confident.

"Another asset is rumored to be coming in," Greg said. "No changes for your flight, though." He walked toward the tail of the Caravan and looked inside at the load. "Just two pallets low drop right into the camp." He turned to look at Rawley. "Nile has done this many many times, so he'll walk you through it. Don't stay down any longer than you need to, and you'll be safe."

Rawley and Nile both nodded in agreement.

"The asset?" Rawley asked.

"Oh yeah. He may have a prisoner, so the QRF will take it," Greg said. "Just giving you a heads up."

Once the plane was loaded and moved outside, Rawley and Nile climbed aboard and checked their gear. Nile was wearing a vest that seemed to carry every piece of survival gear he had been issued. Rawley had her mother's Colt in a shoulder holster, and that was it. Everything else was in the gear bag beside her seat.

In a short time, they were climbing out of kay jay on their preplanned route. Even at ten thousand feet, they both watched the ridge lines and roads below. After an hour at altitude, they both removed their headsets and put on their ballistic helmets.

"Check," Nile said over the com.

"Roger," Rawley responded.

"When the time comes, I'll be in the back, pushing the pallets out," Nile said. "Level off at two hundred and fifty feet and stay there for two minutes. That's all it will take."

Rawley was nodding as she looked at the altimeter.

"When I say clear or you feel that second pallet leave, climb straight out to a thousand then a right forty-five and up to eight. I'll close up and be back in the front before you clear fifteen hundred."

Nile methodically went through the procedure step by step. "I'll need about five minutes in the back to get things ready," he said. With that, he looked at a paper chart then made an adjustment to one of the radio frequencies.

"If anything goes wrong, we need to crash in that camp or as close as possible." Nile was now looking out the window at the rugged terrain. "As you can see, there aren't many fields or straight roads around here, and the locals are not friendly."

"What brought you over here, Nile?" Rawley asked as she also scanned the terrain.

"I was flying a corporate jet, and you know, I was just looking for some adventure and excitement."

Rawley laughed and shook her head. "Wow!" she said.

"What?" Nile sounded a bit defensive. "I know I'm not a military guy."

Rawley turned toward Nile. "No, don't get upset. You were flying a luxury jet, I was flying a fighter jet, and here we are in a plane that couldn't do two hundred knots downhill, in a place where everyone would like to see us dead. And we think we are on a friggin' adventure!"

Nile laughed. "Oh well. We're here," he said as he removed his safety harness. "That's our valley ahead. Let's do a steady descent to five hundred feet above the ground. We are dropping on yellow smoke; we abort on anything else."

Rawley nodded as she inhaled hard then let it out slow.

"Your airspeed should be about one twenty during the drop, no flaps," said Nile as he turned to look into the back of plane.

"All right, don't fall out," Rawley said as she scanned the valley ahead.

"Good plan!" Nile said as he leaned between the seats then plugged his helmet into a long communication cable. "You got it?"

"Yeah, I got it," she replied.

As the Caravan approached the valley, many thoughts raced through Rawley's head. Mostly she thought, Don't screw up.

As the aircraft passed one thousand feet, they were well inside the valley. It was relatively straight but definitely too tight for a larger aircraft. "You know, after this you'll be qualified to fly freight at home!" Nile said as he pushed the first pallet to the open rear door.

"Good retirement plan," Rawley said as she scanned ahead for smoke. "Less than six minutes. I'm taking it down."

Nile didn't respond, and Rawley kept her attention ahead and to the sides. "If you've done this, Nile, you can land on a carrier," Rawley said as the ground continued to rise and the cliffs closed in on both sides. "Yellow smoke, stand by."

"OK, get us to two fifty," said Nile as he looked forward at the camp and rising smoke.

Rawley could now see the camp. It was like a small tent city with sandbag-covered bunkers everywhere. "Three hundred, one hundred twenty knots," she said. "Two fifty, speed is good!" Rawley looked ahead then to the side. She could now see a line of men, vehicles, and a several horses staked out. The first pallet left the aircraft, followed closely by the second. Nile called "Clear!" over the com, and Rawley added power and eased back on the yoke.

The aircraft was climbing at a rate of about seven hundred feet per minute, and everything was normal.

Rawley set her climb rate to six hundred feet per minute, and Nile climbed back into his seat and buckled up. Just ahead Rawley could see the valley turning slightly to the right. She added forty-five degrees to her heading and continued the climb.

"That's a cargo drop. Let's hope they are all that benign," Nile said as he removed his helmet and vest.

Like many things in aviation, there were moments of intense excitement preceded or followed by long intervals of monotony. This evolution was exactly that, Rawley thought.

CHAPTER 40

———◆———

BEFORE RAWLEY LEVELED OFF, SHE could hear talk over the coalition radio frequency. It was obvious from the conversations that the QRF from kay jay had launched in support of an attack someplace. Within minutes she could hear Gil checking in with kay jay as he left Kabul.

"Something big happening," Nile said.

Rawley pushed the nose over when she reached ten thousand feet. They both listened as coordinating instructions went out from kay jay.

The attack was on a forward operating base between Kabul and kay jay. There were confirmed casualties, and the fight seemed to be ongoing. Rawley and Nile couldn't do anything but continue on to kay jay and listen to the action.

A minute later Nile and Rawley heard their call sign over the kay jay frequency. Nile selected the correct radio and responded. "Roger, this is Shaker O 5, go."

Rawley's first thought was to take over the com to communicate in a more military fashion, but she resisted.

"Shaker O 5, say fuel status."

Nile looked at the panel as he keyed his microphone. "OK, stand by."

"What's that look like to you?" he asked Rawley.

Rawley was already doing the math in her head. "We have seventeen hundred pounds, maybe five hours no reserve," she said.

"Classic Work, Shaker O 5, we have approximately five hours no reserve."

"Roger, O 5, proceed to following coordinates and stand by."

"They are not sending us into the fight," Nile said aloud but to himself.

Nile listened and copied the coordinates he was given then keyed them into the navigation computer. Rawley watched as a cyan line appeared on the moving map. She was already turning to intercept the track when Nile told her to turn to one zero zero.

Nile panned the map. "Chagar Raz," he said. "Crap, that's real bad-guy country. Someone's coming in."

"Coming in?" Rawley asked.

"Yeah, no doubt an asset coming in," Nile said.

Rawley could hear in his voice he was less than pleased. In contrast Rawley was suddenly excited.

"Talk about bad timing," Nile said as he looked ahead over the nose of the plane.

Soon the radio was alive, and kay jay was asking other aircraft the same questions. As planes reported in, most were too far or too low on fuel to assist. Nile knew Joe and Caleb would be prepped but held in reserve.

"Well, we are twenty minutes from the hold. Let's set up at four thousand," Nile said. "If we have to get this guy it means landing on a road. It will be kind of the same drill you went through with Caleb, except nobody around. Hopefully."

"The asset will check in with kay jay; they in turn will give us instructions. There are usually three suitable points within ten miles of each other."

Rawley was listening as she flew and Nile continued to talk. Maybe it calmed him down, Rawley thought.

"Shaker O 5, Classic Work."

Rawley keyed her mic and answered. "Skaker O 5."

"Roger, O 5, this is what we know. Your passenger is on the run in a technical with a prisoner headed to pick-up point Quebec two. No compromise reported. QRF more than thirty minutes out. Get close; be prepared to respond, over."

"Quebec Two, WILCO," Rawley said as she turned to Nile.

Nile was opening a manila envelope that held classified contingency plans for such an occasion.

"It must be the Kraken," Nile said as he looked over the plan for Quebec two.

"Kraken?" Rawley asked. "Code name, he was supposed to be in yesterday." Nile said as he keyed more numbers into the navigation computer. The cyan line moved, and Rawley responded. Rawley immediately thought back to the ledger entry in her room.

"Let's go to two thousand," Nile said as he reached for his ballistic flight helmet.

Rawley set the aircraft up for a shallow descent then put her own helmet back on. Nile was looking through his bag, checking his weapon. "Have you done this before?" Rawley asked.

"Yeah, it's my least-favorite thing," he said.

Rawley just smiled. "OK, so we're looking for a technical," she said as she steadied her gaze on a road far off to her left. Technical was a term used for any militarized civilian pickup truck or SUV. Some carried anti-aircraft guns or machine guns, and some just carried personnel. The carcasses of technicals littered Afghanistan from border to border.

"I have dust over here," she said, pointing toward the horizon.

Nile keyed his microphone. "Classic Work, Shaker O 5, we are in the hold for Quebec two, have a dust trail in sight."

"Roger, O 5, we had com and lost it five minutes ago. He may burn the vehicle for recognition. QRF now ten to fifteen out."

"Shaker O 5 standing by," Nile said as he continued to watch the dust. In another minute the vehicle became more visible. "Let's hope the big guns get here," he said, again talking to himself.

Rawley looked, but she could not see anyone in the back of the small truck. That alone was odd for Afghanistan, where nobody traveled alone. It had to be the asset, she thought, based on the location and timing. Without saying anything she turned toward the vehicle.

"What are you doing?" Nile asked.

She could tell from his voice he was stressed. Before Rawley could answer, she pointed beyond the speeding vehicle to another dust trail. "Crap! We have two more vehicles coming fast. Call it in," Rawley said. "They definitely look like they're in pursuit."

"Crap is right!" Nile said. "Classic Work, Shaker O 5, we have what appears to be a close-pursuit situation; advise!"

"O 5, roger, help is coming, but we need that asset alive. Use your best judgement. Also be advised you have two own-company gunships making best speed to your posit."

Rawley knew that had to be Gil and Brett, and she knew they would be listening.

"Gil, say your ETA," Rawley said over the same frequency.

"Sweetheart, we are five minutes out, coming hot and locked, darlin'!"

"We wanted excitement; here it comes," Rawley said. "They will overtake the lead vehicle in less than five minutes," she said. "I'm going to fly by and see what the reaction is from the guy being chased."

Nile slumped momentarily into his seat. "All right, you're the doctor, he said as he sat back up and tightened his shoulder straps.

Rawley knew she was visible to all three vehicles now, and she could clearly see the driver and maybe a passenger as she closed on the lead technical. As they flew by, the driver waved emphatically. "You wouldn't recognize this Kraken from here, would you?" she asked as she banked the Caravan around hard.

"Not quite a fighter jet, is it?" Nile said, trying to keep his eyes on the Kraken. Rawley just smiled. "No way! I can't tell if it's him," Nile said.

"He didn't shoot at us, and he's clearly being chased," Nile said. "What do you want to do? Remember, they don't give us medals," he said.

Rawley didn't answer as she lined up behind what she hoped was the Kraken.

"Landing, get ready," she said. She reached forward and pushed the DA button on the panel. Nile watched and didn't question her. He keyed his microphone one last time.

"All stations, Shaker O 5 landing to retrieve asset; request immediate assistance."

"Roger, O 5, we have your signal. Godspeed. Classic Work, standing by."

"Two minutes, darlin', we are coming down, but you have six not two vehicles in pursuit," Gil said. Rawley could hear in his voice he was thrilled to be involved. At that moment she was thrilled to have him there.

"Get here, Gil" was all Rawley said as her wheels cleared the racing truck by inches.

Stall speed for the Cessna Caravan was seventy miles per hour. She was doing just over one hundred and ten and estimated the truck was doing seventy-five to eighty. Even at this rate, she would be a quarter mile ahead of the truck when she stopped.

She had her right hand on the throttle and worked the yoke back and forth with her left hand, fighting a wicked crosswind to keep the big plane over the road. It was ironic, she thought, that it was Gil who had taught her to land in a strong crosswind using the worst-case scenario. A biplane. It was hands, feet, and eyes, he'd say. "You know the Afghan Caravans carry Hellfire missiles?" Rawley calmly said as the main wheels touched the ground.

Nile strained to look back through the fuselage side windows. "If you are trying to distract me so I feel less stressed, it's not working!" he said. Rawley touched down harder than she had intended and the big plane bounced once then met the dirt road again as Rawley slowed the aircraft using brakes and reverse thrust.

Before the plane came to a stop, Nile pulled his automatic pistol from its holster then he quickly climbed between the seats. He was pushing the door up when the small truck skidded to a stop. The driver emerged, and Nile yelled out to Rawley. "It's him!" Just as she had with Caleb, Rawley watched from side to side and ahead of the plane, never once looking back.

The driver ran to the passenger side of the truck and pulled out a man whose hands were bound. The Caravan filled with swirling dust and Nile reached for the prisoner's shoulders and pulled while the man known only to Nile as the Kraken pushed. Nile drug the man forward and began strapping him to the floor as the Kraken jumped into the plane.

"Go, go, go!" Nile yelled over the com.

"Go!" Rawley pushed the throttle forward, and the Caravan began to roll.

Over the radio she could hear Gil and Bart excitedly talking to each other as they engaged the vehicles pursuing the Kraken.

"Rawley, you have one truck coming at you!" Brett said.

Rawley was now at full power, and she could tell by the feel of the yoke they would soon leave the ground.

Nile was guarding the prisoner, and the Kraken was lying on the floor, shooting through the open cargo door at a technical that was racing next to them with two men who were shooting back.

Gils voice was calm but emphatic as he came over the radio. "I have no shot; they're too close!" "Take the damn shot Gil!" Rawley half yelled over the com. Her voice betrayed her anxiety as she fought the strong wind blowing directly across the road.

In Rawley's peripheral vision, she saw a Tractor fly by just a few feet off the ground then bank up and to the left. Just as she felt the wheels come off the ground, alarms rang out and smoke started coming from the cowling. Indicators on the panel were dropping, and she knew they would not be flying away.

Rawley cursed aloud as she pulled the power and pushed the nose back over. "We're hit!" she screamed to the men in the back.

"Shaker O 5 going down," Rawley transmitted once in the blind, then concentrated on the flying the plane.

She pulled the emergency fuel shutoff to the rear and pulled the flap lever to full. Even though they had little altitude, she was still doing close to eighty knots over the ground, and she knew she would have no reverse thrust to slow them once her wheels touched.

Thoughts raced through her head, but she stayed composed. Nile was between the seats looking forward but not talking. The Kraken continued to engage the enemy, and windows broke as small arms fire came through the fuselage.

"Hold on!" Rawley yelled out. The second the wheels touched the ground, she pushed hard on the brakes, and everyone was thrown forward. The nose went down, and dust was everywhere. Rawley used her rudder to straighten the plane as it had already weathervaned into the wind when the lifted off. Gil and Brett were talking over the radio non-stop, coordinating with each other as they came around to engage the enemy technical closest to the Caravan. The Kraken was struggling to return fire as the aircraft bounced through potholes on the dirt road.

On the radio Rawley heard a voice she knew as the kay jay communicator.

"All stations, QRF three to five minutes out."

"Help is coming!" Rawley yelled out. With the engine shut down, she could hear gunfire all around then the roar of the Tractors as they raced by.

As the Caravan finally came to a stop, the gunfire ceased, and it was suddenly quiet.

"Baby doll, you need to get clear of that bullet trap. We got bad guys all around; move your ass." It was the last voice she would hear on the radio. She hoped it was not the last voice she would ever hear.

Rawley reached for her bag then pushed her door open. Even in the duress of the moment, she remembered all the things she had forgot to do before ditching.

She took one quick glance to see that everyone was out before pulling the red handles to start the thermite ignition process then she jumped from the plane and ran toward the others who were huddled together less than forty feet away. As Rawley reached the group, gunfire again erupted, and she ducked down and pulled her rifle from its bag.

Their current location provided a small amount of cover, and all three were firing in different directions.

In an instant the gunfire was drowned out when the Caravan erupted into a roar flames. The heat was intense, and they all knew they needed to move.

CHAPTER 41

KEJAHN OP CENTER

———◆———

As Rawley, Nile, and the Kraken fought for their lives, an unarmed drone relayed the chaotic scene to the OP Center at kay jay.

Dave Mayer had left his office and was watching the scene along with everyone else in Intel. One man was tracking the QRF as they raced from one battle to assist the retrieval of the Kraken and his prisoner.

"They are about a minute out!" he said to nobody specific. As Mayer and the others watched the fight raged on, they could see Rawley and the others in a small perimeter, shooting. They could see Gil and Brett making pass after pass, providing cover, and they could see the Caravan fully engulfed in flames and a cloud of thick, black smoke.

"All stations, all stations, this is Cordial One. Be advised we are out of ammo. I repeat, we are out of ammo." Gil was straightforward over the radio. There was no humor, no drama. Just a message.

Gil and Brett had expended everything, and still they made pass after pass over the enemy positions, hoping to draw fire or distract.

"Everyone will be out of ammo in a minute," Mayer said. He walked forward to a communications panel and picked up a headset.

Before he could call the QRF, he heard them calling in. "Cowboy, this is Scepter. Clear out; we are coming in."

At that moment Mayer and everyone in the room could see two of the four Apaches assigned to the QRF come into view on the main screen as they approached the burning Caravan.

"Light 'em up, Scepter; your targets are thirty meters east and west of the fire," Brett said as he made his final pass and pulled up hard.

"They aren't safe yet," Mayer said. "Keep this feed in-house for the time being."

"Will do," Lerner said as he continued to watch the screens.

"Did we get anything from Rip at all?" Mayer asked.

Lerner didn't answer; he just shook his head to indicate a negative response.

"I hope we don't lose him," said Mayer as he pulled a seat from the closest desk and sat for the first time since he entered the room.

CHAPTER 42

———————•———————

As the shooting on the ground continued, it became obvious to Rawley the Tractors were out of ammunition. The Kraken's only weapon was an old AK47, and he had a single magazine left. Nile was to the Kraken's right, and he was watching the prisoner. Rawley was ten feet away from both of them using a large rock for cover.

"I've got two mags left," she said.

But before Nile or the Kraken could answer, more shots rang out, and the ground around them erupted. It was more indirect fire than anything, but they were pinned down, and eventually they would have nothing left to fight with.

As the first Tractor came in for what would be his last pass, he rocked his wings from side to side then pulled up abruptly and departed, inverted to the west. An instant later the second Tractor made a low pass and flew straight out and up. As the noise from the Tractors turbine engine died, it was replaced with the familiar chopping noise of a helicopter. Two helicopters, in fact. Nile looked toward the noise then let out a heavy sigh of relief. At that moment the Kraken yelled for smoke.

Nile grabbed his bag and tossed it toward Rip. Even with the noise and incoming gunfire, Rawley froze. That voice. She ducked down and turned back toward Nile and the others.

Nile was now on a knee, firing his weapon, and the Kraken had his back to her as he tossed a green smoke downwind and about twenty feet away.

For a second Rawley was confused and distracted. Suddenly the ground around her came alive, and she turned back to her field of fire and let go a short burst of automatic gunfire. The insurgents were getting desperate now; a few tried to get closer to the perimeter but were gunned down. Everyone knew who came with the helicopters, and they knew they needed to act fast and depart if they hoped to get their friend back. As the Apaches came in, one was low and one was high on each side of the perimeter.

The ground on both sides of their position came alive as the Apaches opened fire. Shrapnel from exploding rocks went everywhere. Nile rolled to the ground, and the Kraken continued to fire. Rawley saw four insurgents rise and begin running in her direction. "Help here!" she yelled out. Nile turned toward her and opened fire.

"Out of ammo!" the Kraken yelled, and again Rawley heard the voice. Without turning she pulled her mother's Colt Commander and tossed it toward the Kraken, then continued to return fire.

By now the first two helicopters had pinpointed the insurgents, and they opened fire with rockets and twenty-millimeter canons. The noise level went up, and the dust cloud thickened. Rawley barely noticed the heat or smoke from the burning Caravan. By now the interior of the plane glowed red and yellow, and a thick cloud of black smoke was carried by the wind. Each time a helicopter made a pass, the smoke swirled and momentarily changed directions until the wind once again took over.

The insurgent gunfire finally subsided as two MH60 Blackhawks touched down for mere seconds. Then as quickly as they had arrived, they were gone in a deafening roar. In seconds Rawley and the others were surrounded by Navy SEALs and other members of the elite QRF.

While the SEALs made a perimeter around the group, two men took control of the prisoner and two Air Force PJs, or paramedics, quickly went between the Kraken, Nile, and Rawley, checking to see if they had been wounded. Rawley said she had not been injured, but a PJ whose face could not be seen behind his black helmet visor reached for her weapon then coaxed her to the ground.

Without a word, he injected her leg with morphine then cut and ripped the leg of her flight suit open. "Are you wearing underwear?" he asked over the noise.

Several men looked in their direction and laughed.

Rawley looked down and saw her leg covered in blood. She suddenly felt lightheaded but aware. Men were screaming orders and again the deafening roar of a large helicopter approached. This time it was it was the largest of the special forces helicopters, an MH53 Pavelow.

"Is she stable?" someone asked.

Rawley became more lightheaded as helicopters raced by and sporadic gunfire continued to ring out in all directions. Rawley and the others were now engulfed by smoke and dust.

"Define stable. She's about an eight crazy, I'd say, but good to go!" the PJ said as he waved off a stretcher. Instead he threw Rawley over his shoulder and raced to the rear of the waiting MH53. The ramp was down and a crewman who was tethered to the helicopter emphatically waved them all aboard.

The second Rawley's butt touched the deck, she felt like she was in a violent earthquake. The Helo deck shook and vibrated, and the engine noise increased a hundredfold. In an instant the nose of the big helicopter pitched down as they accelerated. Just as the helicopter rotated and surged forward, a crewman manning a minigun on the ramp and two miniguns in the front of the helicopter opened fire. Rawley was momentarily distracted and mesmerized by the distinctive buzzing sound as flames shot out from the spinning barrels.

The PJ who had brought her aboard continued to attend to her wound, then he pulled her sleeve back and inserted an IV into her hand. "Just saline," he said. "It's a flesh wound, by the way, no bone issues. Nothing to fret about."

Several operators, along with Nile and the Kraken, had followed her aboard the helicopter. Rawley leaned back against the padded interior and looked around. She was groggy but far from incoherent. The PJ was trying everything to engage her in conversation, and all she could do was stare at the man now sitting directly across from her. He was wearing traditional Afghan clothing from head to toe, and his thick, dark beard and long hair looked as if it had not been washed in weeks.

He was wearing a flight helmet now, and the shaded visor was down. As she watched she could tell he was clearly talking to someone. His facial expressions and gestures made her think he was telling a story. A debriefing maybe.

She knew he was the Kraken, and she was now very sure he was the man in the photo in Alaska. As she stared, the man behind the visor looked at her then gave her a thumbs-up.

The PJ was changing her bandage, and she suddenly snapped from her trance. "Thank you," she yelled as she touched his shoulder. "You guys are freaking awesome!"

The PJ was smiling now as he continued to wipe blood and dirt off her leg.

"You'll be dancing soon, but I'd rule out Miss America. You're going to have a nasty scar," he said, trying to keep things light.

Rawley looked at her leg then around the helo then she breathed in and exhaled hard.

She had only been here two weeks, and she had destroyed one air-craft, killed a few insurgents, and got wounded.

Maybe Greg was right, she thought. I do need to pace myself. Now the Kraken was also laying back. He was no longer talking, his eyes were closed, and his arms were crossed on his chest. Rawley saw the familiar black handle of her mother's Colt sticking out of his coat pocket. If she could reach it, maybe she could shoot him, she thought.

In the ass would be appropriate, she imagined. Verlie would approve of that.

The PJ was persistent if nothing else. "You know we watched that whole scene coming in," he said, in a voice loud enough to be heard over the roaring turbines.

"Watched?" Rawley asked.

"Yeah, there was a drone overhead the whole time. We were rooting for you guys! Who taught you to shoot like that? You're a real operator!"

Rawley looked at him for a minute and smiled. If there was a drone, her father must know or may have watched everything. That would mean her mother must also know.

"Hey. You there?" the PJ said as he snapped his fingers in front of her face.

"Yeah, sorry, I lived with a lot of Marines, and they all taught me to shoot and move. It's all we would do when we weren't drinking and having sex."

The medic's mouth fell open, and he sat back. That wasn't really what he thought he'd hear. He just nodded. "Cool," he said, then happily for Rawley, the conversation was over.

CHAPTER 43

FORWARD OPERATING BASE, KEJAHN

———◆———

DAVE MAYER SAT AT HIS desk, staring at his phone. He had spent fifteen minutes on the radio with Rip, so he knew Rawley's wound was minor.

He sat another twenty minutes, thinking about what he had witnessed before he picked up the phone and called Bud. The conversation between Bud and Mayer was atypically short; he just wanted to let Bud know his daughter was safe and that he was happy he wasn't delivering bad news. Secretly Mayer hoped she would now go home or just on to something else. He knew after watching the firefight he never wanted to tell an old friend his child was dead.

He thought less of it, but it was the same with Rip McGuin. Mayer knew his entire family, and this was the first close call he had experienced involving Rip. At least in Rip's case his work here was finished. He had been compromised, so there would be no going back in the field doing undercover work.

Dave sat for a moment staring at the screens when the silence was interrupted by his phone.

"Dave, I heard you have some news." It was Brick Wellen at Langley.

"The PI weapon sounds credible," Mayer said.

"No, we don't think so here," Brick said. "We think it's a weapon that was lost off Whidbey Island in Washington State."

There was a pause as Mayer gathered his thoughts. "Brick, that weapon was picked up, I thought," Mayer said as he leaned back in his chair.

"No, it was just reported found, and it wasn't as big as we all believed. It went in the sound, and there has been some speculation that it could be viable," Wellen said.

"The Philippine weapon, if it's even in the Philippines, would be trash by now. There would be some radiation or something. We just don't think it's worth running around searching for."

Wellen stopped, and Mayer sat quiet for a second.

"Brick, we gather information, and we piece together clues. Right here, right now. That's what we do."

Wellen could tell Mayer was upset, and he was in no mood for a lecture.

"Dave, stop! Stop! You have some info, act on it. OK? I'll give you some latitude here."

Mayer listened and exhaled. He knew that meant sending an unsupported team or person into the field on what might be nothing more than a vacation, or as he called it, a junket.

"All right," Mayer said. "I have a guy. I'll send him over and look into it. Talk later."

With that Mayer hung up the phone then dialed another number. "Are they back yet? OK, let me know," he said, then again hung up the phone and leaned back in his chair, staring at the walls and thinking.

After a few minutes, Mayer poured himself a drink, just as he often did while trying to solve a problem. Just the little information he heard from Rip convinced him the Philippines lead was worth chasing down.

His phone rang, and again he could see it was Wellen. "Yeah, Brick."

"We watched that feed from the extract, and we want that female pilot to move to ground. Just letting you know," Wellen said.

Mayer cut him off. "She's wounded, so I don't know what her future is."

"Well, send her to Langley as soon as she can travel, will you? We want to talk to her. We need a woman like that on a go team we are putting together. Send her!" As he often did, Brick abruptly ended his thought and hung up the phone.

Mayer picked up the scotch and made his drink a double. Here in this capacity, he saw firsthand the effects of war and terror, and he was expected to make the right decisions every day. Decisions that affected the lives of several people and the war effort. To men like Wellen, who never left the comfort and safety of their offices, the war on terror and other field operations were just a game played by anonymous role payers. To Wellen, people were pawns, no matter who they were or where they fell out in the government-service food chain.

Mayer took a long drink then called Bud's number again. "Sorry to bother, but I have a proposal for you," he said.

Mayer told Bud about his call from Brick Wellen, and then he broached an idea he had that would take Rawley out of Afghanistan and out of circulation for a few weeks. Bud listened and agreed to go along. The call ended with Mayer and Bud making a plan to get together soon for something fun.

When Mayer hung up, he was relieved and content. His idea would kill two birds with one stone, he thought.

CHAPTER 44

———◆———

As the helicopters in the QRF approached kay jay, Rawley and several
others were asleep or in a meditative state. She could tell they were landing, but it was like a dream.

The morphine had kicked in, and she felt no pain. The ramp was
down, and as Rawley looked aft across the open ramp, she could see
familiar landmarks as they descended. Soon there was a bump, and the
helo settled into a roll as they taxied to the hangar.

"You're gonna hate this, I'm sure," the PJ said as he stood up. "We
need to roll you down to the clinic in a wheelchair or carry you on a
stretcher."

Rawley was shaking her head even as he spoke. "No way," she said. "I
can walk; I'm walking." She was adamant.

"Suit yourself," the PJ said as he began gathering his gear.

"I have your stuff, Rawley," Nile said as he jumped to his feet.

"I'll walk her to the dispensary," Rip said, his back to Rawley.

Rawley looked up at Rip and didn't say anything. "Thanks, Nile. I'll
see you for dinner."

When the helo came to a stop, Rawley walked off the ramp and
headed to the closest hangar. She looked a mess with her bloodied, ban-
daged leg and torn flight suit. She had her Gentex flight helmet in one
hand and her rifle in the other.

"Can I take your helmet or weapon?" Nile asked.

"No, I may need them," she said as she walked away without looking back. A minute later she heard his voice again.

"Hey, Fly Girl, how many Marines are we talking about? Several? A few? Just wondering how many I need to kill is all."

Rawley stopped but didn't turn around. "You have my forty-five. I'd like it back."

"Yeah, right, like I'm going to give you another weapon right now." Rip stopped a few feet behind her.

After taking a deep breath, Rawley turned around, and they looked at each other. Even with his long hair, thick beard, and heavy clothes, she now knew it was really him. She could see it in his eyes and hear it in his voice.

"Why? Why did you do that to me?" Rawley asked. Her voice was pained.

Rip said nothing; he just clenched his teeth and raised his hands. "You had a dream. I was already hired," he said. "I just thought the last thing you needed was a distraction."

By now Rawley was regretting her decision to walk. Her leg hurt, her head hurt, and her heart was aching. She was looking at the man who had caused her pain and confusion for almost eight years. Rip was still silent and looking at her when Rawley turned to walk away. Suddenly she stopped again. "Did my father know that I might see you here?" she asked.

"No way. He doesn't know I'm here or what I do. Nobody does," Rip said, with a tone of sincerity.

"Your parents?" asked Rawley.

"Yeah, they know, but they are both retired from the agency," he said.

Rawley's head dropped. "How can people be so cruel?" she said, more as a statement than a question.

Rawley again started walking toward the dispensary when a golf cart pulled up.

"You need to get some medical help right now." It was the PJ who had taken care of her wound.

Rawley looked back at Rip as they drove away. "You know that guy?" the PJ asked. "My name is Jim, by the way." He held out his hand.

"He's someone I used to know," she said, without offering her name or shaking his hand.

"Stop, Jim, go back," Rawley said as she turned her head to see if Rip was still there. Jim said nothing as he turned the golf cart around. Rip had not moved from where she left him.

"Why didn't you contact me later?" Rawley asked as they came to a stop. "You had to know I was finished with school and made it to where I wanted to be."

Rip looked at her and shook his head. "Look," he said. "I did sail, just like I said I would, but I was working. My first assignment was two years out of the country. After that I did some military training, and I've been here almost nonstop for the past four years." Rip paused and looked at the ground. "I guess it just seemed easier to leave you to your life."

"Easier?" Rawley said. "My father said that when I asked why he duped me for so many years about his life. Give me my gun," she said as she held out her hand. Rip dropped the magazine and cleared the chamber before handing Rawley the 45 automatic.

"OK, Jim, let's go." She said.

As Rip turned to walk away, he saw Dave Mayer coming toward him from the hangar. Then he stopped and turned around to watch Rawley disappear while waiting for Mayer.

"Welcome back!" Mayer said, smiling. "That was some ordeal, was it not!"

Rip was smiling but less than jovial.

"What's wrong?" Mayer asked.

"Women, or at least that one, anyway," said Rip.

"I know she just saved your life and all, but hell, you just met her," Mayer said.

Rip shook his head. "No, you don't understand. We have a history."

"Aw. How far back?" Mayer asked. "Not here?"

"No," Rip said. "College, I just let it go and kind of vanished."

"Until today you mean?" Mayer said as watched the gold cart carrying Rawley disappear into a hanger. "That's a hell of way to get back together."

"Tell me about it," said Rip.

"Well, this is a real small world, Rip," said Mayer. "I flew with her father in the Navy, and I was overseas with your parents when you were in middle school."

Rip threw his head back. "No way."

"Way!" Mayer said. "And the plot's about to thicken."

"How so?" Rip asked.

"No need to discuss it here. How bad is she hurt?" Mayer asked.

"Her?" Rip scoffed. "The only reason she in medical right now is because she's that PJ's current wet dream and he won't leave her alone. She's tougher than we are."

"Good! Good! Glad to hear it," Mayer said as he reached to put his arm on Rip's shoulder.

"Listen, Rip, you need to get cleaned up. You really stink. Seriously, you stink."

Rip was smiling. "Yeah, I know."

Mayer started to walk away. "You're done here, by the way," he said. "Burn the clothes, get a haircut and a shave, pack your shit. Let's debrief, then I'll tell you my new plan! See you for dinner, say, seven."

Mayer was leaving, and Rip was still standing in the same place she had left him. He felt confused, and that was a new feeling for him, and his life working undercover in Afghanistan was over, and that was something else he had not anticipated.

CHAPTER 45

---◆---

DINNER WITH DAVE MAYER USUALLY meant dining in his office, and tonight was no exception. When Rip arrived at Mayer's office, he found Jack Lerner from Intel and Dave already seated at the table, drinking scotch. The mood seemed almost festive.

"What's the occasion?" Rip asked as he pulled up a chair.

"Let's call it your going-away party, shall we?" Mayer said as he handed Rip a drink. "One ice cube and a shot of Macallan Scotch Whisky. To you, my friend." Mayer raised his glass. "Cheers."

"Macallan Scotch? Wow, isn't that stuff expensive?" Rip asked as he took a sip.

"Sixteen thousand for that bottle, to be exact," Mayer said. "An inappropriate gift from an Afghan friend. We're just getting rid of the evidence."

Rip raised his glass and looked at it. "God bless graft and corruption," he said. "I suspect this will be my first and last shot of this fine whisky!"

"Rip, let's cut to the chase," Mayer said. "Langley disagrees with your assessment and thoughts on the Philippine weapon. They think the chatter is about a bomb lost off Whidbey Island in the late fifties."

"I've looked at these nuke losses online," Rip said. "That one was actually lost in deep water offshore, wasn't it?" He sipped his drink.

"A PBM carrying the nuclear mine made a precautionary landing about a hundred miles west of the Washington-Oregon border," said Lerner. "That part's true."

"They knew they would be coming back into Whidbey with a questionable aircraft, so they made the decision to dump the mine offshore rather than risk a crash with it onboard. That's the story that was released. What really happened was the cradle malfunctioned in what would turn out to be a cascading series of errors and bad luck."

Rip and Mayer listened as Lerner read the information from a classified brief he pulled up.

"They got the plane in the air, and about twenty miles from Whidbey—this part is disputed—the mine casing got loose and dropped into Puget Sound. They did the best they could to pinpoint their location, but the only thing they knew for certain was they were over water."

Lerner turned a page on his notepad. "It was dark, overcast, with light rain, and they still weren't sure the plane would make NAS Whidbey. They decided to return to base immediately."

Lerner went on. "The entire situation was compounded by communication issues, meaning they could not notify anyone until after they landed."

"Wow," Rip said.

Mayer sipped his drink then leaned back. "What else?"

"So, let's see." Lerner continued. "First they released to the public that it was jettisoned one hundred miles offshore in extremely deep water, then they said it was not actually armed with the nuclear charge."

"This report contradicts all that, of course. They did attempt a discreet search in the stretch of water known as the Strait of Georgia but failed to turn up anything."

"OK," Mayer said. "Moving on. Langley thinks some recent diving activity in that area is an indicator that they are after that weapon. It's relatively small and could be moved around easy enough if it were located.

"Rip, you say it's the one in the Philippines. I have been given the go-ahead to at least look into that possibility. I don't want to send in the Marines and have the Internet filled with more stories of old lost nuclear weapons abandoned by Uncle Sam."

Mayer paused long enough to take another drink when there was a knock at the door.

"Come in!" Mayer said as he rotated in his seat.

"Dinner, sir."

"OK, set it up. I'll make a head call."

When Mayer returned he picked up where he left off. "I'm sending you and one other person to snoop around," Mayer said.

"Who's going?" Rip asked as he filled his plate.

"A military pilot with enough details to validate the wreckage. That is, of course, if you find it." Mayer pushed his plate away and refilled his glass.

Rip was nodding his approval of the plan. "Who's the pilot?"

Mayer looked at Lerner. "We don't know yet. You leave as soon as we can get a plane in here. We'd like to sweat your guy a little more and see what we might find. Revisit your intel, stuff like that."

"Use the time to relax; you deserve it. Maybe by then Langley will verify their lead or drop it."

At that same moment in the common dining area, Rawley, Joe, and Caleb were enjoying their dinner while listening to Nile recount every detail of the day's events.

"It's hard to believe all that happened in a single day," Nile said. He was animated and clearly enjoyed the spotlight.

Rawley said little but smiled and laughed when it was appropriate. "I feel bad about the Caravan," she finally said.

"A Twin Otter is coming in from Kandahar," said Joe. "I heard it will be here in the morning."

"Great!" Caleb said. "Bigger and slower—just what we need!"

"I flew one in Africa for two years," Nile said. "It's a slug; there's no doubt about that."

"Good, you can own it," said Caleb.

Rawley looked at Caleb across the table and decided she really didn't like him at all.

"How's the leg?" Joe asked.

"A flesh wound," Rawley said. "They think it was a ricochet or maybe a flying rock. They told me it's not a typical bullet wound."

"You're lucky," Nile said.

As usual Caleb said nothing unless it was a snide or sarcastic remark. And as usual he sat in his corner, watching people in the room.

"What are you looking for Caleb?" Rawley asked.

"I'm waiting for one of our local friends to go nuts and open fire; that's what I'm looking for."

Nile and Joe looked at Rawley and then they all slowly turned to look into the dining area. Rawley pushed her chair back, then as she stood up to leave, Greg walked in.

"You need to call your dad, if you will," he said as he approached Rawley and the others.

"We just got an urgent tasker, no details but it involves you," he said.

"What's up?" Rawley asked.

Greg just shrugged as he took a seat at the table. "No clue, it came in from Langley through your father. It sounds classified." He looked at the others.

"OK," she said. "I'll give him a call." With that, she took one last slow look around the dining hall, specifically at the locals, then she walked out.

As soon as she got back to her to her room Rawley dialed Gil's number. She was a bit surprised when he answered on the first ring. "I wanted to thank you for saving my life." She said. "Well let's call it even since you saved me first sweetheart." Rawley smiled. "I didn't even get a shot off at Laskar you were out of there so fast but thank you." "I mean when you didn't send me home." Gil said. Then there was a short silence. "Let's get together when you get back and have a few drinks to being alive!" "You know I'm leaving?" She asked. "Your pop filled me in." Rawley just shook her head. "OK" Rawley added. "My best to Brett, I guess I'll call dad and find out what everyone apparently knows already." Before hanging up

Gil brought up some information he had heard about the Air Tractors and a told Rawley about a potential job in Africa teaching others how to fly it.

It would be an opportunity for Gil to move on to a relatively safer environment where he could teach pilots the ins and outs of the aircraft. Rawley loved the idea, and she already knew her father would go along.

Before calling Bud, Rawley stretched out on the bed and stared at the ceiling. She also looked at the ledger on the dresser that held the signature of the Kraken. Then she looked at her watch and calculated the time in Montana. She would take a nap, she thought, before calling home. A minute later she was asleep.

———◆———

CHAPTER 46

INTERROGATORS SPENT TWENTY-FOUR HOURS WORKING on the prisoner Rip had brought in. The information they gained was added to what Rip had reported, and analysts began to develop a theory about the possibility of a lost nuclear weapon being found.

Mayer read the report then called for Rip and Lerner to join him for a debrief.

When Rip and Lerner walked into Mayer's office, they could already see the bulleted lists of details on the screens.

Rip had been through countless debriefs and rehash sessions of the intel he had gathered. He knew it was just a matter of giving everything a sanity check before anything was placed in motion.

"Screen three," Mayer said, pointing to the wall. On the screen was a simple list of discoveries and assumptions.

"Skip to line four," Mayer said. "First a cellular intercept. We have two guys discussing the possibility of a 'big' weapon coming on the market. That weapon is what they have been 'waiting so long for'—a quote. We assume nuke, but nobody is actually saying that." Mayer stopped talking, and Rip and Lerner turned to look at him.

"Why not chem bio?" Mayer asked.

"More chemical weapons have been lost, abandoned, or falsely reported destroyed than any weapon in history." Lerner pointed at the screen. "Line seven—Great flash, or what we translated to mean 'a great flash'—came from the guy we are sweating downstairs."

"OK." Mayer continued. "Let's talk location." Again, he stopped. "The word 'Cuyo' was recorded in two conversations." He pointed at the screen. "A location?"

"Sersi made a comment about trading the help for new models," Rip said. "Everyone in his home is from the Philippines, Pakistan, or Turkey. I'm thinking with Southeast Asia in the conversation, it has to be the PI." Rip stopped, and Lerner looked at Mayer but said nothing.

"Well." Mayer was looking at the screen. "That's pretty damn thin, Rip. What else do we have on the location, Jack?"

Lerner turned his chair and pointed back to the screen then picked up another folder and turned a few pages. "We looked at every 'Cuyo' in the world and came up with several, but the most logical is Cuyo Palawan in the Philippines. The island of Cuyo is a few hundred miles south of the rhumb line track from Bihn Thuy, Vietnam, to Guam, but the lost C-130 would have been fighting a major storm north of their route from the moment they left the ground." Lerner turned another page.

"That plane had a nonstop range of twenty-three hundred miles without supplemental fuel. Bihn Thuy to their destination at Anderson Air Force Base in Guam is two thousand two hundred and ninety-five miles as the crow flies."

"There's no record of how the plane was configured, but we have to assume drop tanks or a planned but undocumented fuel stop at Subic Bay." Lerner looked up from his notes.

"It's academic now. We know they never stopped or contacted Subic, and it is highly unlikely they would have chosen a track to the north of Manila." Lerner closed his notes, and all three looked back at the brief on the screen.

"Line ten. Rip's guy said poison," Mayer interrupted. "Everyone would be poisoned, or something to that effect. Poison, chem bio again." Lerner was shaking his head while Mayer spoke.

"The weapon that plane was carrying was a very low yield and moderately dirty. It was designed to be diver delivered to a port or shipping area to sink or heavily damage anything in a one- to two-mile radius and temporarily deny access to an area for up to six months or more. When you detonate a weapon like that underwater, there are many factors that multiply the impact of fallout but limit the scope of the damage." Lerner paused to look at his notes.

"Hiroshima and Nagasaki experienced maximum destruction but little in the way of long-term fallout and radiation because the detonation happened high above both cities. The mushroom cloud carried the majority of the bad stuff up and away." Lerner stopped, then turned to face Mayer.

"The destructive capability and intended use of the SADAM is well documented in declassified notes on the Internet, and it's been featured in several TV documentaries. Detonated on the ground, it has a kill radius of maybe two or three miles and then a fallout dissipation rate that's a fraction of the Japan bombs." Lerner paused.

"All these lost weapons are close to sixty years old," Lerner added. "Most if not all were lost in the ocean. Who knows what state they are in now."

"It hasn't been detected yet, so in all likelihood it's intact. This thing isn't Armageddon, but it is the perfect terror tool. It's small." Mayer was talking while looking at the screen for something he might have missed.

Lerner and Rip looked up to see what Mayer might be looking at.

"Let's say you can't initiate the firing sequence," Rip said. "How dangerous is it if the core is breached? I mean, like you said, it's almost sixty years old, and it may have been in the water or exposed to weather the whole time it's been lost." Rip looked at Lerner for an answer.

"You could use another charge to pop it open in an inopportune place, and you would still have a poison cloud with a moderate kill or contamination radius," Lerner said as he once again paged through his notes.

"There are several incidents of low-order detonations during testing of nukes where the firing mechanism worked but the chain reaction failed. There can be serious radioactive fallout in a small area," said Lerner.

Mayer pushed his chair back then folded his hands behind his head.

"Give him the package," he said to Lerner. Mayer again started talking as Rip pulled the contents from the envelope he was given.

"Rip, when the plane arrives, it will have a lot of equipment you might need. Anything else you need will come from Sherman Craig's office at Langley. You need logistics support, money, muscle, whatever, you contact him first."

Rip nodded his understanding.

"Sherman will keep me posted," Mayer said.

"If you find the thing, contact Sherman; he'll get the right response team in there fast," Mayer added. "The plane has all the kit you'll need to detect radiation and some TLDs for your team."

"Wear them. And lead-lined underwear if you ever hope to have kids," Lerner added.

TLDs were small devices used by X-ray technicians and personnel assigned to jobs where they might be in contact with radiation. They recorded radiation exposure as a precautionary measure to keep workers safe.

The room was momentarily quiet as Rip thumbed through the envelope. He could see black-and-white photos of a very old Air Force C-130 and posed photos of men in Air Force and Marine Corps uniforms, along with a list of names.

"Twenty-six men who didn't come home," Rip said.

Lerner spoke up. "It's just possible the crash was found, or even salvaged, but improperly documented. It's happened more than once with mass casualties in remote areas."

"We're talking about this crash site like the plane is intact," said Rip. "I haven't seen many wrecks, but I'm thinking it's spread out all over if it impacted the water."

Mayer and Lerner just shrugged.

"I did reach out to JPAC in Hawaii to see if any name on that list has been repatriated. But," Lerner said, "I have not heard back yet." JPAC, or the Joint POW/MIA Accounting Center, housed a forensic laboratory whose sole mission was to identify and bring home the remains of POWs and others listed as missing in action due to combat or other causes.

Anytime remains were found and suspected of being those of a member of the US Armed Forces, a small task unit from the JPAC would be dispatched to retrieve and protect the remains as well as gather any information that might assist in the identification of those service members who were found. It was often a daunting task but one taken very seriously by those who provided the service.

"We still have sixteen hundred servicemen unaccounted for in that theater from the Vietnam War and another thousand found but unidentified. There are three JPAC dets besides Hawaii working the leads. So, I don't expect an answer before you depart," Lerner said as he looked back at the screen, then again at a notebook he carried.

"What about the pilot going with me?" Rip asked as he stood up.

"They'll be on the plane," Mayer said as he reached for Rip's hand. "Good hunting, son."

CHAPTER 47

THE SUN WAS BARELY UP when Rawley walked to the dining area. There were only a few people sitting around, and most of them had just come off a shift.

Rawley got a cup of coffee and made her way to the usual corner table. Just as she sat down, Nile walked through the door then bypassed the coffee and came straight to where she was sitting. Rawley noticed that he looked tired.

"You're up early," he said as he sat down. As Nile bent forward, Rawley noticed he had a small-frame automatic pistol in a holster on his belt. Perhaps that was new, or she hadn't noticed it before.

"You too," she said. "Up early, I mean."

"Yeah, I couldn't sleep," Nile said as he slumped into his chair. "My brain was too active."

Rawley smiled. "Adrenaline," she said as she sipped her coffee.

"What?" Nile asked.

"Adrenaline. We both had enough in our blood to run a marathon."

"I guess you're right. That was some deal, wasn't it?" Nile said. Rawley just nodded. The truth was she had also been awake most of the night thinking about what had transpired, and she could not help but think about what she might have done differently or better.

She wondered what Gil might have done if he would have suffered the same fate. Could she have done anything else while taking off that might have let them fly away?

"I'm going away for a little while," she said as she watched more people come and some leave the dining room.

"Going where?" Nile asked.

"I'm going to the Philippines for some company business. It will give me a chance to heal, I guess."

Nile nodded as he also watched the others in the room come and go.

"What are you watching?" she asked?

Nile laughed. "I won't lie," he said. "I'm really on edge."

"Yeah, I can see that," Rawley said as she looked down at Nile's lap. "Did you just start carrying that?"

Nile put his hand on the weapon. "No, I carried it for weeks when I first got here, then I started leaving it in my room, then yesterday happened and Caleb had to spout off...I guess I'm thinking too much," he said.

Rawley continued to look at him as she spoke. "Don't overthink it. Do whatever makes you feel safe," she said. Then she reached down and pulled the right side of her shirt up. There in her waistband was her mother's Colt Commander. Nile laughed, and Rawley smiled.

"I guess you will be flying the Otter with Brett," she said. "He's bringing it from Kandahar this afternoon."

Nile nodded and relaxed back into his seat.

"I feel a little bad," Rawley said. "When I heard he would be flying the Tractor, my first thought was that he was a rotary guy. I guess he showed me yesterday that he can do anything." Rawley's voice trailed off as the doors opened and the SEALs came into the room. The volume in the dining area instantly went up as they made their way to the food line.

"We were in Africa together when Brett first got out of the Navy," Nile said. "We were flying for a State Department–funded famine-relief group. It was before this job came along." Nile relaxed as he spoke. "We were flying an Otter and a DC4 that had at least one engine shut down on every flight." Nile was shaking his head as he remembered.

"We never got shot at, but every flight had some element of terror. If wasn't mechanical issues, it was weather. Or we were moving livestock, and they were loose in the plane, changing our CG constantly." Nile stopped for a second then continued. "Brett was steady as a rock through it all." Nile stopped talking, but it was obvious he was remembering.

"You are full of surprises," Rawley said. "I honestly had no idea. I went from college to the Navy. I didn't really think about how on edge real bush flying is. My dad made it seem romantic and fun and like one big adventure."

Nile was shaking his head. "Old planes, underfunded maintenance, drunks, druggies, you name it," Nile said. "You see it all in Africa and South America. This place is heaven for guys like me. I tried flying a corporate jet for a while, but that just killed me, it was so dull.

"Speaking of surprises," Nile said as he turned toward Rawley. "What's the deal with you and the Kraken? Just curious of course, unless you don't want to talk about it."

Before he could finish, Rawley cut him off. "No, I don't want to talk about it." she said as she finished her coffee. "Nile," Rawley said, then paused. "This place really will kill you if you aren't careful."

"I have six thousand hours in kites that should have been in museums," said Nile. "I've been flying here for two years. Yesterday was the first crash or actual hot anything I've ever been involved in here. I'll take my chances for a little while longer."

As the SEALs fanned out in the dining room, several waved at Rawley. Then two came to the table and asked to sit down. "You mind?" the first guy asked as he walked up.

"Be my guest," Rawley said as she slid her own chair back so Nile could leave. "I'll see you before you go, hopefully," he said.

"Where are you headed?" one of the SEALs asked.

"Out of here for a few weeks, I guess." That was all Rawley offered.

"That was some shit, wasn't it? You ever been in anything like that before?" the second SEAL asked. Then he looked around the table at her legs. "How's the wound?"

"No," Rawley said, shaking her head. "I have never seen anything like that, and the leg is fine. Just a flesh wound, really."

"Well, you kicked ass! Way to go!" he said as he started eating.

"I have to pack, so enjoy your breakfast." "Thanks for getting there." Rawley said as she stood to leave.

The two SEALs nodded but didn't get up. Then they looked at each other and shrugged. As Rawley walked away, the Air Force PJ who attended to her wound passed her on the way to the table.

"She's kind of icy, isn't she?" he said aloud, watching her cross the room. The SEALs laughed. "She is definitely a manhater," said one.

"She has a connection to the Kraken, I don't know what it is, but they have something going on." the PJ said as he turned his attention to breakfast.

"That dude was in my training class." one of the SEALs offered, without looking up. "I'll get the word from him."

"Really?" the PJ said. "I didn't know he was a team guy."

"Technically he's not; he was a civilian when he went through," the SEAL said. "The agency has been sending guys through for years, but only a few make it all the way. He's a good mug."

"Why Kraken?" the PJ asked. Both SEALs laughed.

"We were in the dive tower doing night knot tying, and some cat that didn't graduate got tangled up. Rip was on his way up and out of breath, but he stopped to help the guy. Doc Young said he looked like a friggin Kraken the way his arms were flailing as he swam to the surface. It just kind of stuck," the SEAL said. Everyone laughed.

As Rawley walked to her room, she passed Greg. "Your plane will be in around noon," he said. Then he offered her his hand. "That was short and sweet. But I hear you're coming right back, so I'll be here."

"Thanks, Greg, be safe," she said. As Rawley walked into her room, her phone was ringing. She looked and saw it was Susan Williams. Rawley sat on the bed and talked for nearly thirty minutes without saying anything specific. Susan filled her in on the latest gossip and goings on at the Lagopus. She said Verlie had a room for her anytime she wanted to come back.

After Susan hung up, Rawley looked at her watch. She wished it was noon. When her father first told her she was leaving, she was conflicted. She had not seen Rip for nearly eight years. Then to meet under such incredulous circumstances was almost beyond comprehension.

Now he had been aware she was at kay jay for thirty-two hours and fifteen minutes, and he had not once tried to contact her. She would leave without seeing him, she decided. It was a decision she was making, and she was content with that.

CHAPTER 48

RAWLEY WALKED INTO THE HANGAR, and she could see the PC12 was gone. That meant Caleb and Joe were also gone. Just outside the hangar doors, she saw the twin Otter with a few men, including Brett, standing nearby.

As she approached the aircraft, Rawley heard the unmistakable roar of a jet slowing to a stop. That had to be her ride, she thought. Just before stepping outside, Rawley took another look around the hangar, then she walked to Brett.

"I owe you many, many beers, my friend!" she said as she hugged him. "You guys were a happy sight."

"Thank God we made it!" Brett said. "How's the leg?"

She reached down and touched the area of the wound. "Just a good story now, and nothing else. How's Gil?" she asked. "Is he happy to be going to Africa?"

"Oh, who knows," Brett said, laughing. "He found out he can't walk around armed, so he's having second thoughts. By the way," Brett said as he walked toward some bags near the Otter, "I have mail from your mother."

"Thanks," Rawley said, smiling. "I love mail from my mother!" Before she could speak again, she heard someone call her name. Rawley turned and saw it was a security guard. "You're wanted in the dining hall if have a moment," he said.

"Who is it?" she asked.

"Not sure, I was just asked to find you."

Rawley turned then waved to Brett. "If I miss you, be safe," she said. Brett waved and returned the sentiment.

As Rawley approached the dining facility, she couldn't help but wonder if she would find him waiting. She wanted to be mad, but then she couldn't. She was thinking about what she might say, but then she wondered why he would come down here to meet. She knew the Intel assets were never in this part of the building.

Maybe he heard she was leaving, but why meet here of all places? Her mind was still cycling through scenarios when she walked in the door and saw Dave Mayer standing by the classified briefing room. Mayer waved then walked into the room. As Rawley walked through the door, she was instantly disappointed, even if she didn't show it.

It was just her and Mayer. Nobody else. A feeling came over Rawley that she had not experienced in many years, and she felt silly if not stupid.

"Rawley, how's the leg?" he asked.

"It's great really. I guess I was lucky," she said.

Mayer motioned to a chair. "Sit, please," he said. "I want to tell what you are doing on this trip."

Mayer pushed a folder toward her. As Rawley opened the folder, she could see the same photos Rip had seen of the C-130 known as Valiant 06.

"We have an urgent tasking to locate and positively identify that aircraft if we can." As Mayer spoke he watched her expression and body language.

"Aren't there people who do that for a living?" she asked.

Mayer nodded. "That's true, but this particular aircraft has a tie to something going on here, so we are sending two people to look into it."

"You'll be accompanied by one of our Intel case officers." Mayer paused as Rawley thumbed through the photos.

"Your role in this," he said, "is to confirm the identification of the wreckage as a United States Air Force, Vietnam vintage C-130. We need positive confirmation of that, so a serial number or other positive proof would be really helpful." Mayer paused again. "Water?" He slid a bottle of water toward her.

"Do you have anything stronger?" Rawley asked as she pushed the photos back into the folder.

"We needed a pilot right now," Mayer said. "We are launching this from here, and we have you. We want to keep this low key, but of course if you find something, the right people can come in and take over." Mayer stopped.

Rawley shrugged. It seemed odd to her that with all the resources of the US government, she would be chosen for this task. But then she had never known the government to make logical decisions.

"Everything else will be considered need to know, so you'll get more information as it's required," Mayer said.

"Seems simple enough," Rawley said. "That's it?"

"That's it," Mayer said.

When Rawley got back to the hangar, she could now see the Global Express outside being refueled. She could also see Jeff doing a walkaround. There was nobody waiting to board or anyone else around except the refueling crew.

Just as she had done before, Rawley stopped and took one last look around the hangar, then she picked up her bags and headed to the aircraft.

Jeff saw Rawley and rushed toward her. "Now I'm taking your bags!" he said.

Rawley didn't resist or protest. Instead she just handed them over. "Thanks," she said.

Ry was on the flight deck working on the route when Rawley came aboard. She looked around, and the cavernous plane was mostly empty except for a few unmarked boxes that were strapped to the floor.

Jeff put Rawley's bags aboard, then yelled out, "Look who's here!"

Ry turned around and smiled. "Welcome back!" he said. "I guess you had to get shot to get out of this hellhole."

Rawley smiled and nodded. "Yeah, I had to do something creative, so I burned down a plane and prayed for a flesh wound."

Ry and Jeff both laughed.

"Where are the others?" she asked. "Just waiting on one," Ry said. "Then we are out of here."

"Do you mind taking a turn in the front?" Jeff asked.

"Love to! What's the flight plan?" Rawley asked as she opened the refrigerator.

Ry turned back then pushed a button on the navigation computer. "Looks like six hours total," he said. "We'll scoot across southern China then down to Puerto Princessa, Palawan. No weather on the route. How about taking the right seat out of here with Jeff?" Ry stepped up from his seat.

Rawley didn't answer; she just moved to the right seat in the cockpit.

"Sit and relax," Jeff said as he took Ry's place in the left seat.

Rawley got settled in and put on her headset. "Check," she said over the internal com.

"Loud and clear," Jeff said. Then he handed her a small binder. "That's our written OPORDER, if you want to look over it." Jeff kept talking while setting up the plane for taxi and takeoff.

Jeff looked down and out the left window. "Looks like our guy is here," he said.

Ry met their passenger at the top of the stairs. "Welcome aboard! All that belongs to you," he said, pointing to the boxes that were strapped to the deck. "Put your things anyplace, and make yourself comfortable." Ry took one last look around then pushed a switch that would close the door.

"This plane makes the world pretty small," Ry said. "We are only six hours in the air. You can sleep in the back, the galley is there, and you can communicate with anyone from our com center up front."

Rip looked around and nodded. "How about a toilet and a place to lay down?" he said as he dropped his bags.

"There is a cabin in the back. We will be out of here in five minutes."

Ry checked the door after it closed then put his own headset on. "All set back here," he said. "Our guest is napping, apparently."

Rawley looked out at the men standing around the hanger and she could see Greg. He waved then went back inside.

Nile had just left his third debriefing regarding the events surrounding the extraction of the Kraken, and he was racing toward the hangar when Greg came around the corner. "Is she still here?" Nile asked.

"They closed up a few minutes ago," Greg said.

"Damn, I wanted to say good-bye." Nile was clearly disappointed.

As Greg started to walk away, he stopped. "She said she left something for you in her room."

"Thanks. I'll go by there," Nile said.

When Nile opened the door to Rawley's room, he saw a well-worn paperback and a note sitting on the desk. Nile picked up the book and looked at the title. It was *Wind, Sand and Stars* by Antoine de Saint-Exupery.

Nile looked at the note.

Not sure if you've read this, but I return to it often to remind myself why I fly. Be safe but not too safe. Caution leads to a false sense of security. See you soon, my friend.

Rawley

As Nile turned to leave, he saw the room ledger and picked it up. He turned the pages, wondering what words of wisdom she might have left behind. On the last page, he saw just two entries, and it made him smile. At the top he saw simply, "The Kraken," and one line below it, "Fly Girl."

CHAPTER 49

———— ◆ ————

THEY HAD BEEN IN THE air four hours when Ry relieved Rawley in the cockpit. "I'm making lunch. Who wants what?" she asked.

Ry and Jeff placed their orders, and she did the best she could with the food available. Just as she sat down to eat, an alarm went off, indicating a secure satellite message traffic was being received.

"Rawley, can you wake that guy up? This stuff is for him," Jeff said.

Rawley left her plate in the galley and made her way to the cabin in the rear. She knocked once, then again. Hearing nothing, she opened the cabin door. She could see a man lying with his back to her. She called out again, but he didn't stir. Finally, she walked forward and touched his shoulder.

Rip startled awake, and as he turned, Rawley felt like she would fall over.

"You!" they both said at the exact same time.

Rawley stepped back until she was in the cabin door. Rip was clean shaven, and his hair was short. He looked more like she remembered him in years past.

Neither spoke; they just looked at each other for an awkward moment that seemed to go on and on. Rawley took another step back then closed the door and stormed to the front of the plane.

Her mind raced as she thought through every scenario. Mayer talked to her father. Her father had to know Rip was here. Her participation in this trip made no sense, so why would they send her unless there was some crazy conspiracy?

Once again, the men in her life were manipulating her. Deceiving her, she thought. But why!

Rawley walked straight to the cockpit. "Do you guys know who that is back there, or why I am even here?" She was clearly upset.

Ry and Jeff looked at each other, then at Rawley. They were both confused and shaking their heads. "No, I don't believe so," Jeff said. "Why?"

"My father didn't say anything to you about who was going on this trip or about me?"

"Nothing except we were picking you up with another guy and flying to the Philippines," said Ry.

"Is there something we should know? A problem?" Jeff asked.

Rawley looked at both of them, paused for a second, then abruptly turned and went back to a seat.

Ry and Jeff looked at each other, then put their headsets back on and turned their attention to the plane. "Do you think he's dead?" Ry asked.

"No but if he isn't here in five, no fifteen minutes, I'll check on him, or you can," said Jeff.

A few minutes later, Rip walked forward through the cabin. He could just barely see the back of Rawley's head over a seat. He thought about stopping and talking to her, then he decided to just walk by and go forward.

As he passed Rawley looked out a window at the passing clouds far below.

In the cockpit Ry and Jeff could see his reflection as Rip walked forward. Jeff turned around and offered him a headset. Then everyone introduced themselves.

"You had several messages come in a few minutes ago," Jeff said as he slid his seat back. "Everything comes up on that screen there." He pointed at a display. "It functions like any computer terminal. You can reply, and it will go out secure. You can also print if you like."

Rip looked over the com station as Jeff went through all the equipment, including secure voice and real-time satellite images of Cuyo Island.

"OK, great!" Rip said as he slid his chair to the desk and began reading messages. "Let me know before you go to voice; we'll isolate you," Ry said.

Then Ry looked back at Rip. "Do you and Rawley have some...something?" Ry asked.

Rip looked back at Rawley, then at Ry and Jeff, who were now looking at Rip. "Can she hear us?" Rip asked.

Jeff looked back at Rawley and shook his head. "No, she can't hear anything," he said.

"We dated in college but haven't seen each other until that plane crash the other day when she picked me up," Rip said.

"I kind of disappeared for seven or eight years without saying anything." Rip looked at Rawley one more time then looked back at the first message on the screen, and Ry and Jeff both nodded but said nothing. "How long until we land?" Rip asked.

"One hour and fifty-eight minutes, give or take," Ry said.

"OK, go ahead and isolate me on com," Rip said as he read the first message from Sherman Craig. Sherman had been an analyst then promoted to program manager. His specialty was WMD, or weapons of mass destruction. Rip had spent a considerable amount of time working with Sherman during various training exercises and actual operations targeting persons actively trying to procure a WMD of any type, including military explosives and gas, civilian explosives, or homemade bombs, regardless of their makeup.

Rip checked the time then dialed Sherman's secure line.

After one ring, Sherman answered. "Hey, pal! I've been waiting for your call."

"Sherm, what's new, brother?" Rip was happy to hear his voice. The last deployment had been long, and there were few people he could talk to at kay jay.

"Home front or where you're headed?" Sherman asked.

"How about where we're headed first?" Rip said.

"We have a twist in this puzzle you're working on," Sherman said.

"Lay it out," Rip said as he opened another message.

"I'll just go through what I know, and you take from it what you will," Sherman said.

"First the word is out that an object fitting the description of something like a bomb was seen in the wreckage of a military aircraft. No details yet, and nobody actually said 'bomb.' Someone with a phone traced to Palawan is trying to get paid to disclose the location of the wreck.

"JPAC says they have scoured that area several times and there is no US wreckage or hint of wreckage there or anyplace near there.

"Some calls went back and forth between Sersi, who you know, and a guy believed to be Abu Sayaaf, or some other group sympathetic to the cause. You know the cause, right?" Sherman asked.

"I'm at a loss here, Sherm," Rip said.

"We all are dude!" Sherman said. "Who knows what the freaking cause is! Where was I?"

"Sayaaf," Rip said.

"Oh yeah, some asshole, possibly Sayaaf, will assist the handoff between the Palawan guy and Sersi for some money."

Sayaaf refereed the Philippines radical Islamic terror group known as Abu Sayaaf. They were responsible for numerous acts of terror including murders, kidnapping, extortion, and bombings, as well as drug trafficking. Their most infamous act of terror was the attack on Superferry 14, which resulted in the death of 116 passengers.

"What will humans not do for money!" Sherman said.

Rip figured Sherman must be exhausted because he was acting giddy. Sherman paused again then went on.

"As near as we can tell by the phone conversations, nobody has actually gone to Cuyo or Puerto Princessa yet. They seem to be haggling over money." Sherman paused.

"We may have beaten them to the punch. If it's really there." Sherman yawned loudly. "You do know what time it is here, right?" Sherman said, without waiting for an answer. "And!" He continued. "It's a little complicated on my end because nobody believes that thing is there."

"I know. I know," Rip said. "What's the development?" Rip asked.

"Development?" Sherman asked.

"Your last message, Sherman. You said 'development,' then you said 'twist, late breaking'…something like that." Rip paused and looked back at the message on the screen.

"Oh yeah, yeah, development! Got it!" Sherman said. "Someone traced to the Tokyo area is talking to Sersi. They're talking money and stuff to the effect of getting control of the bomb, weapon, or thing. You know, buying it once it's been procured."

"Tokyo?" Rip asked. "Do they have a lot of unhappy insurgents there?"

"Rip, they are everywhere, dude!" Sherman said. "Look around you right now. If you are with five people, one of them is contemplating homicide." Sherman laughed.

Rip glanced to where Rawley was sitting and smiled. "What else, Sherman?"

Sherman summarized his list. "Money, Princessa, Cuyo, Japan…You are meeting a guy named Raoul Sabatan in Cuyo. He's a trusted agent, if the wreck is there, he knows where it is. The money you need for him is on the plane. I guess that's it for now."

"If Sabatan isn't the guy making the deal for Sayaaf, how do we know he has the info we need?" Rip asked.

"We've been cultivating this dude for a long time on some other stuff," Sherman said. "He's a producer and loyal! And if he's right on this, he gets his golden ticket to America! House in a gated community, citizenship, 7-Eleven, the whole deal."

Rip was just nodding as he listened. "OK. Is that it?"

"No!" Sherman said.

"Who's the girl?"

"Girl?" Rip said, trying to sound vague.

"Don't play that game, old buddy. The word is out some killer pilot chick saved your ass, and now the front office wants her in ground division, like tomorrow. I heard she's on her way here already. What's she look like? Would I like her?" Sherman asked.

Rip was quiet for a moment. "I'll tell you what she looks like, Sherman," said Rip. "In my little group here, she's the one contemplating a homicide."

Sherman laughed out loud. "All right, dude, watch your back! We're clear!" Sherman said.

Then before Rip could say another word, the line went dead.

CHAPTER 50

PUERTO PRINCESSA, PALAWAN, PHILIPPINES

RIP STOOD UP AND LOOKED ahead into the vast blue sky and solid cloud base far below. Then he turned and looked at Rawley. She was reclined with her eyes closed. As Rip looked at her, he could not help but remember how young and energetic she was when they were last together.

He also remembered their last night together. It was not what he had hoped for after the summers of fun and adventure.

Rip took a step toward her then hesitated. He wanted to talk to her and maybe explain what had happened and where he had been all these years. He also wanted to know about her life. He had followed her career through friends for a short time, but once he was assigned to intelligence gathering, his life was one of constant travel. Just keeping an apartment was challenging enough, much less tracking another person, even if it was only through anecdotes and stories.

He slowly took another step, then another. Soon he was standing next to her. She was still asleep, so he sat in the seat across the aisle from her. He looked at his watch then out the window. Once again, he looked at Rawley. She looked peaceful, he thought. Her long black hair fell forward over her shoulders, framing her face. As he studied her face, he could see the small scar he had accidently given her while training with the Georgetown fencing team. Then he looked down at the long scar on his left wrist and hand and remembered how she had given him that a second later.

They were both chastised for not using safety equipment. They feigned remorse but thought little of the wounds they had received.

What started as playful sparring turned into a tit-for-tat bloodletting. Rip realized then she was aggressive with a quick temper and an instinct to fight rather than flee.

Rawley yawned then looked at her watch. "If you have something to say, you've got twenty minutes to spit it out," she said, without looking at Rip.

Rip grinned and shook his head. "I don't know where to begin."

"How about where you said you were going sailing and you would be back in a few weeks."

Rips jaw tightened as she spoke.

"OK, I was offered a job in the CIA right out of college because my parents and two uncles had been working there for years. I had grown up with that secret and it was never mentioned. When the time came to go, my first assignment was crew on a government sailboat that was working in the Mediterranean around Syria and Lebanon." Once Rip started talking, he went on in what must have sounded like one run-on sentence.

Rawley was listening but showing no emotion.

"We would go into Izmir, Turkey, then Athens to maintain the appearance of a research boat working for a university," Rip said. "All I did was dive and collect samples and write reports about pollution and the sea life we encountered. It was all in support of preserving the cover.

"One month turned into a year turned into two years. Then I was sent to join a crew working out of Malaysia covering the Strait of Malacca.

"We had a similar cover, but we were targeting pirates and getting into occasional gunfights. It was a crazy, hectic existence, and again time flew by.

"When I came home, I was offered a billet at the Navy's SEAL training then assignment to gathering in Afghanistan. I had already mastered several dialects of Arabic, and before I knew it, more time had passed."

Rip paused for a moment and looked at Rawley. If she was listening, she seemed unmoved. Even uninterested.

"I thought about reaching out to you so many times," he said. "I felt like all I would be doing was saying hello and good-bye in the same sentence. And I could never really be honest about what I was doing." Rip stopped and looked at Rawley.

Finally, she looked at him. She still had no expression; she just studied his face. "Kraken?" she asked.

"Oh, well, when I was in SEAL training, someone gave me that name because I looked so...you know...ominous in the water, I guess." Rip looked away from her for the first time.

Rawley just nodded. By now they were descending into Palawan, and Jeff's voice came over the loudspeaker. "Buckle up, folks; we need to punch through some clouds. Maybe fifteen more minutes."

Rip didn't know if he should go on or just stop. "We do need to work together on this effort, so I hope we can put aside our issues for just a day or two, then I'll be going someplace and you somewhere else," he said.

Rawley looked at Rip. "You haven't talked to my father in all these years?" she asked.

"Not once, honest. Why?" he asked.

"It just seems odd, that's all. Me being kind of coerced into this job, being on this trip, you work for Mayer, he's my dad's friend." Rawley shrugged. "Just seems odd.

"I guess I've just been conditioned lately to think all men suck. Thanks for doing that," Rawley said as pushed her lap belt aside. Rip swallowed hard then turned forward and leaned back into his chair and tightened his seatbelt.

Rawley got up and went to the cockpit, where she lowered a jump seat behind the pilots then put on a headset. By now the Global was coming out of the sky at a rate of thirty-five hundred feet per minute, and the plane shook every time clouds engulfed the windscreen. "Tell me about Palawan," she said. "Have you guys been here?"

"I landed a C2 here fifteen years ago," Jeff said. "It was austere, at best."

"They have a new terminal that opened in April last year," Ry added. "We'll be met by some US embassy pogue out of Manila and a Marine Corps V22 Osprey," said Jeff as he dialed up different frequencies on the com stack.

"The Osprey will take you guys to Cuyo while we wait," Ry added as he adjusted the power.

"Did you know Palawan is home to one of the one the 'New Seven Wonders of the World'?" Ry asked.

"And what would that be?" Rawley asked.

"It's an underground river," said Ry. "I don't think you'll have time to visit, but it's kind of cool."

In an instant, the ride went from bumpy to smooth, and the ambient light in the cockpit became extremely bright again as the cloud layer went from solid to broken to widely scattered.

"There's our island." Ry was pointing off to the right. "And there's the airport about in the middle," he said. "Read that page you got from the State Department," Ry said as he looked at Jeff.

Jeff shuffled through some papers then found the one he was looking for. "Palawan is listed as one of the top twenty most beautiful islands on earth, and in the Philippines, it is known as the 'last ecological frontier.' Palawan archipelago is made up of nearly eighteen hundred islands, with Palawan being the largest, and Palawan itself is half desert and mostly undeveloped." Jeff scanned down the page. "There are white-sand beaches, limestone walls, and jungle!" Jeff turned and handed the page to Rawley.

She looked it over then looked ahead. "It's breathtaking," she said. "If ever I wanted to disappear..."

Ry and Jeff continued to prepare for landing, and Jeff was now talking to the tower at Puerto Princessa.

As they turned into a long, straight final, Rawley could see the V22 Osprey sitting on the tarmac. In this pristine vacation setting, it looked starkly out of place.

In every direction there were long, skinny boats on the water fishing or underway. The "bonka boat," as they were often called, was the primary mode of transportation on the water. They were narrow and long like a canoe and usually made of wood. The engine was almost always a large gas lawnmower engine with the propeller at the end of the long pole.

If the boats were larger, they might have a single-cylinder diesel engine that made an unmistakable sound when running. That sound could be best described as a *bonka, bonka, bonka* noise. Hence, every boat around here was referred to as a bonka boat.

While the Global rolled out, Rawley could see several aircraft, big and small, representing the various airlines that provided service to and from Manila and the other islands. Most of the aircraft had carried the name of one or more airlines in their lifetime.

"Follow that pickup," Jeff said, after acknowledging instruction from the ground controller.

They were being led toward the Marine Corps Osprey, and they could see a small gathering of people standing around the aircraft. Rip was now standing next to Rawley and looking ahead as well. "We have suits and flight suits and shorts!" Rip was shaking his head at the sight. "At least we are discreet."

"We used to pull in here occasionally while I was working in Malaysia." Rip wasn't talking to anyone specific, just talking. "I always wanted to come back on vacation.

"I'll talk to the embassy guy then the Osprey crew. That group on the right wearing shorts will move the cargo to the Osprey," he said.

"I'll handle that," Rawley said.

Rip nodded then looked at the computer screen. There were no new messages from Sherman.

CHAPTER 51

───◆───

AFTER A LONG DISCUSSION WITH the US embassy rep and then the Osprey aircrew, Rip was ready to depart. Rawley had overseen the loading of all the boxes from the Global. Rip watched her as she handed out cash and thanked everyone for their help. No matter what their personal issues might be, she was clearly engaged in the mission.

The Marines had brought along a four-man security detail and enough equipment to set up a camp for a week if required. As Rip sat down and settled into one of the nylon jump seats on the V22, he motioned for Rawley to join him. The ambient noise in the Osprey was building as the pilots worked through the startup sequence.

Rawley looked around the interior of the plane then turned to Rip. "So, what does a sixty-year-old plane crash have to do with Afghanistan?" she asked.

Rip leaned toward Rawley to ensure only she could hear him. "If this plane is here at all, and if it's the one we are looking for, it was carrying a very small, very special weapon made for special forces," Rip said. "Everything we see or discover is kept between us." He looked around the aircraft at the men onboard.

Soon the Osprey left the ground and banked hard as it picked up the course for Cuyo. The ride would take less than forty minutes as the Osprey transitioned from helicopter to airplane.

Rip leaned toward Rawley. "We are meeting a guy who supposedly will take us to the wreckage. Apparently, it's been looked for many times since the Vietnam War but never located until now."

Rawley listened, and Rip kept talking. "None of this is confirmed except that a plane was lost and it was carrying what we hope to find. It's all based on some intercepted phone conversations."

Rip sat back and closed his eyes for a moment, then he felt his satellite phone ringing. He could see it was Sherman Craig.

Rip pushed a button to answer then held the phone tight to his ear. "I can only listen, but we land in twenty-five minutes," Rip said. Sherman spoke for ten minutes before hanging up.

Rawley looked at Rip, and he was clearly troubled. "What's the matter?" she asked.

"That was our guy back home who is tracking this situation, and he said a large Japanese-owned yacht was anchored at Cuyo for two days and left about thirty-five hours ago. He just found out."

"There must be hundreds of Japanese-owned yachts in these waters," Rawley said.

Rip shook his head. "This one has a link to somebody we are monitoring." Rip folded his arms and leaned back into the seat. Rawley also sat back then breathed in hard and exhaled. This entire situation was taking on a surreal feeling. She was here with Rip not as a pilot but as a tagalong on a CIA mission looking for a weapon that was lost during the Vietnam War.

"What if they have it? What next?" Rawley asked. She was intrigued and suddenly could not get enough information.

Rip looked at her. "Well, we need confirmation on several things. The plane ID for one. Confirmation that what we want is or was onboard. If we can't find the weapon, positive ID of the plane will trigger a bunch of events that will likely take this out of our hands. I'll go back to whatever I am going back to, and you…" Rip paused as if he was thinking. "I guess you go back to flying or Langley." Rip turned his head back to the front.

"Why Langley?" Rawley asked.

Rip looked at her again. "You don't know?" he asked. Rawley was puzzled by his comment.

"What should I know?" she asked.

The Osprey was slowing and descending. As the big turbines transitioned, the noise changed dramatically. Marines were moving around in the fuselage, and two crewmen pulled the slack out of their gunner's belt to ensure they were secure, then walked to the end of the open ramp.

"Know what?" Rawley asked again.

Rip raised his voice as he looked at her. "Somebody wants you in Langley so they can plug you into a ground team."

Rawley looked at Rip. Again, she was the last to know something that involved her. It was a common theme that was constantly putting her on edge.

"What's a ground team?" she asked.

"They saw the video from the firefight and they, whoever 'they' are, want you on a team that goes in behind the military and picks up intel and interviews locals and prisoners."

Rawley was silent and just processing the information.

"Someone made the call to send you here instead of Langley," Rip said.

"It had to be Mayer. Or my dad," Rawley said. "The word came through him." Rawley sat back into the seat as the wheels of the Osprey touched down.

The aircraft's two thirty-eight-foot-diameter rotors were angled back to taxi the aircraft as dust, grass, and trash blew everywhere, including into the fuselage through the open ramp. As the engines spooled down, the four Marines assigned to security duty exited the Osprey and formed a perimeter around the plane.

Within minutes two rusty old police cars raced up, and local police carrying very old M16 rifles exited the cars. Another car came, and two more men joined the armed group of police.

Rip walked toward the group and asked who was in charge. One man identified himself as the chief of police, and Rip gave the man a letter from the US embassy and endorsed by the president of the Republic of the Philippines.

The police chief looked over the letter then said something to the group in the Philippine language of Tagalog.

The men with the M16s lowered their weapons, and the chief turned back to Rip. Before anyone could speak, another car raced up, but this time with only one man inside. By now at least a hundred locals, including men, women, and children, gathered all around the Osprey. Several people approached the Marines, offering to sell everything from water and fruit to clothes. Although everyone here might have seen a helicopter before, the Osprey must have looked like something from a science-fiction movie. Against the protests of the Marines, children walked directly to the ramp of the Osprey and looked inside.

The last man to arrive left his car and walked directly to the police chief, then after a very brief discussion, he turned and walked to Rip.

As they came together, they reached for each other's hands. Rip intentionally said the man's name wrong. "Raphael Saban?" Rip asked.

"Raoul Sabatan, sir," the man replied, smiling. "And you are?"

"Rip, and that's Rawley," Rip said as he motioned to Rawley, who was now standing near but to one side.

Raoul was a slightly built man in his late sixties. He looked every bit the classic Filipino businessman with his pressed slacks and traditional embroidered shirt known as a barong. Like most, if not all Filipinos, his hair was jet black, he was tall and thin, and he spoke perfect English with only a hint of his native accent.

Rip motioned him aside and called for Rawley. "I hear a boat has been to the aircraft," Rip said. "Is that true?"

Raoul was shaking his head while looking down at Rip's hands, then at Rawley, and then past her to the Osprey. "There are many boats that come and go here. I don't believe any have been near the wreckage," Raoul said, again looking around.

"I have your money," Rip said. "How far away is the wreck?"

"Close, maybe twenty minutes," Raoul said. "It is in the water, maybe fifteen meters. Did you bring equipment?"

"Yeah, we have it." Rip said as he turned toward Rawley. "We need another vehicle, can you—?"

Before Rip finished his request, Rawley walked into the group of police, and after some money changed hands, a radio call was made.

Less than ten minutes later, a small pickup trailing a cloud of black smoke pulled up and was directed to the back of the Osprey.

Rip checked in with Sherman, and by the time he was done, the gear was transferred to the truck. Rip then payed Raoul, and they were off.

What Raoul had described as a twenty-minute drive lasted nearly an hour, over poorly maintained dirt roads rife with potholes and trash and an occasional water buffalo. As they drove along, they passed hundreds of small huts.

Although smoldering piles of rubbish could be seen everywhere, the area around the huts was swept clean several times a day. Clothes could be seen drying nearby, and anyone near the road stopped what they were doing to watch them pass.

The island of Palawan, with its near constant flow of tourists, seemed rich in comparison to Cuyo. Here, most people fished or made crafts that were sent to Palawan for pennies compared what they sold for in the shops and resorts there.

Finally, the thick tropical forestation opened up to the ocean, and before them lay a narrow beach. Raoul stopped his car before the sand became soft and pointed out to sea.

On the beach were two long, narrow wooden boats with one driver each standing by. "OK," Rip said. "How far from here?"

"Very close," Raoul said. "Just easier by boat."

"I have gear for two, but it's your call," Rip said, looking at Rawley.

"I'm diving," she said. "It's why I'm here." She began opening gear bags.

Once they had everything on the boats, they were pushed off the beach. Raoul directed the driver of the first boat to point north and approximately nine hundred yards off the beach.

The water was pristine, and visibility was easily one hundred feet or more. Raoul directed the boats to stop, and the first driver dropped a very large and heavy canvas bag full of stones over the side to act as an anchor.

Rawley and Rip both looked into the water, then Rip put on his mask and jumped over the side.

Rip scanned the bottom from side to side. The bottom was covered in dark rocks and seagrass, but he saw nothing that looked like wreckage of an aircraft. Finally, he lifted his head and looked at Raoul. "What am I missing?" Rip asked. "The water here is twice the depth you said, and there isn't anything here."

"Caverns," Raoul said. "This place is called Playa Kuweba, Beach of the Caverns. It is famous for its massive underwater caverns. You go in here and swim toward the beach maybe two one zero degrees. You will see."

Rip said nothing, but he was trying to imagine a C-130 aircraft in a cavern. It was impossible or at least improbable, he thought. Once they were suited up, Rip signaled to Rawley, and they slowly slid beneath the surface.

CHAPTER 52

——◆——

As Rawley and Rip made their descent, Rawley was instantly reminded of many summers past on the Island of Saint Croix in the US Virgin Islands. It was there she had learned to dive with Rip and some other friends from the university.

Rawley spent a month with Rip sailing, diving, and working at one of the waterfront bars in Christiansted. Many nights they would look out over the anchorage toward the Island of Saint Thomas and talk about one day buying property there. Rawley looked around and ahead as she kicked hard to stay with Rip. She could tell he was clearly on a mission to find the wreckage.

As they swam toward the beach, Rip checked his compass then adjusted his course. Soon the water became shallower, and Rip swam toward the bottom while periodically stopping to look around. Finally they came across the first cavern. As Rip shined his light into each one, he doubted he would find anything that resembled a C-130 aircraft here. The only thing the caverns held now were sharks. Every place they looked, there were one or more blacktip reef sharks or several nurse sharks of all sizes. When Rip looked at his depth gauge, they were just entering thirty-five feet of water. Rip stopped and looked ahead. There he saw the largest cavern yet. The opening was close to sixty feet wide and fifteen feet high. The cavern was so deep and dark, they could not see but a few feet inside.

Rip slowly approached and shined his light ahead. When he stopped again, Rawley came to his side and also shined her light into the cavern.

When their beams came together, the light passed over what could only be a section of aircraft fuselage. They both held their lights in one place, and Rawley felt a shiver. Rip looked at Rawley, then opened the bag he was towing. He reached inside and handed Rawley a small device on a lanyard. It was the radiation-absorbing pendant. Rawley didn't know what she had been given, but she tied it to her buoyancy compensator. Then Rip pulled a small Geiger counter from his bag.

Just before he swam into the wreckage, Rip checked Rawley's air then his own and looked at his watch. The interior of the wreck was a maze of hanging wires, cables, and hoses, all overgrown or encrusted with a very thin layer of coral and other sea life. For a fleeting second, Rip wondered how it came to rest here and why nobody had located it for all these years.

As Rip swam deeper into the remains of the fuselage, he was sweeping the detector and his light from right to left. Rawley swam through the hanging debris to what looked like the forward part of the wreck, looking for anything that might yield a clue about the aircraft's identity.

Fifteen minutes passed when Rip used his knife to tap on his tank. He could see Rawley's light bouncing around amid the debris, but he could not see her. Rawley heard the distinctive noise and shined her light in Rip's direction. As Rip moved about, still sweeping for any trace of radiation, he also looked for signs of human remains or personal equipment that might also help positively identify the aircraft. Near the left side of the fuselage and covered in marine growth, Rip saw a weapon that looked like an M16. He looked at it briefly, thinking maybe he could see a serial number.

Rip looked again at his air and decided they would need to return to the surface in a few minutes. He swam to the other side, shining his light as he went. Suddenly his light danced across a small section of the deck that was remarkably clean, as if something had recently been sitting there. Close by there was a pile that was clearly rotting nylon straps with corroded metal ends.

As he surveyed the site, he knew the box they sought had been there, and now it had to be on the boat that was seen in the area. Rip swept the clean section of deck repeatedly, but no radiation was detected.

Rip looked up as Rawley swam toward him, holding the remnants of a leather bag that was also partially covered with a very thin layer of bush coral.

Rawley was signaling with her thumb to relay that she had found what she was looking for. As they exited the back of the wreckage, Rip stopped and swept the interior one more time with his light.

Rip and Rawley were quiet as they climbed back into the boats. Raoul asked a few questions, but Rip declined to answer.

As soon as they got back to the beach, Rip put the Geiger counter in one bag. "Raoul, this stays with me. You can have the rest of the gear. Get us to the helicopter, quick," Rip said as he threw the bag into the back of Raoul's car.

Raoul was speeding along the dirt road while Rawley carefully rubbed the bush coral off the flap where pilots usually had their name and rank embossed. When she finally brushed enough coral away, she was able to see the leather and all that remained of two gold letters. An uppercase *M* and a lowercase *i*. Rawley remembered the crew list from the documents she had been given and determined the bag belonged to Aircraft Commander Morris.

"No doubt that's Valiant 06," she said as Rip dialed Sherman's number on his sat phone.

"We found it, Sherm. No doubt whatsoever, it's the plane. But no weapon and no trace." He said.

"Way to go brother." "What else you got?" Sherman asked.

Rawley listened to Rip. And she started piecing the puzzle together. A special weapon, and the detector Rip used. It was then she realized the pendant was a radiation absorbing TLD and also knew what kind of weapon they were looking for.

"I am going to say it was there and recently removed based on what I saw," Rip said. "I found a pile of cargo straps that were cut, not torn apart, not rotted apart."

Rip stopped talking and listened to Sherman. "Recently cut, I'm positive." Rip answered. "The straps would have been scattered or just gone. And there was a three-by-two spot on the floor that had no growth."

Rip stopped and again listened to Sherman while he looked at Rawley. She was looking at him and hanging on every word.

"It was pushed nose first into a cavern, no tail, no wings," Rip said. "Yes, a cavern, and it was recently in water deeper that one hundred sixty feet. Maybe a storm brought it up. See when the last typhoon came through there." Rip paused and looked at his watch. As Sherman talked Rip was shaking his head. "I know from working over here that certain types of coral grow above one hundred and sixty feet, and all there is on that wreck is some thin bush coral and nothing else. It's been deep. We need to find that boat, Sherm. What can you do?"

"I'll get into it right now," Sherman said. "They are taking down the dive boat in Washington in the morning. No matter what they find there, this discovery should spark some conversation."

Rip was still looking at Rawley while he listened.

"All right," Sherman said. "I'll do what I can on my end. How soon can you fly?"

Rip looked at his watch again. "We can be in Princessa in a few hours and fly out of there by ten local. Hey, can you get the location information to the JPAC guys in Hawaii? We can preserve the evidence we found. We will leave it with Raoul."

"OK, Rip, give me about four hours to see where we go from here. Great job!" Sherman said, then hung up.

Rip slid back into his seat and looked at Rawley. "Wow! I wasn't expecting that when I started this trip."

Rawley didn't answer; she just held up the TLD pendant. "Does this mean what I think it means?" she asked.

Rip put his index to his mouth and nodded. Raoul looked at Rip and Rawley in the rearview mirror while he drove. If it wasn't obvious to Rip, Rawley could see that Raoul was taking everything in.

CHAPTER 53

———◆———

AFTER LANDING BACK AT PUERTO Princessa, Rip called Sherman again. It had only been two hours, but he was hoping for some or any information.

He was sure whatever was on that aircraft wreckage now had to be on the yacht. Sitting alone he was on the satellite phone for over thirty minutes. Rawley waited in the cockpit with Jeff and Ry, talking about what they had found, but she made no mention of the weapon, whatever it might be.

When Rip came back to the plane, he was clearly disheartened by his conversation. He called for Rawley to come into the cabin. "The yacht we think has the weapon is in Manila," Rip said. "It's been cleared, and nothing was found. The yacht is owned by a company that is controlled by a Japanese National named Masogi. We still don't know anything about Masogi, but there was an aircraft in Manila yesterday owned by Masogi Corp. And, there was a cellular intercept between a confirmed Masogi associate and a known terror suspect that mentioned Havana. So, uh, I'd say it's gone."

"What do we do?" Rawley asked. "Is that it?"

Rip shrugged. "They believe we have confirmed the existence of the SADAM, and they believe Masogi is the go-between getting it to the US or wherever they are headed. What happens next doesn't concern us now because the WMD Task Force has been assigned, and we have been ordered back to Langley." Rip put his hands up as if to surrender.

Rawley shook her head. "It's a nuke, right? Is that what you are not telling me?"

Rip was nodding the affirmative. "Yeah, a SADAM is a very small, low-yield nuke that probably can't even be detonated."

"We aren't quitting just like that, are we?" Rawley was emphatic. "We're in this now; let's follow the damn thing."

"They have a several-hour head start," said Rip. "By the time we get to Havana, they will be someplace else."

Rawley said nothing. She just turned and went to the cockpit. "Get us out of here and head to Havana at your best speed," she said.

"Rawley, we don't know they are going to Havana for a fact. That's an intercept. They know we are listening."

Rawley looked at Rip as he spoke. "Let's roll the dice, and go," Rawley said. "We're headed in that direction anyway."

Ry and Jeff immediately set about prepping for departure. "We should be airborne in fifteen minutes," Ry said as he began dialing up Havana on the flight computer.

Rawley went back into the cabin and retracted the airstairs then closed the door. "We can't just fly to Havana," Rip said. "I have orders."

"I was hired to fly, Rip. We're flying. Find out everything you can about the plane they are using," Rawley said. "We might just beat them there."

Rip said nothing. For a moment he just stared at Rawley.

"It's a nuclear weapon, Rip. Are you really going to just quit and hope someone else solves the problem? Let's go to Havana. That's the least we can do," Rawley said before going back to the cockpit.

Jeff was talking to the tower and maneuvering the aircraft for take-off. Ry turned around in his seat. "If everything works in our favor, we will make Havana nonstop in twelve hours."

"Worst case, we bounce in Mobile for fuel," Ry said. "Go?"

"Best speed, go!" said Rawley.

Rip sat down at the communication center.

"Get the info, Rip," Rawley said. "Let's stay with this."

Rip looked at Rawley and then looked at his watch. There was a twelve-hour time difference between their location and Washington DC.

Rawley touched Ry on the shoulder to get his attention as the Global pulled onto the runway. "I'm laying down. I'll relieve someone in four hours."

Ry held up his thumb then pushed back into his seat as they started to roll.

Rip crafted a short message with several questions for Sherman. "Can you guys isolate me on com?" he asked as he dialed Sherman's number.

It was now close to six in the morning Washington time, but Sherman answered the phone.

"Rip, what's happening?" he said.

"I just sent you some mail. Can you look into that stuff for me and keep my whereabouts between us for now?"

"Let me guess," Sherman said. "You're headed to Havana. Right?"

"Yeah, I have to go," Rip said.

"All right then, yeah, let's keep it between us," Sherman said. "I'll look over that message and get back to you."

Rawley was in bed for almost three hours, but she found it impossible to sleep. As she walked back to the cockpit, she could see Rip reclined in a chair staring out a window into the darkening sky. Before she passed him, she could see an amber light illuminate near the cockpit. That meant message traffic had been received.

"Rip," Rawley said as she touched his shoulder, "you have a message."

Rip rubbed his eyes and yawned then looked at his watch. It would be close to ten o'clock in the morning in Washington, he thought.

Jeff pushed back, and Rawley took his place in the left seat. She scanned the instruments and looked at the GPS. They were doing seven hundred and twenty knots over the ground. "How long have we been doing that?" she asked.

Ry looked at the nav computer. "Since we leveled off," Ry said. "Is Rip coming up?"

"Yeah, he's coming," Rawley said as she turned and looked aft.

Rip read the message from Sherman then printed a copy and handed it to Rawley.

As she read it to herself, Rip read it aloud. "The plane is a Falcon 50EX, whatever that is. I've been temporarily assigned to the stay on the trail at least to Cuba. That's good news," he said.

Rip looked at the remaining answers in the message. "They are trying get shootdown authority. And lots of chatter in all the usual places." Rip stopped reading and turned his chair toward Rawley.

"What's a Falcon 50EX mean to us?" he asked. Rawley looked back at Rip. "It means almost five hundred knots for three thousand miles. They could be landing anytime," she said, shaking her head.

"Depending on their route of flight, that's about eighteen hours in the air, but they wouldn't go into US airspace then out to Havana. That makes no sense at all." Rawley was thinking as she spoke and trying to understand why they were flying to Havana of all places with a weapon that would certainly be used in the United States.

Another ten hours went by, and there were only sporadic messages from Sherman. Most were discussing intercepted cellular conversations. The biggest piece of the puzzle remained the current destination.

"They plan to wait for a specific date. They are selling it. They are…"

Rip was shuffling the printed messages and going through the possibilities out loud but not speaking specifically to anyone. He was still trying to come up with a plausible reason for taking the weapon to Havana. If in fact the weapon was on the plane at all.

"What if the Falcon is a decoy?" Rip asked. "And why would a Japanese National be in league with terrorists? That is another mystery." Now all three pilots were in the cockpit, but nobody answered.

Before Rip could say another word, the phone rang. Rip looked at the number as he answered.

"Sherman, what do you have?" Rip asked.

"Hey, buddy, that plane went into Mexico then over to a private airstrip north of Bayamo, about four hundred miles south of Havana."

"Our guys are there but fighting restrictions. We have an official group and several undercovers working the issue," Sherman said, before pausing.

"Coming in the way you guys are, you'll have to be official and on record. There's no other way unless you go to Gitmo, but then you are another twenty-hour drive from Havana."

Gitmo was the US Navy base on the southwestern end of Cuba.

Rip was nodding as he listened. "OK," he finally said. "Give me the rundown on the chatter." Rip opened the last message he received and read along.

"Masogi is in his eighties, maybe older, a severely crippled, blind guy who runs several conglomerates. No history with the law, no history at all, really. In fact," Sherman said, "the guy is a recluse with no known family. No kids, maybe a wife. The current belief is someone inside his organization is hijacking his assets." Sherman paused like he always did.

"Key words we keep picking up are the usual, 'revenge,' 'retribution,' etcetera, and somebody on the Japanese side said 'poison.' Rip, I floated the decoy idea, but when the plane landed at a private strip and left in twenty minutes...let's just say it has everyone's attention. When do you land?"

"Less than an hour," Rip said. "I'll brief the guys on what we found. Beyond that...I don't know what to tell you." The line went quiet for a moment. "You still there, Sherman?"

"Yeah, I'm here, dude. We need to find that thing," Sherman said. "We are looking at everything coming and going from Cuba now. The coast guard and Navy have the water and air between us and Cuba covered, but they can't stop every boat. Planes are a different story, they have diverted a few already to a remote strip in the Bahamas"

"OK," Rip said. "Who are we meeting?" Rip frowned as he wrote down a familiar name then hung up.

CHAPTER 54

TOKYO, JAPAN

———◆———

DAIKI MASOGI SAT SILENTLY IN the constant darkness that surrounded him. His sight was just another casualty of a war he never fully understood as a child but one that his family dutifully joined. Now at age eighty-five, staying alive was a daily struggle. For eighty years he had lived with a constant reminder of a fateful day in August 1945. While every friend and family member over the age of fifteen worked in support of one of the four Mitsubishi war factories that resided in his hometown of Nagasaki, Daiki studied and played like every other child his age.

Perhaps he was somewhat aware of the war because of where he lived, but Nagasaki had been spared from the tactical firebombing for geographic reasons, and his mother kept him away from any talk of invasion or other conversations that might prove unsettling to a young child.

On August 9, 1945, fate, clouds, and drifting smoke would transform Daiki Masogi's life into a nightmarish ordeal that would leave him terrified, burned, and broken. Nagasaki was the secondary target for the second atomic weapon used against Japan, and the one that would end World War Two. Masogi's home was just past the zone of destruction when the plutonium implosion bomb that would become famously known as "Fat Man" exploded five hundred meters above the city. Thirty-nine thousand Japanese citizens were killed instantly, and another fifty to one hundred thousand residents around Nagasaki were doomed to an excruciating slow death or lifelong pain and suffering as a result of radiation sickness.

The only members of Masogi's family who would survive the initial blast were those not on duty at one of the Mitsubishi factories.

The use of atomic weapons would fuel a debate that would last a lifetime. The decision to drop the weapons was based on potential lives lost during an allied invasion versus the relatively small number of casualties that might result from dropping an atomic weapon.

Although there had been testing and scientific data, little was known about the long-term effects of such weapons of mass destruction on humans who were exposed and survived. At the time of their deployment, the most important thing on people's minds around the world was the simple fact that the war was finally over.

For those not directly affected by the fallout or part of the Japanese Allied occupation effort, the realization of what happened in Hiroshima and Nagasaki would not be fully realized for months or maybe years. For those like Masogi, who survived the blasts, life was a living hell. They would suffer or die from leukemia and other cancers, and most would forever carry painful wounds from radiation burns.

Growing up, Masogi watched his surviving family members, including his mother, mercifully pass after years of agony. He knew from history that his country had been the antagonist in the war, and he knew of the atrocities carried out by Japanese troops. He also knew the incredible devastation caused by the first bomb dropped on Hiroshima had caused such widespread destruction and chaos that communication between that city and Tokyo was so completely severed that news of the bombing was likely unknown to the emperor. Had anyone in a position of power been aware, perhaps the second bomb might never had been needed, and his story would have been vastly different.

Now all of that was conjecture and best left to the historians. Masogi only knew what had happened to him and his family and friends, and he was bitter. His hatred was focused not on the decisions made in his own country but those made by the enemy of his country.

He had suffered greatly, and for too long he had dreamed of revenge. Perhaps now he had found a way to avenge his ancestors. In Masogi's mind he was following the Samurai code.

To him this was his Akō vendetta, and he was a modern-day rōnin. He felt no guilt, no apprehension or hesitation about the events he was placing in motion. To Masogi this was a business deal in support of a higher cause. A deal for which he would gladly give his life to consummate.

This would be the perfect end to his life here on earth and from here the kami, or Japanese spirits, would be his guide. Avenging his family came first; avenging Japan was second. But given the circumstances and his financial means, he would avenge.

———◆———

CHAPTER 55

JEFF AND RY WERE BACK at the controls and talking to Havana air traffic control. Rawley and Rip looked ahead as the island of Cuba came into view.

"I always wanted to come down here," Rip said. "You ever been?"

Rawley just shook her head.

Jeff turned in his seat. "We'll taxi to terminal two. Your party will meet you there."

Rip nodded as he took the seat at the com station and buckled up. Rawley pulled down a jump seat behind Jeff.

The Jose Marti airport had a single thirteen-thousand-foot runway built to accommodate Russia's largest bombers and cargo planes. No matter what Fidel Castro's thoughts might have been for postrevolution Cuba, his future and that of Cuba would forever reside in a political no-man's-land between the United States and Russia. As long as the two superpowers maintained their love-hate relationship, countries like Cuba, and dictators like Castro, would be nothing more than pawns. The real losers were the citizens of Cuba. They were forced to live within a socialist structure where they would never prosper and never have a voice.

Although money would often trickle into Cuba and allow for some modernization, Cubans suffered from the lack of many things a free society would have to offer. All Russia cared about was their own freedom to come and go as they pleased, with their warships and planes just ninety miles from America.

America, in the meantime, maintained a naval outpost on the island of Cuba at Guantanamo Bay, or Gitmo, as it was referred to by those who visited or worked there.

Gitmo was leased by the United States in 1903 from Tomas Palma, the first president of Cuba at a time when warships burned coal and required forward bases to provide refueling.

The lease was reaffirmed in a 1934 Cuban-American Treaty that increased the yearly lease payment of two thousand dollars in gold coins to $4,085. The 1934 treaty stipulated that the only way the lease could be broken was if both parties agreed or the property was abandoned by the United States.

Previous visitors to Guantanamo Bay included Christopher Columbus, the British Navy, the Spanish, the French, and the bay's original inhabitants, the Tainos Indians.

When the days of coal-fired warships came to an end, the strategic value of Guantanamo Bay ceased to exist, and the US occupation of the base became as much a political issue as anything else. It's remote location on foreign soil afforded the United States government with a place suitable for detaining prisoners and processing asylum seekers who might have a legal case for coming to America but posed a perceived threat. Such was the case in the 1990s, when more than thirty thousand HIV-positive Haitians were interned on the base in a facility that would be named Camp X-Ray.

As Jeff maneuvered the Global toward terminal 2, Rawley looked out at all the Russian aircraft parked around the field. She was reminded of Kabul and other airports she had visited around the world that had become the final resting place for so many tired and broken airframes.

Rip was also looking, but it was a person he sought. When they finally came to a stop, he could see a small group of men clearly waiting for their arrival. "That guy in the blue shirt is Brad Smith," he said to

Rawley. "An old acquaintance, not really a friend. He'll have the conversation with you turned to sex in five minutes or less if you let him."

"So what? I'm single," Rawley said, still looking across the field. Ry and Jeff looked at each other, and Rip looked at the back of Rawley's head but said nothing else.

As the plane came to a stop, Rawley opened the door and lowered the stairs. Below were several Cubans in tan coveralls. "Let's see what he has to say," Rip said.

Brad Smith was a career government field agent who had worked for several agencies and thought of himself as more of a politician than a blunt instrument. He always had a neat appearance, like he had just left a barber shop, and he always wore clothing that was native to the country he was in.

Rawley could only smile when she saw his shiny white leather shoes and guayabera shirt. He looked like a character from a bad movie, she thought. "He is very handsome!" she said as she descended the stairs behind Rip.

"He's an ass," Rip said under his breath.

As usual Brad dragged along some dubious official. Today he was joined by a uniformed and highly decorated Cuban officer. Or someone portraying a Cuban officer.

"Welcome to Havana!" Brad said as he reached for Rip's hand. "This is Colonel Seville, our host." He nodded toward the officer standing to his right.

After introductions were made, the group moved into the terminal and then to a small VIP room.

Once inside Brad pulled a folder from a day pack he carried. "I understand you confirmed the ID of the aircraft. Is that one hundred percent?" he asked Rip.

Rawley nodded and answered the question. "Yeah, it's definitely the plane we were sent to find."

"Rip and Rawley. Rip and Rawley. You two could be a singing act." Brad said with a grin. Then he looked directly at Rawley and reached to shake her hand. "OK, young lady, that's all I need from you. You're free to go." Brad paused for a moment then looked her over from head to toe. "Maybe dinner later," he said.

Rawley refused his handshake and didn't answer. Instead she deliberately panned Brad from his head to his feet. There was a brief awkward moment where nobody spoke.

Rip looked at Rawley, then at Brad and the Cuban. "She stays," he said. "She's assigned."

Brad pulled his hand back and turned to Rip. "Whatever," he said. "The National WMD Task Force is in charge, and you guys have done your part. So, maybe we can all have dinner later."

Rip looked down at the folder Brad was holding. "You have some more info, we're cleared, so how about humoring us?"

Brad stared at Rip for a second then pulled back a chair. "Have a seat," he said.

"The weapon is an old special forces tactical nuke," Brad said as he looked at the first page of his notes.

"We know that much," Rip said. "What else?"

"Well, let's see," Brad said. "We have been assured the thing can't be detonated, but we've been told its very dirty if it were popped open."

Rip nodded.

"We have acknowledged the existence of the weapon to certain parties and let it be known that it can't be detonated. What we don't know is if anyone believes that." Brad continued to look over the notes he was holding as he spoke.

"Why is it here?" Rip asked.

Brad looked at the Colonel. "We think there is a former Russian scientist here who could be helping them. If that's true, he'll know right off that a chain reaction is impossible."

"I assume he's under surveillance," Rip said.

Brad again looked at Colonel Seville before he spoke. "We 'think' he's here," Brad said. "Colonel Seville has men working on that now.

The Colonel didn't speak but instead sat quietly, smiling.

Brad stopped talking and leaned back in his seat, looking at Rawley. "If you guys are spending the night, maybe we can explore the town." Brad never looked away from Rawley, and Rip couldn't help but notice.

"Colonel, you wouldn't mind showing us the town, would you?" Brad asked, still looking at Rawley.

"It would be my great pleasure," Colonel Seville said in a distinctly Cuban accent. "El Floridita has food, music, salsa, and the finest daiquiris in Cuba."

Rawley was smiling for the first time since she entered the room. "Rip is a great salsa dancer," she said.

"Bravo, Rip!" the Colonel said, still smiling broadly.

"They can't set it off, but it's real value as a terror weapon is the radiation poison if it's breached," Rip said, trying to get the conversation back on track.

"I would love to see Havana with a local guide," Rawley said. "I'll need to get cleaned up and find something to wear."

Rip glared at Rawley. Then he looked back at Brad. "Poison," he said. "It's been documented from a conversation."

Brad finally turned his attention away from Rawley. "Yeah, I have that in my notes, Rip. If the intent was exposure, it says in here you would need to be practically in the same room for any real harm to come to you. When that cloud hits the air, it's diluted rapidly." Brad shrugged as if to dispel the threat.

"Right now, all they have is an old weapon that they can exploit for propaganda purposes," said Brad.

Then there was a pause.

"Look, Rip," Brad said, with some finality. "It's a minor threat. It will, in all likelihood, never leave this island. You've done your part." Brad pushed his notes back into his bag, indicating he was finished talking.

Rip was remembering past encounters he'd had with Brad and how much he disliked the man.

"All right," Rip said as he pushed his chair back. Then he looked at Rawley, who was looking at Brad. "I guess it's daiquiris and salsa!" he said.

"I will need to file a quick report to tie things up. It won't take but thirty minutes or so," Brad said as he moved to the door.

"Can we make it an hour?" Rawley said as she stood up. "I'll clean up on the plane, then, Colonel, you may take me shopping."

"I will meet you both in perhaps an hour in front of this terminal," the Colonel said as he looked at his watch. "Later you will be guests at my villa," he added.

"See you all at the Floridita," Brad said as he walked out.

CHAPTER 56

As SOON AS RIP AND Rawley returned to the plane, Rawley briefed Jeff and Ry. Rip went to the aircraft's com station to call Sherman.

After talking for twenty minutes, Rip hung up the phone and printed the last message he received. In it were details from recent cellular intercepts between a new player in Afghanistan and the man believed to be associated with Masogi.

"Read this," Rip said as he handed the page to Rawley. "These are excerpts from conversations just in the past four hours."

Rawley looked over the message. "White House confirmed." She looked up at Rip.

"Right." Rip said. "It's definitely leaving this island, and they mentioned the date."

Rawley looked back at the message. "That's two days from now," she said.

"Brad knew all that while we were talking," Rip said. Then he shrugged. "I hate it, but he's right about it being out of our hands. There must be a thousand people working this now. I was on that task force before. When it reaches this level, things are coordinated and orchestrated, and all we would do is run the risk of tipping someone off or really pissing someone off."

For a moment Rawley and Rip sat in silence. Rawley looked at the message Rip had given her.

"The plane leaves tomorrow," she said, without looking up. "It's been tasked."

"Yeah, I heard." Rip said as he looked out the window at the activity on the tarmac. Then he looked at his watch. "You may as well get ready for your date."

Rawley looked at her watch also. "I'll be ready in ten minutes," she said.

While visiting shops with Colonel Seville, Rawley was enjoying the moment, and Rip was preoccupied and distracted. Rawley didn't know if the Colonel's presence influenced the situation, but everyone she met was gracious and kind. She could see for herself how poor the people in Cuba actually were. The Cuban government tried their best to keep certain areas of Havana clean and bright, but some things were impossible to hide. Like the way the locals dressed or the weariness in their eyes.

Rawley was looking for one dress, but she bought several. She also bought many other things that might never make it home, but she felt compelled. Shop clerks weren't begging to make a sale, but they were clearly hopeful. Rawley understood the situation, and she had seen it many times. Every member of the armed forces who traveled abroad knew what being poor looked like. After an hour of following Rawley and the Colonel from shop to shop, Rip announced he had seen all the dresses he cared to see.

"I'll meet you at the Floridita," he said as he walked out the door.

The Colonel watched Rip walk away, then turned and looked at Rawley as she held up another dress while looking in the mirror.

"That man feels he is your protector. I can see he cares for you very much," the Colonel said.

Rawley turned to the left while still looking in the mirror. "I once thought so, Colonel," she said as she held the dress up and nodded to another anxious store clerk who hovered near by. Then she abruptly turned to the Colonel. "I do hope I'm not keeping you from your duties."

"Many others are attending to my responsibilities tonight. So, enjoy Havana, as I will be!"

Rawley smiled and turned back to the clerk.

"I too have enjoyed enough shopping," the Colonel said. "My assistant will remain with you and bring you to join us when you are ready. Please take all the time you need!"

On the street, Rip walked from the dress shop and into the first bar he came to.

It was a small place filled with locals smoking cigars and talking loudly. In every corner of the room, there were fans circulating the stale air. As he approached the bar, people moved aside to give him a clear path. It was obvious to everyone that he was not a local, and everyone knew visitors came to Havana to spend money. Bothering a paying customer was never tolerated. It was like an unwritten rule in Havana. Never molest or cause an issue with a paying customer in any place of business. Outside on the street was another matter. Tourists on the street were fair game for anyone with something to sell, and everyone had something to sell. Tourists on the street could be duped into paying too much for any service or item, and they often were. It was a buyer-beware situation, where the police were never on the side of the visitor.

Pickpockets and grab-and-run gangs were everywhere, along with those hoping to lure the unsuspecting away from the relative safety of the busy streets of downtown Havana. In spite of all this, Havana still remained one of the safest and most popular destinations in the Caribbean and still the most desirable location for anyone with the means of getting here.

After a few beers, Rip walked toward the Floridita. The streets of Havana were filled with old Russian and American automobiles. There were brightly painted trucks, old scooters, and vehicles modified in every manner imaginable. Most emitted a trail of visible exhaust as they sped by, and some seemed to move slower than a man could walk. Amid the traffic were handcarts and wheelbarrows with loads that seemed impossible to carry. Music could be heard from every doorway, and most places had a least one person, normally a buxom, raven-haired woman, beckoning all who passed to come inside.

Walls, posts, and any surface that might hold a tack or staple were covered with posters and notices. Some were political, but most advertised entertainment or sporting events. Cubans were passionate about many things, but entertainment and sporting events were part of everyone's life. One colorful notice that caught Rip's eye had a sailboat over a map that showed a line between Key West, Florida, and Havana. It was a welcoming poster for the Key West to Havana Sailing Rally. Rip looked at the date and realized it was in town today, and the major local sponsor happened to be his destination.

After a few more stops, Rip spied the Floridita. Taxi cabs were everywhere, picking up and dropping off while the Policia maintained a visible presence. In the 1930s the Floridita was a favorite hangout of the famous author and fisherman Ernest Hemingway. Although he had not stepped foot in the establishment for more than sixty years, his image was everywhere. On one wall a large banner heralded the arrival of the Key West Rally sailors. Rip paused before crossing the street and watched as tourists came and went. Most came to the Floridita for a single purpose, and that was to get the requisite photo next to the famous writer whose bronze image stood near the bar.

When Rip finally walked through the door, he immediately saw Brad surrounded by three local women and a short, balding Cuban in a colorful polyester suit with broad lapels. It was a look that went out with the seventies but would likely live on in Cuba forever. He could also see the sailors associated with the rally. They were loud, happy, and animated.

Rip was about ten feet from Brad, and he did nothing to conceal his presence. Under the circumstances he was not surprised to see that Brad hadn't notice him. At one time Brad may have been a great field operative, but he had clearly lost the edge. Rip knew the secret to staying alive was situational awareness. That included knowing who came and went near you, no matter what or who might be distracting you. It seemed impossible to Rip, but Brad had completely lost that quality.

Collection and awareness were a curse to Rip. His mind never stopped taking everything in, and he lived in a constant state of déjà vu. If Rip met someone or saw them cross the street or across a crowded room, they were logged away in a file in his brain. They were categorized by characteristics such as height, weight, hair, eyes, nose, gait, mannerisms. Anything and everything was a data point locked away.

How a person moved or acted could be a clue as to their ultimate intentions. Everyone was a threat until they were classified otherwise, and the process took milliseconds for some and minutes for others. It was crazy at times, but the fact was that it had no off switch, and ignoring the voices while abroad often resulted in death. That much was a fact proven in locations such as El Salvador, Brazil, the Middle East, and countless locations in Southeast Asia. Pay attention or perish. That was the mantra of anyone working away from home in the intelligence community.

CHAPTER 57

———◆———

RIP TURNED HIS ATTENTION FROM Brad and moved to the bar. Hemingway was surrounded by the rowdy crowd of sailors, but each time a person requested room for a photo, his or her wish was graciously respected. Sailors were loud, fun, and loved to party, but they were also a friendly group.

Like most drinking establishments in Cuba, cigar smoke was circulated up into the vaulted ceiling by a series of fans. Latin music played constantly and people danced, talked, and watched. Clearly many tourists were here simply to say they had been.

After getting a local beer, Rip relaxed and leaned on the bar among the sailors, eavesdropping on their stories. As the sailors talked and laughed, he could hear all the familiar terms that went with any high-seas sailing tale.

For a moment he felt a twinge of jealousy and envy. Sailing was a passion he had abandoned for too long, he thought. Then as he turned back to the bar, a woman squeezed next to him and hailed one of the bartenders. She was maybe in her midforties, fit, tan, and confident. Her long, dirty-blond hair was tied in a ponytail, and she was wearing tight shorts and the same red shirt as the other rally sailors.

The crowd at the bar forced them together, and Rip turned sideways to give her more room. Without thinking he looked down at her feet then up toward her shoulders.

"Did you just check me out?" the stranger asked as the bartender handed her a Bucanero beer in a can. Rip tossed his head back and his mouth opened, but nothing came out. "Well?" she asked again.

"Yeah, look, I'm sorry," Rip said. "I know it's rude. I just got out of jail and haven't actually seen many women lately."

"And?" she asked.

"And what?" Rip asked back.

"Your assessment? What do you think?"

"Um...great! Nice lines!" Rip held his beer up to toast. "Rip."

"Catherine," the stranger said as she touched his beer with hers.

"Is there a Mr. Catherine I need to be worried about in here?" Rip asked as he looked quickly around.

Catherine smiled and shook her head. "An ex, a wannabe, and some dreamers. Other than that, no."

"Here's to dreaming!" Rip said as he once more held up his beer. Catherine nodded and smiled.

"Bucanero in a can?" Rip asked, referring to her beer. "You look more like the wine or champagne type," he said.

"It keeps a certain class of dreamers away," she said. "What man wants a beer-swilling, foul-mouthed wench ruining a society luncheon?"

"Is that a trick question?" Rip said. "Wow. You are rapidly turning into the woman of the year!"

"What boat are you on? I don't recognize you," Catherine asked, looking around at the group of sailors.

"I actually flew in on business, but that's over, so here I am." Rip panned the room then looked back at Catherine.

"I guess I'll go home," he said as he motioned for another beer.

"You look like a sailor," Catherine said. "More so than most of these kids."

"Well, I used to sail, but sadly work has kept me away from it for too long." Rip reached for his beer as the bartender slid a fresh glass across the well-worn oak bar. Again, Rip turned and looked at the crowd of racers. He could almost guess what boat class people were racing in by the way they looked. "I love sailors! They know how to have fun."

As he looked around the bar, he noticed two thirty-something, olive-skinned men with short dark hair standing close to each other but not talking. They were wearing rally shirts but looked out of place. Rip thought it was odd but nothing more.

"We have several boats that could use a hand if you'd like a ride to Key West," Catherine said. "I'll introduce you to some people."

"You don't have to do that," a man said as he walked up behind Rip.

Rip instantly knew the voice, and he broke into a broad smile as he turned. "Hey, brother!" Rip said.

The man was Jake Wing, someone Rip had spent many months with when he first left college. "C. Ripley McGuin!" the man said.

"Jake, what are you doing here?" Rip asked.

"Warning you is what I'm doing," Jake said as he nodded toward Catherine.

"Screw you, Jake," she said as she raised her beer.

"Did I hear you need a ride?" Jake asked Rip.

"Why the hell not? I'm off the clock for a few days," he said.

"Still on that same clock?" Jake asked.

Rip just smiled.

Jake motioned across his left shoulder with his head toward Brad, who was still spinning tales for an adoring crowd of women. "You with that slipknot?"

"It's complicated, but you know, end-of-the-world shit."

Jake laughed and reached out to hug Rip. "It's great to see you, man!"

"C?" Catherine asked.

"Classified," Rip said, smiling. "Old family name I try to forget." As Rip turned toward the front of the bar, there standing in the open doorway was something he had not seen in many years.

Silhouetted by the sun, Rawley stopped and surveyed the room. She was wearing a red-and-yellow flower-print sundress and her long, black hair was down and fell forward over her shoulders. Other men stopped what they were doing and looked in her direction as well. In a crowd full of nondescript tourists, she was a stunning sight.

Catherine looked at Rip and Jake, then turned to see what held their attention. "Mrs. Rip?" she asked.

"She wishes," Rip said as he waved to Rawley.

"Who is that?" Jake asked.

"She's the one who gave me this scar," Rip said as he held up his left forearm.

"I wonder where she keeps her rapier in that outfit?" Jake said as he gently brushed someone aside to make room for Rawley.

"Oh, she can kill you with her wit," Rip said as he turned to get the bartender's attention. Rip looked at Rawley in the mirror behind the bar.

"What'll you have?" Rip asked as Rawley stopped directly behind him.

"Cuba Libre would be nice," she said as she looked first at Catherine then at the lack of space between Rip and Catherine.

"I'm a beer drinker myself," Catherine said.

"It gives me gas. I'm sure you have the same issue," Rawley said.

"Rawley, this is Jake. Jake, Rawley. Jake, can you maybe stand between Catherine and Rawley?"

"With pleasure!" Jake held out his hand. "It's nice to meet you after all these years," he said. "I always wanted to meet the woman who gave the Kraken that scar and broke his heart."

"I assure you the heart thing was the other way around," Rawley said.

Catherine put her hand on Rip's back as she moved from the bar. "See you at the finish line, Kraken."

Rip nodded to Catherine. "Key West, I'll be there," he said, then he turned back to Rawley.

"I did some research, Rip, and that guy in Japan is a hibakusha," Rawley said as she took her drink.

"A what?" Rip asked.

"He's a World War Two nuclear survivor. They were labeled. One of only maybe a hundred and sixty thousand left alive. It's revenge; that's what is happening. He wants revenge."

Rip looked at Rawley, and Jake looked at both of them.

"You two are working together?" Jake asked.

"No, she's just a pilot," Rip said. "Listen, Rawley. Every day, some crazy with an idea threatens our safety. We have contingency plans and people who live for that stuff. We're just a cog in the wheel. We did our part."

Rip stopped talking and took a drink. "First op?" Jake asked Rawley.

"Something like that," she said.

"We know all about it," said Jake. "I don't know what you two are into right now, but you have to let it go when it transitions out of your hands. Rip is right; it's the cycle." Jake stopped talking and squeezed into the bar.

Before another word was spoken, Rip could hear Brad calling out to him. Rip turned to see Brad moving through the crowd toward them. "Hey, guys! Did you just get here? I've been over by the door watching for you!" Brad said as he rudely elbowed his way toward Rawley.

"Just walked in," said Rip.

Brad stopped and looked at Jake but didn't say anything. It was clear he remembered the face but not the name. Jake was happy to leave it at that, and he turned his attention to Rip.

"I'm out of here, Rip," Jake said as he finished his beer. "I can use you if you want a spot."

"What's the ride?" Rip asked.

"I have tired old fifty-foot race boat, three guys, all good. We are first in class but just fun racing."

"I'm in," Rip said. "Where and when?"

"Marina Hemingway, four in the morning, ready to go. Or find us tonight if you need a place to sleep. Follow the women!" Jake said. Then he slapped Rip on the shoulder and nodded toward Rawley, and he was gone.

CHAPTER 58

———◆———

RIP WATCHED JAKE LEAVE THEN turned to Rawley. Brad had his right arm on the bar and his body shielding anyone from getting close to her from the left. He was talking nonstop, and Rawley was sipping her drink and looking through him like he was invisible.

Rip looked over Brad's shoulder and caught her eye. "Dance?" he asked.

For a few seconds, she just looked at Rip's face.

"Hey!" Brad said. "I thought I had the first dance."

Rawley narrowed her eyes and looked directly at Brad. "See that scar on Rip's arm?" she asked. "I'll do that to your throat if you don't move."

Brad held both hands up as if to surrender. "Relax, relax. I'll take the next one."

Rip reached for Rawley's hand and walked her to the corner where others were dancing.

"Do you remember how to do this?" Rawley asked.

Rip stopped and spun around then pulled Rawley's right hand into the air and pulled her close. "On two?" Rip asked, in reference to the popular Puerto Rican salsa style.

Rawley picked up Rip's left hand, then they both paused for second to pick up the beat. Rip looked down into Rawley's eyes as he held her close. Then, as if they had danced just yesterday, they began to step in unison to the music.

Rip spun Rawley once then again pulled her body into his then pushed her back.

"I am impressed," Rawley said as she stayed with him.

"I've been watching everybody while I was waiting for you," he said.

"I'm surprised the sailing babe didn't have you out here," she said.

Rip just smiled and kept moving Rawley across the dance floor. When the song ended, several people clapped. "One more?' Rip asked. "Or you can run back to Brad and the Colonel."

Rawley looked toward the bar, and she could see the Colonel had arrived. They were both watching Rawley and grinning. "Oh crap!" Rawley said as she reached for Rip and started dancing again. "What was that about Key West?"

"I'm taking a week off," said Rip as he turned Rawley around and pulled her into his chest then shuffled to the side. Rip's hands slid down Rawley's side to her buttocks, and she pushed into his hand. "Jake is an old friend from work, and he's racing. I'm sailing with him to Key West tomorrow. It's like a six-hour ride on his boat. How did you find out all that about Masogi?" Rip asked.

"I called a guy who used to be an intel officer," Rawley said as she raised her hands over her head and twirled. "He just found that stuff on the Internet." She turned into Rip and flipped her hair into his face. Rip grabbed her waist and jerked her back into his chest.

"Interesting. Langley wants you badly; maybe it's a good fit for you," said Rip. "Meet me in Key West for a couple days. I can tell you all about the job. It's a great town," Rip added as he pushed her away while holding her left hand.

"I've been there on det many times in the Navy," Rawley said. "I'll show you around."

"So, a deal then?" Rip asked, pulling her in one more time as the song ended. Rip held Rawley close and leaned toward her. Just as their lips were about to meet, Rawley put her hands on his chest and tilted her head back.

"We'll get some sun, have some fun, and we'll be nine hundred miles from the White House, just in case," said Rip.

"That's a pleasant thought," Rawley said as she left the dance floor.

As Rip led her back to the bar, Rawley was feeling a sense of dread. She was reminded of an awful blind date. Now there would be small talk with an extremely annoying man and awkward questions with another stranger twice her age.

"Rawley, you look fabulous!" the Colonel said as he reached to embrace her.

Rawley returned the embrace but kept the distance between them just enough to send a signal most men would understand. Although, she wasn't sure if that message would be received here.

"Rip and I will be vacationing starting tomorrow in Florida," she said as she sent another message to Brad that he needed to back off. "I'm meeting Rip in Key West."

"Where to from there?" the Colonel asked. "I travel often to Miami."

Rawley shook her head and smiled as the Colonel spoke. "Oh, we don't know yet," she said. "It will be spontaneous!"

Brad apparently got the clue, or not. Either way, it didn't matter, as he walked away shouting to another woman across the crowded bar.

"When you are ready, we can all go to my villa. It is a short ride from here," the Colonel said as he smiled at Rawley then looked her over from head to toe. "We can use the pool. You will find it most relaxing!"

Rip was to the Colonel's right and behind him drinking another beer but taking it all in. After hearing the Colonel's plans he subtly signaled Rawley by shaking his head.

"Colonel," Rawley started, "I am afraid we will have to take a rain check. Our aircraft must leave tonight, and I need to be on it."

"Well," the Colonel said as he turned and reached for Rip's hand, "you are a lucky man indeed. I wish I were twenty years younger. We would spar for this woman's affection."

"Thanks, Colonel. Estar mas sano de un pera," Rip said, in the Colonel's native tongue.

The Colonel laughed. "Thank you very much for the kind compliment, but I think I shall still pass.

The Colonel then turned to Rawley. "Buena suerte y Dios las bendiga, my dear." He pulled her hand up and kissed it before walking away.

"What was that all about?" Rawley asked. "My Spanish is a little rusty."

"I told him I'd trade you for a box of Cubans." Rip grinned and leaned back on the bar.

"Seems fair," Rawley said.

"Happy?" Rip asked.

Rawley clenched her teeth and looked at Rip. "I don't know if I'm happy or what. I am supposed to be flying for my father in Afghanistan, but I was clearly sent away from there. Anyone, including you, could have identified that plane. I don't know what to think right now." She crossed her arms and again silently looked at Rip.

"Do you want to get a room?" he asked. Before Rip could finish his question, she was shaking her head.

"I'll meet you in Key West tomorrow," she said. "Let's not make any promises and go from there."

"Fair enough," Rip said, nodding his head. "How about I escort you back to the plane?"

Rawley shook her head again. "No, I'll jump in a cab." As she turned to leave, she stopped. "Get some rest," she said. "You might need it. For the race, I mean."

CHAPTER 59

KEY WEST, FLORIDA

RAWLEY WAS SITTING BETWEEN JEFF and Ry, looking ahead as Key West came into view. They were descending through fifteen thousand feet through scattered clouds, and she could clearly see the Key West airport ahead and to their right Boca Chica Naval Air Station.

Rawley had flown here several times while she was in the Navy, and no matter how many times she returned, she always loved scanning the water and horizon. Not much changed, but it didn't matter. The water surrounding Key West was like a painting made from a hundred shades of blue and green. There were shoal areas as far as the eye could see to the west and deep water beyond the reef to the south.

To the west of the island were several schooners on various points along a triangle course they plied three times a day with excited sunburned tourists. To the north were small boats towing parasails. To the east were a thousand boats anchored in three separate mooring fields.

Along the northern generally protected shoreline were docks for cruise ships, marinas, and government vessels.

The prime land owner in Key West had historically been the government and more specifically the US Navy. At different times predating the Civil War, the military had maintained a strong presence in Key West to combat piracy. During the Civil War, the island had a large Union footprint, surrounded by Rebel spies and sympathizers and the Navy occupied Fort Taylor to prevent Confederate ships from using the island to find refuge.

By the midforties there was a school for military divers known as Underwater Swim School. The school had a fifty-foot dive tower visible from most places in town, and it was a popular attraction for the conch trains as they hauled tourists through the streets pointing out various historical points. By the mid-sixties there were destroyers and submarines.

The most famous street in Key West and the state of Florida was named for William Pope Duval, the first territorial governor of Florida. The street was just under a mile and a half long and ran from north to south.

Duval Street was lined with bars, restaurants, and shop after shop selling the same island-themed art, T-shirts, jewelry, and henna tattoos.

Key West had long embraced their unique location and history, and tourists were lured by theme weeks, fishing tournaments, and other activities on the water including a week-long sailboat regatta simply known as Race Week.

Amid all the week-long celebrations, the most famous event by far was Fantasy Fest. It was an event that rivaled Mardi Gras and featured body painting, parades, and beads thrown from balconies. Fantasy Fest had its own yearly theme and drew thousands to the tiny island city nicknamed "The Conch Republic."

The Key West airport was small by any standards. Its single four-thousand-nine-hundred-foot runway often made for exciting landings, and there were no jetways, just mobile stairways, adding to the tropical-island sensation.

Visitors were greeted by sun, wind, and an occasional tropical shower as they made the short walk to a small terminal with its indoor tiki hut serving rum punch. A colorful sign above the entry welcomed all to the Conch Republic. The airport was just a small part of the charm of Key West.

If the aircraft Rawley was on were smaller, air-traffic control would have turned them in right over the downtown area. But due their size, they were sent west toward the Dry Tortugas and set up for a long three-mile straight-in final.

Ry left little runway behind as the main landing gear touched down between the threshold hash marks and the numbers. As soon as the nosewheel touched the ground, the powerful engines slowed the aircraft to a near stop in less than nine hundred feet.

"They're parking us to the left by cargo," Jeff said. On the tarmac were three Boeing 737s from different airlines and two small commuter aircraft. Next to the general aviation parking area, Key West Seaplanes operated a maintenance facility for their amphibious Otters and Caravans.

Parking was tight and extremely crowded during holidays, when hundreds of private planes arrived often in a matter of hours.

"We're cleared, Rawley, so you can head straight out," Ry said as he pushed his seat back.

"Do you need to leave anything with us? We are headed to Edenton," Jeff offered.

"I left a bag with a weapon in it. Can you put that in the Mustang?"

"Will do," Ry said as reached for her hand.

"It's been fun," Jeff said.

CHAPTER 60

MARINA HEMINGWAY, HAVANA, CUBA

———◆———

MORE THAN ONE HUNDRED SAILBOATS participating in the Key West Havana Rally departed Marina Hemingway over the course of an hour, beginning just as the sun came up. The narrow channel was bordered by coral and shallows and was poorly marked, making any low-light passage especially hazardous for sailboats.

Like all regattas, the slowest classes were called to the line first. Most of the cruising boats who were along for the adventure would make the single-leg, eighty-five-mile passage to the finish line in fifteen hours or less. The faster cruising boats would come in under twelve hours, and the boats built for ocean racing would be on a two-leg, one-hundred-and-twenty-mile course. With the prevailing wind, the last thirty miles should be directly downwind for the boats on the longest route, and most if not all of the fastest boats would finish under spinnaker, making them easy to see from the Key West beaches.

Among the sailboats heading out of the marina were several sport-fishing yachts and few high-performance powerboats who signed on as committee boats. Participating in sanctioned events was an easy way to visit Havana, and the sailing rallies and regattas were like a large floating party once the sailing was done. Enlisting support for races to Havana was always the simple part. Getting through the government red tape was a months-long and frustrating task for organizers.

Rip and Jake were on a boat known as an Open 50. The boat was purposely built for ocean racing, and many of the Open class boats had gone around the world with a crew of one person or more. Boats of this type carried a tremendous amount of sail area, had minimal wetted surface, and most if not all were outfitted with an articulating keel—three characteristics needed for speed on the open ocean.

"Nice boat!" Rip said as he looked around. "When did you get it?"

"About six months after I got back from our last trip together. A guy I sailed with before you showed up raced it around the world twice, singlehanded, for Iberia Airlines. It's a little tired, but it will still do fifteen to twenty, easy. All carbon fiber and a swing keel."

"I'm impressed!" Rip said. "You still have the place in Wyoming?"

"Yeah, I'm going back and forth between Jackson Hole and the boat. I'm a bit limited in where I can tie this up because of the draft, but I have a few places I enjoy. Boston in the summer. You can't beat it!" "How about you?" Jake asked. "Still living aboard?" "I've got Beneteau 50 in National Harbor but I haven't seen much of it lately." Rip said as he pulled line from a winch.

Once they cleared the channel and entered the Gulf of Mexico, there would be little to no small talk until they were across the start line and well on their way. Jake and at least one other crewman would be watching all the other boats and several instruments that indicated wind direction and speed as well as hull speed through the water and speed over ground. Rip and the other two crewmen stood by in case they needed to quickly adjust or move the sails as Jake maneuvered for position.

The main committee boat was anchored on the right flank of the starting line. All the boats monitored a specific radio frequency, and the various classes remained well clear of the start line until they were called.

In all sailboat races, the start was often the most perilous time for most of the boats, and collisions were common, especially when relatively inexperienced sailors, overaggressive sailors, and boats of all sizes and capabilities were mixed together. A steady wind would mean the first classes to leave should at least be away from the line, making for a less congested start. Different headings for the fastest class also helped.

Jake looked around and decided it was most important to get across the line without an incident rather than get across first. With that in mind, he maneuvered into a point where he might be third or fourth across the line but not blocked by anyone. If the race were shorter or the competitors were unknown to him, he might handle the start differently but he knew all the boats in his class, and barring a catastrophe he could afford to be conservative.

The radio was alive with messages from the committee boat, and racers were maneuvering close enough to talk from deck to deck. There were catcalls, taunts, and bets going back and forth. The wind was a steady fifteen knots from the southeast, so that would make for an easy reach to the turn then mostly downwind under asymmetrical or spinnaker to the finish line. That plan of course was predicated on nothing changing.

"Ease the jib!" Jake called out. Rip slipped the jib sheet until Jake ordered him to stop. If the boat didn't change course, Rip knew they would slow slightly.

"I'm letting these guys on my left pass, then we'll jibe," Rip said as he looked from side to side and behind. Just as the other boat's stern came even with Jake's bow, he called out, "Stand by to jibe! Jibe, oh!" Rip turned the helm hard left. A jibe would bring the wind directly across they stern of Jake's boat. The boom was centered and tight, so the main sail simply snapped over, and the port main sheet immediately went under tension.

As the bow veered hard to port, Rip slacked the port jib sheet as another crewmember pulled the starboard sheet as fast as he could until the jib shifted between the headstays. Once the sail was through to the other side, the same crewman winched the sheet until Jake called it good.

"Great job, everyone!" Jake said. "Same drill in five minutes or less!"

CHAPTER 61

KEY WEST, FLORIDA

——◆——

AFTER CHECKING IN TO A hotel, Rawley took a ride around Key West then headed down Duval Street. One of the longest north-south streets in Key West, Duval touched the Straits of Florida on the southern end and the Gulf of Mexico on the northern end. By noon Duval would be filled with tourists, but at this hour there were only deliveries and walkers and chickens. After passing one of Key West's most famous landmarks, Sloppy Joe's, Rawley headed over to Pepe's for some breakfast and gossip.

Pepe's was opened in 1909, and for many years it was considered the original city office. In days past, if a decision had to be made regarding Key West, it was probably made at Pepe's over breakfast, lunch, or dinner.

As soon as Rawley walked in, she recognized the bartender and a few of the staff rushing around the restaurant. Over the years Pepe's had grown to include a covered patio surrounding a very large mahogany tree that was often home to a very large cat. The uneven cobblestone floor and open-air dining area was distinctly Old Key West.

Rawley looked around the restaurant as she walked through the dining area to the bar. At Pepe's it would be rare for a visitor to be seated at the bar before nine o'clock. Those seats were almost always occupied by local characters who met very early in the morning to discuss all the events from the previous day. News in Key West traveled fast, and it always traveled by word of mouth, or as the song said, "the coconut telegraph."

It didn't matter how trivial the news might be or how important; it was always debated at Pepe's over hot bread and coffee.

As soon as Rawley approached the bar, she was recognized. "Move over, everyone, move over!" the bartender shouted. Without waiting for anyone to move, Cathy, the bartender, was pushing plates aside. "Make room for the jet pilot!"

Rawley just smiled and those seated at the bar glanced back at her then turned and picked up right where they left off with their stories. There were six people at the bar, and no less than four different stories being told. At least one person was listening to someone on either side and commenting.

"Thanks, Cathy," Rawley said as she squeezed into the corner seat. There was only enough room for one elbow per person on the bar. It was tight but always friendly.

"Coffee, two eggs scrambled, and whatever the bread of the day is," Rawley said as she looked around. Cathy was pouring the coffee, and one of the staff nearby was already relaying the order to the kitchen.

"How's Navy life?" one of the men asked as he leaned back and blew smoke toward the ceiling.

"It hasn't changed much since you were in, except the ships run on oil now," Rawley said. The man laughed and launched into a story from his past life on a destroyer that had been stationed in Key West in the 50s. Rawley looked in his direction as he talked, but like most everyone she was pretending to listen.

"Where have you been since we last saw you?" Cathy asked.

"I have been in Virginia and California and Arizona," Rawley said. Before Rawley finished talking, Cathy had turned to fill someone's cup. Rawley never bothered to get into details, even when she was in Key Wet doing flight training and eating here regularly. Few people really listened anyway, and the details would be lost in a moment. At Pepe's small talk was always about respect for each other whether you flew a multimillion-dollar fighter jet, owned a business, or lived under a tree.

"What's going on in town right now?" Rawley asked.

As expected three people started talking at once. "It's dead!" said one. "Too many kids and foreigners," someone else said.

"It's not dead; it's crowded!" Cathy said, shaking her head and rolling her eyes. The area behind the bar began to fill up as more people showed up and waited for a table. Rawley ate her breakfast and contemplated the day.

She knew she needed to check in with her parents at some point. The events of the last few days had left her somewhat confused. She also knew she needed to return to Afghanistan, and she wanted to spend time with Rip, even if she hadn't told him. That part was a struggle, and she wished it would get settled in her mind.

"There's a sailboat race coming back from Havana today. Does anyone know where the boats are coming in?" Rawley asked the group.

"Schooner's."

"Stock Island."

"The waterfront."

Three people answered her question in unison with three different answers. Rawley just shook her head and looked at Cathy, smiling.

"They're tying up all over, but the meeting point is at Zero Duval," Cathy said pointing in the direction she was referring to.

"They have the whole dock bar reserved for today and tomorrow," she added, before turning away again.

"Thanks. Everyone have a wonderful day!" Rawley said as she stood up to leave.

"Stay away from Caroline and Front," someone yelled out. "They have some big deal going on at Truman's summer home."

Rawley stopped on the sidewalk outside Pepe's. To her left she saw two men having their photo taken in front of the café's front door, and across the street she could see the tall masts of the sunset cruise boats in the historic port basin.

She looked at her watch. It was now half past ten. A good time to find a quiet place and call home, she thought.

CHAPTER 62

STRAIT OF FLORIDA
23° 56' NORTH
81° 12' WEST

———◆———

JAKE HAD JUST TURNED TO the final downwind leg toward Key West. The spinnaker was set, and everyone was on edge. On the reach they were averaging eighteen knots; now they had accelerated to over twenty. The seas were running just one to two feet, and although the boat was riding well, at this speed anything could happen and often did when sailors became complacent—or even if they didn't.

"So, uh, what's with the girl?" Jake asked.

Rip looked at Jake for a moment. "I hadn't seen her in almost eight years," he said. "I was coming out the field south of Kabul, and she flew in and picked me up. A minute later our plane was burning, and we were fighting for our lives."

"Apparently you survived," Jake said as he scanned the instruments then the horizon in every direction.

"Yeah, we made it," Rip said, smiling.

"And what's got the world ending now?" Jake asked.

"About sixty years ago, we lost a little underwater flashlight in a plane that was coming out of Vietnam, and we think the jihadis found it," Rip said, while also looking up at the giant sail dragging them downwind.

"And they took it to Havana?" Jake asked skeptically.

"I don't know, Jake. We think so. Brad was spewing so much double talk and BS. He said there was an old Russian scientist there who might help make the thing work."

"Maybe a wind shift, boys!" Jake yelled.

Rip stood up looked out at the water, and the others did the same.

"If we can't hold this line, we'll go to the asymmetrical," Jake said, referring to the asymmetrical spinnaker. It was still a downwind sail, but it was less likely to collapse as the wind shifted from directly over the stern to the quarter.

"Rip, you're in the sewer!" Jake said, still watching the wind and surface of the water.

Rip immediately went below deck into the bow. Once the spinnaker came down, it would need to be pulled inside as fast as possible to keep it from going over the side and fouling on the keel.

"It's shifting!" Jake yelled. As he veered off course to follow the wind, the big spinnaker was already luffing. "Ready?" Jake asked.

Nobody on the bow spoke. Instead, arms went in the air to indicate the affirmative. Rip yelled from below the he was ready, and the last member of the crew stood by the main halyard.

"Stand by! We'll shadow it with the main." Jake said as he took in all the information at his disposal. "Ease the main halyard!" Jake said, as he turned just enough to port to send the spinnaker behind the giant mainsail that was now nearly perpendicular to the hull.

"Douse it now!" Jake yelled. On the bow the men pulled down on a line that would pull a sock over the collapsing spinnaker and dump the remaining air, making it easier to handle. Once the spinnaker was in the bag, they would have to get the pole disconnected. On many boats this was a time of great peril. In a real race, valuable seconds were often lost due to mishandling lines and sails, and there was always a chance someone could go overboard.

In sailboat racing spinnaker handling was also the most common trigger for strife. Tempers often flared, and mistakes were common, even among the most well-trained crews. Jake didn't suffer from such issues. He was here for fun and to win, but fun first. Nobody had to say it, but everyone on the crew subscribed to the famous skydiving mantra: "Slow is fast." Mistakes cost valuable time and put people in jeopardy, and mistakes came from rushing and inattention to detail. Slow and methodical would always beat fast and reckless.

Rip braced himself in the bow and waited for the hatch above his head to open. As soon as it opened, line fell at his feet and he began to pull until he saw the sock that held the spinnaker. Once he had that in hand, he pulled it down as fast as it would come.

On deck Jake was yelling his intentions as he turned back on course. On the bow the asymmetrical was already going up. Unlike the spinnaker the asymmetrical was wound up on a continuous furler, so it needed only to be hoisted, pulled tight, then attached to a few lines before it could be unfurled.

Before Rip was on deck, the new sail was fully inflated, and the boat speed was coming back up. "We're on course!" Jake said. "Great job, everyone."

"Well that wasn't so bad," Jake said to Rip as he took a seat at the starboard helm. "We are maybe one hour to the finish line," Jake called out.

"Any word on if we'll be searched going in?" Rip asked.

"Nothing yet," Jake said. "It makes sense if it was really on the island," he added.

"It was there," Rip said.

CHAPTER 63

KEY WEST, FLORIDA

———•———

RAWLEY WALKED DOWN THE BOARDWALK that ran the length of the harbor until she came to an area where there were no people watching tarpon or looking for manatees. It was about as much privacy as you could get on the streets of Key West at this hour.

She first dialed her mother's cell number, and Sally answered on the first ring. "I hoped you would call soon," she said. "Is everything all right?" Sally always asked the same questions, and Rawley always gave the same answers.

"I'm fine, Mom," Rawley said.

If Rawley was troubled, happy, or tired, her mother always knew no matter how Rawley answered or what she said. "I hope you aren't taking any chances," she said.

"None, Mom. I'm in Key West now. I think I'll stay for two days, if Dad doesn't have a problem with it."

"I can assure you he won't have a problem," Sally said. "Who's with you?"

Rawley was quiet for just a second. "Rip is here, he…he's sailing. Racing actually, from Havana," Rawley said as she looked down at the water.

"Rip, your old boyfriend? That Rip?" Sally asked.

"Yeah, that one, Mom. I ran across him on this trip."

"You love to sail. I'm surprised you didn't go along," her mother said.

Rawley hesitated as she spoke. "He's with an old friend, and I didn't want to intrude."

"Another woman friend?" Sally asked.

"No, Mom, a man he used to work with. Is Dad around today?" Rawley was preoccupied, and Sally could tell.

"Yes, he's in his office, expecting your call. We haven't been doing much since you had the accident," Sally said.

"It wasn't really an accident, Mom. It was more of a..." Rawley let her thought trail off. Her mother knew it wasn't an accident; she was just being Sally.

"You're sure you are all right?" Sally asked one more time.

"I'm fine, Mom. I'll call Dad. Love you."

"I love you too, dear," Sally said. "Have some fun; you deserve it, and tell Rip I said hello."

"Thanks, Mom." Rawley hung up the phone and smiled. Her mother always had a way of making everything seem so simple.

After a minute Rawley called her father. Talking to Bud was much different than talking to her mother. Bud was a warrior and a pilot, and Rawley had proven beyond a doubt she was his equal in that regard. For many years now, Bud spoke to her like a friend or another pilot rather than as his daughter. More than any man on earth, he knew she could handle any challenge put before her.

Except maybe the truth about a few key things like the family business or why she was sent out of Afghanistan after the crash. She was sure he had orchestrated her involvement with the lost C-130; she just wasn't sure why.

"Hey, Rawley! Where are you?" Bud asked.

"Key West, Dad. Rip is sailing from Havana, and I'm meeting him here this afternoon. You did know I was with Rip, right?" she asked.

"Rip, you mean your Rip, from school? That Rip?" Bud asked.

Rawley paused for a second. He sounded sincere, she thought. "Yes, that Rip. That's who I was picking up when we got shot down." Again, Rawley paused.

"I had no idea that's who you were with," Bud said. "I just knew you were going with someone to identify a lost aircraft. What happened with that?" Bud asked. "I saw you made a heck of trip from Afghanistan to the PI to Havana."

"We found it, then Rip thought we needed to go to Havana, so we did." Rawley was mindful that she was on a nonsecure phone call and left out any details.

"I'd like to spend a day or two here then drive to Norfolk before heading back to Afghanistan," Rawley said.

"Of course!" Bud said. "Take a week. Take two! I'll have you meet Gil in Africa. He may be over his head, teaching close air support with the Tractor."

"Sounds like a fun change of pace," Rawley said. "So." Rawley stopped for a second. "You didn't know Rip was over there or with me?"

"No clue, dear. Who could have known? Do you want the Mustang delivered to Key West?" Bud asked.

"No, I think I'll drive and see a few friends along the way, but thanks," Rawley said as she looked at boats in the Old Harbor area.

"Great job with that lost plane, sweetheart. It was important to a lot of people, especially the families," Bud said. "Have some in fun in Key West; you earned it! You know, when your Uncle Sid was in the Army Air Corps, he flew Harry Truman down there several times," Bud said. "Tell Rip I said hello. Love you; glad you're safe."

Before Rawley could say another word, the line was dead.

After talking to her parents, Rawley walked aimlessly around Old Key West for nearly two hours. Finally, she looked at her watch and headed toward the northern end of Duval Street and the boardwalk.

At the northern end of Duval Street, known by locals as Zero Duval, a hotel and bar sat on a pier overlooking the main harbor channel and Sunset Key. It was a popular spot for private parties, such as the wrap-up for the Key West Havana Rally.

As she approached the end of Duval, she could see a large white tent over the dock bar. Flags and banners from various sailing sponsors were everywhere, and island music could be heard coming from the pier.

Before she went to the tent, Rawley stopped and looked at a sign with the schedule of events. One name caught her eye as she looked at the list of entertainers scheduled to perform. Cory Young was a musician she knew well from her Navy time in Key West. He was popular local singer and the son of a Navy SEAL. Cory lived on a boat with his family and played at every big event in town. Rawley looked at her watch, and she could see from the schedule Cory was expected to start playing within the hour. The entrance to the pier was roped off, and several people stood around a table. The mood was festive, and the weather was beautiful as usual. If she could just reconcile things in her mind, maybe she could have some fun, she thought.

After watching the crowd for a few more minutes, she decided to join the party. At the main table, two women appeared to be checking passes.

"Excuse me, my friend is on one of the boats, but I don't know the name of it. I think it's a fast boat, and the captain's name is Jake...something. Would you possibly know who that is? I know it's silly, but I don't know any more details than that," she said.

The two women, who appeared to be in their late forties, looked up at Rawley. "Can you describe the captain, dear?" one of the women asked.

"Short, dark hair, bushy mustache, big, like muscular, maybe fifty years old, this tall." Rawley held her hands up to indicate his height.

Both women were smiling before she finished. "That pirate is Jake Wing, but he tends to use a different last name depending on whose wife he's talking to." The woman closest to Rawley was talking while the other woman laughed.

"His boat is the *Reckless Rogue*," the other women added.

"Aptly named," they both said, in near harmony. Then the women looked at each other and laughed again. Rawley was smiling and shaking her head as she recalled Jake's image in her mind.

"Honestly, I expected no less," Rawley said.

"They are through the finish gate, and they'll be docking in twenty minutes or less over there," one of the women said, pointing to an area behind the stage. "The first finisher in every class has a spot here."

Rawley looked in that direction. "OK, thanks," she said. "Can I pay to join the—"

"Have fun!" the woman said, waving her through before Rawley finished her question.

CHAPTER 64

———◆———

"WE DID GREAT!" JAKE SAID as he steered past historic Fort Zachary Taylor. "We'll sail down to the Coast Guard piers, turn it into the wind, and furl," he said.

Just past the fort, two cruise ships were tied up end to end. When the cruise ships were in town, the city was swarming with thousands of tourists, and businesses thrived. The prevailing wind would normally make for a nice reach along the boardwalk, but when the giant ships were in port, they blocked or fouled the wind for a distance of nearly half a mile to a height of more than two hundred feet.

As soon as the *Rogue* came into the shadow of the first cruise ship, the jib began to flutter, and the main relaxed. "Screw it," Jake shouted as he started the engine. "Roll it up and drop the main. Let's go drinking!"

In minutes the crew had the jib rolled around the headstay, and when the main was dropped, it effortlessly fell into the lazy jacks.

"I'm surprised we weren't searched," Rip said. "Knowing what we know, don't you think that was odd?" he asked Jake.

Jake shrugged. "Yeah, if it really was in Cuba, or maybe they got it. You know they would have had that island covered with SPECOP guys."

"Maybe you're right," Rip said.

"Or it's gone, or never really there at all." Jake shrugged. "Give yourself a break Rip. You earned it brother!" Rip took a long slow look at the Key West shoreline then he sat down for the time in hours.

As they approached the end of Duval, the party tent came into view, and they could hear music echoing across the water. Over a loudspeaker they heard a woman's voice announce their arrival.

"I think I know her!" Jake said. People all along the boardwalk waved just to be waving, and every other person was taking their photograph. "Portside tie, bow in," Jake said as he slowed their speed.

Rip looked at the crowd. He hadn't talked to Rawley before he left Cuba, but he hoped she would be here.

About two hundred feet from the basin, they heard a long horn blast, announcing the departure of the glass-bottomed boat. It was the only boat left in the basin where they were headed, and Jake could see it coming from where he needed to go.

"We'll let them clear then head in," Jake said as he pulled the throttle to neutral. Even though he had been here several times, Jake watched the depth finder as they turned out of the main channel. The *Reckless Rogue* drew eleven feet when the keel was fully down, and Jake was always cautious in port or close to shore. He knew it would be bad form to run aground in front the cheering crowd.

On the pier Rawley watched the *Rogue* as Jake maneuvered to make the hard right turn into the narrow opening. As they came close, she purposely stood back for a moment, watching Rip.

Standing here in the cheering crowd and seeing Rip like this on a boat made the events of the past week seem a thousand miles away. It also conjured memories she had long ago pushed aside. Tonight would be a new beginning, or it would finally be the end. That much she knew. As Jake passed between the two piers, Rawley moved to the end of the railing, where she could be seen. She held her drink high to toast their arrival. Jake saw her and waved as he blew three short blasts on the horn. Rip crossed the cockpit to the starboard side and smiled, then touched his right index finger to his lips. Without thinking, Rawley smiled and returned the gesture. A throwback to their college days, it was their non-verbal acknowledgment whenever they saw each other in passing.

"I guess she doesn't hate you," Jake said.

"Maybe not," Rip said as he went forward help tie up. After weaving through the crowd, Rawley approached the boat, and she could see Rip talking to the musician, Cory Young, like they were old friends.

"You two know each other?" Rawley asked as she walked up.

"Hey! Rawley!" Cory said as he pulled her close. "I saw you walk by earlier, but you got lost in the crowd."

"His dad was an instructor of mine at SEAL training," Rip said.

"Dad gave him the nickname Kraken when he saw Rip flailing to the surface in the dive tower. Dad said he looked like a crazy sea monster," Cory said, grinning.

"So that's where that came from." Rawley said as she looked at Rip.

Rip just shrugged. "I prefer my story actually," he said. "How do you two know each other?"

"Just people you meet when you're barhopping in Key West," Cory said before Rawley could answer. "I gotta play in a few minutes. Let's have a drink later."

"Look forward to it," Rip said as he put his arm around Rawley and pulled her close.

"How was sailing?" Rawley asked.

"It was fantastic," Rip said as a conch horn went off on the dock, heralding the arrival of another boat.

"You made it!" Jake yelled out as he climbed over the railing.

"Did you guys win?" Rawley asked.

"It was just a fun thing, not really a race, but yeah, we won it! Let's celebrate with a drink!" Jake said as he led the way to the bar.

While sitting at a table on the pier, more boats came in, and other sailors arrived by bus. In minutes the crowd seemed to double in size. Above the chatter Cory was on stage, going back and forth between island music and old rock 'n' roll. As was usually the case in Key West, people were dancing and drinking and generally having a great time.

Jake made a toast, but he was clearly preoccupied watching the crowd.

"Are you looking out for husbands or wives?" Rawley asked.

Jake just smiled. "You been talking to some old friends, I see."

"Just casual conversations, Jake."

"It's all lies and exaggeration, sweetheart."

"It usually is," Rawley said as she also panned the crowd.

"Any word on what we were chasing?" Rawley asked Rip. "I'm trying to let it go in my mind." she said. Rip shook his head. "They must have solved it," he said. "I expected to be searched coming in, but nothing happened. If they didn't know for sure where it was, they would never have let us go from Havana to here without searching every boat."

"Rip's right," Jake said. They would have lined us up miles out and went boat to boat. There wasn't so much as a hint of that."

Rawley smiled and shrugged. "That's a relief."

As Cory finished his song, he asked for everyone's attention. "Folks, as a longtime resident of Key West, I'd like to dedicate this next song to one of our most famous visitors, and for a change it's not Ernest Hemingway."

"In honor of the Truman family reunion, here's an old song by Chicago. 'Harry Truman.'"

Cory started singing, and the crowd cheered and applauded.

"My father just told me today that my uncle used to fly Harry Truman down here," Rawley said as she turned back to face Rip. "He said hello, by the way. So did my mother"

"How are they?" Rip asked.

"They're doing great," she said. As Cory sang the words to the song, Rawley started thinking again. "A Truman family reunion here. Did you know he spent so much time in Key West they named his place 'The Little White House'?"

"Seriously?" Rip asked.

"Yeah, it's true," Rawley said. "I took the tour a few years ago."

Rawley and Rip looked at each other as Cory sang the final verse to the song.

The words "America is calling Harry Truman" came from the speakers, and the crowd was clapping and shouting before Cory finished singing.

"Jake, do you have a weapon on the boat?" Rip asked.

"Of course I do," Jake said. "What are you thinking?"

Without answering Rip got up and started walking toward the *Rogue,* Jake and Rawley followed close behind.

CHAPTER 65

RIP PUSHED A NINE-MILLIMETER HANDGUN Jake had given him into his waist-band as he walked toward the tourist information stand at the end of the dock.

"When is the Truman family reunion?" Rip asked the clerk.

"Starts tomorrow or tonight," the man said. "I'm not sure."

"Take me to the Little White House," Rip said to Rawley.

"What are you thinking?" she asked as she led the way down Duval Street.

Rip just shook his head. "I'm having so many thoughts, I don't know where to begin."

"Do you have a phone?" Rip asked as he followed Rawley through the crowded streets. Rawley pulled out her cell phone and handed it to Rip.

"We are about five minutes away," she said.

Rip dialed Sherman Craig's desk number, but there was no answer. Next he tried Sherman's mobile number. "Sherman, it's Rip. I'm in Key West," he said. Sherman started to talk but Rip interrupted him. "Yeah, it's great, listen."

While talking Rip stayed behind Rawley as she moved through the streets at a brisk walk. "There is a Truman family reunion in Key West today or tomorrow."

"Truman?" Sherman asked.

"Harry Truman, the president, it's his family. They're coming here," Rip said.

"OK, dude, so there's a reunion. They must do that all the time," Sherman said.

"The place is called the 'Little White House,' Sherman."

"Stop, wait a minute," Sherman said. "If this is about the thing you were following, it's gone. Masogi's plane flew back into Cuba and left for Venezuela yesterday. We're seventy to ninety percent sure if it was there it left on that plane."

"It's a decoy, Sherman!" Rip was insistent. "Sherman, Masogi is a hiba…" Rip paused, trying to remember what Rawley had told him.

"Hibakusha," said Rawley, without looking back.

"He's a Hibakusha, Sherman," Rip said.

"OK, I'll bite," said Sherman. "What's that?"

"He's a nuclear survivor from Nagasaki."

"There it is!" Rawley said as she stopped walking.

Rip stopped talking as he looked ahead at the building known as 'The Little White House.' There were cones across the street blocking traffic, but no police cars or obvious law enforcement presence.

"Dude, let it go," Sherman said. "It's in Venezuela or who knows where, but it's not in Key West. We would know." Sherman stopped talking and listened. "Are you there?"

"Yeah, I'm here, Sherman," Rip said.

"Rip, every president had a place called the Little White House or the Other White House. There's one in every vacation spot in America."

"That's true, Sherman, but this is the only one close to Havana. I just sailed here from Havana, along with a hundred other boats, and nobody checked them here or there before we left. I think it's here, and he's targeting the Truman clan. It makes sense if you add up all the clues," said Rip as he continued to look down the street at the building.

"It's a hunch, Rip. And a thin one at that. Anyone I talk to will want a lot more than that before they sound the alarm."

"They said 'poison' in more than one intercept, Sherman. Masogi is alive, but he was poisoned by nuclear radiation. Truman did that. Think about it! They plan to break that weapon open in the house and expose the entire family to radiation." Rip stopped talking as he looked up and down both sides of the street.

Sherman was silent.

"Sherman, all I'm saying is, we should at least alert the family and let them decide. I'm here now," Rip said. "I'll look around and call you back."

"OK, call me back," Sherman said, then they both hung up.

"What do we do now?" Rawley asked.

Rip exhaled and dropped his shoulders. "Here's your phone," he said.

"Let's just see if we can approach the place and see what the response is." Rip crossed the street, and Rawley followed.

A large sign indicated the entrance was in the rear. As Rip and Rawley rounded the final corner on the walkway, a man in a suit came toward them with his hand in the air.

"The place is closed," he said. "You will have to leave."

Rip stopped and looked at the man. "Wait here," Rip said to Rawley, then he walked toward the man.

As Rip got closer, the agent pushed his coat aside to expose a badge and a weapon. "You really need to leave now, sir," the man said. "This place is off limits."

Rip stopped a few feet from the agent and identified himself. After talking for a few minutes, Rip turned and walked back to where Rawley was waiting.

"What did you tell him?" Rawley asked.

"Nothing really," Rip said.

"I can't tell him I think there is a nuke on its way but that I don't know how, when, or where from."

With Rawley following, Rip crossed the street and stopped. "I'll call Sherman back later and see what he thinks. My gut just tells me this is going to happen."

Rip looked down the street. "I know a great bar close by. We can always go to the Green Parrot," he said.

"Let's sit on this bench and think it over," Rawley said. "When you said poison, what did you mean?"

"Nobody believes the bomb can be detonated like a nuclear reaction," Rip said. "But they can break it open with a small explosive charge and release a cloud of radioactive poison. That's what we think is going on. Or what I think, anyway."

Rip and Rawley were sitting on the bench for twenty minutes when Rip noticed something across the street that caused him to take notice.

Four men with dark hair walked in the direction of the Little White House. Two were dressed in slacks and looked well groomed. The other two wore shorts and T shirts. One of the men in shorts was pulling a suitcase. Rip watched as they walked. There was no conversation between them, and they moved like they had a purpose.

"What is it?" Rawley asked.

"It's in that suitcase," Rip said.

"What's in the suitcase?" Rawley asked as she looked toward the men.

"I saw those two men wearing shorts in the bar when we were at the Floridita," Rip said. "I'm sure of it. They were totally out of place there, and together all four of them look out of place here."

"Are you sure?" Rawley asked.

"No," Rip said. "Honestly, I still don't know what I'm sure of."

Rip and Rawley watched as the men continued down the street. Just as they arrived at the first gate to The Little White House, they separated into pairs. The men with the suitcase stopped, while the other two followed the walkway toward the building.

"That's it!" Rip said. "Hit redial and tell Sherman it's happening. He needs to stop the Truman family and get help here now."

"What are you going to do?" Rawley asked as she pulled out her phone.

"You stay here. I'm going in. Tell the police I'm in there," Rip said as he pulled Jake's nine-millimeter pistol from his waistband and put a round in the chamber.

"I'm not staying here; I'm going with you!" Rawley said as she followed Rip.

Rip stopped in the street and turned around. "Listen!" he said. "You got lucky in Afghanistan. and you still got hurt. You're just a pilot. Now stay here and call! I'm trained for this; you aren't."

Rip was emphatic, and Rawley was angry.

"Stay here and tell the police or whoever arrives I'm in there with at least one other agent and I'm wearing a blue shirt."

Rip didn't wait for Rawley to answer as he turned and began walking quickly toward the gate. As he got closer, he could see that the two men who had stayed behind with the suitcase were now missing.

Rawley stopped on the sidewalk and hit redial on her phone, then waited for an answer.

"Sherman, this is Rawley West," she said. "I'm with Rip, and he followed four men into the White House. The bomb is here."

"Did you see it?" Sherman asked.

"No, he recognized two men from Cuba, and they had a suitcase and went inside. Rip is—"

Before Rawley could complete her thought, shots rang out.

"Sherman, there's gunfire. I need to go! Send help now, and stop the Truman family!"

Rawley hung up and moved quickly toward the first gate.

CHAPTER 66

———◆———

As Rawley reached the first gate, she heard two more shots from inside the building. She felt her phone vibrating as she broke into a run, but she didn't stop to answer. When she came around the last corner where they had previously been stopped by the agent, she saw the man lying on the ground in a pool of blood.

Rawley bent down to check his pulse, and she could tell he was dead. She pulled his coat back and took the agent's automatic pistol from its holster.

The entry to The Little White House was approximately in the middle of the building, and Rawley was trying to remember the layout. As she slowly entered, she first looked left then right.

She remembered the biggest room in the house was to the right at the end of the building. Truman had often played poker there. To the right was a round poker table, and to the left there was a bar. That room would seem the most likely place to plant the bomb, she thought.

Rawley moved slowly down the narrow corridor, stopping frequently to listen. Just before she went through the last door, she heard another gunshot. For a moment Rawley froze. The shot clearly came from the room she was about to enter, and she knew once she opened that door, there was no going back.

Rawley pushed the door inward and raised her weapon. As the door opened, she could see Rip was down near the poker table, and there was a man standing over him about to fire his weapon at Rip's head.

"Hey!" Rawley yelled. As the man turned around, she fired twice.

The man fell to floor, and Rawley looked to her left then quickly moved along the wall toward Rip. Her mind raced, and she struggled to calm herself. She kept her weapon trained to the left toward the room, but she looked at Rip then at the man she had shot. When she reached Rip, she went down on one knee, then while holding her weapon in her left hand, she reached down and touched him with her right.

Rip grabbed her arm. "I can't walk," he said in a labored voice. "You need to get out of here now!"

Rawley didn't answer as she continued to watch the room ahead of her. Instinctively she reached down and picked up the handgun dropped by the man she had killed.

For a second her mind had stopped racing. Her breathing slowed, and she began to think about what she needed to do.

As she stood up she made one quick scan for the suitcase or anything that might be a bomb, but it was not there. Again, she thought about the layout of the building. There were several narrow hallways, more than ten rooms, at least two sets of stairs leading to the second floor, and three terrorists somewhere.

Help should arrive soon, she thought, but the terrorists would surely set the bomb off in desperation now that they were compromised. Rawley knew she needed to act quickly. Just as she took her first step, Rip grabbed her leg.

"Get out now!" he said. "Get out!"

Rawley froze. She could drag Rip from the building, but if the bomb went off, they would still not be safe. If she acted quickly, maybe she could stop them. Without looking down Rawley pulled her leg from Rip's grasp and moved forward.

With her eyes following her weapon, she moved toward the farthest exit from the room. As she moved she systematically cleared every corner, every potential hiding place, until she came to the first hallway going left.

Moving as quietly as she could, she cautiously pushed open the door. Just as she looked through the door, she saw movement in the hallway directly ahead of her. As she came around the door, a shot went off and wood splinters hit her in the face. She instinctively pointed her weapon in the direction of the movement and pulled the trigger three times.

She could see one of the men who was wearing shorts fall backward and collapse. As she approached the man, she fired one more shot into his sternum then leaned back against the wall.

Her breathing was rapid again, and she knew she needed to calm down. Then she slowly squatted and picked up the dead man's weapon and pushed it into her waistband.

Before she started moving again, she thought about what was behind her. There was no way for anyone to come from that direction without going past Rip, she thought.

Rawley looked ahead and down the hall, and she saw the first staircase leading up to the southern bedrooms and a straight hallway toward the northern end of the house. Her instincts told her to go up.

When she reached the midpoint of the staircase, Rawley stopped and quickly formulated a plan. The attack was clearly foiled, and they would set the bomb off regardless, she thought.

If the attackers had done their homework, they would know President Truman's living quarters were on the second floor at the northern end of the building. It would be a symbolic suicidal end, she decided. Now she moved quickly up the remaining stairs, watching up and ahead as she went.

When she reached the second floor, she knew it would take too long to go from room to room. As she stood looking at the closed door at the northern end of the hall, she fought to keep her breathing under control. She knew they had to be there.

Moving deliberately down the hall, she tried to listen for any sign of movement behind her or in the rooms she passed.

She pulled one of the other weapons from her waistband and held them both in front of her. As she got close to the room, she could see a shadow moving under the door. Rawley stopped and slowly went to one knee. In the gap between the floor and the door, she could see the white soles of what appeared to be boating shoes. Rawley stood up, swallowed hard, then took the last step toward the door.

Two feet from the door, she stopped and leaned against the wall, looking back down the hall behind her. If the other men were in any of those rooms, she would likely be dead.

Then she turned back toward the door and fired four shots. She could hear what had to be a body hit the floor, then she kicked the door inward. As the heavy door swung into the room, it hit the body of the man who was standing behind it then the door came back and hit her hard on her left side, knocking the handgun out of her left hand.

Rawley pushed back against the door and quickly scanned the room. To her right stood the last man, and in front of him on the bed sat an open suitcase with the weapon they had been chasing.

The weapon looked exactly as she had imagined it would look after sitting on the ocean floor for nearly sixty years: a rust-covered ball that could hardly be mistaken for a bomb or anything of importance.

For a second Rawley and the man looked at each other. The terrorist was unarmed, but in his hands he held what must have been a detonator. It was small plastic box wired to a package taped to the corroded nuclear weapon.

"Who are you?" the man asked in a distinctly Hispanic accent. "FBI? CIA?"

She slowly shook her head as he spoke. In her mind Rawley could hear Mike Crabbes distinctive voice instructing her to focus on the front sight of her handgun. She drew a deep breath and placed the iridium dot on the front of her weapon squarely on the young terrorists face.

She could hear sirens now, but they were still far off. The sun was nearly down, and shadows were everywhere in the room. Although the standoff seemed to last for minutes, it was in fact only seconds since she had come through the final door.

The man she looked at was young, and he looked tired and desperate. For a split second, Rawley thought about pleading with him. As they stared at each other, she could see there would be no simple solution and no compromise. A saga that had traversed the world all came down to this moment, and whether she had been trained for this or not, the situation had become hers to solve.

"I'm nobody," Rawley said. "I'm just a pilot." As Rawley spoke she gently squeezed the trigger.

With one fatal shot to the head, the young terrorist instantly collapsed into a heap on the floor. Rawley kept her weapon trained on his crumpled body as she walked around the end of the bed.

After staring at him for another second, she pointed the gun at his heart and pulled the trigger one more time. Only then did she realize the slide was locked back and her weapon was empty.

Rawley looked at the rust covered bomb sitting on the bed. Then she looked at the empty weapon she held and realized her hands weren't shaking. She wasn't breathing hard; she wasn't excited. She felt calm and devoid of emotion. The entire sequence of events since she entered the building seemed like a surreal dream.

She bent down and picked up the detonator. It was not high tech or military in nature. It looked like common parts from a hardware store, she thought as she gently placed it on the bed. The sirens came closer, and the sound brought her back to reality.

Rawley threw her weapon on the bed and ran back to where Rip lay wounded. Just as she ran into the room, it was like the whole world descended on The Little White House. Doors flew open, and window glass shattered as the Key West Police flooded the building.

"He's wounded, and the bomb is upstairs," Rawley said.

The first officer to come into the room held his weapon on Rawley as others yelled for medical assistance.

"Your man is down but alive," another said over the radio.

Soon men and women wearing vests emblazoned with the letters "FBI" swarmed the building. Three men went directly to Rip, and she was relieved to see he was still alive and coherent. Rawley stood back and watched as an EMT put an oxygen mask on his face while another attended to Rip's wounds. She could see he had been shot in both legs, and he appeared to have a wound in his right shoulder. Rip was trying to look up at Rawley, but the EMTs restrained him as they injected him with morphine. More men were running through the room when once again someone asked who she was and what she was doing there.

Rawley looked around the room and then at Rip. "I'm just a pilot," she said. "I heard the shooting and came in to find him lying there."

"OK, get her out of here," an FBI agent said. "I want this place locked down."

As Rawley was led from the building, her phone rang again. She pulled it from her pocket and saw it was Sherman Craig calling. She thought about answering but just let it ring. The officer led Rawley to a vehicle near the gate then told her to wait for someone to take her statement. After five minutes she realized she had been left alone. She watched as more and more people arrived from the police and fire departments and the military, and there were others she couldn't identify.

When the ambulance carrying Rip pulled away, Rawley looked at her hands and realized they were now trembling. She also realized she had clearly been forgotten.

Rawley walked through the gate without looking back, and nobody called after her. On the street officers stood by to keep everyone away. Rawley looked right then left down Front Street, and then she started walking.

The Green Parrot was exactly what she needed, she thought.

CHAPTER 67

———✦———

THE GREEN PARROT WAS THE first bar outside the main gate at Truman Annex. It was an open-air bar that billed itself as a "Key West icon." Built in 1890 as a grocery store, it eventually turned into the Brown Derby and became a home away from home for submarine and destroyer sailors stationed at the Navy base. When the Navy left Key West in the seventies, the bar went through a few transformations until it became what it was today, a symbol of old Key West. For years Navy men from the fifties and sixties returned to Key West and went immediately to the Green Parrot to relive old memories of the Derby. Locals embraced the bar to avoid the crowds on Duval and everyone else came so they could say they had been there. The bar was and remains in every sense of the word an icon of Key West, old and new.

For the next two hours, Rawley sat under the multi-colored military parachute that hung over the bar, eavesdropping on everyone's version of what had transpired at The Little White House. Cars and trucks with lights flashing and sirens wailing continued to race by. There was speculation of kidnappers, robbers, and assassins waiting for the Truman family, but no mention of a bomb or terrorists.

All anyone knew was that a hero FBI agent had foiled whatever plot there might have been, but he was killed in the process. In true Key West fashion, the excitement quickly died down, and by the time the band started playing, all was forgotten.

As the band got louder and the crowd grew larger, conversations at the bar ended, or they were simply drowned out. Rawley was now alone with her thoughts amid the constant roar of the ambient noise. Her phone continued to ring, and she continued to ignore it. She thought about Rip, but she knew he was in good care, and he was clearly stable when she left. She thought about finding Jake.

As she looked around the bar, Rawley could see the wild-eyed tourists dancing in place to the music or taking photographs and the staff weaving through the crowd, delivering drinks. The scene looked almost chaotic, but it was an orchestrated event that repeated itself every twenty-four hours, seven days a week. As the crowd grew and thinned in an endless cycle, Rawley could see one group who looked unaffected by the noise and the ebb flow of customers bouncing off each other as they moved about the bar. These were the locals who came here each night. They did not come to be entertained or be social; they came because it was home. It was where they fit in no matter how they looked or how detached from society they might be. In a town that often raged to the early hours of the morning, this was their sanctuary.

As she looked across the bar, Rawley thought of her mother and Apisto, and she understood why people needed a place where they could clear their minds and mend their hearts.

Everyone needed their own sanctuary, however that was defined, she thought.

CHAPTER 68

———————◆———————

IT HAD BEEN NEARLY FORTY-EIGHT hours since Rawley left the Green Parrot and the Florida Keys. For a moment she stood in silence and looked around at her environment. It was as far from Key West and the chaos at Truman Annex as she could get. Then she looked at her phone and realized it had not rang in hours. Rawley decided she needed to get one question answered.

When Sherman answered her call, she could tell he was exasperated. "Babe, where have you been? Where are you?"

"Is he OK?" Rawley asked.

"He's great, thanks to you! Listen, you are on the most-wanted list right now. Your fingerprints are on everything. The director wants you in his office immediately they're talking APB."

"I'm sure," Rawley said as she looked up at the blue sky and the mountains that surrounded her.

"I'll be back, but I need some time," she said.

"Yeah, OK, I get it. Do whatever you need to do," Sherman said. "They probably just want to give you a medal so they can tell you to keep your mouth shut anyway."

For a second, they were both quiet. Then Sherman spoke. "Those guys with the weapon were an odd mix. They came from Yemen, Iran, and Venezuela. A pure money job, all financed by the guy in Japan. I think you knew that." Sherman stopped talking and listened, but Rawley was quiet. "Well, take care of yourself, kid. You did a great job." Sherman listened for another second and the line went dead.

Rawley turned her phone off then crossed the muddy street and paused to look at the door that was in front of her. Then, after looking up and down the busy street, she slowly stepped forward and pushed it open. As she stood in the doorway, backlit by the bright morning sun, she looked at her sanctuary and immediately felt a sense of calm.

"Welcome back to the Lagopus, dear!" said Verlie.

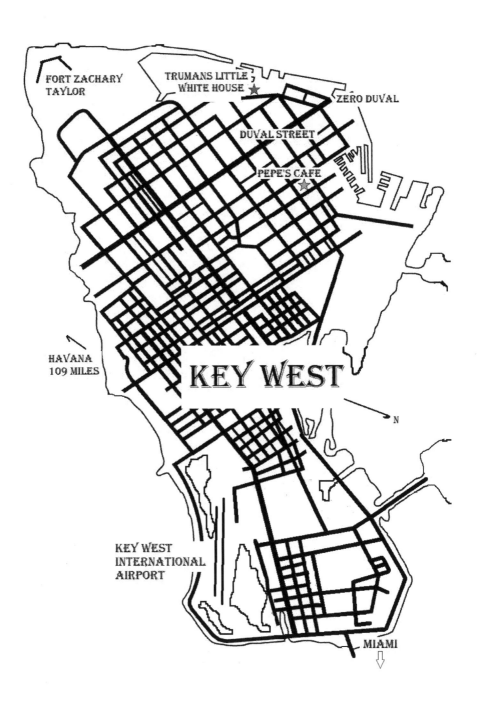

FORT ZACHARY
TAYLOR

TRUMANS LITTLE
WHITE HOUSE

ZERO DUVAL

DUVAL STREET

PEPE'S CAFE

HAVANA
109 MILES

KEY WEST

N

KEY WEST
INTERNATIONAL
AIRPORT

MIAMI

ACKNOWLEDGMENT

———◆———

THERE IS A LONG AND distinguished list of friends and family who I should thank for encouraging me to see this writing effort through to the end. I must give thanks to Debbie and Walter who have made the last seventeen years of my life a nonstop, worldwide adventure of the highest caliber and encouraged me to write. Thanks to the author of the *Wolf Series* and other fine stories, Craig Macintosh, for his guidance and invaluable advice, and to best-selling author, Nicole Morgan, who has been an inspiration! Thanks to Brett Hellman, my most honest critic, and Sarah Derrick for your valuable time. And most important, thank you to Debra Sue Waters and Fred Miner for your artistic contributions.

Special thanks to Verlie Davis and Dale Coopwood. Without them Rawley's journey to Alaska might never have happened. And of course, Jessica. Thank you for donning a flight suit and giving Rawley a face. We can't thank you enough.

My entire adult life has been one fantastic adventure that any action writer would envy. There has been world travel, ocean sailing, skydiving, flying, scuba diving, shooting, fast boats, submersible boats, warfighting, cold beer, hot women, danger, intrigue, and desperate missions both in the military and in business. I would never say my life has been dull, but no matter what has gone on in the past, I still long for the next adventure, whatever that might be.

Fly Girl was born in the mind of my creative partner and partner for life, Sali Gear. Her life experiences and mine were blended into this fictional tale. Like all great adventurers, Sali's life story has heroes and villains, highs and lows, and events that should have turned her into a memory. Happily, like our character, she has survived. Today she still pursues a life in the cockpit while rescuing dogs, horses, donkeys, and people. To Sally Stanwood Gear Doggett, you are gone but never forgotten. And to my greatest fan, my mother, love you!

For my warrior friends who have passed and those still risking it all, until Valhalla. LLTB

66917525R00183

Made in the USA
Middletown, DE
16 March 2018